Ironpass
THE BLACKWOOD
Dolth
Rodez
Ran
Euper
Romney
Tiburn
Sadara
Silden
Bas-Tyra
Cheam
Rillanon
Timons
THE KINGDOM OF ROLDEM
THE KINGDOM SEA
Deep Taunton
Mallow Haven
Pointer's Head
THE PEAKS OF TRANQUILLITY

Silverthorn

by Raymond E. Feist

DOUBLEDAY & COMPANY, INC.
GARDEN CITY, NEW YORK
1985

This book is dedicated to my nephews and niece,
Benjamin Adam Feist,
Ethan Aaron Feist,
Alicia Jeanne Lareau,
little magicians, all.

Library of Congress Cataloging in Publication Data
Feist, Raymond E.
Silverthorn.
Sequel to: Magician.
I. Title.
PS3556.E446S5 1985 813′.54

ISBN 0-385-19210-X
Library of Congress Catalog Card Number 83-27471

Printed in the United States of America
First Edition

ACKNOWLEDGMENTS

I am once more indebted to many people for this book's existence. My deep thanks to:

The Friday Nighters: April and Stephen Abrams, Steve Barrett, Anita and Jon Everson, Dave Guinasso, Conan LaMotte, Tim LaSelle, Ethan Munson, Bob Potter, Rich Spahl, Alan Springer, and Lori and Jeff Velten, for too many reasons to list.

Susan Avery, David Brin, Kathie Buford, and Janny Wurts for giving me their thoughts on a work in progress.

My friends at Doubleday, to which list I am pleased to add the names of Pat LoBrutto and Peter Schneider.

Al Sarantonio, for playing the jukebox in Chicago.

Again, Harold Matson, my agent.

And, as always, Barbara A. Feist, my mother.

Raymond E. Feist
San Diego, California
April 1984

SYNOPSIS

OUR STORY SO FAR . . .

Upon the world of Midkemia, the mighty Kingdom of the Isles arose, beside the vast Empire of Great Kesh to the south. The Kingdom was then nearing an era of greatness; the nation spanned a continent, from the Kingdom Sea to the Endless Sea.

In the twelfth year of the reign of Rodric the Fourth, in the westernmost province of the Kingdom, the Duchy of Crydee, an orphan kitchen boy named Pug was made apprentice to the magician Kulgan. An indifferent student of magic, he rose to high station, for he saved the daughter of Duke Borric conDoin, Princess Carline, from a dire fate and became a squire of the Duke's court. Pug then found himself the object of Carline's girlish infatuation and, as a result, rival to young Squire Roland, a member of the court.

With his best friend, Tomas, Pug discovered the wreckage of an alien vessel and a dying man of unknown nationality. The Duke's priest, Father Tully, used his magic to learn that the dying man was from another world, Kelewan, dominated by a mighty empire of warriors, the Tsurani. They had reached Midkemia by a magic gate, a rift in space, and might be preparing the way for invasion. Duke Borric took council with the Elf Queen, Aglaranna, who agreed that some strange menace was approaching the Far Coast of the Kingdom; the elves had seen strange warriors mapping the West, men who vanished mysteriously.

Fearing this a prelude to invasion, Lord Borric and his younger son, Arutha, led a company of men to warn King Rodric of the possible attack, leaving Crydee to the care of his elder son, Lyam, and Swordmaster Fannon. The company numbered Kulgan the magician, Pug and Tomas, Sergeant Gardan, and fifty soldiers of Crydee. In the forest called the Green Heart the Duke's party was attacked by the dreaded moredhel, the dark elves known as the Brotherhood of the Dark Path. After a long, bloody fight, the Duke and the other survivors were saved by Dolgan, a dwarven chief, and his companions.

Dolgan led them through the mines of Mac Mordain Cadal, where a wraith attacked, separating Tomas from the others in the company. Tomas fled deep into the ancient mine, while Dolgan led the others to safety.

Dolgan returned into the mine to find Tomas, discovering that the boy had been given refuge by one of the last of the mighty golden dragons, ancient and near death. The dragon, Rhuagh, told of his life, of his encounter with the strange sorcerer Macros the Black, and of other wonders. Rhuagh vanished in a wondrous final moment of glory, a boon of Macros, and left Tomas with a special gift, magic golden armor.

Duke Borric's company reached the city of Bordon, where they took ship for Krondor, capital of the Western Realm of the Kingdom. They were driven by a storm to Sorcerer's Isle, home of the legendary Macros the Black. There Pug met a mysterious hermit, discovered later to be Macros. He hints they shall meet again, but warns them not to seek him out.

In Krondor, Prince Erland, the King's uncle and heir apparent, instructed the Duke to continue on to Rillanon, capital of the Kingdom, to see King Rodric. While in Krondor, Pug met Princess Anita, Erland's only child, and learned she was expected to marry Prince Arutha when she grew up.

In Rillanon, Duke Borric discovered the King to be a man of vision, also a man of doubtful sanity, given to outbursts of temper and rambling discourse. Duke Caldric of Rillanon, Borric's uncle by marriage, warned that the burden of repelling the Tsurani, should they come, would fall to the western lords. The King distrusted the Prince of Krondor, dreaming of plots against the crown, and was even leery of Borric, who followed after Erland in the succession. He refused to allow the Armies of the East to leave the Eastern Realm. Then came the Tsurani invasion, and Rodric put aside his suspicions, giving Borric command of the Armies of the West. Borric and his companions rushed westward as the Riftwar began.

During the early part of the war, a raid into Tsurani-held territory was mounted, and Pug was captured.

Tomas was with Dolgan's force of dwarves, among the first to resist the invaders. Something alien had manifested itself in Tomas's armor, and while wearing it he became a warrior of awesome power. Haunted by strange visions, he was slowly changing in appearance. In a frantic battle in the dwarven mines, the Tsurani forced Tomas and Dolgan's company to flee into the forests. Having no safe haven, the dwarves struck out for Elvandar, home of the elves, seeking to ally themselves with the elves. Reaching the court of the Elf Queen, they were made welcome. Something in Tomas's appearance caused the old elven Spellweavers to be fearful, though they would not speak of it.

Lyam left Crydee to join his father, and Swordmaster Fannon assumed command of the castle, with Arutha his second-in-command. Carline grieved over Pug's loss and turned to Roland for comfort. The Tsurani raided Crydee, using a captured ship; during the battle, Arutha rescued Amos Trask, the ship's captain, a former pirate.

The Tsurani besieged Crydee and were repulsed many times. During a battle, Swordmaster Fannon was wounded and Arutha assumed command. After a terrible underground battle between Arutha's men and Tsurani sappers, Arutha ordered the garrisons surrounding Crydee to coordinate for a final battle against the Tsurani. But before that battle could commence, the Tsurani commander, Kasumi of the Shinzawai, received orders to return home with his command.

Four years passed, and Pug was working as a slave in a swamp camp on Kelewan, the Tsurani homeworld, with a newcomer, Laurie of Tyr-Sog, a minstrel. After trouble with the camp overseer they were taken by Hokanu, younger son of the Shinzawai, to his father's estate. They were ordered to train Kasumi in every aspect of Kingdom culture and language. There Pug also met a slave girl, Katala, with whom he fell in love. The brother of the Lord of the Shinzawai, Kamatsu, was one of the Great Ones, magicians of power, beings who were a law unto themselves. One night the Great One, Fumita, learned Pug had been apprenticed as a magician on Midkemia. He claimed Pug for the Assembly, the brotherhood of magicians, and they vanished from the Shinzawai estate.

Tomas by then had grown to a figure of stunning power, made so by his ancient armor, once worn by a Valheru—a Dragon Lord—one of the legendary first people of Midkemia, masters of all. Little was known about them save that they were cruel and powerful and had kept the elves and moredhel as slaves. Aglaranna, her son, Calin, and Tathar, her senior adviser, feared that Tomas was being consumed by the power of Ashen-Shugar, the ancient Dragon Lord whose armor he wore. They feared an attempt at a return of Valheru domination. Aglaranna was doubly troubled, for besides fearing Tomas, she was falling in love with him. The Tsurani invaded Elvandar and were driven back by Tomas and Dolgan's forces, aided by the mysterious Macros the Black. After the battle, Aglaranna admitted her feelings to Tomas and took him as her lover, thereby losing her power to command him.

Pug was cleansed of his memory by the teachers of the Assembly and after four years of training became a magician. He learned he was a gifted follower of the Greater Path, a magic nonexistent upon Midkemia. Kulgan was a Lesser Path magician, so he had been unable to teach Pug. Pug was given the name Milamber when he became a Great One. His teacher, Shimone, watched as Milamber passed the final test, standing upon a thin spire at the height of a storm while the history of the Empire of Tsuranuanni was revealed to him. There he was steeped in the first duty of a Great One, to serve the Empire. Pug met his first friend in the Assembly, Hochopepa, a shrewd magician who instructed Pug in the pitfalls of Tsurani politics.

By the ninth year of the war, Arutha feared they were losing the struggle, then learned from a captive slave that new troops were arriving from Kelewan. With Martin Longbow, his father's Huntmaster, and Amos Trask, Arutha traveled to Krondor to seek additional aid from Prince Erland. During the journey, Amos discovered Martin's secret, that he was Lord Borric's bastard. Martin made Amos swear never to reveal the secret until Martin allowed it. In Krondor, Arutha discovered the city under the control of Guy, Duke of Bas-Tyra, and avowed enemy of Lord Borric. Guy was clearly embarked on some plan to gain the crown for himself. Arutha then ran afoul of Jocko Radburn, Guy's henchman and head of the secret police, who chased Arutha, Martin, and Amos into the arms of the Mockers, the thieves of Krondor. There they met Jimmy the Hand, a boy thief; Trevor Hull, a former pirate turned smuggler; and his first mate, Aaron Cook. The Mockers were hiding Princess Anita, who had fled the palace. Jocko Radburn was furiously trying to recapture Anita before Guy du Bas-Tyra returned from a border skirmish with the neighboring Empire of Great Kesh. With the Mockers' help, Arutha, his companions, and Anita fled the city. During a sea chase, Amos lured Radburn's ship onto the rocks and the head of the secret police drowned. Upon returning to Crydee, Arutha learned that Squire Roland had been killed in a skirmish. By then Arutha was in love with Anita, though he would not admit as much to himself, counting her too young.

Pug, now Milamber, returned to the Shinzawai estate to claim Katala, and discovered he was a father. His son, William, had been born during his absence. He also learned that the Shinzawai were involved in a plot with the Emperor to force peace upon the Tsurani High Council, which was dominated by the Warlord. Laurie was to guide Kasumi, who had by then mastered the language and customs of the Kingdom, to the King, bearing the Emperor's offer of peace. Pug wished them well and took his wife and child to his home.

Tomas underwent a great change, bringing the forces of the Valheru and the human into balance, but only after almost killing Martin Longbow. In a titanic inner battle, the human was nearly overcome, but at the end he mastered the raging thing that once was a Dragon Lord and at last discovered peace within his soul.

Kasumi and Laurie came through the rift and made their way to Rillanon, where they discovered that the King had become thoroughly mad. He accused them of being spies, and they fled with the aid of Duke Caldric. The Duke advised them to seek out Lord Borric, for it seemed civil war would surely come. Reaching Borric's camp, Laurie and Kasumi met Lyam, who informed them Borric was close to death from a wound.

Milamber, as Pug was known, attended the Imperial Games, given by the Warlord to commemorate his smashing victory over Lord Borric. Milamber became enraged at the wanton cruelty, especially the treatment of Midkemian prisoners. In a fit of rage he destroyed the arena, shaming the Warlord, thereby throwing the politics of the Empire into shambles. Milamber then fled with Katala and William back to Midkemia, a Tsurani Great One no longer, but once again Pug of Crydee.

Pug returned in time to be at Lord Borric's side when he died. The Duke's last act was to legitimize Martin. The King then arrived, angered by his commanders' inability to end the long war. He led a mad charge against the Tsurani and, against all odds, broke their front, driving them back into the valley where they held their rift machine, their means of travel between the worlds. The King was mortally wounded and, in a rare lucid moment, named Lyam, the eldest conDoin male, his heir.

Lyam sent word to the Tsurani he would accept the peace offer Rodric had spurned, and the date for the truce talks was set. Macros then went to Elvandar, warning Tomas to expect deception at the peace meeting. Tomas agreed to bring his warriors, as would the dwarves.

At the peace meeting, Macros created an illusion, bringing chaos and battle where peace was the intent. Macros arrived, and he and Pug destroyed the rift, stranding four thousand Tsurani under Kasumi's command on Midkemia. He surrendered them to Lyam, who granted them freedom if they swore fealty.

All returned to Rillanon for Lyam's coronation, save Arutha, Pug, and Kulgan, who visited Macros's isle. There they discovered Gathis, a goblin-like servant of the sorcerer, who gave them a message. Macros, it appeared, had died in the destruction of the rift. He left his vast library to Pug and Kulgan, who planned to start an academy for magicians. He explained his treachery by saying that a being known only as the Enemy, a vast and terrible power known to the Tsurani in ancient times, could find Midkemia by means of the rift. That was why he had forced a situation where the rift had to be destroyed.

Arutha, Pug, and Kulgan went on to Rillanon, where Arutha discovered the truth about Martin. Since he was the eldest of Borric's sons, Martin's birth clouded Lyam's inheritance, but the former Huntmaster renounced any claim to the throne, and Lyam became King. Arutha was made Prince of Krondor, as Anita's father had died. Guy du Bas-Tyra was in hiding and in his absence was banished as a traitor. Laurie made the acquaintance of Princess Carline, who seemed to return his interest.

Lyam, Martin, who became Duke of Crydee, and Arutha left for a tour of the Eastern Realm, while Pug and his family, along with Kulgan, traveled to the island of Stardock, to begin the construction of the academy. For nearly a year, peace reigned in the Kingdom. . . .

Book III

Arutha and Jimmy

Their rising all at once was as the
sound
Of thunder heard remote.

—MILTON, *Paradise Lost,*
BOOK II, l. 476

PROLOGUE

TWILIGHT

The sun dropped behind the peaks.

The last rays of warmth touched the earth and only the rosy afterglow of the day remained. From the east, indigo darkness approached rapidly. The wind cut through the hills like a sharp-edged blade, as if spring were only a faintly remembered dream. Winter's ice still clung to shadow-protected pockets, ice that cracked loudly under the heels of heavy boots. Out of the evening's darkness three figures entered the firelight.

The old witch looked up, her dark eyes widening slightly at the sight of the three. She knew the figure on the left, the broad, mute warrior with the shaved head and single long scalp lock. He had come once before, seeking magic signs for strange rites. Though he was a powerful chieftain, she had sent him away, for his nature was evil, and while issues of good and evil seldom held any significance for the witch, there were limits even for her. Besides, she had little love for any moredhel, especially one who had cut out his own tongue as a sign of devotion to dark powers.

The mute warrior regarded her with the blue eyes unusual for one of his race. He was broader of shoulders than most, even for one of the mountain clans, who tended to be more powerful of arm and shoulder than their forest-dwelling cousins. The mute wore golden circle rings in his large, upswept ears, painful to affix, as the moredhel had no lobes. Upon each cheek were three scars, mystic symbols whose meaning was not lost upon the witch.

The mute made a sign to his companions, and the one to the far right seemed to nod. It was difficult to judge, for he was clothed in an all-concealing robe, with a deep hood revealing no features. Both hands were hidden in voluminous sleeves that were kept together. As if speaking from a great distance, the cloaked figure said, "We seek a reading of signs." His voice was sibilant, almost a hiss, and there was a note of something alien in it. One hand appeared and the witch pulled away, for it was misshapen and scaled, as if the owner possessed talons covered with snakeskin. She then knew the creature for what it was: a priest of the Pantathian serpent people. Compared to the serpent people, the moredhel were held in high regard by the witch.

She turned her attention from the end figures and studied the one in the center. He stood a full head taller than the mute and was even more impressive in bulk. He slowly removed a bearskin robe, the bear's skull providing a helm for his own head, and cast it aside. The old witch gasped, for he was the most striking moredhel she had seen in her long life. He wore the heavy trousers, vest, and knee-high boots of the hill clans, and his chest was bare. His powerfully muscled body gleamed in the firelight, and he leaned forward to study the witch. His face was almost frightening in its near-perfect beauty. But what had caused her to gasp, more than his awesome appearance, was the sign upon his chest.

"Do you know me?" he asked the witch.

She nodded. "I know who you appear to be."

He leaned even farther forward, until his face was lit from below by the fire, revealing something in his nature. "I am who I appear to be," he whispered with a smile. She felt fear, for behind his handsome features, behind the benign smile, she saw the visage of evil, evil so pure it defied endurance. "We seek a reading of signs," he repeated, his voice the sound of ice-clear madness.

She chuckled. "Even one so mighty has limits?"

The handsome moredhel's smile slowly vanished. "One may not foretell one's own future."

Resigned to her own likely lot, she said, "I require silver."

The moredhel nodded. The mute dug a coin from out of his belt pouch and tossed it upon the floor before the witch. Without touching it, she prepared some ingredients in a stone cup. When the concoction was ready, she poured it upon the silver. A hissing came, both from the coin and from the serpent man. A green-scaled claw began to make signs, and the witch snapped, "None of that nonsense, snake. Your hot-land magic will only cant my reading."

The serpent man was restrained by a gentle touch and smile from the center figure, who nodded at the witch.

In croaking tones, her throat dry with fear, the witch said, "Say you then truly: What would you know?" She studied the hissing silver coin, covered now in bubbling green slime.

"Is it time? Shall I do now that which was ordained?"

A bright green flame sprang from the coin and danced. The witch followed its movement closely, her eyes seeing something within the flame none but she could divine. After a while she said, "The Bloodstones form the Cross of Fire. That which you are, you are. That which you are born to do . . . do!" The last word was a half-gasp.

Something in the witch's expression was unexpected, for the moredhel said, "What else, crone?"

"You stand not unopposed, for there is one who is your bane. You stand not alone, for behind you . . . I do not understand." Her voice was weak, faint.

"What?" The moredhel showed no smile this time.

"Something . . . something vast, something distant, something evil."

The moredhel paused to consider; turning to the serpent man, he spoke softly yet commandingly. "Go then, Cathos. Employ your arcane skills and discover where this seat of weakness lies. Give a name to our enemy. Find him."

The serpent man bowed awkwardly and shambled out of the cave. The moredhel turned to his mute companion and said, "Raise the standards, my general, and gather the loyal clans upon the plains of Isbandia, beneath the towers of Sar-Sargoth. Raise highest that standard I have chosen for my own, and let all know we begin that which was ordained. You shall be my battlemaster, Murad, and all shall know you stand highest among my servants. Glory and greatness now await.

"Then, when the mad snake has identified our quarry, lead forth the Black Slayers. Let those whose souls are mine serve us by seeking out our enemy. Find him! Destroy him! Go!"

The mute nodded once and left the cave. The moredhel with the sign on his chest faced the witch. "Then, human refuse, do you know what dark powers move?"

"Aye, messenger of destruction, I know. By the Dark Lady, I know."

He laughed, a cold humorless sound. "I wear the sign," he said, pointing to the purple birthmark upon his chest, which seemed to glow angrily in the firelight. It was clear that his was no simple disfigurement but some sort of magic talisman, for it formed a perfect silhouette of a dragon in flight. He raised his finger, pointing upward. "I have the power." He made a circular motion with his upraised finger. "I am the foreordained. I am destiny."

The witch nodded, knowing death raced to embrace her. She suddenly mouthed a complex incantation, her hands moving furiously through the air. A gathering of power manifested itself in the cave and a strange keening filled the night. The warrior before her simply shook his head. She cast a spell at him, one that should have withered him where he stood. He remained, grinning at her evilly. "You seek to test me with your puny arts, seer?"

Seeing no effect, she slowly closed her eyes and sat erect, awaiting her fate. The moredhel pointed his finger at her and a silver shaft of light came forth, striking the witch. She shrieked in agony, then exploded into white-hot fire. For an instant her dark form writhed within the inferno, then the flames vanished.

The moredhel cast a quick glance at the ashes upon the floor, forming the outline of a body. With a deep laugh he gathered up his robe and left the cave.

Outside, his companions waited, holding his horse. Far below he could see the camp of his band, still small but destined to grow. He mounted and said, "To Sar-Sargoth!" With a jerk on the reins he spun his horse and led the mute and the serpent priest down the hillside.

ONE

REUNION

The ship sped home.

The wind changed quarter and the captain's voice rang out; aloft, his crew scrambled to answer the demands of a freshening breeze and a captain anxious to get safely to port. He was a seasoned sailingmaster, nearly thirty years in the King's navy, and seventeen years commanding his own ship. And the *Royal Eagle* was the best ship in the King's fleet, but still the captain wished for just a little more wind, just a little more speed, since he would not rest until his passengers were safely ashore.

Standing upon the foredeck were the reasons for the captain's concern, three tall men. Two, one blond and one dark, were standing at the rail, sharing a joke, for they both laughed. Each stood a full four inches over six feet, and each carried himself with the sure step of a fighting man or hunter. Lyam, King of the Kingdom of the Isles, and Martin, his elder brother and Duke of Crydee, spoke of many things, of hunting and feasting, of travel and politics, of war and discord, and occasionally they spoke of their father, Duke Borric.

The third man, not as tall or as broad of shoulder as the other two, leaned against the rail a short way off, lost in his own thoughts. Arutha, Prince of Krondor and youngest of the three brothers, also dwelt upon the past, but his vision was not of the father killed during the war with the Tsurani, in what was now being called the Riftwar. Instead he watched the bow wake of the ship as it sliced through emerald-green waters, and in that green he saw two sparkling green eyes.

The captain cast a glance aloft, then ordered the sails trimmed. Again he took note of the three men upon the foredeck and again he gave a silent prayer to Kilian, Goddess of Sailors, and wished Rillanon's tall spires were in sight. For those three were the three most powerful and important men in the Kingdom, and the sailingmaster refused to think of the chaos that would befall the Kingdom should any ill chance visit his ship.

Arutha vaguely heard the captain's shouts and the replies of his mates and crew. He was fatigued by the events of the last year, so he paid little attention to what was occurring about him. He could keep his thoughts only upon one thing: he was returning to Rillanon, and to Anita.

Arutha smiled to himself. His life had seemed unremarkable for the first eighteen years. Then the Tsurani invasion had come and the world had been forever changed. He had come to be counted one of the finest commanders in the Kingdom, had discovered an unsuspected eldest brother in Martin, and had seen a thousand horrors and miracles. But the most miraculous thing that had happened to Arutha had been Anita.

They had been parted after Lyam's coronation. For nearly a year Lyam had been displaying the royal banner to both eastern lords and neighboring kings, and now they were returning home.

Lyam's voice cut through Arutha's reverie. "What see you in the wave's sparkle, little brother?"

Martin smiled as Arutha looked up, and the former Huntmaster of Crydee, once called Martin Longbow, nodded toward his youngest brother. "I wager a year's taxes he sees a pair of green eyes and a pert smile in the waves."

Lyam said, "No wager, Martin. Since we departed Rillanon I've had three messages from Anita on some matter or other of state business. All conspire to keep her in Rillanon while her mother returned to their estates a month after my coronation. Arutha, by rough estimate, has averaged better than two messages a week from her the entire time. One might draw a conclusion or two from that."

"I'd be more than anxious to return if I had someone of her mettle waiting for me," agreed Martin.

Arutha was a private person, ill humored when it came to revealing deep feelings, and he was doubly sensitive to any question involving Anita. He was impossibly in love with the slender young woman, intoxicated with the way she moved, the way she sounded, the way she looked at him. And while these were possibly the only two men on all Midkemia to whom he felt close enough to share his feelings, he had never, even as a boy, shown good grace when he felt he was the butt of a jest.

As Arutha's expression darkened, Lyam said, "Put away your black looks, little storm cloud. Not only am I your King, I'm still your older brother and I can box your ears if the need arises."

The use of the pet name their mother had given him and the improbable image of the King boxing the ears of the Prince of Krondor made Arutha smile slightly. He was silent a moment, then said, "I worry I misread her in this. Her letters, while warm, are formal and at times distant. And there are many young courtiers in your palace."

Martin said, "From the moment we escaped from Krondor, your fate was sealed, Arutha. She's had you in her bow mark from the first, like a hunter drawing down on a deer. Even before we reached Crydee, when we were hiding out, she'd look at you in a certain way. No, she's waiting for you, have no doubt."

"Besides," added Lyam, "you've told her how you feel."

"Well, not in so many words. But I have stated my fondest affection."

Lyam and Martin exchanged glances. "Arutha," said Lyam, "you write with all the passion of a scribe doing year-end tax tallies."

All three laughed. The months of travel had allowed a redefinition of their relationship. Martin had been both tutor and friend to the other two as boys, teaching hunting and woodcraft. But he had also been a commoner, though as Huntmaster he stood as a highly placed member of Duke Borric's staff. With the revelation that he was their father's bastard, an elder half brother, all three had passed through a time of adjustment. Since then they had endured the false camaraderie of those seeking advantage, the hollow promises of friendship and loyalty from those seeking gain, and during this time they had discovered something more. In the others, each had found two men who could be trusted, who could be confided in, who understood what this sudden rise to preeminence meant, and who shared the pressures of newly inflicted responsibilities. In the other two, each had found friends.

Arutha shook his head, laughing at himself. "I guess I have known from the first as well, though I had doubts. She's so young."

Lyam said, "About our mother's age when she wed Father, you mean?"

Arutha fixed Lyam with a skeptical look. "Do you have an answer for everything?"

Martin clapped Lyam on the back. "Of course," he said. Then softly he added, "That's why he's the King." As Lyam turned a mock frown upon Martin, the eldest brother continued. "So when we return, ask her to wed, dear brother. Then we can wake old Father Tully from before his fireplace and we can all be off to Krondor and have a merry wedding. And I can stop all this bloody travel and return to Crydee."

A voice from above cried out, "Land ho!"

"Where away?" shouted the captain.

"Dead ahead."

Gazing into the distance, Martin's practiced hunter's eye was the first to perceive the distant shores. Quietly he placed his hands upon his brothers' shoulders. After a time all three could see the distant outline of tall towers against an azure sky.

Softly Arutha said, "Rillanon."

The light tapping of footfalls and the rustle of a full skirt held above hurrying feet accompanied the sight of a slender figure marching purposefully down a long hallway. The lovely features of the lady rightly acknowledged the reigning beauty of the court were set in an expression of less than pleasant aspect. The guards posted along the hall stood face front, but eyes followed her passage. More than one guard considered the likely target of the lady's well-known temper and smiled inwardly. The singer was in for a rude awakening, literally.

In a most unladylike fashion, Princess Carline, sister to the King, swept past a startled servant who tried to jump aside and bow to her at the same time, a feat that landed him on his backside as Carline vanished into the guest wing of the palace.

Coming to a door, she paused. Patting her loose dark hair into place, she raised her hand to knock, then halted. Her blue eyes narrowed as she became irritated by the thought of waiting for the door to open, so she simply pushed it open without announcing herself.

The chamber was dark, as the night curtains were still drawn. The large bed was occupied by a large lump beneath the blankets that groaned as Carline slammed the door behind her. Picking her way across the clothing-strewn floor, she yanked aside the curtains, admitting the brilliant midmorning light. Another groan emitted from the lump as a head with two red-rimmed eyes peeked out over the bedcovers. "Carline," came the dry croak, "are you trying to wither me to death?"

Coming to stand over the bed, she snapped, "If you hadn't been carousing all night, and had been to breakfast as expected, you might have heard that my brothers' ship had been sighted. They'll be at the dock within two hours."

Laurie of Tyr-Sog, troubadour, traveler, former hero of the Riftwar, and lately court minstrel and constant companion to the Princess, sat up, rubbing at tired eyes. "I was not carousing. The Earl of Dolth insisted on hearing every song in my repertoire. I sang until near dawn." He blinked and smiled up at Carline. Scratching at his neatly trimmed blond beard, he said, "The man has inexhaustible endurance, but also excellent taste in music."

Carline sat on the edge of the bed, leaned over, and kissed him briefly. She deftly disengaged herself from arms that sought to entangle her. Holding him at bay with her hand upon his chest, she said, "Listen, you amorous nightingale, Lyam, Martin, and Arutha will be here soon, and the minute Lyam holds court and gets all the formalities done with, I'm talking to him about our marriage."

Laurie looked around as if seeking a corner in which to disappear. Over the last year their relationship had developed in depth and passion, but Laurie had a near-reflexive avoidance of the topic of marriage. "Now, Carline—" he began.

" 'Now, Carline,' indeed!" she interrupted with a jab of her finger into his bare chest. "You buffoon, I've had eastern princes, sons of half the dukes in the Kingdom, and who knows how many others simply begging for permission to pay court to me. And I've always ignored them. And for what? So some witless musician can trifle with my affections? Well, we shall have an accounting."

Laurie grinned, pushing his tousled blond hair back. He sat up and, before she could move, kissed her deeply. When he pulled away, he said, "Carline, love of my being, please. We've covered this ground."

Her eyes, which had been half-closed during the kiss, instantly widened. "Oh! We've covered this ground before?" she said, infuriated. "We will be married. That is final." She stood up to avoid his embrace again. "It has become the scandal of the court, the Princess and her minstrel lover. It's not even an original tale. I am becoming a laughingstock. Damn it all, Laurie, I'm nearly twenty-six. Most women my age are eight, nine years married. Would you have me die a spinster?"

"Never that, my love," he answered, still amused. Besides the fact of her beauty, and the slim chance of anyone's calling her an old maid, she was ten years his junior and he regarded her as young, a perception constantly furthered by her outbursts of childish temper. He sat up fully and spread his hands in a gesture of helplessness as he stifled his mirth. "I am what I am, darling, no more or less. I've been here longer than I've been anywhere when I was a free man. I'll admit, though, this is a far more pleasant captivity than the last." He was speaking of the years he had been a slave on Kelewan, the Tsurani homeworld. "But you'll never know when I'll want to roam once more." He could see her temper rising as he spoke, and was forced to admit to himself that he was often what brought out the worst in her nature. He rapidly changed tack. "Besides, I don't know if I'd make a good . . . whatever the husband of the King's sister is called."

"Well, you'd better get used to it. Now get up and get dressed."

Laurie grabbed the trousers she tossed to him and quickly put them on. When he was finished dressing he stood before her and put his arms around her waist. "Since the day we met I have been your adoring subject, Carline. I have never loved, nor will I love, anyone as I love you, but—"

"I know. I have had months of the same excuses." She jabbed him in the chest again. "You've always been a traveler," she mocked. "You've always been free. You don't know how you would fare being tied to one spot—though I've noticed you've managed to endure settling down here in the King's palace."

Laurie cast his eyes heavenward. "This is true enough."

"Well, lover mine, those excuses may serve you as you bid farewell to some poor tavern keeper's daughter, but they'll do you little good here. We shall see what Lyam thinks of all this. I should imagine there is some old law or other in the archives dealing with commoners becoming involved with nobles."

Laurie chuckled. "There is. My father is entitled to a golden sovereign, a pair of mules, and a farm for your having taken advantage of me."

Suddenly Carline giggled, tried to smother it, then laughed aloud. "You bastard." Tightly hugging him, she rested her head upon his shoulder and sighed. "I can never stay angry with you."

He cradled her gently in the circle of his arms. "I do give you reason upon occasion," he said softly.

"Yes, you do."

"Well, not all that often."

"Look you well, boyo," she said. "My brothers are nearing the harbor as we speak, and you stand here arguing. You may dare make free with my person, but the King may take a dim view of things as they stand."

"So I have feared," Laurie said, with obvious concern in his voice.

Suddenly Carline's mood softened. Her expression changed to one of reassurance. "Lyam will do whatever I ask. He's never been able to say no to anything I've truly wished for since I was tiny. This is not Crydee. He knows things are different here, and that I'm no longer a child."

"So I have noticed."

"Rogue. Look, Laurie. You're no simple farmer or cobbler. You speak more languages than any 'educated' noble I have known. You read and write. You have traveled widely, even to the Tsurani world. You have wits and talents. You are much more able to govern than many who are born to it. Besides, if I can have an older brother who was a hunter before becoming a duke, why not a husband who was a singer?"

"Your logic is impeccable. I simply don't have a good answer. I love you without stint, but the rest—"

"Your problem is you have the ability to govern, but you just don't want the responsibility. You're lazy."

He laughed. "That's why my father tossed me out of the house when I was thirteen. Said I'd never make a decent farmer."

She pushed away from him gently, her voice taking on a serious note. "Things change, Laurie. I've given this much consideration. I thought I was in love before, twice, but you're the only man who could get me to forget who I am and act this shamelessly. When I'm with you, nothing makes sense, but that's all right, because then I don't care if the way I feel makes sense. But now I must care. You'd better make a choice, and make it soon. I'll bet my jewels Arutha and Anita will announce they are betrothed before my brothers are in the palace a day. Which means we'll all be off to Krondor for their wedding.

"When they are wed, I'll return here with Lyam. It will be up to you to decide if you will be coming back with us, Laurie." She locked gazes with him. "I have had a wonderful time with you. I've feelings I couldn't imagine possible when I dreamed my girl's dreams of Pug and then Roland. But you must get ready to choose. You are my first lover, and will always be my dearest love, but when I return here you will be either my husband or a memory."

Before he could answer, she walked to the door. "In all ways I love you, rogue. But time is short." She paused. "Now come along and help me greet the King."

He came to her side and opened the door for her. They hurried to where carriages were waiting to take the reception committee to the docks. Laurie of Tyr-Sog, troubadour, traveler, and hero of the Riftwar, was acutely aware of the presence of this woman at his side and wondered how it would feel to be denied that presence for good and all. He felt decidedly unhappy at the prospect.

Rillanon, capital of the Kingdom of the Isles, waited to welcome home her King. The buildings were bedecked in festive bunting and hothouse flowers. Brave pennants flew from the rooftops and bold banners of every color were strung between the buildings over the streets the King would travel. Called Jewel of the Kingdom, Rillanon rested upon the slopes of many hills, a marvelous place of graceful spires, airy arches, and delicate spans. The late King, Rodric, had embarked upon a restoration of the city, adding lovely marble and quartz stone facing to most of the buildings before the palace, rendering the city a sparkling wonderland in the afternoon sunlight.

The *Royal Eagle* approached the King's dock, where the welcoming party waited. In the distance, upon those buildings and hillside streets affording a clear view of the dock, throngs of citizens were cheering the return of their young King. For many years Rillanon had abided under the black cloud of King Rodric's madness, and though Lyam was still a stranger to most of the city's populace, he was adored, for he was young and handsome, his bravery in the Riftwar was widely known, and his generosity had been great. He had lowered taxes.

With a master's ease, the harbor pilot guided the King's ship into its appointed place. It was quickly made secure and the gangway run out.

Arutha watched as Lyam was the first to descend. As tradition dictated, he dropped to his knees and kissed the soil of his homeland. Arutha's eyes scanned the crowd, seeking Anita, but in the press of nobles moving forward to greet Lyam he saw no sign of her. A momentary cold stab of doubt struck him.

Martin nudged Arutha, who, protocol dictated, was expected to be the second to disembark. Arutha hurried down the gangway, with Martin a step behind. Arutha's attention was caught by the sight of his sister leaving the side of the singer, Laurie, to rush forward and fiercely hug Lyam. While others in the reception committee were not as free with ritual as Carline, there was a spontaneous cheer from the courtiers and guards awaiting the King's pleasure. Then Arutha had Carline's arms about his neck as she bestowed a kiss and hug on him. "Oh, I've missed your sour looks," she said happily.

Arutha had been wearing the dour expression he exhibited when lost in thought. He said, "What sour looks?"

Carline looked up into Arutha's eyes and, with an innocent smile, said, "You look as if you'd swallowed something and it moved."

Martin laughed aloud at that, then Carline was hugging him in turn. He stiffened at first, for he was still less comfortable with a sister than with two brothers, then he relaxed and hugged her back. Carline said, "I've grown bored without you three around."

Seeing Laurie a short distance off, Martin shook his head. "Not too bored, it seems."

Carline playfully said, "There's no law that says only men can indulge themselves. Besides, he's the best man I've met who's not my brother." Martin could only smile at that while Arutha continued looking for Anita.

Lord Caldric, Duke of Rillanon, First Adviser to the King, and Lyam's great-uncle, smiled broadly as the King's huge hand engulfed his own in a vigorous shake. Lyam nearly had to shout over the cheers from those nearby. "Uncle, how stands our Kingdom?"

"Well, my King, now that you've returned."

As Arutha's expression grew more distressful, Carline said, "Put away that long face, Arutha. She's in the eastern garden, waiting for you."

Arutha kissed Carline's cheek, hurried away from her and a laughing Martin, and as he dashed past Lyam, shouted, "With Your Majesty's permission."

Lyam's expression ran quickly from surprise to mirth, while Caldric and the other courtiers were amazed at the Prince of Krondor's behavior. Lyam leaned close to Caldric and said, "Anita."

Caldric's old face beamed with a sunny smile as he chuckled in understanding. "Then you'll soon be off again, this time for Krondor and your brother's wedding?"

"We'd sooner hold it here, but tradition dictates the Prince weds in his own city, and we must bow before tradition. But that won't be for a few weeks yet. These things take time, and we have a kingdom to govern in the meantime, though it seems you've done well enough in our absence."

"Perhaps, Your Majesty, but now that there is a King again in Rillanon, many matters held in abeyance this last year will be unloosed for your consideration. Those petitions and other documents forwarded to you during your travels were but a tenth part of what you will see."

Lyam gave a mock groan. "We think we shall have the captain put to sea again at once."

Caldric smiled. "Come, Majesty. Your city wishes to see its King."

The eastern garden was empty save for one figure. She moved quietly between well-tended planters of flowers not quite ready to send forth blooms. A few heartier varieties were already beginning to take on the bright green of spring and many of the bordering hedges were evergreen, but the garden still seemed more the barren symbol of winter than the fresh promise of spring, which would manifest itself within a few weeks.

Anita looked across the vista of Rillanon below. The palace sat atop a hill, once the site of a large keep that still served as its heart. Seven high-arched bridges spanned the river that surrounded the palace with the loops of its meandering course. The afternoon wind was chill, and Anita drew a shawl of fine silken material close about her shoulders.

Anita smiled in remembrance. Her green eyes misted over slightly as she thought of her late father, Prince Erland, and of all that had occurred in the last year and more: how Guy du Bas-Tyra had arrived in Krondor and attempted to force her into a marriage of state, and how Arutha had come to Krondor incognito. They had hidden together under the protection of the Mockers—the thieves of Krondor—for over a month until their escape to Crydee. At the end of the Riftwar she had traveled to Rillanon to see Lyam crowned. During all those months she had also fallen deeply in love with the King's younger brother. And now Arutha was returning to Rillanon.

The tread of boots upon flagstone caused her to turn. Anita expected to see a servant or guard, come to tell of the King's arrival in the harbor. Instead a weary-looking man in fine but rumpled traveler's clothing approached across the garden. His dark brown hair was tousled by the breeze and his brown eyes were ringed with dark circles. His near-gaunt face was set in the half-frown which he assumed when he was dwelling upon something serious, and which she found so dear. As he neared, she silently marveled at the way he walked, lithe, almost catlike in his quickness and economy of movement. As he came up to her, he smiled, tentatively, even shyly. Before she could muster years of court-taught poise, Anita found tears coming to her eyes. Suddenly she was in his arms, clinging tightly to him. "Arutha" was all she said.

For a time they stood saying nothing, holding each other tight. Then he slowly tilted her head back and kissed her. Without words he spoke of his devotion and longing and without words she answered. He looked down at eyes as green as the sea and a nose delightfully dusted by a small scattering of freckles, a pleasing imperfection upon her otherwise fair skin. With a tired grin he said, "I've returned."

Then he was laughing at the obvious remark. She laughed as well. He felt buoyant to be holding this slender young woman in his arms, smelling the faint scent of her dark red hair, which was caught up in some complex fashion popular at court this season. He rejoiced to be with her again.

She stepped away but held tightly to his hand. "It has been so very long," she said softly. "It was only to be for a month . . . then another, then more. You've been gone over half a year. I couldn't bring myself to go to the dock. I knew I'd cry at sight of you." Her cheeks were wet from tears. She smiled and wiped them away.

Arutha squeezed her hand. "Lyam kept finding more nobles to visit. The business of the Kingdom," he said with a wry note of deprecation. From the day he had met Anita, Arutha had been unable to articulate his feelings for the girl. Strongly attracted to her from the first, he had wrestled with his emotions constantly after their escape from Krondor. He was powerfully drawn to her and yet saw her as little more than a child, only about to come of age. But she had been a calming influence on him, reading his moods like no one else, sensing how to ease his worry, stem his anger, and draw him from his dark introspection. And he had come to love her soft ways.

He had remained silent until the night before he had departed with Lyam. They had walked in this garden, speaking late into the night, and while little of consequence had been said, Arutha had left feeling as if an understanding had been reached. The light, and occasionally somewhat formal, tone of her letters had caused him worry, fear that he had misread her that night, but now, looking down at her, he knew he had not. Without preamble he said, "I have done little but think of you since we left."

He saw tears come again to her eyes, and she said, "And I of you."

"I love you, Anita. I would have you always at my side. Will you consent to marry me?"

She squeezed his hand as she said, "Yes," then embraced him again. Arutha's mind reeled under the sheer weight of happiness he felt. Holding her close, he whispered, "You are my joy. You are my heart."

They stood there for a time, the tall, rangy Prince and the slender Princess, whose head barely reached his chin. They spoke softly and nothing seemed of importance except the other's presence. Then the self-conscious sound of someone clearing his throat brought them both out of their reverie. They turned to find a palace guardsman standing at the entrance to the garden. He said, "His Majesty approaches, Your Highnesses. He will be entering the great hall within a few minutes."

Arutha said, "We shall go there at once." He led Anita by the hand past the guard, who fell in behind them. Had Arutha and Anita looked over their shoulders, they would have seen the experienced palace guardsman fighting hard to overcome a broad grin.

Arutha gave Anita's hand a final squeeze, then stationed himself next to the door as Lyam entered the grand throne room of the palace. As the King moved toward the dais upon which his throne rested, courtiers bowed to him, and the Court Master of Ceremonies struck the floor with the iron-shod butt of his ceremonial staff. A herald shouted, "Hearken to me! Hearken to me! Let the word go forth: Lyam, first of that name and by the grace of the gods rightwise ruler, is returned to us and again sits upon his throne. Long live the King!"

"Long live the King!" came the response of those gathered in the great hall.

When he was seated, his simple gold circlet of office upon his brow and his purple mantle upon his shoulders, Lyam said, "We are pleased to be home."

The Master of Ceremonies struck the floor again and the herald shouted out Arutha's name. Arutha entered the hall, Carline and Anita behind him, and Martin behind them, as protocol dictated.

Each was announced in order. When all were in place at Lyam's side, the King motioned to Arutha.

Arutha came to his side and leaned over. "Did you ask her?" said the King.

With a lopsided smile Arutha responded, "Ask her what?"

Lyam grinned. "To marry, jackanapes. Of course you did, and from that sloppy smile, she said yes," he whispered. "Go get back in place and I'll make the announcement in a moment." Arutha went back to Anita's side and Lyam motioned Duke Caldric over. "We are weary, my lord Chancellor. We would be pleased to keep the day's business brief."

"There are two matters I judge require Your Majesty's attention this day. The balance may wait."

Lyam indicated that Caldric should proceed. "First, from the Border Barons and Duke Vandros of Yabon, we have reports of unusual goblin activity in the Western Realm."

Arutha's attention was drawn from Anita at this. The Western Realm was his to govern. Lyam looked over toward him, then Martin, indicating they should attend.

Martin said, "What of Crydee, my lord?"

Caldric said, "No word from the Far Coast, Your Grace. At this time we've only reports from the area between Highcastle to the east and the Lake of the Sky to the west—steady sightings of goblin bands moving northward, and occasional raids as they pass villages."

"Northward?" Martin glanced at Arutha.

Arutha said, "With Your Majesty's permission?" Lyam nodded. "Martin, do you think the goblins move to join the Brotherhood of the Dark Path?"

Martin considered. "I would not dismiss such a possibility. The goblins have long served the moredhel. Though I would have thought it more likely the Dark Brothers would be moving south, returning to their homes in the Grey Tower Mountains." The dark cousins to the elves had been driven northward from the Grey Towers by the Tsurani invasion during the Riftwar. Martin said to Caldric, "My lord, have there been reportings of the Dark Brotherhood?"

Caldric shook his head. "There have been the usual sightings along the foothills of the Teeth of the World, Duke Martin, but nothing extraordinary. Lords Northwarden, Ironpass, and Highcastle send their usual reports, nothing more, regarding the Brotherhood."

Lyam said, "Arutha, we shall leave it to you and Martin to review these reports and determine what may be required in the West." He looked at Caldric. "What else, my lord?"

"A message from the Empress of Great Kesh, Your Majesty."

"And what has Kesh to say to Isles?"

"The Empress has ordered her ambassador, one Abdur Rachman Memo Hazara-Khan, to Isles for the purpose of discussing ending whatever contention may exist between Kesh and Isles."

Lyam said, "That news pleases us, my lord. Overlong has the issue of the Vale of Dreams prevented our Kingdom and Great Kesh from treating fairly with one another in other matters. It would prove doubly beneficial to our two nations if we could settle this matter for all time." Lyam stood. "But send word that His Excellency will have to attend us in Krondor, for we have a wedding to celebrate.

"My lords and ladies of the court, it is with profound pleasure that we announce the forthcoming wedding of our brother Arutha to the Princess Anita." The King turned to Arutha and Anita, taking them each by the hand and presenting them to the assembled court, who applauded the announcement.

From where she stood next to her brothers, Carline threw Laurie a dark frown, went to kiss Anita's cheek. While good cheer reigned in the hall, Lyam said, "This day's business is at an end."

TWO

KRONDOR

The city slumbered.

A mantle of heavy fog had rolled in off the Bitter Sea, enshrouding Krondor in dense whiteness. The capital of the Western Realm of the Kingdom never rested, but normal night sounds were muffled by the nearly impenetrable haze cloaking the movements of those still traveling the streets. Everything seemed more subdued, less strident than usual, almost as if the city were at peace with itself.

For one inhabitant of the city the night's conditions were nearly ideal. The fog had turned every street into a narrow, dark passageway, each block of buildings into an isolated island. The unending gloom was punctuated slightly by streetlamps at the corners, small way stations of warmth and brightness for passersby before they once more plunged into the damp and murky night. But between those small havens of illumination one given to working in darkness was granted additional protection, as small noises were deadened and movements were masked from chance observation. Jimmy the Hand went about his business.

About fifteen years of age, Jimmy was already counted among the most gifted members of the Mockers, the Guild of Thieves. Jimmy had been a thief nearly all his short life, a street boy who had graduated from stealing fruit from peddlers' carts to full membership in the Mockers. Jimmy's father was unknown to him, and his mother had been a prostitute in the Poor Quarter until her death at the hands of a drunken sailor. Since then the boy had been a Mocker, and his rise had been rapid. The most astonishing thing about Jimmy's rise was not his age, for the Mockers were of the opinion that as soon as a boy was ready to try thieving, he should be turned loose. Failure had its own rewards. A poor thief was quickly a dead thief. As long as another Mocker was not put at risk, there was little loss in the death of a thief of limited talents. No, the most astonishing fact of Jimmy's rapid rise was that he was nearly as good as he thought he was.

With stealth bordering on the preternatural he moved about the room. The night's quiet was broken only by the deep snores of his unsuspecting host and hostess. The faint glow from a distant streetlamp, entering the open window, was his only illumination. Jimmy peered around, his other senses aiding his search. A sudden change in the sound of the floorboards under Jimmy's light tread, and the thief found what he was looking for. He laughed inwardly at the merchant's lack of originality in hoarding his wealth. With economical movement the boy thief had the false floorboard up and his hand into Trig the Fuller's hideaway.

Trig snorted and rolled over, bringing a responding snore from his fat wife. Jimmy froze in place, barely breathing, until the two sleeping figures were quiescent for several minutes. He then extracted a heavy pouch and gently placed the booty in his tunic, secured by his wide belt. He put the board back and returned to the window. With luck it might be days before the theft was discovered.

He stepped through the window and, turning backward, reached up to grip the eaves. A quick pull, and he was sitting on the roof. Overhanging the edge, he closed the window shutters with a gentle push and jiggled the hook and twine so the inside latch fell back into place. He quickly retrieved his twine, silently laughing at the perplexity sure to result when the fuller tried to figure out how the gold had been taken. Jimmy lay quietly for a moment, listening for sounds of waking inside. When none came, he relaxed.

He rose and began making his way along the Thieves' Highway, as the rooftops of the city were known. He leaped from the roof of Trig's house to the next, then sat down upon the tiles to inspect his haul. The pouch was evidence the fuller had been a thrifty man, holding back a fair share of his steady profits. It would keep Jimmy in comfort for months if he didn't gamble it all away.

A slight noise caused Jimmy to drop to the roof, hugging the tiles in silence. He heard another sound, a scuffle of movement coming from the other side of a gable halfway down the roof from where he lay. The boy cursed his luck and ran a hand through his fog-damp curly brown hair. For another to be upon the rooftops nearby could only spell trouble. Jimmy was working without writ from the Nightmaster of Mockers, a habit of his that had earned him reprimands and beatings the few times he had been found out, but if he was now jeopardizing another Mocker's nightwork, he was in line for more than harsh words or a cuffing around the room. Jimmy was treated as an adult by others in the guild, his position hard won by skill and wit. In turn he was expected to be a responsible member, his age being of no account. By his risking the life of another Mocker, his own could be forfeit.

The other alternative could prove as bad. If a freebooting thief was working the city without permission from the Mockers, it was Jimmy's duty to identify and report him. That would somewhat mitigate Jimmy's own breach of Mocker etiquette, especially if he gave the guild its normal two thirds of the fuller's gold.

Jimmy slipped over the peak of the roof and crawled along until he was opposite the source of the noise. He need only glimpse the independent thief and report him. The Nightmaster would circulate the man's description and sooner or later he would be paid a visit by some guild bashers who would educate him in the proper courtesies due the Mockers by visiting thieves. Jimmy edged upward and peered over the rooftop. He saw nothing. Looking about, he glimpsed a faint movement from the corner of his eye and turned. Again he saw nothing. Jimmy the Hand settled down to wait. There was something here that provoked his sensitive curiosity.

That acute curiosity was one of Jimmy's only weaknesses when it came to work—that and an occasional irritation with the need to divide his loot with the guild, which took a dim view of this reluctance. His upbringing by the Mockers had given him an appreciation of life—a skepticism bordering on cynicism—far beyond his years. He was uneducated but canny. One thing he knew: sound does not issue from thin air—except when magic is in play.

Jimmy settled down a moment to puzzle out what he didn't see before him. Either some invisible spirit was squirming about uncomfortably on the roof tiles, which while possible was highly unlikely, or something more corporeal was hidden deep within the shadows of the other side of the gable.

Jimmy crawled along until he was opposite the gable and raised himself slightly to look over the peak of the roof. He peered into the darkness and when he heard another faint scuffling was rewarded with a glimpse of movement. Someone was deep within the gloom, wearing a dark cloak. Jimmy could locate him only when he moved. Jimmy inched along below the peak to gain a better angle to watch, until he was directly behind the figure. Again he reared up. The lurker moved, adjusting his cloak around his shoulders. The hair on the back of Jimmy's neck stood up. The figure before him was dressed all in black and carried a heavy crossbow. This was no thief but a Nighthawk!

Jimmy lay rock still. To stumble across a member of the Guild of Death at work was not likely to enhance one's prospects of old age. But there was a standing order among the Mockers that any news of the brotherhood of assassins was to be reported at once, and the order had come down from the Upright Man himself, the highest authority in the Mockers. Jimmy chose to wait, trusting in his skills should he be discovered. He might not possess the nearly legendary attributes of a Nighthawk, but he had the supreme confidence of a fifteen-year-old boy who had become the youngest Master Thief in the history of the Mockers. If he was discovered, it would not be his first chase across the Thieves' Highway.

Time passed and Jimmy waited, with a discipline unusual for one his age. A thief who cannot remain still for hours if need be does not remain a living thief long. Occasionally Jimmy heard and glimpsed the assassin moving about. Jimmy's awe of the legendary Nighthawks steadily lessened, for this one displayed little skill in staying motionless. Jimmy had long before mastered the trick of quietly tensing and relaxing muscles to prevent cramping and stiffening. Then, he considered, most legends tend to be overstated, and in the Nighthawks' line of work it was only to their advantage to keep people in awe of them.

Abruptly the assassin moved, letting his cloak fall away completely as he raised his crossbow. Jimmy could hear hoofbeats approaching. Riders passed below, and the assassin slowly lowered the weapon. Obviously those below had not included his intended prey.

Jimmy elbowed himself a little higher to gain a better view of the man, now that his cloak didn't mask him. The assassin turned slightly, retrieving his cloak, exposing his face to Jimmy. The thief gathered his legs under him, ready to spring away should the need arise, and studied the man. Jimmy could make out little, except that the man had dark hair and was light-complexioned. Then the assassin seemed to be looking directly at the boy.

Jimmy's heart pounded loudly in his ears and he wondered how the assassin could fail to hear such a racket. But the man turned back to his vigil, and Jimmy dropped silently below the roof peak. He breathed slowly, fighting back a sudden giddy urge to giggle. After it passed, he relaxed slightly and chanced another look.

Again the assassin waited. Jimmy settled in. He wondered at the Nighthawk's weapon. The heavy crossbow was a poor choice for a marksman, being less accurate than any good bow. It would do for someone with little training, for it delivered a bolt with thundering force—a wound less than fatal from an arrow could kill if from a bolt, because of the added shock of the blow. Jimmy had once seen a steel cuirass on display in a tavern. The metal breastplate had a hole in it the size of Jimmy's fist, punched through by a bolt from a heavy crossbow. It had been hung up not because of the size of the hole, which was usual for the weapon, but because the wearer had somehow survived. But the weapon had its disadvantages. Besides being inaccurate past a dozen yards, it had a short range.

Jimmy craned his neck to watch the Nighthawk and felt a tic in his right arm. He shifted his weight slightly to his left. Suddenly a tile gave way beneath his hand and with a loud crack it broke. It fell away, clattering over the roof to crash down on the cobbles below. To Jimmy it was a thunder peal sounding his doom.

Moving with inhuman speed, the assassin turned and fired. Jimmy's slipping saved his life, for he could not have dodged fast enough to avoid the bolt, but gravity had provided the necessary speed. He struck the roof and heard the quarrel pass over his head. For a brief instant he imagined his head exploding like a ripe pumpkin and silently thanked Banath, patron god of thieves.

Jimmy's reflexes saved him next, for rather than standing, he rolled to his right. Where he had lain a moment before, a sword came crashing down. Knowing he couldn't gain enough of a lead to outrun the assassin, Jimmy leaped up into a crouch, pulling his dirk from his right boot top in a single motion. He had little love for fighting, but he had realized early in his career that his life might depend upon his use of the blade. He had practiced diligently whenever the opportunity had presented itself. Jimmy only wished his rooftop foray had not precluded his bringing along his rapier.

The assassin turned to face the boy, and Jimmy saw him teeter for a brief instant. The Nighthawk might have quick reflexes, but he was not used to the precarious footing the rooftops offered. Jimmy grinned, as much to hide his fear as from any amusement at the assassin's unease.

In a hissing whisper the assassin said, "Pray to whatever gods brought you here, boy."

Jimmy thought such a remark odd, considering it distracted only the speaker. The assassin lashed out, the blade slicing the air where Jimmy had been, and the boy thief was off.

He dashed along the roof and leaped back to the building wherein lived Trig the Fuller. A moment later he could hear the assassin landing also. Jimmy ran nimbly until he was confronted by a yawning gap. In his hurry he had forgotten there was a wide alley at this end of the building and the next building was impossibly distant. He spun about.

The assassin was slowly approaching, his sword point leveled at Jimmy. Jimmy was struck by a thought and suddenly began a mad stomping dance upon the roof. In a moment the noise was answered by an angry voice from below. "Thief! I am undone!" Jimmy could picture Trig the Fuller leaning out his window, rousing the city watch, and hoped the assassin had the same picture in mind. The racket below would surely have the building surrounded in short order. He prayed the assassin would flee rather than punish the author of his failure.

The assassin ignored the fuller's cries and advanced upon Jimmy. Again he slashed and Jimmy ducked, bringing himself inside the assassin's reach. Jimmy stabbed with his dirk and felt the point dig into the Nighthawk's sword arm. The assassin's blade went clattering to the street below. A howl of pain echoed through the night, silencing the fuller's shouts. Jimmy heard the shutters slam closed and wondered what poor Trig must be thinking, hearing that shriek right over his head.

The assassin dodged another thrust by Jimmy and pulled a dagger from his belt. He advanced again, not speaking, his weapon held in his left hand. Jimmy heard shouts from the street below and resisted the urge to cry for aid. He felt little confidence about besting the Nighthawk, even if the assassin was fighting with his off hand, but he was also reluctant to explain his presence upon the fuller's roof. Besides, even should he shout for aid, by the time the watch arrived, gained entrance to the house, and reached the roof the issue would be decided.

Jimmy backed to the end of the roof, until his heels hung in space. The assassin closed, saying, "You have nowhere left to run, boy."

Jimmy waited, preparing a desperate gamble. The assassin tensed, the sign Jimmy had watched for. Jimmy crouched and stepped backward all at once, letting himself fall. The assassin had begun a lunge, and when his blade did not meet the expected resistance, he overbalanced and fell forward. Jimmy caught the edge of the roof, nearly dislocating his shoulder sockets with the jolt. He felt more than saw the assassin fall past, silently speeding through the darkness to crash on the cobbles below.

Jimmy hung for a moment, his hands, arms, and shoulders afire with pain. It would be so simple just to let go and fall into soft darkness. Shaking off the fatigue and pain, he urged protesting muscles to pull himself back onto the roof. He lay gasping for a moment, then rolled over and looked down.

The assassin lay still on the cobbles, his crooked neck offering clear evidence he was no longer alive. Jimmy breathed deeply, the chill of fear finally acknowledged. He suppressed a shudder and ducked down as two men rushed into the alley below. They grabbed the corpse and rolled it over, then picked it up and hurried off. Jimmy considered. For the assassin to have confederates about was a certain sign this had been a Guild of Death undertaking. But who was expected down this street at this hour of the night? Casting about for a moment, he weighed the risk of staying a little longer to satisfy his curiosity against the certain arrival of the city watch within a few more minutes. Curiosity won.

The sound of hoofbeats echoed through the fog, and soon two riders came into the light that burned from the lantern before Trig's home. It was at this moment that Trig decided to open his shutters again and resume his hue and cry. Jimmy's eyes widened as the riders looked up toward the fuller's window. Jimmy had not seen one of the men in over a year, but he was well known to the thief. Shaking his head at the implications of what he saw, the boy thief judged it a good time to depart. But seeing that man below made it impossible for Jimmy to consider this night's business at an end. It would most likely be a long night. He rose and began his trek along the Thieves' Highway, back toward Mockers' Rest.

Arutha reined in his horse and looked up to where a man in a nightshirt shouted from a window. "Laurie, what is that all about?"

"From what I can make out between the wails and screams, I judge that burgher to have recently been the victim of some felony."

Arutha laughed. "I guessed that much myself." He did not know Laurie well, but he enjoyed the singer's wit and sense of fun. He knew there was now some trouble between Laurie and Carline, which was why Laurie had asked to accompany Arutha on his journey to Krondor. Carline would be arriving in a week with Anita and Lyam. But Arutha had long ago decided that what Carline didn't confide in him wasn't his business. Besides, Arutha was sympathetic to Laurie's plight if he had fallen into her bad graces. After Anita, Carline was the last person Arutha would wish angry with him.

Arutha studied the area as a few sleepy souls in neighboring buildings began shouting inquiries. "Well, there's bound to be some investigation here soon. We'd best be along."

As if his words had been prophecy, Arutha and Laurie were startled to hear a voice coming out of the fog. "Here now!" Emerging from the murk were three men wearing the grey felt caps and yellow tabards of the city watch. The leftmost watchman, a beefy, heavy-browed fellow, carried a lantern in one hand and a large nightstick in the other. The center man was of advancing years, close to retirement age from appearances, and the third was a young lad, but both had an air of street experience about them, evidenced in the way they casually had their hands resting on large belt knives. "What passes this night?" the older watchman said, his voice a mixture of good-natured humor and authority.

"Some disturbance in that house, watchman." Arutha pointed toward the fuller. "We were simply passing by."

"Were you now, sir? Well, I don't suppose you'd object to remaining for a few moments longer until we discover what this is all about." He signaled to the young watchman to look around.

Arutha nodded, saying nothing. At that point a red-faced puffball of a man emerged from the house, waving his arms while he shouted, "Thieves! They stole into my room, my very room, and took my treasure! What's to be done when a law-abiding citizen isn't safe in his bed, his own bed, I ask you?" Catching sight of Arutha and Laurie, he said, "Are these then the thieves, the vicious thieves?" Mustering what dignity he could while wearing a voluminous nightshirt, he exclaimed, "What have you done with my gold, my precious gold?"

The beefy watchman jerked on the shouting man's arm, nearly spinning the fuller completely around. "Here now, watch your shouting, churl."

"Churl!" shouted Trig. "Just what, I ask, gives you the right to call a citizen, a law-abiding citizen, a—" He stopped, and his expression changed to one of disbelief as a company of riders appeared out of the fog. At their head rode a tall, black-skinned man wearing the tabard of the captain of the Prince's Royal Household Guard. Seeing the gathering in the streets, he signaled for his men to rein in.

With a shake of his head, Arutha said to Laurie, "So much for a quiet return to Krondor."

The captain said, "Watchman, what is all this?"

The watchman saluted. "That is what I was just undertaking to discover this very minute, Captain. We apprehended these two. . . ." He indicated Arutha and Laurie.

The captain rode closer and laughed. The watchman looked sidewise at this tall captain, not knowing what to say. Riding up to Arutha, Gardan, former sergeant of the garrison at Crydee, saluted. "Welcome to your city, Highness." At these words the other guards braced in their saddles, saluting their Prince.

Arutha returned the salute of the guardsmen, then shook hands with Gardan while the watchmen and the fuller stood speechless. "Singer," said Gardan, "it is good to see you again, as well." Laurie acknowledged the greeting with a smile and wave. He had known Gardan for only a brief while before Arutha had dispatched him to Krondor to assume command of the city and palace guards, but he liked the grey-haired soldier.

Arutha looked to where the watchmen and the fuller waited. The watchmen had their caps off and the seniormost said, "Beggin' Your Highness's pardon, old Bert didn't know. Any offense was unintended, Sire."

Arutha shook his head, amused despite the late hour and the cold weather. "No offense, Bert the Watchman. You were but doing your duty, and rightly so." He turned to Gardan. "Now, how in heaven's name did you manage to find me?"

"Duke Caldric sent a full itinerary along with the news that you were returning from Rillanon. You were due in tomorrow, but I said to Earl Volney you'd most likely try to slip in tonight. As you were riding from Salador, there was only one gate you'd enter"—he pointed down the street toward the eastern gate, unseen in the fog-shrouded night—"and here we are. Your Highness arrived even earlier than I had expected. Where is the rest of your party?"

"Half the guards are escorting the Princess Anita toward her mother's estates. The rest are camped about six hours' ride from the city. I couldn't abide one more night on the road. Besides, there's a great deal to be done." Gardan looked quizzically at the Prince, but all Arutha would say was "More when I speak to Volney. Now"—he looked at the fuller—"who is this loud fellow?"

"This is Trig the Fuller, Highness," answered the senior watchman. "He claims someone broke into his room and stole from him. He says he was awakened by the sounds of struggle on his roof."

Trig interrupted. "They were fighting over my head, over my . . . very . . . head . . ." His voice trailed off as he realized who he was speaking to. ". . . Your Highness," he finished, suddenly embarrassed.

The heavy-browed watchman threw him a stern look. "He says he heard some sort of scream and, like a turtle, pulled his head back in from the window."

Trig nodded vigorously. "Like someone was doing murder, doing bloody murder, Your Highness. It was horrible." The beefy watchman visited Trig with an elbow to the ribs at the interruption.

The young watchman came from the side alley. "This was lying atop some trash on the street the other side of the house, Bert." He held out the assassin's sword. "There was some blood on the grip, but none on the blade. There's also a small pool of blood in the alley, but no body, anywhere."

Arutha motioned for Gardan to take the sword. The young watchman, observing the guards and the obvious position of command assumed by the newcomers, handed up the sword, then doffed his own cap.

Arutha received the sword from Gardan, saw nothing significant in it, and returned it to the watchman. "Turn your guards around, Gardan. It is late and there's little sleep left this night."

"But what of the theft?" cried the fuller, shaken loose from his silence. "It was my savings, my life savings! I'm ruined! What shall I do?"

The Prince turned his horse and came alongside the watchmen. To Trig he said, "I offer my sympathies, good fuller, but rest assured the watch will do their utmost to retrieve your goods."

"Now," said Bert to Trig, "I suggest you turn in for what's left of the night, sir. In the morning you may enter a complaint with the duty sergeant of the watch. He'll want a description of what was taken."

"What was taken? Gold, man, that's what they took! My hoard, my entire hoard!"

"Gold, is it? Then," said Bert, with the voice of experience, "I suggest you turn in and tomorrow begin to rebuild your treasure, for as sure as there's fog in Krondor, you'll not see one coin again. But do not be too disconsolate, good sir. You are a man of means, and gold quickly accrues to those of your station, resources, and enterprise."

Arutha stifled a laugh, for despite the man's personal tragedy, he stood a comic figure in his nightshirt of linen, his nightcap tipping forward to almost touch his nose. "Good fuller, I will make amends." He pulled his dagger from his belt and handed it down to Bert the watchman. "This weapon bears my family crest. The only others like it are worn by my brothers, the King and the Duke of

Crydee. Return it to the palace tomorrow and a bag of gold will be placed in its stead. I'll have no unhappy fullers in Krondor on the day of my homecoming. Now I bid you all good night." Arutha spurred his horse and led his companions toward the palace.

When Arutha and his guards had vanished into the gloom, Bert turned to Trig. "Well then, sir, there's a happy end to it," he said, passing the Prince's dagger over to the fuller. "And you may take some added pleasure in knowing you are one of the few of common birth who may claim to have spoken with the Prince of Krondor, albeit under somewhat strange and difficult circumstances." To his men he said, "Let us back to our rounds. There'll be more than this one little bit of fun in Krondor on a night like this." He signaled for his men to follow and led them off into the white murk.

Trig stood alone. After a moment his expression brightened and he shouted up to his wife and any others who still looked out their windows, "I've spoken to the Prince! I, Trig the Fuller!" Feeling emotions somewhat akin to elation, the fuller trudged back into the warmth of his home, clutching Arutha's dagger.

Jimmy made his way through the narrowest of tunnels. The passage was part of the maze of sewers and other underground constructions common to that part of the city, and every foot of those underground passages was controlled by the Mockers. Jimmy passed a tofsman—one who made his living gathering up whatever of use could be found in the sewers. He used a stick to halt a jumble of debris carried along on the waters of the sewer. The floating mass was called a tof, that which tofleets, in a corruption of language. He picked at it, looking for a coin or anything else of value. He was in fact a sentry. Jimmy signaled to him, ducked under a low-hanging timber, apparently a fallen brace in an abandoned cellar, and entered a large hall carved out among the tunnels. Here was the heart of the guild of thieves, Mockers' Rest.

Jimmy retrieved his rapier from the weapons locker. He sought out a quiet corner in which to sit, for he felt troubled by the conflict he faced. By rights he should own up to his unauthorized pilfering of the fuller's house, split the gold, and take whatever punishment the Nightmaster meted out. By tomorrow afternoon the guild would know the fuller had been boosted, anyway. Once it was clear that no freebooting thief was at work, suspicion would fall upon Jimmy and the others known to occasionally go for a night's foray without leave. Any punishment forthcoming then would be doubly harsh for his not having confessed now. Still, Jimmy couldn't consider only his own interests, since he knew the assassin's target had been none other than the Prince of Krondor himself. And Jimmy had spent enough time with Arutha when the Mockers had hidden the Prince and Princess Anita from du Bas-Tyra's men to have developed a liking for the Prince. Arutha had given Jimmy the very rapier the boy thief wore at his side. No, Jimmy couldn't ignore the assassin's presence, but he was not clear where his best course lay.

After long moments of quiet consideration, Jimmy decided. He would first attempt to get warning to the Prince, then pass along the information about the assassin to Alvarny the Quick, the Daymaster. Alvarny was a friend and allowed Jimmy a little more latitude than Gaspar daVey, the Nightmaster. Alvarny would make no mention to the Upright Man of Jimmy's tardiness in reporting, if the boy didn't take too long to come forth. Which meant Jimmy would have to reach Arutha quickly, then return at once to speak with the Daymaster—before sundown tomorrow at the latest. Any later than that, and Jimmy would be compromised beyond even Alvarny's ability to look the other way. Alvarny might be a generous man, now that he was in his twilight, but he was still a Mocker. Disloyalty to the guild was something he would not permit.

"Jimmy!"

Jimmy looked up and saw Golden Dase approaching. While young, the dashing thief was already experienced in parting rich older women from their wealth. He relied more on his blond good looks and charm than on stealth. Dase made a display of the valuable clothing he wore. "What think you?"

Jimmy nodded in approval. "Taken to robbing tailors?"

Golden aimed a playful, halfhearted cuff at Jimmy, who ducked easily, then sat next to the boy. "No, you misbegotten son of an alley cat, I have not. My current 'benefactor' is the widow of the famous Masterbrewer Fallon." Jimmy had heard of the man; his ales and beers had been so highly prized they had even graced the table of the late Prince Erland. "And given her late husband's and now her far-reaching business concerns, she has received an invitation to the reception."

"Reception?" Jimmy knew Golden had some tidbit of gossip he wished to unfold in his own good time.

"Ah," said Golden, "did I fail to mention the fact of a wedding?"

Jimmy rolled his eyes upward but played along. "What wedding, Golden?"

"Why, the royal wedding of course. Though we shall be seated away from the King's table, it will not be at the table most remote."

Jimmy sat bolt upright. "The King? In Krondor!"

"Of course."

Jimmy gripped Golden by the arm. "Start at the beginning."

Grinning, the handsome but not terribly perceptive confidence man said, "The widow Fallon was informed by no less a source than the purchasing agent at the palace, a man she has known for seventeen years, that extra stores were required within a month's time for, and I quote, 'the royal wedding.' One is safe in assuming a king would be in attendance at his own wedding."

Jimmy shook his head. "No, you simpleton, not the King's. Anita and Arutha's."

Golden seemed ready to take umbrage at the remark, but then a sudden glimmer of interest showed in his eyes. "What makes you say that?"

"The King weds in Rillanon. The Prince weds in Krondor." Golden nodded, indicating this made sense. "I hid out with Anita and Arutha; it was only a matter of time before they wed. That's why he's back." Seeing a reaction at that, Jimmy quickly added, ". . . Or will be back soon."

Jimmy's mind raced. Not only would Lyam be in Krondor for the wedding, but so would every noble of importance in the West, and no small number from the East. And if Dase knew of the wedding, then half of Krondor did as well and the other half would know of it before the next sundown.

Jimmy's reverie was interrupted by the approach of Laughing Jack, the Nightwarden, senior lieutenant to the Nightmaster. The thin-lipped man came to stand before Jimmy and Dase and, with hands upon hips, said, "You look like you've something on your mind, boy?"

Jimmy had no affection for Jack. He was a dour, tight-jawed man given to violent tempers and unnecessary cruelty. The only reason for his high place in the guild was his ability at keeping the guild's bashers and other hotheads in line. Jimmy's dislike was returned in kind by Jack, for it had been Jimmy who had appended "Laughing" to Jack's name. In the years Jack had been in the guild, no one could remember hearing him laugh. "Nothing, really," said Jimmy.

Jack's eyes narrowed as he studied Jimmy, then Dase, for a long minute. "I hear there was some fuss over near the east gate; you weren't thereabouts this night, were you?"

Jimmy maintained an indifferent expression and regarded Dase, as if Jack had asked both the question. Golden shook his head in the negative. Jimmy wondered if Jack already knew about the Nighthawk. If he did, and if someone else had caught sight of Jimmy nearby, Jimmy could expect no mercy from Jack's bashers. Still, Jimmy suspected that if Jack had proof, he would have come accusing, not questioning. Subtlety was not Jack's hallmark. Jimmy feigned indifference as he said, "Another drunken argument? No, I was asleep most of the night."

"Good, then you'll be fresh," said Jack. With a jerk of his head he indicated Dase should absent himself. Golden rose and left without comment and Jack placed his boot upon the bench next to Jimmy. "We've got a job this night."

"Tonight?" said Jimmy, already counting the night half done. There was barely five hours left until sunrise.

"It's special. From himself," he said, meaning the Upright Man. "There's a royal do on at the palace and the Keshian ambassador's coming. A load of gifts arrived late tonight, gifts for a wedding. They'll be straight off for the palace by midday next at latest, so tonight's our only chance to boost them. It's a rare chance." His tone left no doubt in Jimmy's mind that his presence was not requested but required. Jimmy had hoped to get some sleep tonight before heading for the palace, but now there was no chance of that. With a note of resignation in his voice, he said, "When and where?"

"An hour from now at the big warehouse one street over from the Fiddler Crab Inn, near dockside."

Jimmy knew the place. He nodded and without another word left Laughing Jack. He headed up the stairs toward the street. The question of assassins and plots would have to wait a few hours more.

Fog still overwhelmed Krondor. The warehouse district near the docks was usually quiet in the early morning hours, but this night the scene was otherworldly. Jimmy wended his way among large bales of goods, of too little value to warrant the additional expense of storage inside, and therefore safe from the threat of thievery. Bulk cotton, animal fodder to be shipped, and stacked lumber created a maze of maddening complexity through which Jimmy moved quietly. He had spied several dock watchmen, but the night's dampness and a generous bribe kept them close to their shed, where a fire burned brightly in a brazier, relieving the gloom. Nothing short of a riot would get them away from the warmth. The Mockers would be long removed from this area before those indifferent guardians stirred.

Reaching the designated meeting place, Jimmy looked about and, seeing no one in sight, settled in to wait. He was early, as was his habit, for he liked to compose his mind before the action began. Additionally, there was something in Laughing Jack's orders to him that made him wary. A job this important was rarely a last-minute affair, and even rarer was the Upright Man's allowing anything to tempt the Prince's wrath—and purloining royal wedding gifts would bring Arutha's wrath. But Jimmy was not placed highly enough in the guild to know if everything was on the up and up. He would simply have to remain alert.

The soft hint of someone approaching caused Jimmy to tense. Whoever was coming was moving cautiously, as was to be expected, but with the faint footfalls he had heard a strange sound. It was the slight clicking of metal on wood and, as soon as recognition registered, Jimmy leaped away. With a loud thud and an eruption of wood splinters, a crossbow bolt ripped through the side of a crate, where Jimmy had stood a moment before.

An instant later, two figures, dark silhouettes in the grey night, appeared from out of the gloom, running toward him.

Sword in hand, Laughing Jack rushed Jimmy without a word, while his companion furiously cranked up his crossbow for another shot. Jimmy drew weapons and executed a parry of an overhand slash by Jack, diverting the blade with his dirk, then lunging with his rapier in return. Jack skipped to one side, and the two figures squared off.

"Now we'll see how well you can use that toad sticker, you snotty little bastard," snarled Jack. "Watching you bleed just might give me something to laugh about."

Jimmy said nothing, refusing to engage in distracting conversation. His only reply was a high-line attack that drove Jack back. He had no illusions about being a better swordsman than Jack; he simply wanted to keep alive long enough to gain a chance to flee.

Back and forth they moved, exchanging blows and parries, each looking for an opening to finish the contest. Jimmy tried for a counterthrust and misjudged his position, and suddenly fire erupted in his side. Jack had managed to cut Jimmy with the edge of his sword, a painful and potentially weakening wound, but not fatal, at least not yet. Jimmy looked for more room to move, feeling sick to his stomach from the pain, while Jack pressed his advantage. Jimmy backed off from a furious overhand slashing attack as Jack used the advantage of his heavier blade to beat down Jimmy's guard.

A sudden shout telling Jack to get out of the way warned Jimmy the other man had reloaded his crossbow. Jimmy circled away from Jack, trying to keep moving and put Jack between himself and Jack's accomplice. Jack slashed at Jimmy, turning him back rapidly, and then hacked downward. The force of the blow dropped Jimmy to his knees.

Abruptly Jack leaped backward, as if a giant hand had seized him by the collar and yanked. He slammed against a large crate and for an instant his eyes registered shocked disbelief, then rolled up in his head as limp fingers lost their grip on his sword. Jimmy saw that, where Jack's chest had been, a bloody, pulped mass was left by the passage of another crossbow bolt. But for the sudden fury of Jack's attack, Jimmy would have received it in the back. Without a sound Jack slumped, and Jimmy realized he was pinned to the crate. Jimmy rose from his crouch, spinning to confront the nameless man, who had tossed away the crossbow with a curse. He pulled his sword and rushed Jimmy. The man aimed a blow at Jimmy's head and the boy ducked, catching his heel. He fell heavily backward into a sitting position while the man's swing took him off balance slightly. Jimmy tossed his dirk at the man. The man took the point of the long dagger in the side and looked down at the wound, more an inconvenience than an injury. But the brief distraction was all Jimmy needed. An expression of uncomprehending surprise crossed the nameless man's face as Jimmy got to one knee and ran him through.

Jimmy yanked away his blade as the man fell. He pulled his dirk from the dead man's side, then wiped off and resheathed his blades. Slowly examining himself, he found he was bleeding but would live.

Fighting off nausea, he walked to where Jack hung against the crate. Looking at the Nightwarden, Jimmy tried to gather his thoughts. He and Jack had never cared a whit for each other, but why this elaborate trap? Jimmy wondered if this was somehow tied up with the matter of the assassin and the Prince. It was something he could dwell on after he spoke to the Prince, for if there was a direct relationship, it boded ill for the Mockers. The possibility of a betrayal by one as highly placed as Laughing Jack would shake the guild to its foundation.

Never losing his perspective, Jimmy relieved Jack and his companion of their purses, finding them both satisfactorily full. As he finished looting Jack's companion, he noticed something around the man's neck.

Reaching down, Jimmy came away with a gold chain, upon which hung an ebony hawk. He studied the charm for a few moments, then stuck it away in his tunic. Looking around, he spied a likely-looking place to deposit the bodies. He plucked Jack from off the bolt, dragged him and the other man over to a nook formed by crates, and tipped some heavy sacks down on top of them. He turned two damaged crates so the intact sides were revealed. It might be days before someone uncovered the corpses.

Ignoring his angry side and fatigue, Jimmy looked around to make sure he was still unobserved, then vanished into the foggy gloom.

THREE

PLOTS

Arutha attacked furiously.

Laurie exhorted Gardan to better efforts as the Prince forced his dueling companion into a retreat. The singer had willingly surrendered the honor of the first bout to Gardan, for he had been Arutha's partner every morning upon the journey from Salador to Krondor. While the practice had sharpened sword skills grown rusty in the King's palace, he had tired of always losing to the lightning-quick Prince. At least this morning he would have someone with whom to share his defeat. Still, the old campaigner wasn't without a trick or two and suddenly Gardan had Arutha backing up. Laurie whooped when he realized the captain had been lulling the Prince into a false sense of control. But after a furious exchange the Prince was again on the offensive, and Gardan was crying, "Hold!"

The chuckling Gardan backed away. "In all my years there have been only three men who could best me with the blade, Highness: Swordmaster Fannon, your father, and now yourself."

Laurie said, "A worthy trio." Arutha was about to offer a bout to Laurie when something caught his eye.

A large tree was situated in the corner of the palace exercise yard, where it overhung a wall separating the palace grounds from an alley and the city beyond. Something was moving along the branches of the tree. Arutha pointed. One of the palace guardsmen was already moving toward the tree, his attention drawn there by the Prince's stare.

Suddenly someone dropped from the branches, landing lightly on his feet. Arutha, Laurie, and Gardan all stood with swords held ready. The guardsman took the youth, as they now clearly saw him to be, by the arm and led him toward the Prince.

As they approached, a flicker of recognition crossed Arutha's face. "Jimmy?"

Jimmy executed a bow, wincing slightly at the pain in his side, poorly bandaged by himself that morning. Gardan said, "Highness, you know this lad?"

With a nod, Arutha said, "Yes. He may be a little older and a bit taller, but I know this young rogue. He's Jimmy the Hand, already a legend among brigands and cutpurses in the city. This is the boy thief who helped Anita and me flee the city."

Laurie studied the boy, then laughed. "I never saw him clearly, for the warehouse was dark when Kasumi and I were taken from Krondor by the Mockers, but by my teeth, it's the same lad. 'There's a party at Mother's.' "

Jimmy grinned. " 'And a good time will be had by all.' "

Arutha said, "So you know each other as well?"

"I told you once that when Kasumi and I were carrying the peace message from the Tsurani Emperor to King Rodric, there was a boy who had guided us from the warehouse to the city gate and led away the guards while we escaped Krondor. This was that boy, and I never could remember his name."

Arutha put up his sword, as did the others. "Well then, Jimmy, while I am glad to see you again, there is this matter of climbing walls into my palace."

Jimmy shrugged. "I thought it possible you'd be willing to see an old acquaintance, Highness, but I doubted I could convince the captain's guards to send word."

Gardan smiled at the brash answer and signaled the guard to release his hold upon the boy's arm. "Probably you're right, Jack-a-rags."

Jimmy suddenly became aware he looked a poor sight to these men, used to the well-dressed and -groomed inhabitants of the palace. From his raggedly cut hair down to his dirty bare feet he looked every inch the beggar boy. Then Jimmy saw the humor in Gardan's eyes.

"Don't let his appearance mislead you, Gardan. He's far more capable than his years indicate." To Jimmy, Arutha said, "You throw some discredit upon Gardan's guards by entering in this fashion. I expect you've reason to seek me out?"

"Yes, Highness. Business most serious and urgent."

Arutha nodded. "Well then, what is this most serious and urgent business?"

"Someone has placed a price on your head."

Gardan's face registered shock. Laurie said, "What—how?"

"What leads you to think so?" asked Arutha.

"Because someone has already tried to collect."

Besides Arutha, Laurie, and Gardan, two others listened to the boy's story in the Prince's council chambers. Earl Volney of Landreth had formerly been the assistant to the Principate Chancellor, Lord Dulanic, the Duke of Krondor who disappeared during the viceroyalty of Guy du Bas-Tyra. At Volney's side sat Father Nathan, a priest of Sung the White, Goddess of the One Path, once one of Prince Erland's chief advisers and there at Gardan's request. Arutha did not know these two men, but during the months of his absence Gardan had come to trust their judgment, and that opinion counted for much with Arutha. Gardan had been virtually acting Knight-Marshal of Krondor, just as Volney had been acting Chancellor, while Arutha had been gone.

Both men were stocky, but while Volney seemed one who had never known labor, simply a man always stout, Nathan looked like a wrestler now going to fat. Under that soft appearance strength still waited. Neither spoke until Jimmy had finished recounting his two fights of the night before.

Volney studied the boy thief for a moment, looking at him from under carefully combed, bushy eyebrows. "Utterly fantastic. I simply don't wish to believe such a plot can exist."

Arutha had sat with his hands forming a tent before his face, the fingers restlessly flexing. "I'd not be the first prince targeted for an assassin's blade, Earl Volney." He said to Gardan, "Double the guard at once, but quietly, with no explanation given. I do not want rumors flying about the palace. Within two weeks we'll have every noble in the Kingdom worth mention in these halls, as well as my brother."

Volney said, "Perhaps you should warn His Majesty?"

"No," said Arutha flatly. "Lyam will be traveling with a full company of his Royal Household Guard. Have a detachment of

Krondorian Lancers meet them at Malac's Cross, but no word that it is other than a formal honor company. If a hundred soldiers can't protect him while he rides, he can't be protected.

"No, our problem lies here in Krondor. We have no choice in our options."

"I'm not sure I follow, Highness," said Father Nathan.

Laurie threw his eyes heavenward while Jimmy grinned. Arutha smiled grimly. "I think our two streetwise companions have a clear understanding of what must be done." Turning to face Jimmy and Laurie, Arutha said, "We must catch a Nighthawk."

Arutha sat quietly while Volney paced the dining hall. Laurie, who had seen years enough of hunger to take food when it was available, ate while the stout Earl of Landreth stalked the hall. After watching Volney make another circuit before the table, Arutha, in weary tones, said, "My lord Earl, must you pace so?"

The Earl, who was caught up in his own thoughts, stopped abruptly. He bowed toward Arutha slightly, but his expression was one of irritation. "Highness, I'm sorry to have disturbed you"—his tone showed he wasn't in the least bit sorry, and Laurie smiled behind a joint of beef—"but to trust that thief is sheer idiocy."

Arutha's eyes widened and he looked at Laurie, who returned his amazed expression. Laurie said, "My dear Earl, you should cease being so circumspect. Come, just speak your mind to the Prince. Be direct, man!"

Volney flushed as he realized his gaffe. "I beg your pardon, I . . ." He seemed genuinely embarrassed.

Arutha smiled his crooked half-smile. "Pardon granted, Volney, but only for the rudeness." He studied Volney for a quiet moment, then added, "I find the candor rather refreshing. Say on."

"Highness," Volney said firmly, "for all we know, this boy is but a part of some confidence game designed to capture you, or to destroy you, as he claims others intend."

"And what would you have me do?"

Volney paused and shook his head slowly. "I don't know, Highness, but sending the boy alone to gather intelligence is . . . I don't know."

Arutha said, "Laurie, tell my friend and counselor the Earl that all is well."

Gulping down a mouthful of fine wine, Laurie said, "All is well, Earl." When Arutha threw the minstrel a black look, Laurie added, "In truth, sir, all possible is being done. I know the ways of the city as well as any man can who is not one of the Upright Man's own. Jimmy's a Mocker. He may discover a lead to the Nighthawks where a dozen spies will find none."

"Remember," said Arutha, "I met Guy's captain of secret police, Jocko Radburn, and he was a cunning, ruthless man who stopped at nothing to try to recapture Anita. The Mockers proved his match."

Volney seemed to sag a little, then indicated he required the Prince's permission to sit. Arutha waved him to a chair, and as he sat he said, "Perhaps you are right, singer. It is just that I have no means to answer this threat. The thought of assassins running loose gives me little ease."

Arutha leaned across the table. "Less than myself? Remember, Volney, it appeared I was the intended target."

Laurie nodded. "It couldn't have been me they were after."

"Perhaps a music lover?" countered Arutha dryly.

Volney sighed. "I am sorry if I am acting poorly in all this. I have wished upon more than one occasion to be done with this business of administering the Principality."

"Nonsense, Volney," said Arutha. "You've done a capital job here. When Lyam insisted I make the eastern tour with him, I objected on the grounds that the Western Realm would suffer under any hand but my own—which was because of the effects of Bas-Tyra's rule and no comment upon your abilities. But I am pleased to see this was not the case. I doubt that any could have done better in running the daily affairs of the realm than you have, Earl."

"I thank His Highness," said Volney, somewhat less agitated for the compliment.

"In fact, I was going to ask you to stay on. With Dulanic mysteriously gone, we've no Duke of Krondor to act on behalf of the city. Lyam cannot announce the office vacant—without dishonoring Dulanic's memory by stripping him of the title—for another two years, but we can all assume he is dead at Guy's or Radburn's hands. So for the time being, I think we'll plan on your acting the part of Chancellor."

Volney seemed less than pleased with this news, but took the pronouncement with good grace. He simply said, "I thank His Highness for the trust."

Further conversation was interrupted by the appearance of Gardan, Father Nathan, and Jimmy. Nathan's bull neck bulged as he half carried Jimmy to a chair. The boy's face was drained of color and he was sweating. Ignoring formality, Arutha pointed to a chair and the priest deposited Jimmy there.

"What is this?" asked Arutha.

Gardan half smiled, half looked disapproving. "This young bravo has been running around since last night with a nasty cut in his side. He bandaged it himself and botched the job."

"It had begun to fester," added Nathan, "so I was forced to clean and dress it. I insisted on treating it before we came to see you, as the boy was turning feverish. It takes no magic to keep a wound from putrefaction, but every street boy thinks he is a chirurgeon. So the wound sours." He looked down at Jimmy. "He's a little pale from the lancing, but he'll be fine in a few hours—as long as he doesn't reopen the wound," he added pointedly to Jimmy.

Jimmy looked abashed. "Sorry to put you to the trouble, father, but under other circumstances, I would have had the wound tended."

Arutha looked at the boy thief. "What have you discovered?"

"This business of catching assassins may be even more difficult than we thought, Highness. There is a way to make contact, but it is varied and roundabout." Arutha nodded for him to continue. "I had to cadge a lot with the street people, but here is what I have gleaned. Should you wish to employ the services of the Guild of Death, you must take yourself away to the Temple of Lims-Kragma." Nathan made a sign of protection at mention of the Death Goddess. "A devotion is said and a votive offering placed in the urn marked for such, but with the gold sewn into a parchment, giving your name. You will be contacted at their convenience within one day's time. You name the victim; they name the price. You pay or you don't. If you do, they tell you when and where to drop the gold. If you don't, they vanish and you can't reach them again."

"Simple," said Laurie. "They dictate when and where, so laying a trap will not be easy."

"Impossible, I should think," said Gardan.

"Nothing is impossible," said Arutha, his expression showing he was deep in thought.

After a long moment Laurie said, "I have it!"

Arutha and the others looked at the singer. "Jimmy, you said they will contact whoever leaves the gold within the day." Jimmy nodded. "Then what we need to do is have whoever leaves the gold stay in one place. A place we control."

Arutha said, "A simple enough idea, once it's thought of, Laurie. But where?"

Jimmy said, "There are a few places we might take over for a time, Highness, but those who own them are unreliable."

"I know a place," said Laurie, "if friend Jimmy the Hand is willing to say devotions, so the Nighthawks will be less likely to think it a trap."

"I don't know," said Jimmy. "Things are funny in Krondor. If I'm under suspicion, we might never get another opportunity." He reminded them of Jack's attack, and of his unknown companion with the crossbow. "It may have been a grudge thing; I've known men to get crazy over something even more trivial than a nickname, but if it wasn't . . . If Jack was somehow involved with that assassin . . ."

"Then," said Laurie, "the Nighthawks have turned an officer of the Mockers to their cause."

Jimmy looked upset, as he suddenly dropped his mask of bravado. "That thought has troubled me as much as the thought of someone sticking his Highness with a crossbow bolt. I've been neglecting my oath to the Mockers. I should have told all last night, and certainly I must now." He seemed ready to rise.

Volney placed a firm hand upon Jimmy's shoulder. "Presumptuous boy! Are you saying some league of cutthroats merits even a moment's consideration in light of the danger to your Prince and possibly your King?"

Jimmy seemed on the verge of a retort when Arutha said, "I think that's exactly what the boy said, Volney. He has given oath."

Laurie quickly stepped over to where the boy sat. Moving Volney to one side, he leaned down so his face was level with Jimmy's. "You have your concerns, we know, lad, but things seem to be moving rapidly. If the Mockers have been infiltrated, then speaking too soon could make those who have been placed there cover tracks. If we can get one of these Nighthawks . . ." He left the thought unfinished.

Jimmy nodded. "If the Upright Man will only follow your logic, I may survive, singer. I come close to past the time when I may cover my actions with a facile story. Soon I will be at an accounting. Very well, I'll take a note to the Drawer of Nets' temple. And I will play no mummery when I ask her to make a place for me should it be my time."

"And," said Laurie, "I must be off to see an old friend about the loan of an inn."

"Good," said Arutha. "We will spring the snare tomorrow."

While Volney, Nathan, and Gardan watched, Laurie and Jimmy departed, deep in conversation as they made plans. Arutha followed their departure as well, his dark eyes masking the quietly burning rage he felt. After so many years of strife during the Riftwar he had returned to Krondor hoping for a long, peaceful life with Anita. Now someone dared to threaten that peaceful life. And that someone would pay dearly.

The Rainbow Parrot Inn was quiet. The storm windows had been closed against a sudden squall off the Bitter Sea, so the tap room lay blanketed in haze, blue smoke from the fireplace and a dozen patrons' pipes. To any casual observer the inn looked much as it would have on other rainy nights. The owner, Lucas, and his two sons stood behind the long bar, one of them occasionally moving through the door to the kitchen to get meals and carry them to the tables. In the corner near the fireplace, opposite the stairs to the second floor, a blond minstrel sang softly of a sailor who is far from home.

Close inspection would have revealed that the men at the tables barely touched their ale. While rough in appearance, they didn't have the air of workers from the docks and sailors fresh in from sea voyages. They all possessed a certain hard-eyed look, and their scars were earned in past battles rather than tavern brawls. All were members of Gardan's company of Household Guard, some of the most seasoned veterans of the Armies of the West during the Riftwar. In the kitchen five new cooks and apprentices worked. Upstairs, in the room closest to the head of the stairway, Arutha, Gardan, and five soldiers waited patiently. In total, Arutha had placed twenty-four men in the inn. Arutha's men were the only ones present, as the last local had left when the storm commenced.

In the corner farthest from the door, Jimmy the Hand waited. Something had troubled him all day, though he couldn't put his finger on it. But he knew one thing: if he himself had entered this room this night, his experience-bred caution would have warned him away. He hoped the Nighthawks' agent wasn't as perceptive. Something here just wasn't right.

Jimmy sat back and absently nibbled at the cheese, pondering what was askew. It was an hour after sundown, and still no sign of anyone who might be from the Nighthawks. Jimmy had come straight from the temple, making sure he had been seen by several beggars who knew him well. If any in Krondor wished to find him, word of his whereabouts could be purchased easily and cheaply.

The front door opened and two men came in from the rain, shaking water from their cloaks. Both appeared to be fighting men, perhaps bravos who had earned a fair purse of silver protecting some merchant's caravans. They wore similar attire: leather armor, calf-length boots, broadswords at their sides, and shields slung over their backs, under the protective cloaks.

The taller fellow, with a grey streak through his dark hair, ordered ales. The other, a thin blond man, looked about the room. Something in the way his eyes narrowed alarmed Jimmy: he also sensed something different in the inn. He spoke softly to his companion. The man with the grey lock nodded, then took the ales presented by the barman. Paying with coppers, the two men moved to the only available table, the one next to Jimmy's.

The man with the grey lock turned toward Jimmy and said, "Lad, is this inn always so somber?" Jimmy then realized what the problem had been all day. In their waiting, the guards had fallen into the soldier's habit of speaking softly. The room was free of the usual common-room din.

Jimmy held his forefinger before his lips and whispered, "It is the singer." The man turned his head and listened to Laurie for a moment. Laurie was a gifted performer and was in good voice despite his long day's work. When he finished, Jimmy banged his ale jack hard upon the table and shouted, "Ha! Minstrel, more, more!" as he tossed a silver coin toward the dais upon which Laurie sat. His outburst was followed a moment later by similar shouting and cheering as the others realized the need of some display. Several other coins were tossed. When Laurie struck up another tune, lively and bawdy, a sound not unlike the normal buzz of conversation returned to the taproom.

The two strangers settled back into their chairs and listened, occasionally speaking to each other. They visibly relaxed as the mood in the room shifted to resemble what they had expected. Jimmy sat for a while, watching the two men at the next table. Something about these two was out of place, something that nagged at him as had the false note in the common room only moments before.

The door opened again and another man entered. He looked around the room as he shook water from his hooded great cloak, but he didn't remove the voluminous covering or lower the cowl. He spied Jimmy and crossed to his table. Without waiting for invitation, he pulled out a chair and sat. In hushed tones he said, "Have you a name?"

Jimmy nodded and leaned forward as if to speak. As he did so, four facts suddenly struck him. The men at the next table, despite their casual appearance, had swords and shields close at hand, needing only an instant to bring them to the ready. They didn't drink like mercenaries fresh into town after a long caravan; in fact, their drinks were nearly untouched. The man opposite Jimmy had one hand hidden under his cloak, as he had since entering. But most revealing of all, all three men wore large black rings on their left hands, with a hawk device carved in them, one similar to the talisman taken from Laughing Jack's companion. Jimmy's mind worked furiously, for he had seen such rings before and understood their use.

Jimmy pulled a parchment out of his boot. Improvising, he placed it on the table, to the far right of the man, making him reach awkwardly across himself to reach for it while he kept his right hand hidden. As the man's hand touched the parchment, Jimmy pulled his dirk out and struck, pinning the man's hand to the table. The man froze at the sudden attack, then his other hand came from within his cloak, holding a dagger. He slashed at Jimmy as the boy thief fell backward. Then pain struck the man and he howled in agony. Jimmy, tumbling over his chair, shouted, "Nighthawks!" as he struck the floor.

The room exploded with activity. Lucas's sons, both veterans of the Armies of the West, came leaping over the bar, landing on the swordsmen at the table next to Jimmy as they attempted to rise. Jimmy found himself hanging backward atop the overturned chair and awkwardly tried to pull himself upright. From his position he could see the barmen grappling with the grey-lock man. The other false mercenary had his left hand before his face, his ring to his lips. Jimmy shouted, "Poison rings! They have poison rings!"

Other guards had the hooded man in their grip as he frantically tried to remove his ring from his pinned hand. After another moment he was held tightly by the three men around him, unable to move.

The grey-lock man kicked out at the barmen, rolled away, leaped up, and dashed toward the door, knocking aside two men surprised by the sudden move. For a moment a clear path to the door appeared as curses filled the room from soldiers attempting to navigate the jumble of tables and chairs. The Nighthawk was nearing the door and freedom when a slender fighter interposed himself. The assassin leaped toward the door. With near-inhuman speed Arutha stepped forward and struck the grey-locked man a blow to the head with his rapier's hilt. The stunned man teetered for a moment, then collapsed to the floor, unconscious.

Arutha stood erect and looked about the room. The blond assassin lay with eyes staring blankly upward, obviously dead. The hooded man's cloak was thrown back and he was white with pain as the dagger pinning his hand to the table was pulled loose. Three soldiers held him down, though he looked too weak to stand upon his own feet. When a soldier roughly stripped the black ring from the wounded hand, the Nighthawk screamed and fainted.

Jimmy stepped gingerly around the dead man and came up to Arutha. He looked down to where Gardan was removing the other black ring from the man on the floor and then the boy grinned at Arutha. Holding up his hand, he counted two on his fingers.

The Prince, still flushed from the struggle, smiled and nodded. None of his men appeared wounded and he had two assassins in tow. He said to Gardan, "Guard them closely and let no one who is not known to us see them when you take them into the palace. I'll have no rumors flying around. Lucas and others may be in danger enough when these three turn up missing, should others from the Guild of Death be about. Leave enough of this company to keep up the appearance of normal business until closing, and pay Lucas double the damages, with our thanks." Even as he spoke, Gardan's company was restoring the inn to order, removing the broken table and moving the others about so it would not be noticed missing. "Take these two to the rooms I have chosen and be quick about it. We shall begin questioning tonight."

Guards blocked a door leading to a remote wing of the palace. The rooms were used only occasionally by guests of minor importance. The wing was a recent construction, being accessible from the main buildings of the palace by a single short hall and a single outside doorway. The outside door was bolted from within and was posted with two guards without, who had orders that absolutely no one, no matter who, was to enter or leave by that door.

Inside the wing all the outer rooms had been secured. In the center of the largest room of the suite Arutha studied his two prisoners. Both were tied to stout wooden beds by heavy ropes. Arutha was taking no chances on their attempting suicide. Father Nathan supervised his acolytes, who tended the two assassins' wounds.

Abruptly one of the acolytes moved away from the bedside of the man with the grey lock. He looked at Nathan, his face betraying confusion. "Father, come see."

Jimmy and Laurie followed behind the priest and Arutha. Nathan stepped up behind the acolyte and all heard his sharp intake of breath. "Sung show us the way!" The grey-locked man's leather armor had been cut away, revealing a black tunic beneath embroidered with a silver fisher's net. Nathan pulled away the other prisoner's robe. Beneath that robe was another, of night's black color, also with a silver net over his heart. The prisoner's hand had been bandaged and he had regained consciousness. He glared defiantly at the priest of Sung, naked hatred in his eyes.

Nathan motioned the Prince aside. "These men wear the mark of Lims-Kragma in her guise as the Drawer of Nets, she who gathers all to her in the end."

Arutha nodded. "It fits in. We know the Nighthawks are contacted through the temple. Even should the hierarchy of the temple be ignorant of this business, someone within the temple must be a confederate of the Nighthawks. Come, Nathan, we must question this other one." They returned to the bed where the conscious man lay. Looking down upon him, Arutha said, "Who offers the price for my death?"

Nathan was called to attend the unconscious man. "Who are you?" demanded the Prince of the other. "Answer now, or the pain you've endured will be merely a hint of what will be visited upon you." Arutha did not enjoy the prospect of torture, but he would not stop at any means to discover who was responsible for the attack upon him. The question and the threat were answered by silence.

After a moment Nathan returned to Arutha's side. "The other is dead," he said softly. "We must treat this one cautiously. That man should not have died from your blow to the head. They may have means to command the body not to fight against death, but to welcome it. It is said even a hardy man may will himself to death, given enough time."

Arutha noticed sweat beading upon the brow of the wounded man as Nathan examined him. With concern on his face, the priest said, "He is fevered, and it rises apace. I will have to tend him before there can be an accounting." The priest quickly fetched his potion and forced some fluid down the man's throat as soldiers held his jaws apart. Then the priest began to intone his clerical magic. The man on the bed began to writhe frantically, his face a contorted mask of concentration. Tendons stood out on his arms, and his neck was a mass of ropy cords as he struggled against his confinement. Suddenly he let forth a hollow-sounding laugh and fell back, eyes closed.

Nathan examined the man. "He is unconscious, Highness." The priest added, "I have slowed the fever's rise, but I don't think I can halt it. Some magic agency works here. He fails before our eyes. It will take time to counter whatever magic is at work upon him . . . if I have the time." There was doubt in Nathan's voice. "And if my arts are equal to the task."

Arutha turned to Gardan. "Captain, take ten of your most trusted men and make straight for the Temple of Lims-Kragma. Inform the High Priestess I command her attendance at once. Bring her by force if needs be, but bring her."

Gardan saluted, but there was a flicker in his eyes. Laurie and Jimmy knew he disliked the thought of bearding the priestess in her own halls. Still, the staunch captain turned and obeyed his Prince without comment.

Arutha returned to the stricken man, who lay in fevered torment. Nathan said, "Highness, the fever rises, slowly, but it rises."

"How long will he live?"

"If we can do nothing, through the balance of the night, no longer."

Arutha struck his left hand with his balled right fist in frustration. There was less than six hours before dawn. Less than six hours to discover the cause for the attack upon him. And should this man die, they would be back where they started, and worse, for his unknown enemy would not likely fall into another snare.

"Is there anything else you can do?" asked Laurie softly.

Nathan considered. "Perhaps. . . ." He moved away from the ill man and motioned his acolytes away from the bedside. With a gesture he indicated that one of them should bring him a large volume of priestly spells.

Nathan instructed the acolytes and they quickly did his bidding, knowing the ritual and their parts in it. A pentagram was chalked upon the floor, and many runic symbols laid within its boundary, with the bed at the center. When they were finished, everyone who stood within the room was encompassed by the chalk marks upon the floor. A lighted candle was placed at every point of the design, and a sixth given to Nathan, who stood studying the book. Nathan began waving the light in an intricate pattern while he read aloud in a language unknown to the nonclerics in the room. His acolytes stood quietly to one side, responding in unison at several points during the incantation. The others felt a strange stilling of the air, and as the final syllables were uttered, the dying man groaned, a low and piteous sound.

Nathan snapped shut the book. "Nothing less powerful than an agent of the gods themselves may pass through the boundaries of the pentagram without my leave. No spirit, demon, or being sent by any dark agency can trouble us now."

Nathan then directed everyone to stand outside the pentagram, opened the book again, and began reading another chant. Quickly the words tumbled from the stocky priest. He finished the spell and pointed at the man upon the bed. Arutha looked at the ill man but could see nothing amiss, then, as he turned to speak to Laurie, noticed a change. Seeing the man from the corner of his eye, Arutha could discern a nimbus of faint light around him, filling the pentagram, not visible when viewed directly. It was a light, milky quartz in color. Arutha asked, "What is this?"

Nathan faced Arutha. "I have slowed his passage through time, Highness. To him an hour is now a moment. The spell will last only until dawn, but to him less than a quarter hour will have passed. Thus we gain time. With luck, he will now linger until midday."

"Can we speak to him?"

"No, for we would sound like buzzing bees to him. But if we need, I can remove the spell."

Arutha regarded the slowly writhing, fevered man. His hand seemed poised a scant inch above the bed, hanging in space. "Then," said the Prince impatiently, "we must wait upon the pleasure of the High Priestess of Lims-Kragma."

The wait was not long, nor was there much pleasure evident in the manner of the High Priestess. There was a commotion outside, and Arutha hurried to the door. Beyond it he found Gardan waiting with a woman in black robes. Her face was hidden behind a thick, gauzy black veil, but her head turned toward the Prince.

A finger shot out toward Arutha, and a deep, pleasant-sounding feminine voice said, "Why have I been commanded here, Prince of the Kingdom?"

Arutha ignored the question as he took in the scene. Behind Gardan stood a quartet of guards, spears held across their chests, barring the way to a group of determined-looking temple guards wearing the black and silver tabards of Lims-Kragma. "What passes, Captain?"

Gardan said, "The lady wishes to bring her guards within, and I have forbidden it."

In tones of icy fury the priestess said, "I have come as you bid, though never have the clergy acknowledged temporal authority. But I will not come as a prisoner, not even for you, Prince of Krondor."

Arutha said, "Two guards may enter, but they will stand away from the prisoner. Madam, you will cooperate and enter, now." Arutha's tone left little doubt of his mood. The High Priestess might be commander of a powerful sect, but before her stood the ruler of the Kingdom absolute, save the King, a man who would brook no interference in some matter of paramount importance. She nodded to the two foremost guards, and they entered. The door was closed behind them, and the two guards were taken off to one side by Gardan. Outside, the palace guards kept watchful eyes upon the remaining temple guards and the wicked curved swords carried at their belts.

Father Nathan greeted the High Priestess with a stiffly formal bow, their two orders having little affection for each other. The High Priestess chose to ignore the priest's presence.

Her first remark upon seeing the pentagram upon the floor was "Do you fear otherworld interference?" Her tone was suddenly analytical and even.

It was Nathan who answered. "Lady, we are not sure of many things, but we do seek to prevent complications from whatever source, physical or spiritual."

She did not acknowledge his words but stepped as close to the two men, one dead and the other wounded, as she could. Seeing the black tunics, she faltered a step, then turned to face Arutha. Through the veil he could almost feel her malevolent gaze upon him. "These men are of my order. How do they come to lie here?"

Arutha's face was a mask of controlled anger. "Madam, it is to answer that question that you have been fetched. Do you know these two?"

She studied their faces. "I do not know this one," she said, pointing to the dead man with the grey lock in his hair. "But the other is a priest of my temple, named Morgan, newly come to us from our temple in Yabon." She paused for a moment as she considered something. "He wears the mark of a brother of the Order of the Silver Net." Her head came around, facing Arutha once more. "They are the martial arm of our faith, supervised by their Grand Master in Rillanon. And he answers to none save our Mother Matriarch for his order's practices." She paused again. "And then only sometimes." Before anyone could comment, she continued. "What I do not understand is how one of my temple priests came to wear their mark. Is he a member of the order, passing himself off as a priest? Is he a priest playing the part of a warrior? Or is he neither priest nor brother of the order, but an impostor on both counts? Any of those three possibilities is forbidden, at risk of Lims-Kragma's wrath. Why is he here?"

Arutha said, "Madam, if what you say is true"—she seemed to tense at the implication of a possible falsehood—"then what is occurring concerns your temple as much as it concerns me. Jimmy, speak what you know of the Nighthawks."

Jimmy, obviously uncomfortable under the scrutiny of the Death Goddess's High Priestess, spoke quickly and forwent his usual embellishments. When he finished, the High Priestess said, "Highness, what you say is a deed foul in the nostrils of our goddess." Her voice was cold rage. "In times past, certain of the faithful sought sacrifices, but those practices are long abandoned. Death is a patient goddess; all will come to know her in time. We need no black murders. I would speak to this man." She indicated the prisoner.

Arutha hesitated and noticed Father Nathan shaking his head slightly. "He is close to death, less than hours without any additional stress upon him. Should the questioning prove rigorous, he might die before we can plumb the depths of these dark waters."

The High Priestess said, "What cause for concern, priest? Even dead, he is still my subject. I am Lims-Kragma's ephemeral hand. In her manor I will find truths no living man can obtain."

Father Nathan bowed. "In the realm of death, so you are supreme." To Arutha he said, "May my brothers and I withdraw, Highness? My order finds these practices offensive."

The Prince nodded, and the High Priestess said, "Before you go, remove the prayer of slowness you have called down upon him. It will cause less difficulty than should I do it."

Nathan quickly complied and the man on the bed began to groan feverishly. The priest and acolytes of Sung hurriedly left the room, and when they were gone, the High Priestess said, "This pentagram will aid in keeping outside forces from interfering with this act. I would ask all to remain outside, for within its bounds each person creates ripples in the fabric of magic. This is a most holy rite, for whatever the outcome, our lady will most surely claim this man."

Arutha and the others waited outside the pentagram and the priestess said, "Speak only when I have given permission, and ensure the candles do not burn out, or forces may be loosed that would prove . . . troublesome to recall." The High Priestess drew back her black veil, and Arutha was almost shocked at her appearance. She looked barely more than a girl, and a lovely one at that, with blue eyes and skin the color of dawn's blush. Her eyebrows promised her hair would be the palest gold. She raised her hands overhead and began to pray. Her voice was soft, musical, but the words were strange and fearful to hear.

The man on the bed squirmed as she continued her incantation. Suddenly his eyes opened and he stared upward. He seemed to convulse, straining at the bonds that restrained him. He relaxed, then turned to face the High Priestess. A distant look crossed his face, as his eyes seemed to focus and unfocus in turn. After a moment a strange, sinister smile formed on his lips, an expression of mocking cruelty. His mouth opened and the voice that issued forth was deep and hollow. "What service, mistress?"

The High Priestess's brow furrowed slightly as if there was something askew in his manner, but she maintained her poise and said in commanding tones, "You wear the mantle of the Order of the Silver Net, yet you practice in the temple. Explain this falsehood."

The man laughed, a high shrieking cackle that trailed off. "I am he who serves."

She stopped, for the answer was not to her liking. "Answer then, who do you serve?"

There came another laugh and the man's body tensed once more, pulling against the restraining ropes. Beads of sweat popped out upon his brow, and the muscles of his arms corded as he drew himself against the ropes. Then he relaxed and laughed again. "I am he who is caught."

"Who do you serve?"

"I am he who is a fish. I am in a net." Again came the mad laughter and the near-convulsive straining at the ropes. As the man strained, sweat poured off his face in rivulets. Shrieking, he pulled again and again at the restraints. As it seemed he would break his own bones with exertion, the man screamed, "Murmandamus! Aid your servant!"

Abruptly one of the candles blew out as a wind from some unknown place swept across the room. The man reacted with a single convulsive spasm, bowing his body in a high arch, with only his feet and head touching the bed, pulling against the ropes with such force that his skin tore and bled. Suddenly he collapsed upon the bed. The High Priestess fell back a step, then crossed to look down on the man. Softly she said, "He is dead. Relight the candle."

Arutha motioned and a guard lit a taper from another candle and relit the extinguished one. The priestess began another incantation. While the first had been mildly discomforting, this one carried a feeling of dread, a chill from the farthest corner of some lost and frozen land of wretchedness. It carried the echo of the cries of those without comfort or hope. Yet within it was another quality, powerful and attractive, an almost seductive feeling that it would somehow be wonderful to lay aside all burdens and rest. As the spell continued, the feelings of foreboding increased, and those who waited fought against the desire to run far from the sound of the High Priestess's spell casting.

Suddenly the spell was over, and the room lay as quiet as a tomb. The High Priestess spoke in the King's Tongue. "You who are with us in body but are now subject to the will of our mistress, Lims-Kragma, hearken to me. As our Lady of Death commands all things in the end, so do I now command you in her name. Return!"

The form on the bed stirred but lay silent once more. The High Priestess shouted, "Return!" and the figure moved again. With a sudden movement the dead man's head came up and his eyes opened. He seemed to be looking around the room, but while his eyes were open, they remained rolled back up in his head, only the whites showing. Still there was some feeling that the corpse could yet see, for his head stopped moving as if he was looking at the High Priestess. His mouth opened and a distant, hollow laugh issued from it.

The High Priestess stepped forward. "Silence!"

The dead man quieted, but then the face grinned, a slowly broadening, terrible, and evil expression. The features began to twitch, moving as if the man's face were subject to some strange palsy. The very flesh shivered, then sagged, as if turned to heated wax. The skin color subtly shifted, becoming fairer, almost pale white. The forehead became higher and the chin more delicate, the nose more arched and the ears pointed. The hair darkened to black. Within moments the man they had questioned was gone and in his place lay a form no longer human.

Softly Laurie spoke. "By the gods! A Brother of the Dark Path!"

Jimmy shifted his weight uncomfortably. "Your Brother Morgan is from a lot farther north than Yabon city, lady," he whispered. There was no humor in his tone, only fear.

Again came the chill wind from some unknown quarter, and the High Priestess turned toward Arutha. Her eyes were wide with fear and she seemed to speak, but none could hear her words.

The creature on the bed, one of the hated dark cousins to the elves, shrieked in maniacal glee. With a shocking and sudden display of strength, the moredhel ripped one arm free of its bond, then the other. Before the guards could react, it tore free the bonds holding its legs. Instantly the dead thing was on its feet, leaping toward the High Priestess.

The woman stood resolute, a feeling of power radiating from her. She pointed her hand at the creature. "Halt!" The moredhel obeyed. "By my mistress's power, I command obedience from you who are called. In her domain do you dwell and subject you are to her laws and ministers. By her power do I order you back!"

The moredhel faltered a moment, then with startling quickness reached out and with one hand seized the High Priestess by the throat. In that hollow, distant voice it screamed, "Trouble not my servant, lady. If you love your mistress so dearly, then to her go!"

The High Priestess gripped its wrist, and blue fire sprang to life along the creature's arm. With a howl of pain it picked her up as if she weighed nothing and hurled her against the wall near Arutha, where she crashed and slid to the floor.

All stood motionless. The transformation of this creature and its unexpected attack upon the High Priestess robbed all in the room of volition. The temple guards were rooted by the sight of their priestess humbled by some dark, otherworld power. Gardan and his men were equally stunned.

With another booming howl of laughter the creature turned toward Arutha. "Now, Lord of the West, we are met, and it is your hour!"

The moredhel swayed upon its feet a moment, then stepped toward Arutha. The temple guards recovered an instant before Gardan's men. The two black-and-silver-clad soldiers leaped forward, one interposing himself between the advancing moredhel and the stunned priestess, the other attacking the creature. Arutha's soldiers were only a step behind in preventing the creature from reaching Arutha. Laurie sprang for the door, shouting for the guards without.

The temple guard thrust with his scimitar and impaled the moredhel. Sightless eyes widened, showing red rims, as the creature grinned, a horrid expression of glee. In an instant its hands shot forward and were around the guard's throat. With a twisting motion it broke the guard's neck, then tossed him aside. The first of Arutha's guards to reach the creature struck from the side, a blow that gouged a bloody furrow along its back. With a backhand slap it knocked the guard down. It reached down and pulled the scimitar out of its own chest and with a snarl tossed it aside. As it turned away, Gardan hit it low and from behind. The huge captain encircled the creature with his powerful arms, lifting it from the ground. The creature's claws raked Gardan's arms, but still he held it high, preventing its progress toward Arutha. Then the creature kicked backward, its heel striking Gardan in the leg, causing both to fall. The creature rose. As Gardan tried to reach it again, he stumbled over the body of the fallen temple guard.

The door flew open as Laurie tossed aside the inner bar, and palace and temple guards raced past the singer. The creature was within a sword's thrust of Arutha when the first guard tackled it from behind, followed an instant later by two more. The temple guards joined their lone fellow in forming a defense around the unconscious High Priestess. Arutha's guards joined in the assault upon the moredhel. Gardan recovered from his fall and rushed to Arutha's side. "Leave, Highness. We can hold it here by weight of numbers."

Arutha, with sword ready, said, "How long, Gardan? How can you stop a creature already dead?"

Jimmy the Hand backed away from Arutha's side, edging toward the door. He couldn't take his eyes from the knot of writhing bodies. Guards hammered at the creature with hilts and fists, seeking to bludgeon it into submission. Hands and faces were sticky red as the creature's claws raked out again and again.

Laurie circled around the melee, looking for an opening, his sword pointed like a dagger. Catching sight of Jimmy as the thief bolted toward the door, Laurie shouted, "Arutha! Jimmy shows uncommon good sense. Leave!" Then he thrust with his sword and a low, chilling moan came from within the jumble of bodies.

Arutha was gripped by indecision. The mass seemed to be inching toward him, as if the weight of the guards served only to slow the creature's progress. The creature's voice rang out. "Flee, if you will, Lord of the West, but you shall never find refuge from my servants." As if gifted by some additional surge of power, the moredhel heaved mightily and the guards were cast aside. They crashed into those standing before the High Priestess, and for a moment the creature was free to stand upright. Now it was covered in blood, its face a mask of bleeding wounds. Torn flesh hung from one cheek, transforming the moredhel's face into a permanent, baleful grin. One guard managed to rise and shatter the creature's right arm with a sword blow. It spun and tore the man's throat out with a single rake of its hand. With its right arm dangling uselessly at its side, the moredhel spoke through loose, rubbery lips, its voice a bubbling, wet noise. "I feed on death! Come! I shall feed on yours!"

Two soldiers jumped upon the moredhel from behind, driving it to the floor once more, before Arutha. Ignoring the guards, the creature clawed toward the Prince, its good arm outstretched, fingers hooked like a claw. More guards leaped upon it, and Arutha darted forward, driving his sword through the creature's shoulder, deep into its back. The monstrous figure shuddered briefly, then resumed its forward motion.

Like some giant, obscene crab, the mass of bodies inched slowly toward the Prince. The activities of the guards increased, as if they would protect Arutha by literally tearing the creature to shreds. Arutha took a step back, his reluctance to flee slowly overbalanced by the refusal of the moredhel to be stopped. With a cry, a soldier was tossed away, to land hard, his head striking the stone floor with an audible crack. Another shouted, "Highness, it grows in strength!" A third screamed as he had an eye clawed out by the frantic creature. With a titanic heave, it tossed the remaining soldiers away and rose, with no one between itself and Arutha.

Laurie tugged at Arutha's left sleeve, leading the Prince slowly toward the door. They walked sideways, never taking their eyes from the loathsome creature, while it stood swaying upon its feet. Its sightless eyes followed the two men, glaring from a skull rendered a pulpy red mask devoid of recognizable features. One of the High Priestess's guards charged the creature from behind, and without looking, the moredhel lashed backward with its right hand and crushed the man's skull with a single blow.

Laurie cried, "It has the use of its arm once more! It's healing itself!" The creature was upon them in a leap. Suddenly Arutha felt himself going down as someone shoved him aside. In a blur of images, Arutha saw Laurie ducking away from the blow that would have torn Arutha's head from his shoulders. Arutha rolled away and came to his feet beside Jimmy the Hand. The boy had knocked him out of harm's way. Beyond Jimmy, Arutha could see Father Nathan.

The bull-necked priest approached the monster, his left hand held upright, palm forward. The creature somehow sensed the priest's approach, for it turned its attention from Arutha and spun to face Nathan.

The center of Nathan's hand began to glow, then shine with a fierce white light that cast a visible beam upon the moredhel, which stood transfixed. From its torn lips a low moan was emitted. Then Nathan began to chant.

A high shriek erupted from the moredhel, and it cowered, covering sightless eyes from the glare of Nathan's mystic light. Its voice could be heard, low and bubbling. "It burns . . . it burns!" The stocky cleric took a step forward, forcing the creature to shamble backward. The thing looked nothing mortal, bleeding thick, nearly coagulated blood from a hundred wounds, large pieces of flesh and clothing dangling from its form. It hunkered lower and cried out, "I burn!"

Then a cold wind blew in the room and the creature shrieked, loud enough to startle even seasoned, battle-ready soldiers. Guards looked furiously about, seeking the source of some nameless horror that could be felt on every side.

The creature suddenly rose up, as if new power had come into it. Its right hand shot out, grabbing at the source of the burning light, Nathan's left hand. Fingers and talon-like fingers interlaced, and with a searing sound the creature's hand began to smoke. The moredhel drew back its left hand to strike a blow at the cleric, but as it uncoiled to strike, Nathan shouted a word unknown to the others in the room, and the creature faltered and groaned. Nathan's voice rang out, filling the room with the sounds of mystic prayer and holy magic. The creature froze for an instant, then trembled in place. It seemed to bend back slowly under the power of the priest's grip. Nathan stepped up the urgency of his incantation and the creature reeled as if being struck a mighty blow, and smoke rose from its body. Nathan called down the power of his goddess, Sung the White, the deity of purity, his voice hoarse and strained. A loud moaning, seeming to come from a great distance, escaped from the moredhel's mouth and it shuddered again. Locked in this mystic battle, Nathan lifted his shoulders as if he were struggling to move away a great weight, and the moredhel fell to its knees. Its right hand bent backward as Nathan's voice droned on. Beads of sweat rolled down the priest's forehead and the cords on his neck stood out. Blisters rose on the creature's ragged flesh and exposed muscle and it began an ululating cry. A sizzling sound and the smell of cooking meat filled the room. Thick oily smoke poured off its body, and one guard turned his head and vomited. Nathan's eyes grew wide as he exerted the force of his will upon this creature. Slowly they swayed, the creature's flesh cracking as it blackened and crisped from Nathan's magic. The moredhel bent backward under the force of the priest's grip, and suddenly blue energy coursed over its blackening body. Nathan released his hold and the creature toppled sideways, flames erupting from its eyes, mouth, and ears. Soon flames engulfed the body and reduced it quickly to ashes, choking the room with a foul, greasy odor.

Nathan slowly turned to face Arutha, and the Prince saw a man suddenly aged. The cleric's eyes were wide and sweat poured down his face. In a dry croak he said, "Highness, it is done." Taking one slow step, then another, toward the Prince, Nathan smiled weakly. Then he fell forward, to be caught by Arutha before he struck the floor.

FOUR

REVELATIONS

Birds sang to welcome the new dawn.

Arutha, Laurie, Jimmy, Volney, and Gardan sat in the Prince's private audience chamber awaiting word of Nathan and the High Priestess. The temple guards had carried the priestess to a guest chamber and stood guard while healers summoned from her temple attended her. They had been with her all night, while members of Nathan's order tended him in his quarters.

Everyone in the room had been rendered silent by the horrors of the night, and all were reluctant to speak of it. Laurie stirred first from the numbness, leaving his chair to move to a window.

Arutha's eyes followed Laurie's movement, but his mind was wrestling with a dozen unanswerable questions. Who or what was seeking his death? And why? But more important to him than his own safety was the question of what threat this posed for Lyam, Carline, and the others due to arrive soon. And most of all, was there any risk to Anita? A dozen times over the last few hours Arutha had considered postponing the wedding.

Laurie sat down on a couch next to the half-dozing Jimmy. Quietly he asked, "Jimmy, how did you know to fetch Father Nathan when the High Priestess herself was helpless?"

Jimmy stretched and yawned. "It was something I remembered from my youth." At this, Gardan laughed and the tension in the room lessened. Even Arutha ventured a half-smile as Jimmy continued. "I was given into the tutelage of one Father Timothy, a cleric of Astalon, for a time. Occasionally one boy or another is allowed to do this. It's a sign the Mockers have great expectations for the boy," he said proudly. "I stayed only to learn my letters and numbers, but along the way I chanced to pick up a few other bits of knowledge.

"I remembered a discourse on the nature of the gods Father Timothy had given once—though it had almost put me to sleep. According to that worthy, there is an opposition of forces, positive and negative forces that are sometimes called good and evil. Good cannot cancel good, nor evil cancel evil. To balk an agent of evil, you need an agency of good. The High Priestess is counted a servant of dark powers by most people and could not hold the creature at bay. I hoped the father could oppose the creature, as Sung and her servants are seen as being of 'good' demeanor. I really didn't know if it was possible, but I couldn't see standing around while that thing chewed up the palace guards one by one."

Arutha said, "It proved a good guess." His tone revealed approval of Jimmy's quick thinking.

A guard came into the room and said, "Highness, the priest is recovered and sends word for you. He begs you to come to his quarters." Arutha nearly leaped from his chair and strode out of the chamber with the others close behind.

For over a century custom had provided that the palace of the Prince of Krondor contain a temple with a shrine to each of the gods, so that whoever was a guest, no matter which of the major deities he worshipped, would find a place of spiritual comfort close by. The order seeing to the temple's care would change from time to time as different advisers to the Prince came and went. It was Nathan and his acolytes who cared for the temple under Arutha's administration, as they had during Erland's. The priest's quarters lay behind the temple, and Arutha entered through the large, vaulted hall. At the opposite end of the nave a door could be glimpsed behind the bema that contained the shrine to the four greater gods. Arutha strode toward the door, his boots clacking upon the stone floor as he walked past the shrines to the lesser gods on either side of the temple. As he approached the door to Nathan's quarters, Arutha could see it was open and glimpsed movement inside.

He entered the priest's quarters and Nathan's acolytes stepped aside. Arutha was struck by the austere look of the room, nearly a cell without personal property or decoration. The only nonutilitarian item visible was a personal statuette of Sung, represented as a lovely young woman in a long white robe, resting on a small table next to Nathan's bed.

The priest looked haggard and weak but alert. He lay propped up on cushions. Nathan's assistant priest hovered close by, ready to answer any need Nathan might have. The royal chirurgeon waited beside the bed. He bowed and said, "There is nothing physically wrong, Highness, save he is exhausted. Please be brief." Arutha nodded as the chirurgeon, followed by all the acolytes, withdrew. As he left, he motioned for Gardan and the others to remain outside.

Arutha came to Nathan's side. "How do you fare?"

"I will live, Highness," he answered weakly.

Arutha cast a quick glance at the door and saw the alarmed expression on Gardan's face. It confirmed Arutha's impression that Nathan's ordeal had left him changed. Softly Arutha said, "You will do more than just live, Nathan. You'll be back to your old self soon."

"I have lived through a horror no man should have to face, Highness. So you may understand, I must share a confidence with you." He nodded toward the door.

The assistant priest closed the door and returned to Nathan's bedside. Nathan said, "I must now tell you something not commonly known outside the temple, Highness. I take great responsibility upon myself to do this, but I judge it imperative."

Arutha leaned forward the better to hear the tired priest's faint words. Nathan said, "There is an order to things, Arutha, a balance imposed by Ishap, the One Above All. The greater gods rule through the lesser gods, who are served by the priesthoods. Each order has its mission. An order may seem to be in opposition to another, but the higher truth is that all orders have a place in the scheme of things. Even those in the temples who are of lower rank are kept ignorant of this higher order. It is the reason for occasional conflicts erupting between temples. My discomfort at the High Priestess's rites last night was as much for the benefit of my acolytes as from any true distaste. What an individual is capable of understanding determines how much of the truth is revealed to him by the temples. Many need the simple concepts of good and evil, light and dark, to govern their daily lives. You are not such a one.

"I have trained in the Following of the Single Path, the order I am best suited for by my nature. But as do all others who have reached my rank, I know well the nature and manifestations of the other gods and goddesses. What appeared in that room last night was nothing I have ever known."

Arutha seemed lost. "What do you mean?"

"As I battled against the force that drove the moredhel I could sense something of its nature. It is something alien, dark and dread, something without mercy. It rages and it seeks to dominate or destroy. Even those gods called dark, Lims-Kragma and Guis-wa, are not truly evil when the truth is understood. But this thing is a blotting out of the light of hope. It is despair incarnate."

The assistant priest indicated it was time for Arutha to leave. As he moved toward the door, Nathan called out. "Wait, you must understand something more. It left, not because I had bested it, but because I had robbed it of the servant it inhabited. It had no physical means of continuing the attack. I only defeated its agent. It . . . revealed something of itself in that moment. It is not ready yet to face my Lady of the One Path, but it holds her and the other gods in contempt." His face revealed his alarm. "Arutha, it feels contempt for the gods!" Nathan sat up, his hand outstretched, and Arutha returned and took it. "Highness, it is a force that deems itself supreme. It hates and it rails and it means to destroy any who oppose it. If—"

Arutha said, "Softly, Nathan."

The priest nodded and lay back. "Seek greater wisdom than

mine, Arutha. For one other thing did I sense. This foe, this encompassing darkness, is growing in strength."

Arutha said, "Sleep, Nathan. Let this all become just another bad dream." He nodded to the assistant priest and left the room. As he passed the royal chirurgeon, he said, "Aid him," a plea more than a command.

Hours went by as Arutha awaited word of the High Priestess of Lims-Kragma. He sat alone, while Jimmy slept on a low settee. Gardan was off seeing to the deployment of his guards. Volney was busy with running the Principality, as Arutha was preoccupied with the mysteries of the previous night. He had decided against informing Lyam of exactly what had occurred until the King was in Krondor. As he had observed before, with Lyam's retinue numbering in excess of a hundred soldiers, it would take something on the order of a small army to imperil him.

Arutha paused for a moment in his deliberation to study Jimmy. He looked still a child as he breathed slowly. He had laughed off the severity of his wound, but once things had finally quieted down, he had fallen asleep almost instantly. Gardan had gently lifted him onto the couch. Arutha shook his head slightly. The youth was a common criminal, a parasite upon society who had not worked an honest day's labor in his young life. Not much past fourteen or fifteen, he was a braggart, a liar, and a thief, but while he might be many things, he was still a friend. Arutha sighed and wondered what to do about the boy.

A court page arrived with a message from the High Priestess, requesting Arutha's presence at once. The Prince rose quietly, so as not to awaken Jimmy, and followed the page to where the High Priestess was being cared for by her healers. Arutha's guards waited outside the suite and temple guards stood inside the door, a concession Arutha had granted when requested by the priest who had come from the temple. The priest greeted Arutha coolly, as if Arutha somehow bore the responsibility for his mistress's injury. He led Arutha into the sleeping chamber, where a priestess attended the leader of their temple.

Arutha was shocked by the appearance of the High Priestess. She lay propped up by a pile of bolsters, her pale blond hair framing a face drained of color, as if the icy blue of winter had suffused her features. She looked as if she had aged twenty years in a day. But as she fixed her gaze upon Arutha, there was still an aura of power about her.

"Have you recovered, madam?" Arutha's tone showed concern as he inclined his head toward her.

"My mistress has work for me yet, Highness. I will not join her for some time."

"I am pleased to hear that news. I have come as you required."

The woman drew herself upright, until she sat with her back against the pillows. Without conscious thought she brushed back her nearly white hair, and Arutha could see that despite the grim demeanor the High Priestess was a woman of unusual beauty, albeit a beauty without a hint of softness. In voice still strained, the priestess said, "Arutha conDoin, there is peril to our Kingdom, and more. In the realm of the Mistress of Death, only one stands higher than I; she is our Mother Matriarch in Rillanon. Other than herself, none should challenge my power in the domain of death. But now there comes something that challenges the very goddess herself, something that while still weak, while still learning its powers, can overcome my control over one in my mistress's realm.

"Have you any understanding of the importance of my words? It is as if a baby fresh from her mother's teat has come to your palace, nay, the palace of your brother the King, and turned his retinue, his guards, even the very people against him, rendering him helpless in the very seat of his power. That is what we face. And it grows. As we stand speaking, it grows in strength and rage. And it is ancient. . . ." Her eyes grew wide, and suddenly Arutha saw a hint of madness. "It is both new and old. . . . I don't understand."

Arutha nodded toward the healer and turned to the priest. The priest indicated the door and Arutha started to leave. As he reached the door, the High Priestess's voice broke into sobbing.

When they reached the outer room, the priest said, "Highness, I am Julian, Chief Priest of the Inner Circle. I've sent word to our mother temple in Rillanon of what has happened here. I . . ." He appeared troubled by what he was about to say. "Most likely I will be High Priest of Lims-Kragma within a few months' time. We shall care for her," he said, facing the closed door, "but she will never again be able to guide us in our mistress's service." He returned his attention to Arutha. "I have heard from the temple guards of what occurred last night, and I have just heard the High Priestess's words. If the temple can help, we will."

Arutha considered the man's words. It was usual for a priest of one of the orders to be numbered among the councillors of the nobility. There were too many matters of mystic importance to be faced for the nobility to be without spiritual guidance. That was why Arutha's father had been the first to include a magician in his company of advisers. But active cooperation between temple and temporal authority, between ruling bodies themselves, was rare. Finally Arutha said, "My thanks, Julian. When we have a better sense of what we are dealing with, we shall seek out your wisdom. I have just come to understand that my view of the world is somewhat narrow. I expect you will provide valued assistance."

The priest bowed his head. As Arutha made to leave, he said, "Highness?"

Arutha looked back to see a concerned expression on the priest's face. "Yes?"

"Find whatever this thing is, Highness. Seek it out, and destroy it utterly."

Arutha could only nod. He made his way back to his chamber. Entering, he sat quietly, lest he disturb Jimmy, who still lay sleeping upon the settee. Arutha noticed that a plate of fruit and cheese and a decanter of chilled wine had been placed upon the table for him. Realizing he had had nothing to eat all day, he poured himself a glass of wine and cut a wedge of cheese, then sat down again. He put his boots on the table and leaned back, letting his mind wander. The fatigue of two nights with little sleep washed over him, but his mind was too caught up in the events of the last two days to let sleep be considered for even a moment. Some supernatural agent was loose in his realm, some magic thing that threw fear into priests of two of the most powerful temples in the Kingdom. Lyam would arrive in less than a week. Nearly every noble in the Kingdom would be in Krondor for the wedding. In his city! And he could think of nothing he could do to guarantee their safety.

Arutha sat for an hour, his mind miles away as he absently ate and drank. He was a man who often descended into dark brooding when left alone, but when given a problem he never ceased to work on it, to attack it from every possible side, to worry it, tossing it about, as a terrier does a rat. He conjured up dozens of possible approaches to the problem and constantly reexamined every shred of information he had. Finally, after discarding a dozen plans, he knew what he must do. He took his feet off the table and grabbed a ripe apple off the dish before him.

"Jimmy!" he shouted, and the boy thief was instantly awake, years of dangerous living having bred the habit of light sleeping. Arutha threw the apple at the boy and with astonishing speed he sat up and caught the fruit scant inches from his face. Arutha could understand how he had come to be known as "the Hand."

"What?" inquired the boy as he bit into the fruit.

"I need you to carry a message to your master." Jimmy stopped in mid-bite. "I need you to arrange a meeting between myself and the Upright Man." Jimmy's eyes widened in utter disbelief.

Again thick fog had rolled in off the Bitter Sea to blanket Krondor in a deep mantle of haze. Two figures moved quickly past the few taverns still open for business. Arutha followed as Jimmy led him through the city, passing out of the Merchants' Quarter into rougher environs, until they were deep within the heart of the Poor Quarter. Then a quick turn down an alley and they stood before a dead end. Emerging from the shadows, three men appeared as if by magic. Arutha had his rapier out in an instant, but Jimmy only said, "We are pilgrims who seek guidance."

"Pilgrims, I am the guide," came the answer from the foremost man. "Now, tell your friend to put up his toad sticker or we'll deliver him up in a sack."

If the men knew Arutha's identity, they were giving no sign. Arutha slowly put away his sword. The other two men came forward, holding out blindfolds. Arutha said, "What business is this?"

"This is the way you will travel," answered the spokesman. "If you refuse, you will go not one step farther."

Arutha fought down irritation and nodded, once. The men came forward and Arutha saw Jimmy blindfolded an instant before he was roughly denied light himself. Struggling against the urge to pull the blindfold away, Arutha heard the man speak. "You will both be led from here to another place, where others will come to guide you. You may be passed along through many hands before you reach your destination, so do not become alarmed should you hear unexpected voices in the dark. I do not know what your ultimate destination is, for I do not need to know. I also do not know who you are, man, but orders have come down from one most highly placed that you are to be led quickly and delivered unharmed. But be warned: remove your blindfold only at grave risk. You may not know where you are from this moment henceforth." Arutha felt a rope being tied around his waist and heard the speaker say, "Hold tightly to the rope and keep a sure foot; we travel at good pace."

Without further word, Arutha was jerked around and led off into the night.

For more than an hour, or so it seemed to the Prince, he had been led about the streets of Krondor. He had twice stumbled and had bruises to show for the casual care given by his guides. At least three times he had changed guides, so he had no idea whom he would see when the blindfold was removed. But at last he climbed a flight of stairs. He heard several doors open and shut before strong hands forced him to sit. At last the blindfold was removed and Arutha blinked as he was dazzled by the light.

Arrayed along a table was a series of lanterns, with a polished reflector behind each, all turned to face him. Each cast a brilliant illumination into the Prince's eyes, preventing him from seeing anyone who stood behind that table.

Arutha looked to his right and saw Jimmy sitting upon another stool. After a long moment a deep voice rumbled from behind the lights. "Greetings, Prince of Krondor."

Arutha squinted against the light, but could catch no glimpse of who spoke from behind the glare. "Am I speaking to the Upright Man?"

A long pause preceded the answer. "Be satisfied that I am empowered to reach any understanding you may desire. I speak with his voice."

Arutha considered for a moment. "Very well. I seek an alliance."

From behind the glare came a deep chuckle. "What would the Prince of Krondor need of the Upright Man's aid?"

"I seek to learn the secrets of the Guild of Death."

A long silence followed on the heels of this statement. Arutha couldn't decide if the speaker was consulting another person or simply thinking. Then the voice behind the lanterns said, "Remove the boy and hold him outside."

Two men appeared from out of the dark and roughly grabbed Jimmy, hauling him from the room. When he was gone, the voice said, "The Nighthawks are a source of concern for the Upright Man, Prince of Krondor. They trespass upon the Thieves' Highway and their black murders stir up the populace, casting unwelcome light upon the Mockers' many activities. In short, they are bad for business. It would serve us to see them ended, but what cause have you beyond that which normally occupies a ruler when his subjects are being wantonly murdered in their sleep?"

"They pose a threat to my brother and myself."

Again there was a long silence. "Then they set their sights high. Still, royalty often needs killing as much as the commons, and a man must earn a living howsoever he may, even though he be an assassin."

"It should be apparent to you," said Arutha dryly, "that murdering Princes would be especially bad for business. The Mockers would find things a little cramped working in a city under martial law."

"This is true. Name your bargain."

"I ask no bargain. I demand cooperation. I need information. I wish to know where lies the heart of the Nighthawks."

"Altruism accrues little benefit to those lying cold in the gutter. The arm of the Guild of Death is long."

"No longer than mine," said Arutha in a voice devoid of humor. "I can see that the activities of the Mockers suffer greatly. You know as well as I what would happen to the Mockers should the Prince of Krondor declare war upon your guild."

"There is little profit in such contention between the guild and Your Highness."

Arutha leaned forward, his dark eyes gleaming from the brilliant lights. Slowly, biting off each word, he said, "I have no need of profit."

A moment of silence was followed by a deep sigh. "Yes, there is that," said the voice thoughtfully. Then it chuckled. "That is one of the advantages to inheriting one's position. It would prove troublesome to govern a guild of starving thieves. Very well, Arutha of Krondor, but for this risk the guild needs indemnity. You've shown the stick, now what of the carrot?"

"Name your price." Arutha sat back.

"Understand this: the Upright Man is sympathetic to Your Highness regarding the problems posed by the Guild of Death. The Nighthawks are not to be endured. They must be eliminated root and branch. But many risks are involved, and great expense will be incurred; this will be a costly venture."

"Your price?" Arutha repeated flatly.

"For the risk involved to all should we fail, ten thousand golden sovereigns."

"That would put a large hole in the royal treasury."

"True, but consider the alternatives."

"We have a bargain."

"I shall provide the Upright Man's instructions as to the means of payment later," the voice said with a hint of humor in it. "Now there is another matter."

"What is that?" said Arutha.

"Young Jimmy the Hand has broken oath with the Mockers and his life is forfeit. He shall die within the hour."

Without thinking, Arutha began to rise. Strong hands pushed him down from behind as a large thief stepped out of the darkness. He simply shook his head in the negative.

"We would never think of returning you to the palace in less salubrious condition than that in which you arrived," said the voice behind the lights, "but draw a weapon in this room and you will be delivered to the palace gate in a box and we will deal then with the consequences."

"But Jimmy—"

"Broke oath!" interrupted the voice. "He was honor-bound to report the whereabouts of the Nighthawk when he saw him. As he was honor-bound to tell of Laughing Jack's treachery. Yes, Highness, we know of these things. Jimmy betrayed the guild to carry word to you first. There are certain matters that can be forgiven because of age, but these actions cannot."

"I'll not stand by and allow Jimmy to be murdered."

"Then listen, Prince of Krondor, for I have a story to tell. Once the Upright Man lay with a woman of the streets, as he had with hundreds of others, but this whore bore him a son. This is a certainty: Jimmy the Hand is the Upright Man's son, though he is ignorant of his paternity. This presents the Upright Man with something of a quandary. If he is to obey the laws he has made, he must order the death of his own son. But should he not, he will lose credibility with those who serve him. An unpleasant choice. Already the Guild of Thieves is in turmoil from Jack's being shown as an agent of the Nighthawks. Trust is a thin enough commodity at most times; it is nearly nonexistent now. Can you think of another way?"

Arutha smiled, for he knew another way. "In times not far past, it was not unheard of to buy pardon. Name your price."

"For treason? No less than another ten thousand gold sovereigns."

Arutha shook his head. His treasury would be gutted. Still, Jimmy must have known the risks of betraying the Mockers to bring him warning, and that was worth much. "Done," said Arutha sourly.

"Then you must keep the boy with you, Prince of Krondor, for he'll never be one with the Mockers again, though we will not attempt to harm him . . . unless he again transgress against us. Then we shall deal with him as we would any freebooter. Harshly."

Arutha rose. "Is our business then done?"

"Except for one last thing."

"Yes?"

"Also in times not far past, it was not unheard of to buy a patent of nobility for a price in gold. What price would you ask of a father to have his son named Squire of the Prince's court?"

Arutha laughed, suddenly understanding the course of negotiations. "Twenty thousand golden sovereigns."

"Done! The Upright Man is fond of Jimmy; though he has other bastards around, Jimmy is special. The Upright Man wishes Jimmy to remain ignorant of the relationship, but he will be pleased to think his son shall have a brighter future for this night's negotiations."

"He will be placed within my service, without knowing who his father is. Shall we meet again?"

"I think not, Prince of Krondor. The Upright Man guards his identity jealously, and even to come close to one who speaks with his voice brings him dangers. But we will carry clear messages to you when we know where hide the Nighthawks. And we will welcome news of their obliteration."

Jimmy sat nervously. For over three hours Arutha had been closeted with Gardan, Volney, and Laurie, as well as other members of his privy staff. Jimmy had been invited to remain in a room set aside for his use. The presence of two guards at the door and two more below the balcony outside his window gave ample support to the notion that he was, for whatever reason, a prisoner. Jimmy had little doubt he could leave undetected during the night if he had been in fit condition, but after the events of the last few days he felt abused. Also, he was at something of a loss to understand being returned to the palace with the Prince. The boy thief was uneasy. Something in his life had changed and he wasn't sure what, or why.

The door to the room opened and a guard sergeant stuck his head in, waving to Jimmy to come. "His Highness wants you, boy." Jimmy quickly followed the soldier down the hall to the long passage to the council chambers.

Arutha looked up from reading something. About the table sat Gardan, Laurie, and some other men Jimmy didn't know, while Earl Volney stood near the door. "Jimmy, I have something for you here." Jimmy simply looked around the room, not knowing what to say. Arutha said, "This is a royal patent naming you Squire to the Prince's court."

Jimmy was speechless, his eyes wide. Laurie chuckled at his reaction, while Gardan grinned. Finally Jimmy found his voice. "This is a jest, right?" When Arutha shook his head, the boy said, "But . . . me, a squire?"

Arutha replied, "You have saved my life and you are to be rewarded."

Jimmy said, "But, Highness, I . . . thank you, but . . . there's the matter of my oath to the Mockers."

Arutha leaned forward. "That matter has been disposed of, Squire. You are no longer a member of the Guild of Thieves. The Upright Man has agreed. It is done."

Jimmy felt trapped. He had never taken much pleasure in being a thief, but he had taken great pleasure in being a very good thief. What appealed to him was the chance to prove himself at every turn, to show all that Jimmy the Hand was the best thief in the guild . . . or at least would be someday. But now he was to be bound to the Prince's household, and with the office came duties. And if the Upright Man had agreed, Jimmy was forever denied access to the society of the streets.

Seeing the boy's lack of enthusiasm, Laurie said, "May I, Highness?"

Arutha permitted, and the singer came over to place a hand on the boy's shoulder. "Jimmy, His Highness is simply keeping your head above water, literally. He had to bargain for your life. If he had not, you'd be floating in the harbor this hour. The Upright Man knew you'd broken oath with the guild."

Jimmy visibly sagged and Laurie squeezed his shoulder reassuringly. The boy had always thought himself somehow above the rules, free of the responsibilities that bound others. Jimmy had never known why he had been granted special consideration so many times, while others were forced to pay their way, but now he knew that he had stretched privilege too far once too often. There was no doubt in the boy's mind that the singer told the truth, and conflicting emotions surged up within as he considered how close to being murdered he had come.

Laurie said, "Palace life isn't so bad. The building's warm, your clothing'll be clean, and there's ample food. Besides, there'll be plenty to hold your interest." He looked at Arutha and added dryly, "Especially of late."

Jimmy nodded and Laurie led him around the table. Jimmy was instructed to kneel. The Earl quickly read the patent. "To all within our demesne: whereas the youth Jimmy, an orphan of the city of Krondor, has rendered worthy service in preventing injury to the royal person of the Prince of Krondor; and: Whereas the youth

Jimmy is considered to hold us forever in his debt; It is my wish that he be known to all in the realm as our beloved and loyal servant, and it is furthermore wished that he be given a place in the court of Krondor, with the rank of Squire, with all rights and privileges pertaining thereunto. Furthermore let it be known that the title to the estate of Haverford on the River Welandel is conferred upon him and his progeny as long as they shall live, to have and to hold, with servants and properties thereupon. Title to this estate shall be held by the crown until the day of his majority. Set this day by my hand and seal, Arutha conDoin, Prince of Krondor; Knight-Marshal of the Western Realm and of the King's Armies of the West; Heir Apparent to the throne of Rillanon." Volney looked at Jimmy. "Do you accept this charge?"

Jimmy said, "Yes." Volney rolled up the parchment and handed it to the boy. That, apparently, was all that was needed to turn a thief into a squire.

The boy didn't know where Haverford on the River Welandel was, but land meant income, and immediately he brightened. As he stepped away, he studied Arutha, who was obviously preoccupied. Chance had twice thrown them together, and twice Arutha had proved the only person who hadn't wanted anything from him. Even his few friends among the Mockers had tried to gain advantage over the boy at least once until he had shown that to be a difficult task. Jimmy found his relationship with Arutha a novel one. As Arutha read some papers silently, Jimmy decided that if fate was again taking a hand, he'd just as soon stay with the Prince and his lively bunch as go anywhere else he could think of. Besides, he would have income and comfort as long as Arutha lived, though this, he thought somberly, might prove a bit of a problem.

While Jimmy glanced at his patent, Arutha in turn studied him. He was a street boy: tough, resilient, resourceful, and occasionally ruthless. Arutha smiled to himself. He'd get along just fine in court.

Jimmy rolled up the paper as Arutha said, "Your former master works with alacrity." To the entire group he said, "Here I have his word that he has nearly uncovered the nest of the Nighthawks. He states he will send a message at any moment, and he regrets he must withhold any direct aid in stamping them out. Jimmy, what do you think of this?"

Jimmy grinned. "The Upright Man knows how to play. Should you destroy the Nighthawks, business returns to normal. Should you fail, there is no suspicion he took a hand in your attempt. He cannot lose." In more serious tones he added, "He also worries about additional infiltration of the Mockers. Should that be the case, any Mocker participation places the raid in jeopardy."

Arutha took the boy's meaning. "It is come to that serious a pass?"

"Most likely, Highness. There are no more than three or four men with access to the Upright Man himself. These are the only ones he can fully trust. I would guess he has a few agents of his own outside the guild, unknown to any but his most trusted aides, perhaps not even to them. He must be using these to ferret out the Nighthawks. There are over two hundred Mockers and twice that number of beggars and urchins, any of whom could be eyes and ears for the Guild of Death."

Arutha smiled his crooked smile. Volney said, "You have wits, Squire James. You should prove a boon to His Highness's court."

Jimmy looked as if something tasted bad as he muttered, "Squire James?"

Arutha seemed unaware of Jimmy's sour tone. "We could all do with some rest. Until we hear from the Upright Man, the best we can do is recover from the rigors of the last few days." He rose. "I bid you all good night."

Arutha quickly left the chamber and Volney gathered up the papers from the conference table and hurried along on his own errands. Laurie said to Jimmy, "Well, I'd better take you in tow, youngster. Someone should teach you a thing or two about quality folk."

Gardan came over to them. "Then the boy is as good as damned forever to be an embarrassment to the Prince."

Laurie sighed. "It just shows you," he rejoined to Jimmy, "you can put a badge of rank on the man, but once a barracks sweeper, always a barracks sweeper."

"Barracks sweeper!" snapped Gardan, mock outrage on his dark face. "Singer, I'll have you know I come from a long line of heroes. . . ."

Jimmy sighed in resignation as he followed the two bickering men from the hall. On the whole, life had been simpler a week ago. He tried to put on a brighter expression, but at best he resembled a cat who had fallen into a barrel of cream, unsure of whether to lap it up or swim for his life.

FIVE

OBLITERATION

Arutha studied the old thief.

The Upright Man's messenger had waited while the Prince read the missive. Now the Prince's eyes were upon him. "Know you the contents of this?"

"To the specifics, no. He who gave it to me was explicit in instructions." The old thief, now robbed of his agility by age, rubbed absently at his bald pate as he stood before Arutha. "He said to tell you the boy could bring you easily to the place named within, Your Highness. He also said to tell you that word has been passed regarding the boy, and the Mockers consider the matter at a close." The man cast a brief glance at Jimmy and winked. Jimmy, who was standing off to one side, breathed a silent sigh of relief at hearing that. The wink told him that while Jimmy would never be a Mocker again, he at least was not denied the streets of the city and that old Alvarny the Quick was still a friend. Arutha said, "Tell your master I am pleased with this swift resolution. Tell him we shall have an end to this matter tonight. He will understand."

Arutha waved for a guard to escort Alvarny from the hall and turned to Gardan. "Select a company of your most trusted men and any Pathfinders still in the garrison. Any who are new to our service shall be passed over. By word of mouth, tell each to muster at the postern gate, beginning at sundown. By ones and twos I want them sent into the city, using varied routes and with sharp eyes for signs they are being followed. Let them wander and dine, as if they were off duty, though any drinking should be only sham. By midnight they are all to gather at the Rainbow Parrot." Gardan saluted and left.

When Arutha and the boy were alone, the Prince said, "You must think I've dealt harshly with you."

Jimmy's face showed his surprise. "No, Highness. I thought it a bit strange, is all. If anything, I owe you my life."

"I worried you'd resent being taken from the only family you knew." Jimmy shrugged off the remark. "And as for owing a life . . ." He leaned back, finger against his cheek as he smiled. "We are even, Squire James, for had you not acted quickly the other night I'd be shorter by a head."

They both smiled at that. Jimmy said, "If we're even, why the office?"

Arutha remembered his pledge to the Upright Man. "Count it a means of keeping an eye upon you. You are free to come and go, as long as you discharge your duties as a squire, but should I find the gold cups missing from the pantry, I'll personally drag you down to the dungeon." Jimmy again laughed, but Arutha's voice took on a more somber tone. "Also, there's the matter of someone's foiling an assassin upon the roof of a certain fuller's house earlier this week. And you've never said why you chose to come to me with news of that Nighthawk rather than report it as you were warranted to do."

Jimmy looked at Arutha, his gaze older by years than his boyish face. Finally he said, "The night you escaped from Krondor with the Princess, I got caught with a full company of Black Guy's horsemen on the docks between me and freedom. You threw me your sword before you knew you'd be safely away. And when we were closeted in the safe house, you taught me swordplay. You were always as fairly spoken to me as you were to any other." He paused for a moment. "You treated me like a friend. I've . . . I've had few friends, Highness."

Arutha indicated understanding. "I also count few as true friends —my family, the magicians Pug and Kulgan, Father Tully, and Gardan." His expression turned wry. "Laurie has shown himself more than a simple courtier and I think he may prove a friend. I'll even go so far as to name that pirate Amos Trask a true friend. Now, if Amos can be the friend of the Prince of Krondor, why not Jimmy the Hand?"

Jimmy grinned and there was a hint of moisture in his eyes. "Why not indeed?" He swallowed hard and raised his mask again. "Whatever happened to Amos?"

Arutha sat back. "The last I saw of him, he was stealing the King's ship." Jimmy guffawed. "We've not had word of him since. I'd give much to have that cutthroat by my side this night."

Jimmy lost his smile. "I hate to bring this up, but what if we run into another of those damn things that won't die?"

"Nathan thinks it unlikely. He thinks it happened only because the priestess called that thing back. Besides, I can't wait upon the temples' pleasure to act. Only that death priest, Julian, has offered to help."

"And we've seen how much help those who serve Lims-Kragma can provide," Jimmy added dryly. "Let's hope Father Nathan knows of what he speaks."

Arutha rose. "Come, let's get what rest we may, for the night should provide bloody work."

Throughout the night bands of soldiers, dressed in the common garb of mercenaries, had been wending their way through the streets of Krondor, passing one another without a flicker of acknowledgment, until at three hours after midnight over a hundred men were in the Rainbow Parrot. Several were dispensing uniform tabards from large sacks, so the soldiers would again be in the Prince's colors during the raid.

Jimmy entered in the company of two men dressed in simple foresters' garb, members of Arutha's elite company of army scouts, the Royal Pathfinders. The senior Pathfinder saluted. "This youngster has the eyes of a cat, Highness. He spotted our men being followed to the inn three times."

When Arutha looked at them questioningly, Jimmy said, "Two of them were beggars known to me, and they were easy to intercept and chase off, but the third . . . It may have been he simply followed to see if something was up. Anyway, when we blocked his way down a street—subtly, you may be sure—he simply moved off in another direction. It could have been nothing."

"It also could have been something," Arutha said. "Still, there is nothing more we can do. Even if the Nighthawks know we are doing something, they will not know what. Look you here," he said to Jimmy, pointing to a map on a table before him. "This was given me by the royal architect. It is old, but he thinks it a fair accounting of the sewers."

Jimmy studied it for a moment. "Perhaps a score of years ago it was." He pointed to one spot on the map and another. "Here there's been a collapse of a wall, and while the sewage still flows, the passage is too narrow for a man. And here there is a new tunnel, dug by a tanner requiring a more rapid disposal of his waste." Jimmy studied the map a bit longer, then said, "Is there a quill and ink, or charcoal?" A piece of charcoal was forthcoming and Jimmy made marks upon the map. "Friend Lucas has a slip-me-out to the sewers in his basement."

Behind the bar the old owner's mouth dropped at hearing that piece of news. "What? How'd you know?"

Jimmy grinned. "The rooftops aren't the only Thieves' Highway. From here"—he pointed at the map—"companies of men can move to these two points. The exits from the basement of the Nighthawks' stronghold are cleverly located. Each comes out in a tunnel not directly connected with the others. The doors may be only scant yards apart, but it's yards of solid walls of brick and stone, with miles of twisting sewers to travel, to gain one from the next. It would take an hour to find your way from one exit to another. It's this third one that's the problem. It empties out near a large landing with a dozen tunnels to flee down, too many to block."

Gardan, who was looking over the boy's shoulder, said, "Which means a coordinated assault. Jimmy, can you hear if someone is breaking in one of the doors and you're at the other?"

Jimmy said, "I should think. If you slip someone to the top of the stairs, for certain. Especially this time of night. You'd be surprised how many little noises filter down the streets during the day, but at night . . ."

Arutha said to the two Pathfinders, "Can you find these locations from this map?" Each nodded. "Good. Each of you will guide a third of the men to one of these two entrances. The other third will come with Gardan and myself. Jimmy will guide us. You will position men but not enter the basement of that building unless you are discovered first or you hear our party assaulting those within. Then come with all speed. Gardan, those on the streets should be in position. They have their orders?"

Gardan said, "Each has been instructed. At first hint of trouble, no one is allowed to leave that building unless he wears your tabard and is known by sight. I have thirty archers in place on the rooftops on all sides to discourage any seeking quick exit. A herald with a trumpet will sound alarm and two companies of horsemen will exit the palace at the bugle. They will reach us within five minutes. Any in the streets not of our company will be ridden down, that is the order."

Arutha quickly put on a tabard and tossed one each to Jimmy and Laurie. When all were wearing the Prince's purple and black, Arutha said, "It is time." The Pathfinders led the first two groups into the cellar below the inn. Then it was time for Jimmy to lead the Prince's group. He took them to the slip-me-out behind a false cask in the wall and led them down the narrow stairs to the sewers. The stench caused a few soldiers to gasp and utter soft oaths, but a single word from Gardan restored order to the ranks. Several shuttered lanterns were lit. Jimmy motioned for a single line to be formed, and led the Prince's raiders off toward the Merchants' Quarter of the city.

After nearly a half hour walking, past slowly moving channels carrying waste and garbage toward the harbor, they found themselves approaching the large landing. Arutha ordered the lanterns shuttered. Jimmy went forward. Arutha tried to follow his movements but was astonished as the darkness seemed to swallow him up. Arutha strained to hear him, but Jimmy was noiseless. For the waiting soldiers, the strangest thing about the sewers was the stillness, broken only by the sound of slow water lapping. Each soldier had taken care to muffle all armor and weapons, so should there be a Nighthawk lookout he wouldn't be alerted.

Jimmy returned after a moment and signaled that a single guard stood at the bottom of the stairs to the building. With his mouth near Arutha's ear he whispered, "You'll never get one of your men close enough before the guard gives alarm. I'm the only one who stands a chance. Just come running when you hear the scuffle begin."

Jimmy pulled his dirk out of his boot and slipped away. Suddenly there was a painful grunt and Arutha and his men were off, all thoughts of silence discarded. The Prince was the first to reach the boy, who struggled with a powerful guard. The youth had come up behind the man and had leaped and grabbed him around the throat, but had only wounded him with the dirk, which now lay upon the stones. The man was nearly blue from being choked, but had tried to smash Jimmy against the wall. Arutha ended the struggle with a single thrust of his blade and the man slipped silently to the stones. Jimmy let go and smiled weakly. He had taken a terrible battering. Arutha whispered, "Stay here," to him, then signaled his men to follow.

Ignoring his promise to Volney to wait behind while Gardan led the assault, Arutha silently hurried up the stairs. He halted before a wooden door with a single sliding latch, placed his ear next to it, and listened. Muffled voices from the other side caused him to raise his hand in warning. Gardan and the others slowed their approach.

Arutha quietly moved the door's latch and pushed gently. He peeked into a large, well-lit basement. Sitting around three tables were about a dozen armed men. Several were tending weapons and armor. The scene was more reminiscent of a soldiers' commons than a basement. What Arutha found more incredible was that this basement was located below the most richly appointed and successful brothel in the city, the House of Willows, one frequented by most of the rich merchants and no small portion of the minor nobility of Krondor. Arutha could well understand how the Nighthawks could gain access to so much information about the palace and his own comings and goings. Many a courtier would boast of his knowledge of some "secret" or other to impress his whore. It would not have taken more than a chance mention from someone in the palace that Gardan had planned to ride out to the east gate to meet the Prince for the assassin to know Arutha's route that night earlier in the week.

Abruptly a figure entered Arutha's view that made the Prince catch his breath. A moredhel warrior approached a man who sat oiling a broadsword and spoke quietly to him. The man nodded while the Dark Brother continued his discourse. Then suddenly he spun. He pointed directly toward the door and opened his mouth to speak. Arutha didn't hesitate. He shouted, "Now!" and charged into the room.

The basement erupted into a riot of action. Those who had moments before been sitting idly by now grabbed up weapons and answered the assault. Others bolted out doors leading up to the brothel or down to other parts of the sewers. From above, screams and shouts told of customers alarmed by the fleeing assassins. Those who attempted to leave via the exits to the sewers were quickly pushed back up the stairs into the cellar by the other units of Arutha's invading force.

Arutha ducked a blow by the moredhel warrior and leaped to the left as soldiers fought their way into the center of the room, separating the Prince from the Dark Brother. The few assassins who stood their ground charged into Arutha's men with complete disregard for their own lives, forcing the soldiers to kill them. The sole exception was the moredhel, who seemed to be in a frenzy trying to reach Arutha. Arutha shouted, "Take him alive!"

The moredhel was soon the only Nighthawk standing in the room, and he was forced back to the wall and held. Arutha came up to him. The dark elf locked gazes with the Prince, naked hatred upon his face. He allowed himself to be disarmed as Arutha put up his own sword. Arutha had never been this close to a living moredhel before. There was no doubt they were elven kin, though elves tended to be fairer of hair and eyes. As Martin had remarked more than once, the moredhel were a handsome race, if one dark of soul. Then, as one soldier bent to examine the moredhel's boot top for weapons, the creature kneed the guard in the face, pushed away the other, and leaped at Arutha. Arutha had barely an instant to duck away from hands outstretched for his face. He moved to his left and saw the moredhel stiffen as Laurie's blade took him in the chest. The moredhel collapsed to the floor, but with a final spasm tried to reach out and claw at Arutha's leg. Laurie kicked the creature's hands, deflecting the weak clawing motion. "Look well at the nails. I saw them gleam as he let himself be disarmed," said the singer.

Arutha grabbed a wrist and inspected the moredhel's hand closely. "Careful how you handle it," warned Laurie. Arutha saw tiny needles embedded in the Dark Brother's nails, each with a dark stain at the end. Laurie said, "It's an old whore's trick, though only those with some gold and a friendly chirurgeon can get it done. If a man tries to leave without paying or is given to beating his whores, a simple scratch and the man is no longer a problem."

Arutha looked at the singer. "You have my debt."

"Banath preserve us!"

Arutha and Gardan turned to see that Jimmy had crossed to a fallen man, fair and well dressed. He was staring at the dead assassin. "Golden," he said softly.

"You knew this man?" asked Arutha.

"He was a Mocker," said Jimmy. "In my life I would not have suspected him."

"Is there not a one left alive?" demanded the Prince. He was in a fury, for his orders had been to capture as many as possible.

Gardan, who had been taking reports from his men, said, "Highness, there were full thirty and five assassins in this basement and the rooms above. All either fought so our men had no choice but to kill or turned and slew one another, then threw themselves upon their own weapons." Gardan held out something to the Prince. "They all wore these, Highness." In his hand was an ebony hawk on a gold chain.

Then there was an abrupt silence, not as if the men had stopped their movements, but rather as if something had been heard and all had instantly halted to listen, yet there was no sound. An odd dampening of sound occurred, as if a heavy, oppressive presence had entered the room, and an eerieness descended upon Arutha and his men for a brief moment. Then a chill fell over the room. Arutha felt his neck hair rise, as some primordial dread filled him. Something alien had entered the room, an unseen but palpable evil. As Arutha turned to say something to Gardan and the others, a soldier shouted, "Highness, I think this one is alive. He moved!" He sounded eager to please his Prince. Then a second soldier said, "This one, too!" Arutha saw the two soldiers lean over the fallen assassins.

All in the basement gasped in horror as one of the corpses moved, his hand shooting upward to seize the kneeling soldier by the throat. The corpse sat up, forcing the soldier upward. The terrible wet cracking sound of the soldier's throat being crushed echoed in the room. The other corpse sprang upward, sinking his teeth in the neck of the second guard, ripping open his throat while Arutha and his men were rooted in shocked silence. The first dead assassin tossed away the choking soldier and turned. Fixing milk-white eyes upon the Prince, the dead man smiled. As if from a great distance, a voice sounded from the grinning maw. "Again we meet, Lord of the West. Now shall my servants have you, for you have not brought your meddling priests. Rise! Rise, O my children! Rise, and kill!"

Around the room the corpses began to twitch and move and soldiers gasped and offered prayers to Tith, the soldiers' god. One, thinking quickly, hacked the head off the second corpse as it started to rise. The headless corpse shuddered and fell, but began to rise once more while the rolling head mouthed silent curses. Like grotesque marionettes manipulated by a demented puppeteer, the bodies rose, in jerks and spasms. Jimmy, his voice almost quavering, said, "I think we should have waited on the temples' pleasure."

Gardan shouted, "Protect the Prince!" and men leaped at the animated corpses. Like crazed butchers in a cattle pen, soldiers began madly chopping in all directions. Gore spattered the walls and all who stood in the room, but the bodies continued to rise.

Soldiers slipped in the blood and found themselves overwhelmed by cold, slimy hands that gripped arms and legs. Some managed throttled cries as dead fingers closed around their throats or teeth bit hard into their flesh.

Soldiers of the Prince of Krondor hacked and slashed, sending limbs flying through the air, but the hands and arms only flopped madly about the floor like bleeding fish out of water. Arutha felt a tugging at his leg and looked down to see a severed hand gripping at his ankle. A frantic kick sent the hand flying across the room to strike the opposite wall.

Arutha shouted, "Get out and hold closed those doors!" Soldiers swore as they cut and kicked their way through the blood and pulped flesh before them. Many of the soldiers, hardened veterans, were coming close to panic. Nothing in their experience had prepared them for the horror they faced in that basement. Each time a body was knocked down, it would but try to rise once more. And each time a comrade fell, he stayed down.

Arutha led the way toward the door leading upstairs, the closest exit. Jimmy and Laurie followed. Arutha paused to cut apart another rising corpse and Jimmy dashed past the Prince. Jimmy reached the door first and swore as he looked up. Stumbling down the stairs toward them came the corpse of a beautiful woman, wearing a diaphanous gown, torn half away, with a spreading bloodstain at the waist. Her blank white eyes fastened on Arutha at the bottom of the stairs and she shrieked in delight. Jimmy ducked under a clumsy slash and drove his shoulder into her bloody stomach, shouting, " 'Ware the stairs!" They both went down and he was first to his feet, scrambling past her.

Arutha looked back into the basement and saw his men being pulled down. Gardan and several other soldiers had reached the safety of the far doors and were attempting to close them, while stragglers who were frantically attempting to reach them were being pulled down. A few valiant men were pulling closed the doors from inside, ignoring a sure sentence of death. The floor was a sea of gore, wet and treacherous, and many soldiers slipped and fell, never to rise again. Detached body parts seemed somehow to gather together and corpses would stand once more. Remembering the creature in the palace and how it had gained in strength as time passed, Arutha shouted, "Bar the doors!"

Laurie leaped up the stairs and struck at the grinning whore, once more on her feet. Her blond head rolled past Arutha as he raced up the stairs after Jimmy and the singer.

Reaching the ground floor of the House of Willows, Arutha and his companions were greeted with the sight of soldiers struggling with more animated corpses. The horse companies had arrived, cleared the streets, and entered the building. But they, like those below, were unprepared to fight dead opponents. Outside the main door several bodies, impaled with dozens of arrows, were trying to rise. Each time one would gain its feet, a flight of bowshafts would strike it from the dark, knocking it over again.

Jimmy glanced around the room and made a leap atop a table. With an acrobat's spring, he jumped high over a guard being strangled by a dead Nighthawk and grabbed at a wall covering. The tapestry held his weight for a moment, then the room filled with a loud tearing sound as it ripped free of its fastenings high overhead.

Yards of fine cloth fell about Jimmy, and he quickly disentangled himself. He grabbed up as much cloth as he could and dragged the tapestry to the large fireplace in the main room of the brothel. He dumped it in the fireplace and then started overturning anything that would burn onto it. Within minutes flames were spreading out into the room.

Arutha shoved away a corpse and yanked down another tapestry, which he tossed to Laurie. The singer ducked as a dead assassin lunged at him, and tangled the corpse in the fabric. Quickly spinning the dead creature, Laurie wrapped it in cloth and with a kick sent it stumbling toward Jimmy. Jimmy leaped aside and let the cloth-bound thing stumble into the rapidly spreading flames, tripping it as it went past. The dead man fell into the flames and began shrieking in rage.

The heat in the room was becoming unbearable, as was the choking smoke. Laurie ran to the door and halted just before the threshold. "The Prince!" he shouted to the bowmen atop the surrounding buildings. "The Prince is coming through!"

"Hurry!" came the answering shout as an arrow knocked down a rising corpse a few feet away from Laurie.

Arutha and Jimmy came out of the firelit door, followed by a few coughing soldiers. Arutha shouted, "To me!"

At once a dozen guards were dashing across the street, past grooms brought along to hold the cavalry mounts. The stench of blood and burning bodies and the heat from the fire were causing the horses to nicker and tug at their reins as the grooms led them away.

When the guards reached Arutha, several picked up arrow-studded bodies and tossed them through the windows into the fire. The shrieks of the burning corpses filled the night.

A dead Nighthawk stumbled out the door, its left side ablaze, its arms outstretched as if to embrace Arutha. Two soldiers caught at it and hurled it back through the door into the fire, disregarding the burns they suffered as a consequence. Arutha moved from the door while soldiers denied exit to those corpses seeking to flee the inferno. He crossed the street as the most exclusive brothel in the city went up in flames. To a soldier he said, "Send word to those in the sewers to make sure nothing gets out of the basement." The soldier saluted and ran off.

In short order the house was a tower of fire, the surrounding area lit like day. Neighboring buildings spilled their inhabitants into the street as the heat threatened to ignite the block. Arutha called for the soldiers to form bucket lines and douse buildings on both sides of the House of Willows.

Less than a half hour after the blaze began, there came a loud crash and a billowing explosion of smoke as the main floor caved in and the building collapsed. Laurie said, "So much for those things in the basement."

Arutha's face was set in a grim expression as he said, "Some good men remained down there."

Jimmy had stood transfixed by the sight, his face smudged with soot and blood. Arutha placed his hand upon the boy's shoulder. "Again, you did well."

Jimmy could only nod. Laurie said, "I need strong drink. Gods, I'll never get that stench out of my nose."

Arutha said, "Let's return to the palace. This night's work is done."

SIX

RECEPTION

Jimmy tugged at his collar.

Master of Ceremonies Brian deLacy struck the floor of the audience hall with his staff and the boy snapped eyes forward. Ranging from fourteen to eighteen years of age, the squires of Arutha's court were being instructed upon the duties they would be performing during the upcoming celebration of Anita and Arutha's wedding. The old Master, a slow-speaking, impeccably attired man, said, "Squire James, if you can't remain still, we shall have to find something of an active duty for you, say, running messages between the palace and the outer billets?" There was a barely audible groan, for the visiting nobles were forever sending inconsequential notes back and forth, and the outer billets, where many of them were to be housed, were as far away as three-quarters of a mile from the palace proper. Such duty was mainly nonstop running to and fro for ten hours a day. Master deLacy turned to the author of the groan and said, "Squire Paul, perhaps you would care to join Squire James?"

When no answer was forthcoming, he continued. "Very well. Those of you who are expecting relatives to attend should know that all of you will be required to serve such duties in turn." With that announcement, all the boys groaned, swore, and shuffled. Again the staff struck the wooden floor loudly. "You're not dukes, earls, and barons yet! One or two days' duty will not cause your death. There will simply be too many in the palace for the servants, porters, and pages to meet every demand."

Another of the new boys, Squire Locklear, the youngest son of the Baron of Land's End, said, "Sir, which of us will be at the wedding?"

"In time, boy, in time. All of you will be escorting guests to their places in the great hall and in the banquet hall. During the ceremony you'll all stand respectfully at the rear of the great hall, so you'll all get to see the wedding."

A page ran into the room and handed the Master a note, then dashed off without awaiting a reply. Master deLacy read the note, then said, "I must make ready for the reception for the King. All of you know where you must be today. Meet here again once the King and His Highness are closeted in council this afternoon. And anyone who is late will have an extra day of running messages to the outer billets. That is all for now." As he walked off, he could be heard to mutter, "So much to do and so little time."

The boys began to move off, but as Jimmy started to leave, a voice from behind shouted, "Hey, new boy!"

Jimmy turned, as did two others nearby, but the speaker had his eyes locked on Jimmy. Jimmy waited, knowing full well what was coming. His place in the order of squires was about to be established.

When Jimmy didn't move, Locklear, who had also halted, pointed to himself and took a hesitant step toward the speaker. The speaker, a tall, rawboned boy of sixteen or seventeen years, snapped, "Not you, boy. I mean that fellow." He pointed at Jimmy.

The speaker wore the same brown and green uniform of the house squires, but it was of better cut than those of most of the other boys; he obviously had the funds for personal tailoring. At his belt was a jeweled-hilt dagger, and his boots were so polished they shone like bright metal. His hair was straw-colored and cut cleanly. Knowing the boy had to be the resident bully, Jimmy rolled his eyes heavenward and sighed. His uniform fit poorly and his boots hurt and his healing side itched constantly. He was in an ill-tempered mood to begin with. Best to get this over with quickly, he thought.

Jimmy walked slowly toward the older boy, who was called Jerome. He knew Jerome's father was the Squire of Ludland, a town up the coast from Krondor, a minor title, but one that garnered wealth for whoever held it. When Jimmy stood before him, he said, "Yes?"

With a sneer Jerome said, "I don't like much about you, fellow."

Jimmy slowly smiled, then suddenly drove his fist into Jerome's stomach. The taller boy doubled over and collapsed onto the floor. He thrashed about for a moment before, with a grunt, he rose. "Why . . ." he began, but stopped, confronted by the sight of Jimmy standing before him, a dagger in his hand. Jerome reached to his belt for his own dagger and felt nothing. He looked down, then frantically about.

"I think this is what you are missing," Jimmy said cheerfully, holding out the dagger to reveal the jeweled hilt. Jerome's eyes widened. Jimmy tossed the dagger with a flick of his wrist and the blade stood quivering in the floor between Jerome's boots. "And the name isn't 'fellow.' It's Squire James, Prince Arutha's Squire."

Jimmy quickly exited the hall. After a few yards the boy called Locklear caught up and fell into step beside him. "That was something, Squire James," said the other new boy. "Jerome's been making it hard on all the new boys."

Jimmy stopped, in no mood for this. "That's because you let him, boy." Locklear stepped away and began to stammer an apologetic reply. Jimmy held up his hand. "Wait a moment. I don't mean to be short with you. I have things on my mind. Look, Locklear, isn't it?"

"My friends call me Locky."

Jimmy studied the boy. He was a small lad, still looking more the baby he was than the man he would be. His eyes were wide and blue in a face of deep tan, his brown hair shot through with sun-gold. Jimmy knew that no more than a few weeks ago he was playing in the sand with the common boys at the beach near his father's rural castle. "Locky," said Jimmy, "when that fool begins to trouble you, kick him where he lives. That'll sort him out quick enough. Look, I can't talk now. I've got to go meet the King." Jimmy walked quickly away, leaving an astonished boy standing in the hall.

Jimmy fidgeted, hating the too tight collar of his new tunic. One thing Jerome had been good for was to show him he didn't have to put up with poor tailoring. As soon as he could, he'd slip out of the palace for a few hours and visit the three caches he had around the city. He had enough gold secreted there to tailor himself a dozen new outfits. This business of being a noble had drawbacks he hadn't imagined.

"What's the matter with you, boy?"

Jimmy looked up and saw the narrow gaze of a tall old man with dark grey hair. He studied Jimmy with a practiced eye, and Jimmy recognized him as Swordmaster Fannon, one of Arutha's old companions from Crydee. He'd arrived by ship on the evening tide the night before. "It's this deuced collar, Swordmaster. And these new boots hurt my feet as well."

Fannon nodded. "Well, one must keep up appearances, discomfort or no. Now, here comes the Prince."

Arutha walked out of the great doors to the palace, to stand at the center of the throng assembled to meet the King. Broad steps led down to the parade ground. Beyond the ground, past the large iron gates, the great square of the city had been cleared of hawkers' stalls. Krondorian soldiers formed long lines along the route through the city to the palace, and behind them stood the citizens eager to catch a glimpse of their King. Lyam's column had been reported approaching the city only an hour before, but the citizens had been gathering since before dawn.

Wild cheering heralded the King's approach and Lyam was the first to ride into view, sitting astride a large chestnut war-horse, Gardan, as city commander, riding at his side. Behind them rode Martin and the attending nobles from the Eastern Realm, a company of Lyam's Royal Household Guard, and two richly appointed carriages. Arutha's lancers followed, with the baggage train bringing up the rear.

As Lyam reined in his mount before the steps, trumpets sounded flourishes. Grooms rushed to take the King's horse while Arutha hurried down the steps to meet his brother. Tradition held the Prince of Krondor to be second only to the King in rank, and therefore the least deferential noble in the Kingdom, but all protocol was forgotten as the two brothers embraced in greeting. The first to dismount after Lyam was Martin, and in a moment all three stood reunited.

Jimmy watched as Lyam introduced his riding companions while the two carriages rolled up to the steps. The doors to the first carriage opened and Jimmy craned his neck to see. A stunning young woman alighted and Jimmy gave a silent nod of approval. From the greeting she gave Arutha, Jimmy guessed her to be the Princess Carline. Jimmy stole a quick look to where Laurie stood and saw the singer waiting with open worship on his face. Jimmy nodded to himself: yes, that was Carline. Behind her came an old noble, who Jimmy expected would be Lord Caldric, Duke of Rillanon.

The second carriage's door opened and an older woman descended. Immediately after her came a familiar figure and Jimmy smiled. He felt a slight flush at sight of Princess Anita, for he had once harbored a terrible infatuation for her. The older woman would be Princess Alicia, her mother. While they were greeted by Arutha, Jimmy thought back to when Anita, Arutha, and he had all hidden together and the boy grinned unselfconsciously.

"What's gotten into you, Squire?"

Jimmy looked up at Swordmaster Fannon again. Covering his agitation, he said, "Boots, sir."

Fannon said, "Well enough, boy, but you should learn to bear up under a little discomfort. I mean no disrespect to your teachers, but you're poorly prepared as squires go."

Jimmy nodded, his eyes back on Anita. "New to the trade, sir. Last month I was a thief."

Fannon's mouth popped open. After a moment Jimmy took great delight in gently elbowing him in the ribs and saying, "The King's coming."

Fannon's gaze snapped foward, years of military training overcoming any other distractions. Lyam approached first, with Arutha at his side. Martin and Carline and the others followed as befitted their rank. Brian deLacy was presenting members of Arutha's court to the King, and Lyam ignored protocol several times to shake hands vigorously, even embrace several of the people waiting to be presented. Many of the western lords were men who had served with Lyam under command of his father during the Riftwar, and he hadn't seen them since his coronation. Earl Volney seemed embarrassed when Lyam placed his hand upon his shoulder and said, "Well done, Volney. You've kept the Western Realm in good order this last year." These familiarities distressed several of the nobles, but the crowd loved them, cheering wildly each time Lyam acted like a man greeting old friends rather than the King.

When the King came up to Fannon, he caught the old fighter by the shoulders as he began to bow. "No," said Lyam softly enough so that only Fannon, Jimmy, and Arutha could hear. "Not from you, my old teacher." Lyam engulfed the Swordmaster of Crydee in a bear hug and then with a laugh said, "Well now, Master Fannon, how stands my home? How stands Crydee?"

"Well, Majesty, she stands well." Jimmy noticed a faint moisture in the old man's eyes.

Then Arutha was saying, "This young scoundrel is the newest member of my court, Majesty. May I present Squire James of Krondor?" Master deLacy looked heavenward as Arutha usurped his office.

Jimmy bowed as he had been instructed. Lyam gifted the boy with a broad grin. "You I've heard of, Jimmy the Hand," he said as he took a step away. Then Lyam suddenly stopped. "I'd best check to see I've all my belongings." He made a show of patting himself down while Jimmy blushed furiously. Just as he was reaching the height of embarrassment, Jimmy saw Lyam cast a glance his way and wink at him. Jimmy laughed with the others.

Then Jimmy turned and found himself looking into the bluest eyes he had ever seen as a soft, feminine voice said, "Don't let Lyam upset you, Jimmy. He's always been a tease." Jimmy began to stammer, being caught by surprise after the King's jest, then executed a ragged bow.

Martin said, "I'm glad to see you again, Jimmy," and gripped his hand. "We've often spoken of you and wondered if you were faring well."

He presented the boy to his sister. Princess Carline nodded to Jimmy and said, "My brothers and the Princess Anita have spoken well of you. I am pleased to finally meet you." Then they moved off.

Jimmy stared after, overwhelmed at the remarks. "She's had that effect on me for a year," came a voice from behind, and Jimmy turned to see Laurie hurrying to keep abreast of the royal party as it moved toward the palace entrance. The singer touched his forehead in salute to the boy as he hurried to the crowd, having mistaken Jimmy's astonishment at Carline's and Martin's remarks for his being thunderstruck by the Princess's beauty.

Jimmy returned his attention to the passing nobles and his face split into a broad grin. "Hello, Jimmy," said Anita, now standing directly before him.

Jimmy bowed. "Hello, Princess."

Anita returned Jimmy's smile and said, "Mother, my lord Caldric, may I present an old friend, Jimmy." She noted his tunic. "Now a squire, I see."

Jimmy bowed again before the Princess Alicia and the Duke of Rillanon. Anita's mother presented her hand, and Jimmy awkwardly took it. "I've wished to thank you, young Jimmy, since I heard how you aided my daughter," said Alicia.

Jimmy felt eyes upon him and blushed. He found within himself no hint of the braggadocio that had sheltered him for most of his short life. He could only stand awkwardly while Anita said, "We shall visit later." Anita, her mother, and Caldric moved forward. Jimmy stood silently amazed.

No further introductions were made as the other nobles of the

Kingdom passed on toward the great hall. After a short ceremony, Lyam was due to be shown to his private quarters.

Suddenly the square erupted with the sound of drums and shouts as people pointed off to one of the major side streets to the palace. The royal party halted their entrance and waited, then Lyam and Arutha began walking back toward the top of the steps, the other nobles quickly scurrying around as all order to the procession crumbled. The King and Prince moved to where Jimmy and Fannon stood, and into their view rode a full dozen mounted warriors, each wearing a leopard skin over head and shoulders. Perspiration glinted on their dark skin as these fierce-looking men pounded upon drums mounted on either side of their saddles, while carefully guiding their mounts with their knees. Behind came another dozen leopard-skin-covered riders, each blowing on a large brass trumpet that curved over his shoulder. Both drummers and trumpeters moved their horses into two lines and allowed a procession of foot soldiers to come into view. Each soldier wore a metal helm ending in a spike, with a chain neck covering, and a metal cuirass. Ballooning trousers were tucked into knee-high black boots and each carried a round shield with a metal boss and had a long scimitar in his belt sash. Someone behind Jimmy said, "Dog soldiers."

Jimmy said to Fannon, "Why are they called that, Swordmaster?"

"Because in the ancient days in Kesh they were treated like dogs, penned away from the rest of the people until it was time to turn them loose on someone. Now it's said it's because they'll swarm over you like a pack of dogs if you give them the chance. They're a rough lot, boy, but we've taken their measure before."

The dog soldiers marched into place and opened a passage for others to move through. They drew scimitars and saluted as the first figure came into view. He was on foot, a giant of a man, taller than the King and broader of shoulder. His ebon skin reflected the bright sunlight, for he wore only a metal-studded vest above the waist. Like the soldiers, he wore the odd trousers and boots, but at his belt he wore a flasher, a curved sword half again the size of a scimitar. His head was uncovered, and in place of a shield he carried an ornamental staff of office. Four men rode behind him, mounted on the small, fast horses of the desert men of the Jal-Pur.

They wore the dress of desert men, not unseen but rare in Krondor—flowing knee-length robes of indigo silk, open in front to reveal white tunics and trousers, the calf-high boots of horsemen, and head coverings of blue cloth wrapped in such a manner that only their eyes could be seen. Each wore a ceremonial dagger of considerable length in his waist sash, the handle and sheath exquisitely carved from ivory. As the large dark man climbed the steps, Jimmy could hear his deep voice: ". . . before him, and the mountains tremble. The very stars pause in their course and the sun begs his leave to rise. He is the might of the Empire and in his nostrils the four winds blow. He is the Dragon of the Valley of the Sun, the Eagle of the Peaks of Tranquillity, the Lion of the Jal-Pur. . . ." The speaker approached where the King stood, with Jimmy behind, and moved off to one side as the four men dismounted and followed him up the steps. One walked before the others and was obviously the subject of the giant man's discourse.

Jimmy gave Fannon a questioning look and the Swordmaster said, "Keshian court etiquette."

Lyam had a sudden coughing fit and turned his head toward Jimmy behind his hand, and the boy could see the King was laughing at Fannon's remark. Regaining his composure, Lyam looked forward while the Keshian Master of Ceremonies finished his introduction. ". . . He is an oasis to his people." He faced the King and bowed low. "Your Royal Majesty, I have the signal honor to present His Excellency Abdur Rachman Memo Hazara-Khan, Bey of the Benni-Sherin, Lord of the Jal-Pur, and Prince of the Empire, Ambassador of Great Kesh to the Kingdom of the Isles."

The four dignitaries bowed in Keshian fashion, the three behind the Ambassador falling to their knees, briefly touching foreheads to the stone floor. The Ambassador placed his right hand over his heart and bowed from the waist, his left hand extended out and back. As all stood erect, they perfunctorily touched index finger to heart, lips, and forehead, a gesture indicating a generous heart, a truthful tongue, and a mind harboring no deceit.

Lyam said, "We welcome the Lord of the Jal-Pur to our court."

The Ambassador removed his face covering, revealing a gaunt, bearded visage of advancing years, his mouth set in a half-smile. "Your Royal Majesty, Her Most Imperial Majesty, blessings upon her name, sends greetings to her brother, Isles." Dropping his voice to a whisper, he added, "I would have chosen to make a less formal entrance, Majesty, but . . ." He shrugged, with a faint toss of his head toward the Keshian Master of Ceremonies, indicating he had no control over such matters. "The man's a tyrant."

Lyam grinned. "We return warm greetings to Great Kesh. May she always prosper and her bounty increase."

The Ambassador inclined his head in thanks. "If it pleases Your Majesty, may I present my companions?" Lyam nodded slightly, and the Keshian indicated the leftmost man. "This worthy is my senior aide and adviser, Lord Kamal Mishwa Daoud-Khan, Shereef of the Benni-Tular. And these other are my sons, Shandon and Jehansuz, Shereefs of the Benni-Sherin and also my personal bodyguards."

"We are pleased you could join us, my lords," said Lyam.

As Master deLacy attempted to restore some order to the milling nobles, another commotion broke out along a different street leading to the market square. The King and Prince turned away from the Master of Ceremonies and deLacy's hand went up. "What now?" the old man said aloud, then quickly regained his nearly vanished poise.

A drumming more furious than the Keshians' could be heard as brightly colored figures came into view. Prancing horses led a parade of soldiers in green. But each wore a shield of vivid hue upon his arm with strange blazons depicted. Loud pipes played a polytonal melody, alien but bright and infectious in rhythm. Soon many of the citizens of Krondor had taken up the beat with hand clapping or impromptu dancing around the edge of the square.

The first rider came before the palace and his banner blew out in the wind. Arutha laughed and slapped Lyam upon the shoulder. "It's Vandros of Yabon, and Kasumi's Tsurani garrison from LaMut." Then marching foot soldiers came into view, and they could be heard singing loudly.

When the Tsurani garrison of LaMut had come to stand before the Keshians, they halted. Martin observed, "Look at them, eyeing one another like tomcats. I warrant each side would love an excuse to test the other."

"Not in my city," said Arutha, obviously not finding the notion amusing.

Lyam laughed. "Well, it would be a show. Ho! Vandros!"

The Duke of Yabon rode up and dismounted. He hurried up the stairs and bowed. "I beg forgiveness for being tardy, Majesty. We were inconvenienced on the road. We chanced upon a band of goblins raiding south of Zūn."

"How many in the band?" asked Lyam.

"No more than two hundred."

Arutha said, " 'Inconvenienced' he calls it. Vandros, you've been with the Tsurani too long."

Lyam laughed. "Where is the Earl Kasumi?"

"He comes now, Majesty." Carriages could be seen entering the square as he spoke.

Arutha took aside the Duke of Yabon and said, "Tell your men to billet with the city garrison, Vandros. I want them close. When you have them bedded down, come to my quarters and bring along Brucal and Kasumi."

Vandros caught the serious tone and said, "As soon as the men are billeted, Highness."

The carriages from Yabon were halted before the stairs and Lord Brucal, Duchess Felinah, Countess Megan, and their ladies-in-waiting got out. Earl Kasumi, formerly a Force Commander in the Tsurani army during the Riftwar, dismounted his horse and walked quickly up the stairs. He bowed before Lyam and Arutha. Vandros quickly presented his party, and Lyam said, "Unless that pirate the King of Queg is going to arrive in a war galley pulled by a thousand little sea horses, we shall retire." With a laugh he swept past the near-distraught Master of Ceremonies deLacy, who was vainly trying to restore order in the King's procession.

Jimmy hung back, for while he had seen an occasional Keshian merchant, he'd never seen a dog soldier or a Tsurani. For all his wordly ways, outside the usual matters of the city and its life he was still a fifteen-year-old boy.

Kasumi's undercommander was giving orders for the billeting of his men, and the Keshian captain was doing the same. Jimmy sat quietly on the stairs, wiggling his toes to stretch his boots. He stared at the colorful Keshians for a few minutes, then watched the

Tsurani as they mustered to depart the square. Both were certainly exotic, and if Jimmy could judge, both looked equally fierce.

Jimmy was about to leave when something strange behind the Keshians caught his eye. He tried to decide what it was, but couldn't. Some odd itch made him walk down the stairs until he was near the Keshians, all still at parade rest. Then he saw what had caused him to feel something was out of the ordinary. Retreating into the crowd behind the Keshians was a man Jimmy had thought to be dead. Jimmy was rocked to the soul of his being, unable to move, for he had seen Laughing Jack vanish into the press.

Arutha paced. Around his council table sat Laurie, Brucal, Vandros, and Kasumi. Arutha had finished his recounting of the assault upon the Nighthawks. He held out a message. "This is from Baron Highcastle, in response to my query. He says there is some unusual movement northward in his area." Arutha put down the paper. "He goes on to give numbers of sightings, where, and the rest."

"Highness," said Vandros, "we had some movement in our region, but nothing of great note. In Yabon clever Dark Brothers and goblins can avoid the garrisons by turning westward once they're past the northern limits of the elven forests. By skirting to the west of the Lake of the Sky they avoid our patrols. We send few companies into that sector. The elves and the dwarves at Stone Mountain keep that area quiet."

"Or so we like to think," snorted Brucal. The old former Duke of Yabon had resigned his office in favor of Vandros when the latter had married Brucal's daughter. But he was still a fine military mind and had been battling the moredhel all his life. "No, if they move in small bands, the Brotherhood can come and go almost at will through the smaller passes. We've few enough men to keep the trading routes clear and a hell of a lot more ground to cover than that. All they must do is move at night and stay clear of the Hadati clan villages and the major roads. Let's not delude ourselves by thinking otherwise."

Arutha smiled. "That's why I wanted you here."

Kasumi said, "Highness, perhaps it is as Lord Brucal states.

We've had little contact with them in recent times. They may have tired of our steel and now move in small, stealthy bands."

Laurie shrugged. Yabon-born and -raised, the singer from Tyr-Sog knew as much about the moredhel as any in the room. "It is something to consider, that we have all these strange reports of goings on to the north at a time when moredhel hands can be seen involved with the attempts to kill Arutha."

"I would be less troubled," said Arutha, "if I knew that crushing them in Krondor would prove sufficient. Until we've uncovered the mystery of who is behind all this, I think we are not through with the Nighthawks. They may take months to re-form and be a menace, but I think they'll return. And as I sit here, I am certain there's some connection between the Nighthawks and what is occurring in the north."

A knock at the door preceded Gardan's entrance. "I have searched everywhere, Highness, and can find no sign of Squire James."

Laurie said, "Last I saw him, he was standing upon the steps next to Swordmaster Fannon while the Tsurani were making their entrance."

Gardan said, "He was sitting on the steps after I dismissed the troops."

From a high window a voice said, "He's now sitting above you."

All eyes turned to see the boy sitting in a high-arched window overlooking Arutha's chamber. Before anyone could speak, he nimbly leaped down.

Arutha's expression showed mixed disbelief and amusement. "When you asked to explore the roofs, I thought you would be needing ladders and . . . help. . . ."

Jimmy's manner was serious. "I saw little sense in waiting, Highness, and besides, what sort of thief needs ladders or help to climb walls?" He came up to Arutha. "This place is a warren of nooks and niches a man could secrete himself in."

"But first he must get onto the grounds," said Gardan. Jimmy gave the captain a look indicating that that feat presented no difficulty. Gardan lapsed into silence.

Laurie picked up the dropped thread of conversation. "Well,

while we don't know what's behind the Nighthawks, at least they've been destroyed here in Krondor."

"So I thought myself," said Jimmy, looking about the room. "But this afternoon, as the crowd began to break up, I saw an old friend in the square. Laughing Jack."

Arutha looked hard at Jimmy. "It was my understanding you left that traitor to the Mockers dead."

"As dead as any man with a six-inch hole in his chest from a steel bolt is likely to be. It's difficult getting out and about with half your lungs missing, but after what we saw at the whorehouse, if my own dear dead mum came to tuck me in bed tonight I wouldn't be surprised." Jimmy spoke in a distracted fashion as he prowled around the room. With a slightly theatrical show he said, "Aha!" and pressed down on something behind a decorative shield on the wall. With a groan a section of wall, two feet wide and three high, swung open. Arutha went over to the opening and peered in.

"What is this?" he asked Jimmy.

"One of many secret passages throughout the palace. Back when we were hiding out together, Highness, I remember the Princess Anita talking of how she fled the palace with the aid of a serving girl. She once mentioned 'taking a passage,' and I'd thought nothing of it until today."

Brucal looked about the room. "This may have been part of the original keep, or one of the first additions. Back home we had a bolt-hole out of the keep to the woods. I don't know of a keep that doesn't." He looked thoughtful. "There may be more such passages."

Jimmy smiled. "A dozen or more. You walk around the roof a little and you'll see some very wide walls and odd bends in passages."

Arutha said, "Gardan, I want every foot of these passages mapped. Take a dozen men and uncover where this one leads and where else it may empty. And see if the royal architect has a clue if any of these passages are shown in old plans."

Gardan saluted and left. Vandros appeared deeply troubled. "Arutha, in all this I have had little time to adjust to thoughts of assassins and Dark Brothers secretly working with them."

"That's why I wanted this talk before the festivities get under way." Arutha sat down. "The palace is overrun with strangers. Every noble in attendance will have dozens of people in his retinue. Kasumi, I want your Tsurani in every key location. They would be impossible to infiltrate and are above reproach. Coordinate with Gardan, and if needs be we'll have only Tsurani, men I know from Crydee, and my personal guards inside the central palace." To Jimmy he said, "By rights I should have you strapped for this little escapade." Jimmy stiffened until he saw Arutha smile. "But I warrant anyone who tried would end up with a dagger in the ribs to show for his efforts. I heard of your confrontation with Squire Jerome."

"That snot thinks himself boss cocky of the yard."

"Well, his father's very upset, and while he's not a very important member of my vassalage, he is certainly very loud. Look, you leave Jerome to play head rooster all he wants. From now on, you stay close to me. I'll tell Master deLacy you're relieved of further duty until I say otherwise. But keep your prowling under control until you tell Gardan or myself you're going up on the roof. One of my more excitable guards might put an arrow into you before he recognized you. Things have been somewhat tense around here of late, in case you failed to notice."

Jimmy ignored the sarcasm. "The fellow would have to see me first, Highness."

Brucal slapped the table. "Got a tongue in his head, that one," he said with a guffaw and approving nod.

Arutha smiled as well. He found it difficult to stay out of sorts with the young rogue. "Enough. We've receptions and banquets for the next week. Perhaps our concerns are for naught and the Nighthawks are no more."

Laurie said, "Let us hope."

Without further discussion, Arutha and his guests dispersed to their own rooms.

"Jimmy!"

Jimmy turned and saw the Princess Anita coming down the corridor in his direction, accompanied by two of Gardan's guards and two ladies-in-waiting. When she caught up with him he bowed. She presented her hand and he kissed it lightly, as he had been shown by Laurie.

"What a young courtier you've become," she observed as they resumed walking.

"It seems fate has taken an interest in me, Princess. I have never had ambitions above becoming a power in the Mockers, perhaps even the next Upright Man, but now I find my life has much broader horizons."

She smiled while her ladies whispered behind their hands. Jimmy hadn't seen the Princess since her arrival the previous day, and again felt the faint tugging inside he had known the year before. He had put his boyhood infatuation behind, but he still liked her very much.

"Have you developed ambitions, then, Jimmy the Hand?"

In feigned scolding tones he said, "Squire James of Krondor, Your Highness," and they shared a laugh. "Look, then, Princess: this is a time of change in the Kingdom. The long war with the Tsurani robbed us of quite a few men with titles. Earl Volney is acting the part of Chancellor, and there are no Dukes yet in Salador or Bas-Tyra. Three dukedoms without masters! It seems possible for a man of wit and talent to rise high in such an environment."

"Have you a plan?" Anita asked, her delight at the boy's impudence showing in her bright green eyes and her smile.

"Not as yet, not fully at least, but I can see the possibility someday of a title beyond Squire. Perhaps, even . . . Duke of Krondor."

"First Adviser to the Prince of Krondor?" Anita said in mock astonishment.

Jimmy winked. "I am well connected. I am a close personal friend of his betrothed." They both laughed.

Anita touched his arm. "It will be good to have you here with us. I'm pleased Arutha found you so quickly. He didn't think it would be easy locating you."

Jimmy faltered a half-step. It had never occurred to him that Arutha wouldn't tell Anita of the assassin, but now he realized he hadn't. Of course, Jimmy thought to himself, he wouldn't needlessly throw a pall over the wedding. Quickly he recovered his poise. "It was more an accident than anything. His Highness never said anything about looking for me."

"You'll not know how Arutha and I worried about you all the time after we left Krondor. Last we saw you, you were fleeing across the docks from Guy's men. We had no word of you. We passed through Krondor so quickly on our way to Lyam's coronation, we had no way to discover what had happened to you. Lyam sent warrants pardoning Trevor Hull and his men and giving them a commission for helping us, but no one knew what became of Jimmy. I made Arutha promise he would straight away begin inquiries. I didn't think he would make you a squire just yet, but I knew he had plans for you."

Jimmy felt genuinely moved. This revelation added double meaning to Arutha's remark before that he liked to think they were already friends.

Anita halted their walk, indicating a door. "I am to stand for a fitting. My wedding gown arrived from Rillanon this morning." She leaned over and kissed him lightly upon the cheek. "Now I must go."

Jimmy fought down strange, and frighteningly strong, emotions. "Highness . . . I am also glad to be here. We shall have a grand time."

She laughed and passed through the door with her ladies, the guards taking up position outside. Jimmy waited until the door was closed, then walked away whistling a light tune. He reflected upon the last few weeks of his life and judged himself happy, despite assassins and tight boots.

Rounding a corner into a less frequented hallway, Jimmy halted. His dagger was instantly in his hand as he stood regarding a gleaming pair of eyes in the half-shadows before him. Then with a snuffling sound the owner of those nearly glowing red eyes ambled out. Covered in green scales, the creature bulked about the size of a small hound. His head resembled an alligator's, with a rounded snout, and large wings were folded across his back. A long, sinuous neck allowed the creature to look backward past an equally long tail as a young voice shouted from behind, "Fantus!"

A small boy, no more than six years old, came dashing forward to throw his arms around the creature's neck. He looked up at Jimmy with serious dark eyes and said, "He won't hurt you, sir."

Jimmy suddenly felt awkward holding his dagger and quickly put it away. The creature was obviously a pet, albeit an unusual sort. "What did you call it . . . ?"

"Him? Fantus. He's my friend and he's very smart. He knows lots of things."

"I guess he does," agreed Jimmy, still uncomfortable under the creature's gaze. "What is he?"

The boy looked at Jimmy as if he were the living incarnation of ignorance, but said, "A firedrake. We just got here, and he followed from home. He can fly, you know." Jimmy only nodded. "We have to get back. Momma will be angry if we're not in our room." Pulling the creature around, the boy led him away without another word.

Jimmy didn't move for a full minute, then looked around as if seeking someone to validate the vision he had witnessed. Shrugging off his astonishment, the boy thief continued walking along. After a little while he could hear the sound of lute strings being plucked.

Jimmy left the hallway and entered a large garden, where Laurie was tuning his lute. The boy sat upon the edge of a planter, crossing his feet under him, and said, "For a minstrel, you're a sorry sight."

"I'm a sorry sort of minstrel." Laurie did look less than his usual spirited self. He fiddled with his lute strings and began a solemn tune.

After a few minutes Jimmy said, "Enough of this dirge, singer. This is supposed to be a time of cheer. What's gotten you so long in the face?"

Laurie sighed, his head cocked to one side. "You're a bit young to understand—"

"Ha! Try me," interrupted Jimmy.

Laurie put up his lute. "It's the Princess Carline."

"Still wants to marry you, huh?"

Laurie's jaw dropped. "How . . . ?"

Jimmy laughed. "You've been around nobles too long, singer. I'm new to all this. I still know how to talk to servants. More important, I know how to listen. Those maids from Rillanon were fit to bust to tell the maids here all about you and Princess Carline. You're quite an item."

Laurie seemed unamused by Jimmy's mirth. "I suppose you've heard the whole tale?"

Jimmy took on an indifferent manner. "The Princess is a prize, but I grew up in a whorehouse, so my views on women are less . . . idealized." As he thought of Anita, his voice dropped a little. "Still, I must admit princesses seem different from the rest."

"Nice that you noticed," Laurie commented dryly.

"Well, I'll say this: your Princess is the finest-looking woman I've seen and I've seen a lot of them, including your better-paid courtesans, and some of them are pretty special. Most men I know would sell their darling mothers to get her attention. So then, what's your problem?"

Laurie looked at the boy for a minute. "My problem is this business of being a noble."

Jimmy laughed, a genuine sound of amusement. "What problem? You just get to order people around and blame mistakes on someone else."

Laurie laughed. "I doubt Arutha and Lyam would agree."

"Well, kings and princes are a different sort, but most of the nobles around here show me nothing. Old Volney has some wits, but he's not too anxious to be here anyway. The rest just want to be important. Hell, musician, you should marry her. You might improve the breed."

Laurie swung playfully at Jimmy, laughing as the brash youngster easily ducked away, also laughing. A third laugh caused Laurie to turn.

A short, slender, dark-haired man in fine clothing of simple cut stood observing the proceedings. "Pug!" Laurie exclaimed, jumping up to embrace the man. "When did you arrive?"

"About two hours ago. I've had a brief meeting with Arutha and the King. They're off with Earl Volney now, discussing preparations for tonight's welcoming banquet. But Arutha hinted there was something strange going on and suggested I look for you."

Laurie indicated Pug should take a seat, and he sat beside Jimmy. Laurie made the introduction, then said, "I've much to tell, but first: how are Katala and the boy?"

"Fine. She's in our suite now, gossiping with Carline." Laurie again looked depressed at mention of the Princess. "William ran off somewhere after Fantus."

"That thing is yours?" exclaimed Jimmy.

"Fantus?" Pug laughed. "You've seen him, then. No, Fantus belongs to no one. He comes and goes as he pleases, which is why he's here without anyone's leave."

Laurie said, "I doubt he's on deLacy's guest list. Look, I'd best catch you up on matters of importance." Pug glanced at Jimmy, and Laurie said, "This fount of trouble here has been at the center of things since the first. He'll hear nothing he doesn't already know."

Laurie told of what happened, with Jimmy adding a few bits of information the singer missed. When they were done, Pug said, "This business of necromancy is an evil thing. If nothing else you said speaks of dark powers at work, that does. This is more the province of priests than magicians, but Kulgan and I will aid in whatever way we can."

"Then Kulgan came from Stardock as well?"

"There would have been no stopping him. Arutha was his student, remember? Besides, though he'd never admit to it, I think he misses his arguments with Father Tully. And there was no doubt Tully would officiate at Arutha's wedding. I think that's where Kulgan is now, arguing with Tully."

Laurie said, "I've not seen Tully, but he was due to arrive this morning with those from Rillanon traveling at a more sedate pace than the King's party. At his age he tends to prefer things quiet."

"He must be past eighty now."

"Closer to ninety, but he hasn't lost a step. You should hear him around the palace in Rillanon. Let a squire or page fail at his lessons and he'll talk blisters on the boy's back."

Pug laughed. Then as an afterthought, he said, "Laurie, how fare things with you and Carline?"

Laurie groaned and Jimmy hid a chuckle. "That is what we were speaking of when you appeared. Good, bad, I don't know."

Sympathy showed in Pug's dark eyes. "I know the feeling, friend. When we were children, back at Crydee . . . Just remember, you were the one who held me to my promise to introduce you if we ever returned to Midkemia from Kelewan." He shook his head and with a laugh added, "It's good to know some things never change."

Jimmy leaped off the bench. "Well, I must be off. Pleased to make your acquaintance, magician. Cheer up, singer. You'll either marry the Princess or you won't." He dashed off, leaving Laurie struggling with the logic of that statement while Pug laughed aloud.

SEVEN

WEDDING

Jimmy prowled the great hall.

The Prince's throne room was being readied, and the other squires were supervising the activities of the pages and porters as all the last-minute touches were being applied. Everyone had their minds upon the ceremony, due to get under way in less than an hour's time. Jimmy found that the price of his being excused duty was having nothing to do at the last, and as Arutha certainly didn't want him underfoot right now, he was left to find his own distraction.

Jimmy couldn't shake the feeling that in the rush of excitement few were mindful of the past dangers to the Prince. The horrors found at the House of Willows had been hidden behind masses of bridal flowers and festive bunting.

Jimmy noticed a black, sidelong glance from Squire Jerome and, irritated, took a menacing step in the older boy's direction. Jerome immediately had a need to be somewhere else and hurried off.

A laugh sounded from behind. Jimmy saw a grinning Squire Locklear carrying a huge bridal wreath past a Tsurani guard, who carefully checked it. Of all the other squires, only Locky showed Jimmy the slightest hint of friendship. The others were either indifferent or outright hostile. Jimmy liked the younger boy, though he tended to prattle on about the most insignificant things. He's the youngest child, thought Jimmy, his mother's darling. He'd last a fast five minutes on the streets. Still, he was a cut above the rest, whom Jimmy judged a boring lot. The only amusement Jimmy gained from them was their woeful imitations of worldly knowledge. No, Arutha and his friends were far more interesting folk than the squires with their lewd jokes and salacious speculations about this serving girl or that, and their little games of intrigue. Jimmy threw Locky a wave and headed toward another door.

Jimmy waited to pass through the door as one of the porters came through. A small bunch of flowers fell from the man's load. Jimmy bent to pick it up. As he handed it to the porter, Jimmy was struck by a sudden realization. The blooms, white chrysanthemums, shone with a faint amber tint.

Jimmy looked back over his shoulder and upward. A full four stories above, the high vaulted ceiling of the chamber was punctuated by large stained-glass windows, the colors barely noticeable unless the sun was directly behind the panes. Jimmy studied the windows, as his "something is not as it should be" bump was itching. Then he understood. Each window was recessed into a cupola, no less than five or six feet deep, plenty of room to hide a quiet assassin. But how would someone get up there? The design of the hall was such that scaffolding would be needed to clean the windows, and the room had been almost constantly occupied for the last few days.

Jimmy quickly left the hall, walked down a connecting corridor, and went through into a terraced garden that ran the length of the Prince's great hall.

A pair of guards approached, walking post between the distant wall and the main palace complex, and Jimmy halted them. "Pass the word. I'm going to snoop about a bit on top of the great hall."

They exchanged glances, but Captain Gardan had ordered that the strange squire wasn't to be detained should he be seen scampering about the rooftops. One saluted. "Right you are, Squire. We'll pass the word so the archers on the walls don't use you for target practice."

Jimmy paced off alongside the wall of the great hall. The garden was off to the left of the hall as you entered the main doors, assuming you could see through the walls, Jimmy thought to himself.

Now, if I were an assassin, where would I want to climb? Jimmy cast about quickly and spotted a trellis that ran up the connecting hall's outer wall. From there to the roof of the connecting hall would be no difficulty, then . . .

Jimmy left off thinking and acted. He studied the configuration of the walls as he kicked off his hated dress boots. He scampered up the trellis and ran along the roof of the connecting hall. From there he leaped nimbly up to a low cornice that ran the length of the great hall. Moving with astonishing agility, he crawled along, his face pressed to the stones, toward the far end of the great hall. When he reached halfway to the corner, he looked up. One story above awaited the bottoms of the windows, tantalizingly close. But Jimmy knew he needed a better climbing position and continued on until he reached the last third of the hall. Here, outside the portion of the hall given over to the Prince's dais, the building flared, giving Jimmy an extra two feet of wall at a right angle to the wall he hugged. Levering up in the angle was now possible. Jimmy felt about until his fingers discovered a crack between stones. He used his experience to good advantage, shifting his weight as his toes began searching for another hold. Slowly he inched upward, seeming to climb in the angle of the two walls in defiance of gravity. It was a demanding task, requiring total concentration, but after what seemed an eternity he reached up and his fingers touched the ledge below the windows. Only a foot wide, the ledge was still a potentially fatal barrier, for any slip could send Jimmy falling to his death four stories below. Jimmy took a firm grip on the ledge and let go with his other hand. For an instant he dangled by one hand, then he reached upward with the other and with a single smooth pull had a leg over the ledge.

Standing upon the narrow ledge, Jimmy turned the corner above the rear of the dais, faced the window, and peered through. He wiped away some dust and was momentarily blinded by the sun, seen through the window and another on the wall he had just left. He waited for his eyes to adjust again to the interior darkness as he shaded his eyes from the sun. This would prove difficult, he thought, until the angle of the sun changed. Then Jimmy felt the glass move beneath his fingers, and suddenly powerful hands clamped around his mouth and throat.

Shocked by the sudden attack, Jimmy froze a moment and was too tightly held when he began to struggle. A heavy blow to the side of the head stunned him and the world seemed to spin.

When his vision finally cleared, Jimmy could see the snarling face of Laughing Jack before him. The false Mocker was not only alive, but in the palace and, from his expression and the crossbow nearby, ready and willing to kill. "So, you little bastard," he whispered as he adjusted a gag in Jimmy's mouth, "you've turned up where you didn't belong one time too many. I'd gut you here, right now, but I can't risk anyone's noticing blood dripping below." He moved around in the scant area between glass and the open space above the hall that the cupola provided. "But once the deed is done, over you go, boy." He pointed to the hall floor. He tied some cords around Jimmy's hands and ankles, pulling them painfully tight. Jimmy tried to make a sound, but it was lost in the buzz of conversation among the guests below. Jack gave Jimmy another blow to the head, which sent the boy's senses reeling again. Jimmy saw Jack turn to survey the hall below just before darkness overcame him.

Jimmy lay stunned for some unknown time, for when he recovered his wits, he could hear the chanting of the priests entering the hall. He knew the King and Arutha and the other members of the court would be making their entrance once Father Tully and the other priests were in position.

Jimmy felt panic building inside. Since he'd been dismissed from duty, his absence would be overlooked in the excitement of the moment. Jimmy struggled, but Jack, being a Mocker, knew how to make it difficult to slip those bonds. Given time and a willingness to lose some skin and blood, Jimmy would eventually rid himself of the ropes, but time was a precious commodity at present. With his struggling, he only managed to change his position so he was able to see the window. He noticed it had been tampered with to cause a single large panel of glass to swing aside. Someone had prepared this window days before.

A change in the song below told Jimmy that Arutha and the others were in place and Anita was beginning her long walk down the aisle. The boy looked about frantically for a way either to break his bonds or to make enough noise to alert those below. The singing filled the hall with a chorus loud enough to cover a brawl, so Jimmy knew anything as feeble as kicking at the glass would only bring a blow to the head from Jack. Jimmy could hear movement close by, during a lull in the singing, and knew Jack was placing a bolt in the crossbow.

The singing stopped, and Jimmy heard Tully's voice begin the instructions to the bride and groom. He saw Jack taking aim upon the dais. Jimmy was half folded in the narrow window space, forced back against the glass by the kneeling Jack. Jack threw the boy a quick glance as he began to squirm. Jimmy was unable even to kick out at Jack, who paused for a moment, evidently undecided whether to fire at his target or silence Jimmy first. For all the pomp, the ceremony itself was brief, so Jack seemed willing to chance he would be untroubled by the boy a few moments longer.

Jimmy was young, in fit condition, and an expert acrobat from his years of scampering about the roofs of Krondor. He acted without thought and simply flexed his entire body so it bowed upward, head and feet against the sides of the cupola. He half rolled, half flipped himself, and suddenly he sat with his back to the window. Jack spun to look again at the boy and swore silently. He could not afford to lose this single shot. A quick glance downward reassured him the boy had not alerted anyone. Jack raised his crossbow again and took aim.

Jimmy's vision seemed to contract, as if all he could see was Jack's finger on the trigger of the crossbow. He saw the finger begin to close and kicked out wildly. His bare feet glanced off the assassin and the crossbow fired. Jack turned in shock and Jimmy kicked out again with both feet. For a moment Jack looked to be calmly sitting at the edge of the window cupola. Then he began to fall outward, his hands grasping wildly for the sill.

Jack's hands pressed out against the sides of the cupola and halted his fall. He hung in midair, not moving for an instant, then his palms began to slip on the stone. Jimmy recognized something else was strange, then realized the singing, almost constant in counterpoint to the ceremony, had stopped. As Jack began his backward slide into space, Jimmy heard shouts and screams from below.

Then Jimmy felt a shock and his head struck stone. His legs felt as if they were being torn from his hips, and the boy knew Jack had grabbed the only thing he could reach, Jimmy's ankles. Jimmy was dragged outward as Jack's weight moved them both toward death. Jimmy struggled, pressing backward with all his might, bowing his body to slow his slide, but he might as well have had iron heaped upon his feet for the good it did him. Bones and muscles protested, but he could not move an inch to rid himself of Jack. He was dragged outward slowly, his legs, hips, and back scraping on the stone, the cloth of his trousers and tunic keeping skin intact. Then he was suddenly upright, as Jack's weight tipped his balance for an instant, teetering upon the lip of the cupola.

Then they fell. Jack released his hold upon the boy, but Jimmy didn't notice. The stones rushed up to meet them, to crush them in a hard embrace. Jimmy thought his mind must be going at the last, for the stones seemed to slow in their approach, as if some agency had ordered the boy's last seconds of life to be prolonged. Then Jimmy realized some force had control of him and was slowing his descent. With a less than gentle bump he was upon the floor of the great hall, stunned slightly, but decidedly alive. Guards and priests surrounded him and hands quickly lifted him as he wondered at this miracle. He saw the magician Pug moving his hands in incantation, and felt the strange slowness vanish. Guards cut his bonds, and Jimmy doubled in pain as the returning blood flow burned like hot irons in his feet and hands. He nearly fainted. Two soldiers seized his arms and kept him from falling. As his senses cleared, he saw a half-dozen or more holding Jack down, while others searched for the black poison ring or other means of suicide.

Jimmy looked about, his head clearing. All around him the room seemed frozen in horrified tableau. Father Tully stood at Arutha's side, while Tsurani guards surrounded the King, their eyes peering into every corner of the room. Everyone else looked at Anita, who was cradled in Arutha's arms as he knelt upon the stones. Her veils and gown were spread out around her and she seemed to sleep while he held her. She was a vision in pristine white in the late afternoon light, except for the rapidly expanding crimson stain upon her back.

Arutha sat in shock. He leaned forward, elbows on knees, as his eyes stared out into space, unfocused, not seeing any of those with him in the antechamber. He saw only the last minutes of the ceremony, again and again in his mind's eye.

Anita had just pledged her vows, and Arutha was listening to Tully's final blessing. Suddenly she had a strange expression and seemed to stumble, as if shoved hard from behind. He caught her, finding it strange she should fall, for she was so graceful by nature. He tired to think of a witticism that would break the tension, for he knew she would feel embarrassed at stumbling. And she looked so serious, with her eyes wide and her mouth half open as if she wanted to ask some important question. When he heard the first scream, he looked up and saw the man hanging backward out of the cupola high above the dais. Instantly everything seemed to run together. People were shouting and pointing and Pug was rushing forward, incanting a spell. And Anita couldn't seem to stand, no matter how he tried to help her. Then he saw the blood.

Arutha buried his face in his hands and wept. In his life he had never before been unable to control his emotions. Carline placed her arms about him, holding him tight, and her tears fell with his. She had been with him since Lyam and three guards had pulled him from Anita's side, leaving the priests and chirurgeons to their work. Princess Alicia was in her quarters, near-prostrate from grief. Gardan was off with Martin, Kasumi, and Vandros, supervising the guards who were searching the grounds for any other intruders. By Lyam's order, the palace had been sealed within minutes of the assassination attempt. Now the King paced the room silently, while Volney was off in a corner, in quiet conversation with Laurie, Brucal, and Fannon. They all awaited word.

The door to the outer hall opened and a Tsurani guard admitted Jimmy. He walked forward gingerly, for his legs had been strained and scraped badly. Lyam and the others watched as the boy thief came to stand before Arutha.

Jimmy tried to speak, but no words were forthcoming. Like Arutha, he had relived every moment of the attack over and over in his mind while an acolyte of Nathan's order had bandaged his legs. His memory had constantly played tricks on him, as he would see Arutha's face of days ago when he had told Jimmy his feelings of friendship, then suddenly he would see the Prince's face as he had knelt holding Anita, uncomprehending shock on his features. Then

Jimmy would remember Anita standing in the hall before going for a dress fitting. That image would fade and he would once more see Arutha slowly lower her to the floor as priests rushed to her side.

Jimmy again tried to speak as Arutha looked up. The Prince's eyes focused upon the boy, and he said, "Why . . . Jimmy, I . . . didn't see you there."

Jimmy saw the grief and pain in those dark brown eyes and felt something break inside himself. Unbidden tears came to his eyes as the boy spoke softly. "I . . . I tried . . ." He swallowed hard; something seemed to be choking off his breath. Jimmy's mouth worked, but no sound came. Finally he whispered, "I'm sorry." Then suddenly he was on his knees before Arutha. "I'm sorry."

Arutha looked on uncomprehendingly for a moment, then shook his head. He put his hand upon Jimmy's shoulder and said, "It's all right. It wasn't your fault."

Jimmy knelt with his head cradled in his arms upon Arutha's knees, sobbing loudly while Arutha awkwardly tried to comfort him. Laurie knelt beside him and said, "You couldn't have done anything more."

Jimmy raised his head and looked at Arutha. "But I should have."

Carline leaned over and gently ran her hand down the side of his face, wiping away the tears. "You went to investigate, which no one else did. Who knows what would have happened if you hadn't." She left unspoken the thought that Arutha might be lying dead had Jimmy not kicked at Laughing Jack when he fired.

Jimmy was disconsolate. He said, "I should have done more."

Lyam crossed to where Laurie, Carline, and Arutha were clustered around Jimmy. He also knelt beside the boy as Laurie made room. "Son, I've seen men who would fight goblins go pale at the thought of climbing out where you did. Each of us has fears," he said softly. "But when something terrible happens, each of us always thinks, I should have done more." He placed his hand over Arutha's, which still rested upon Jimmy's shoulder. "I've just had to order the Tsurani guards responsible for searching the hall not to kill themselves. At least you don't have that twisted a sense of honor."

Seriously Jimmy said, "If I could trade places with the Princess, I would."

Lyam spoke solemly. "I know you would, son; I know you would."

Arutha, as if slowly returning from some distant place, said, "Jimmy . . . just so you know . . . you did well. Thank you." He tried to smile.

Jimmy, with tears still on his cheeks, hugged Arutha's knees hard, then sat back, wiping at his face, returning Arutha's smile. "I've not cried since the night I saw my mum murdered." Carline's hand went to her mouth and her face turned white.

The door to the antechamber opened and Nathan came through. He wore only his white knee-length undertunic, having stripped off his ceremonial robes to supervise the care of the Princess. He was wiping his hands upon a cloth and he looked haggard. Arutha slowly rose, Lyam holding his arm. Nathan looked grim as he said, "She lives. Though the wound is severe, the bolt struck at a glancing angle that saved her spine. Had the bolt hit full on, death would have been instantaneous. She is young and healthy, but . . ."

"But what?" asked Lyam.

"The bolt was poisoned, Your Majesty. And it is a poison fashioned with foul arts, a concoction using evil spells. We have been able to do nothing to counter it. Alchemy or magic, nothing works."

Arutha blinked. Comprehension seemed to elude him.

Nathan looked at Arutha, his eyes reflecting his sorrow. "I'm sorry, Highness. She's dying."

The dungeon lay beneath sea level, damp and dark, the air musty with the sour smells of molds and algae. A guard moved aside while another pulled open a protesting door as Lyam and Arutha passed through the portal. Martin waited off to one side in the torture chamber, speaking softly with Vandros and Kasumi. This room had not been used since before Prince Erland's time, except for a short period when Jocko Radburn's secret police had used it to interrogate prisoners during du Bas-Tyra's reign.

The room had been cleared of the usual instruments of torture, but a brazier had been returned to its former place and irons were heating within. One of Gardan's soldiers tended the burning coals. Laughing Jack stood chained to a pillar of stone, his hands above his head. Standing in full circle around him were six Tsurani, close enough that the groaning prisoner touched them as he moved. Each faced outward, maintaining a level of vigilance unmatched by even the most loyal of Arutha's Household Guard.

From another part of the chamber, Father Tully left the side of several other priests, all of whom had been present at the wedding. He said to Lyam, "We have established protective spells of the most powerful sort." He pointed at Jack. "But something seeks to gain access to him. How fares Anita?"

Lyam shook his head slowly. "The bolt was poisoned in some arcane fashion. Nathan says her time grows short."

"Then we must question the prisoner quickly," said the old priest. "We have no idea what we are combating."

Jack groaned aloud. Arutha's rage rose up and he nearly choked with fury. Lyam pushed past his brother, motioned for a guard to step aside, and looked the thief in the eyes. Laughing Jack looked back with eyes wide with fear. His body gleamed and sweat dripped off his hooked nose. Each time he moved, he groaned. The Tsurani had obviously not been gentle when they searched him. Jack tried to speak, wet his lips with his tongue, then said, "Please . . ." His voice was hoarse. "Don't let him take me."

Lyam stepped up beside him and grabbed Jack, his hand closing on the man's face like a vise. Shaking Jack's head, he said, "What poison did you use?"

Jack was near tears when he spoke. "I don't know. I swear it!"

"We shall have the truth out of you, man. You had better answer, for we can make it hard on you." Lyam indicated the burning irons.

Jack tried to laugh, but it became a bubbling sound. "Hard? You think I fear irons? Listen you, King of the bloody damn Kingdom, I'll gladly let you burn out my liver if you promise you won't let him take me." The last statement had a hysterical note in it.

Lyam threw a quick glance around the room. "Let who take him?"

Tully said, "He's been yelling for an hour not to let 'him' take him." The priest's expression betrayed a thought. "He's made a compact with dark powers. Now he fears to pay!" he said with sudden certainty.

Jack nodded his head emphatically, eyes wide. With a half-laugh, half-sob, he said, "Aye, priest, as would you if you'd ever been touched by that darkness."

Lyam grabbed Jack by his stringy hair and jerked his head back. "What are you speaking of?"

Jack's eyes grew round. "Murmandamus," he whispered.

Suddenly there was a cold chill in the room and the coals in the brazier and the torches on the wall seemed to flicker and fade. "He's here!" shrieked Jack, out of control. One of the priests began to chant and after a moment the light brightened.

Tully looked toward Lyam. "That was . . . frightening." His face was drawn and his eyes wide. "It has tremendous power. Hurry, Majesty, but speak not that name. It only serves to draw it to its minion here."

"What was the poison?" Lyam demanded.

Jack sobbed, "I don't know. In truth. It was something the goblin kisser give me, the Dark Brother. I swear it."

The door opened and Pug entered, followed by the stout figure of another magician, this one wearing a bushy grey beard. Pug's dark eyes mirrored the somber tone of his voice when he said, "Kulgan and I have established wards around this part of the palace, but something batters them even as we speak."

Kulgan, his face wan as if he had just finished some taxing labor, added, "Whatever is seeking to enter is determined. Given time, I think we could unravel something of its nature, but . . ."

Tully finished the thought. ". . . it will win past us before we can. So time is something we lack." To Lyam he said, "Hurry."

Lyam said, "This thing you serve, or this person, whatever it is, tell us what you know. Why does it seek my brother's death?"

"A bargain!" shouted Jack. "I'll tell you what I know, everything, just don't let him take me."

Lyam nodded curtly. "We shall keep him from you."

"You don't know," Jack screamed, then his voice fell off to a half-sob. "I was dead. Do you understand? That bastard shot me instead of Jimmy and I was dead." He looked at those around the room. "None of you can know. I could feel life slip away, and then he came. When I was almost dead, he took me to this cold, dark place and he . . . hurt me. He showed me . . . things. He said I could live and serve him and he'd give me back life, or he'd . . . he'd let me die and leave me there. He couldn't save me then, for I wasn't his. But now I am. He's . . . evil."

Julian, the priest of Lims-Kragma, came up behind the King. "He lied to you, man. That cold place was of his fashioning. Our mistress's love brings comfort to all who embrace her at the end. You were shown a lie."

"He's the father of all liars! But now I'm his creature," Jack sobbed. "He said I had to go to the palace and kill the Prince. He said I was the only one he had left and the others would arrive too late, wouldn't be here for days. It had to be me. I said I would, but . . . I botched it and now he wants my soul!" The last was a piteous cry, a plea for mercy beyond the power of the King to grant.

Lyam turned to Julian. "Can we do anything?"

Julian said, "There is a rite, but . . ." He looked at Jack and said, "You will die, man, you know that. You died already and you are here because of an unholy compact. What will be will be. You will die within the hour. Do you understand?"

Through tears and spittle Jack sobbed, "Yes."

"Then you will answer our questions and tell us what you know, and die willingly to free your soul?" Jack's eyes screwed shut and he cried like a child, but he nodded his head.

"So tell us what you know of the Nighthawks and this plot to kill my brother," demanded Lyam.

Jack sniffed and gasped for air. "Six, seven months ago, Golden Dase tells me he's tumbled to something that could make us wealthy." As he spoke, Jack's voice lost the hysterical quality. "I asked him if he'd cleared it with the Nightmaster, but he says it's not Mocker business. I'm not sure it's a good idea playing fast and loose with the guild, but I'd not mind an extra sovereign on the side, so I say 'Why not?' and I go with him. We met this fellow Havram, who'd worked with us before, and who asks a bunch of questions but isn't giving with answers, so I get ready to chuck the whole deal, before I even know what's going on, but then he lays this bag of gold on the table and tells me there's more to be had."

Jack closed his eyes and a half-choked sob came from his throat. "I came with Golden and Havram to the Willows, through the sewer. I nearly messed myself when I saw the goblin kissers, two of them, in the cellar. They had gold, though, and I will put up with a lot for gold. So they tell me I've got to do this and that and listen up to what's coming along from the Upright Man and Nightmaster and Daymaster and tell them. I tell them that's a death warrant, then they pull out their swords and tell me it's a death warrant if I don't. I thought I'd go along, then turn my bashers loose on them, but they took me up to another room in the Willows, and this fellow, all in robes, was there. I couldn't see his face but he sounded funny, and he stank. I smelled that stink once when I was a kid, and I'll never forget it."

"What?" said Lyam.

"In a cave once I smelled it. Snake."

Lyam turned to Tully, who gasped. "A Pantathian serpent priest!" The other priests in the room looked aghast and began speaking quietly with one another. Tully said, "Continue; time grows short."

"Then they start doing things like I never seen before. I'm no misty-eyed virgin, thinking the world's pure and lovely, but these blokes were something I've never dreamed of. They brought in a kid! A little girl, no more than eight or nine. I thought I'd seen it all. The one in the robes pulls a dagger and . . ." Jack gulped, obviously fighting down the contents of his stomach. "They drew these diagrams with her blood and took some sort of oath. I'm not one for the gods, but I've always tossed a coin to Ruthia and Banath on the high holidays. But now I'm praying to Banath like I'm robbing the city treasury in broad daylight. I don't know if that had anything to do with it, but they didn't make me take the oath. . . ." His voice broke into a sob. "Man, they were drinking her blood!" He took a deep breath. "I agreed to work with them. Everything went all right until they told me to ambush Jimmy."

"Who are these men and what do they want?" demanded Lyam.

"This goblin kisser tells me one night that there's some sort of prophecy about the Lord of the West. The Lord of the West must die, then something's going to happen."

Lyam shot a glance at Arutha. "You said they called you Lord of the West."

Arutha had regained some measure of self-control and said, "Yes, they have, twice."

Lyam returned to the questioning. "What else?"

"I don't know," said Jack, nearly exhausted. "They would talk among themselves. I wasn't properly one of them." Again the room shuddered and the coals and torches flickered. "He's here!" Jack shrieked.

Arutha came to stand at Lyam's shoulder. "What about the poison?" he demanded.

"I don't know," Jack sobbed. "It was something the goblin kisser gave me. It"—he nodded—"one of the others called it 'Silverthorn.' "

Arutha looked rapidly around the room but could see no one who recognized that name. Suddenly one of the priests said, "It has returned."

Several of the priests began incantations, then stopped, and one said, "It has won past our wards."

Lyam said to Tully, "Are we in danger?"

Tully replied, "The dark powers may directly control only those who have willingly given themselves over to them. We are safe from direct attack here."

The room began to chill as the torches flickered madly, and shadows deepened on all sides. "Don't let him take me!" Jack shrieked. "You promised!"

Tully looked to Lyam, who nodded and indicated that Father Julian should take charge.

The King motioned for the Tsurani guards to give the priest of Lims-Kragma room. The priest stood before Jack and asked, "Do you find in your heart the earnest desire to receive our mistress's mercy?"

Jack couldn't speak for terror. Through tear-filled eyes he blinked, then nodded. Julian began a low, quiet chant and the other priests made quick gestures. Tully came over to Arutha and said, "Stay calm. Death is now among us."

It was over quickly. One moment Jack was sobbing uncontrollably, then abruptly he slumped down, prevented from falling only by the chains. Julian turned to the others. "He is safe with the Mistress of Death. No harm can come to him now."

Suddenly the very walls of the chamber seemed to shake. A black presence could be felt in the room and a high-pitched keening began, as something inhuman shrieked in outrage at being robbed of its minion. All the priests, as well as Pug and Kulgan, mounted a magic defense against the invading spirit, then suddenly everything was deathly quiet.

Tully, looking shaken, said, "It has fled."

Arutha knelt beside the bed, his face a stony mask. Anita lay with her hair falling upon the white pillow like a dark red crown. "She seems so tiny," he said softly. He looked at those in the room. Carline clung to Laurie's arm, while Martin waited with Pug and Kulgan next to the window. In silence Arutha's eyes beseeched them all. All looked down on the princess, except Kulgan, who seemed lost in thoughts of his own. They stood the deathwatch, for Nathan had said the young Princess wouldn't last the hour. Lyam was in another room attempting to comfort Anita's mother.

Suddenly Kulgan moved around the bed and, in a voice made loud by the hushed tones of the others, asked Tully, "If you had a question and you could ask it only once, where would you go to ask it?"

Tully blinked. "Riddles?" Kulgan's expression, his bushy grey eyebrows meeting over his prominent nose, showed he was not attempting some tasteless jest. "I'm sorry," said Tully. "Let me think. . . ." Tully's aged face furrowed in concentration. Then he looked as if some obvious truth had struck. "Sarth!"

Kulgan tapped the old cleric in the chest with a forefinger. "Right. Sarth."

Arutha, who had been following the conversation, said, "Why Sarth? It is one of the least important ports in the Principality."

"Because," answered Tully, "there is an Ishapian abbey near there that is said to house more knowledge than any other place in the Kingdom."

"And," added Kulgan, "if there was any place in this Kingdom where we could discover the nature of Silverthorn, and what would counter it, that would be the place."

Arutha looked helplessly down at Anita. "But Sarth . . . No rider could reach there and return in less than a week and . . ."

Pug stepped forward. "I may be able to help." With sudden authority he said, "Leave the room. All of you, except Fathers Nathan, Tully, and Julian." He said to Laurie, "Run to my rooms. Katala will give you a large red-leather-bound book. Bring it at once."

Without question Laurie dashed off, while the others vacated the room. Pug spoke softly to the priests. "Can you slow her passage through time without harm?"

Nathan said, "I can work such a spell. I did so with the wounded Dark Brother before he died. But it will gain us only a few hours." He looked down at Anita, whose face had already taken on a cold blue appearance. Nathan touched her forehead. "She grows clammy to the touch. She fails fast. We must hurry."

The three priests quickly fashioned the pentagram and lit the candles. Within minutes they had prepared the room and soon the rite was done. The Princess lay, apparently asleep, in a bed engulfed by a rosy glow seen when viewed askance. Pug led the priests from the room and asked for sealing wax to be brought. Martin ordered it and a page ran off. Pug took the book he had asked Laurie to fetch. He reentered the room and paced around it, reading from his tome. When he was finished, he stepped outside and began a long string of incantations.

He finished by placing a seal of wax upon the wall near the door. He then closed the book. "It is done."

Tully moved toward the door, and Pug's hand restrained him. "Do not cross the threshold." The old priest looked at Pug questioningly.

Kulgan shook his head in appreciation. "Don't you see what the boy's done, Tully?" Pug was forced to smile, for even after he'd grown long white whiskers, he'd still be a boy to Kulgan. "Look at the candles!"

The others looked in, and in a moment all could see what the stout magician meant. The candles at the corners of the pentagram were alight, although this was difficult to see in the daylight. But when they were watched closely, it was clear the flames didn't flicker. Pug said to the others, "Time moves so slowly in that room it is nearly impossible to detect its passage. The wall of this palace would crumble to dust before the candles burn a tenth part of their length. Should anyone cross the threshold, he will be caught like a fly in amber. It would mean death, but Father Nathan's spell slows time's ravages within the pentagram and prevents harm to the Princess."

"How long will it last?" said Kulgan, obviously in awe of his former student.

"Until the seal is broken."

Arutha's face betrayed the first flickerings of hope. "She will live?"

"She lives now," said Pug. "Arutha, she exists between moments, and will stay that way, forever young, until the spell is removed. But then time will once again flow for her and she will need a cure, if one exists."

Kulgan gave out with an audible sigh. "Then we have gained that which we needed most. Time."

"Yes, but how much?" asked Tully.

Arutha's voice was firm. "Enough. I shall find a cure."

Martin said, "What do you intend?"

Arutha looked at his brother, and for the first time that day was free of the crippling grief, the madness of despair. Coldly, evenly he said, "I will go to Sarth."

EIGHT

VOW

Lyam sat unmoving.

He studied Arutha for a long moment and shook his head. "No. I forbid it."

Arutha registered no reaction as he said, "Why?"

Lyam sighed. "Because it's too dangerous, and you've other responsibilities here." Lyam rose from behind the table in Arutha's private quarters and crossed over to his brother. Gently placing his hand on Arutha's arm, he said, "I know your nature, Arutha. You hate sitting idly by while matters are moving to conclusion without you. I know you cannot abide the thought of Anita's fate resting in hands other than your own, but in good conscience I cannot allow you to travel to Sarth."

Arutha's expression remained clouded, as it had been since the assassination attempt the day before. But with the death of Laughing Jack, Arutha's rage had fled, seeming to turn inward, becoming cold detachment. Kulgan and Tully's revelation of a possible source of knowledge existing in Sarth had cleansed his mind of the initial madness. Now he had something to do, something that required clarity of judgment, the ability to think rationally, coolly, dispassionately. Fixing his brother with a penetrating look, he said, "I've been away for months, traveling abroad with you, so the business of the Western Realm can endure my absence for another few weeks. As for my safety," he added, his voice rising in inflection, "we've all seen just how safe I am in *my own palace!"* He fell into silence for a moment, then said, "I will go to Sarth."

Martin had been quietly sitting in the corner, observing the debate, listening closely to both his half brothers. He leaned forward in his chair. "Arutha, I've known you since you were a babe and I know your moods as well as my own. You think it impossible to leave vital matters to the care of others. You have a certain arrogance to your nature, little brother. It is a trait, a flaw of character if you will, we all share."

Lyam blinked as if surprised to be included in the indictment. "All . . . ?"

The corner of Arutha's mouth turned up in a half-smile as he let out a deep sigh. "All, Lyam," Martin said. "We're all three Borric's sons, and for all his good qualities, Father could be arrogant. Arutha, in temper you and I are as one; I simply mask myself better. I can think of little to make me chafe more than sitting while others are about tasks I feel better able to accomplish, but at the last, there is no reason for you to go. There are others better suited. Tully, Kulgan, and Pug can set pen to parchment with all the questions required for the Abbot at Sarth. And there are those better suited to carry such messages quickly and without notice through the woods between here and Sarth."

Lyam scowled. "Such as a certain duke from the West, I expect."

Martin smiled his crooked smile, a reflection of Arutha's. "Not even Arutha's Pathfinders are as adept at traveling through the woods as one elven-taught. If this Murmandamus has agents along the woodland trails, there is no one south of Elvandar more likely to win past them than I."

Lyam cast his eyes heavenward in disgust. "You are no better than he." He crossed to the doors and pulled them open. Arutha and Martin followed behind. Gardan waited without, and his company of guards snapped to attention as their monarch left the chamber. To Gardan, Lyam said, "Captain, should either of our half-witted brothers attempt to leave the palace, arrest him and lock him up. That is our royal will. Understood?"

Gardan saluted. "Yes, Your Majesty."

Without another word, Lyam strode down the hall toward his own quarters, his face a mask of worry and preoccupation. Behind him Gardan's guards exchanged astonished glances, then watched Arutha and Martin leave in another direction. Arutha's face was flushed, his anger only partially hidden, while Martin's expression revealed nothing of his feelings. When the two brothers were out of sight, questioning glances passed from soldier to soldier, for they had heard every word exchanged between the King and his brothers, until Gardan spoke in soft but commanding tones. "Steady on. You're at post."

"Arutha!"

Arutha and Martin, who had been speaking softly as they walked, halted as the Keshian Ambassador hurried to overtake them, his retinue following behind. He reached them, bowed slightly, and said, "Your Highness, Your Grace."

"Good day, Your Excellency," Arutha responded somewhat curtly. The presence of Lord Hazara-Khan reminded him there were obligations of office going unmet. Sooner or later, Arutha knew, he would have to return his attention to the mundane concerns of governance. That thought rankled him.

The Ambassador said, "I have been informed, Your Highness,

that I and my party will require permission to quit the palace. Is this so?"

Arutha's irritation intensified, though now it was directed at himself. He had secured the palace as a matter of course, but had done so without considering the often sticky question of diplomatic immunity, that necessary oil in the usually squeaky machinery of international relations. With a note of apology he said, "My lord Hazara-Khan, I am sorry. In the heat of the moment . . ."

"I fully understand, Highness." Looking quickly about, he said, "May I also have a brief moment? We could speak as we walk." Arutha indicated he might, and Martin dropped back to walk with Hazara-Khan's sons and bodyguard. The Ambassador said, "It would be a poor time to pester the King over treaties. I think it a proper time to visit my people in the Jal-Pur. I will stay there awhile. I'll return to your city, or to Rillanon, as needed, to discuss treaties, after . . . things have settled."

Arutha studied the Ambassador. Volney's intelligence on him had revealed that the Empress had dispatched one of her finest minds to negotiate with the Kingdom. "My lord Hazara-Khan, I thank you for considering my own feelings and those of my family at this time."

The Ambassador waved away the remark. "There is no honor in besting those afflicted by sorrow and woe. When this evil business is over, I desire you and your brother to come to the negotiating table with clear minds, when we discuss the Vale of Dreams. I wish to win concessions from the best you have to offer, Highness. Now it would be too simple to gain advantage. You need Kesh's approbation in the matter of the King's forthcoming wedding to the Princess Magda of Roldem. As she is the only daughter of King Carole, and if anything happens to her brother, Crown Prince Dravos, any child of hers would sit the thrones of both the Isles and Roldem, and as Roldem has long been seen as lying within Kesh's traditional sphere of influence . . . well, you can see how we are concerned."

"My compliments to the Imperial Intelligence Corps, Excellency," said Arutha in rueful appreciation. Only he and Martin had known.

"Officially, no such group exists, though we do have certain sources—those wishing to maintain the status quo."

"I appreciate your candor, Excellency. We also must concern our discussions with the question of a new Keshian war fleet being constructed in Durbin in violation of the Treaty of Shamata."

Lord Hazara-Khan shook his head and said with affection, "Oh, Arutha, I look forward to bargaining with you."

"And I with you. I'll order the guards to allow your party to leave at will. I only ask that you ensure that no one not of your retinue slips out in disguise."

"I shall stand at the gate and name every soldier and servant as they pass, Highness."

Arutha had no doubts he would be able to do just that. "No matter what fate brings, Abdur Rachman Memo Hazara-Khan, even should we someday face each other across a battlefield, I will count you a generous, honorable friend." He extended his hand.

Abdur took it. "You do me honor, Highness. As long as I speak with Kesh's voice, she will negotiate only in good faith, toward honorable ends."

The Ambassador signaled for his companions to join him, and after asking Arutha's leave they departed. Martin came to Arutha's side and said, "At least we now have one fewer problem for the moment."

Arutha nodded in agreement. "For the moment. That wily old fox will probably end up with this palace for his embassy and I'll be left with some flophouse near the docks to hold court in."

"Then we shall need to have Jimmy recommend one of the better ones to us." Suddenly struck by a thought, Martin said, "Where is he? I've not seen him since we questioned Laughing Jack."

"Out and about. I had a few things for him to do." Martin indicated understanding and the two brothers continued down the hall.

Laurie spun at the sound of someone entering his room. Carline closed the door behind her, then stopped as she observed the singer's travel bundle resting next to his lute upon his bed. He had just finished tying it and he wore his old travel clothing. Her eyes narrowed and she nodded once, knowingly. "Going somewhere?" Carline's tone was icy. "Just thought you'd take a quick run up to Sarth and ask a few questions, right?"

Laurie raised his hands in supplication. "Just for a while, beloved. I'll be quickly back."

Sitting down on the bed, she said, "Oh! You're as bad as Arutha or Martin. You'd think everyone in the palace didn't possess the brains to blow their noses without one of you telling them how. So you'll get your head lopped off by some bandit, or . . . something. Laurie, I get so angry sometimes." He sat next to her and placed his arm around her shoulders. She leaned her head against his shoulder. "We've had so little time together since we arrived, and everything is so . . . terrible." Her voice broke as she began to cry. "Poor Anita," she said after a while. Defiantly wiping away her tears, she went on, "I hate it when I cry.

"And I'm still angry with you. You were going to run off and leave without a good-bye. I knew it. Well, if you go, don't come back. Just send a message about what you find out—if you live that long—but don't set foot in this palace. I don't ever want to see you again." She rose to her feet and made for the door.

Laurie was after her in an instant. He took her by the arm and turned her to face him. "Beloved, please . . . don't . . ."

With tears in her eyes she said, "If you loved me, you'd ask Lyam for my hand. I'm done with sweet words, Laurie. I'm done with vague unease. I'm done with you."

Laurie felt panic overtake him. He had been ignoring Carline's earlier threat to be through with him or married to him by the time she returned to Rillanon, as much from choice as from the pressure of events. "I wasn't going to say anything until this business with Anita was resolved, but—I've decided. I can't let you leave me out of your life. I do want to marry you."

Suddenly her eyes were wide. "What?"

"I said I want to marry—"

She covered his mouth with her hand. Then she kissed him. For a long silent moment no words were necessary. She pushed away, a dangerous half-smile on her face. Shaking her head in the negative, she spoke softly. "No. Say nothing more. I'll not have you fog my mind again with honeyed words." She slowly walked to the door and opened it. "Guards!" she called and in an instant a pair appeared. Pointing at an astonished Laurie, she said, "Don't let him move! If he tries to leave, sit on him!"

Carline vanished from sight down the hall, and the guards turned amused expressions on Laurie. He sighed and sat down quietly upon his bed.

A few minutes later the Princess was back, an irritated Father Tully in tow. The old prelate had his night robe hastily gathered about him, as he had been almost ready for sleep. Lyam, looking equally inconvenienced, followed his sister. Laurie fell backward onto the bed with an audible groan as Carline marched into the room and pointed at him. "He told me he wants to marry me!"

Laurie sat up. Lyam regarded his sister with an astonished expression. "Should I congratulate him or have him hung? From your tone it's difficult to tell."

Laurie bolted upright as if stuck by a needle and moved toward the King. "Your Majesty—"

"Don't let him say anything," interrupted Carline, pointing an accusatory finger at Laurie. In a menacing whisper, she said, "He is the king of all liars and a seducer of the innocent. He'll talk his way out of it."

Lyam shook his head as he muttered, "Innocent?" Suddenly his face clouded. "Seducer?" He fixed his gaze upon Laurie.

"Your Majesty, please," began Laurie.

Carline crossed her arms and impatiently tapped her foot on the floor. "He's doing it," she muttered. "He's talking his way out of marrying me."

Tully interposed himself between Carline and Laurie. "Majesty, if I may?"

Looking confused, Lyam said, "I wish you would."

Tully looked first at Laurie, then at Carline. "Am I to understand, Highness, that you wish to wed this man?"

"Yes!"

"And you, sir?"

Carline began to say something, but Lyam cut her off. "Let him speak!"

Laurie stood blinking at the sudden silence. He shrugged as if to say he didn't understand the commotion. "Of course I do, father."

Lyam looked close to the end of his patience. "Then what is the difficulty?" He said to Tully, "Post bans, oh, next week sometime. After the last few days we should wait a bit. We'll have the wedding after . . . things settle a bit. If you have no objections, Carline?" She shook her head, her eyes moist. Lyam continued, "Someday, when you're an old married lady with dozens of grandchildren, you'll have to explain this all to me." To Laurie he said, "You're a braver man than most," then, with a glance at his sister, added, "and luckier than most." He kissed her on the cheek. "Now, if there's nothing else, I'll retire."

Carline threw her arms around his neck and gave him a fierce hug. "Thank you."

Still shaking his head, Lyam left the room. Tully said, "There must be a reason for this urgent need of betrothal at this late hour." He held his hands palms out and quickly added, "But I'll wait to hear it some other time. Now, if you'll excuse me—" He gave Carline no opportunity to say anything as he almost dashed from the room. The guards followed after, closing the door behind them. Carline smiled at Laurie after they were alone. "Well, it is done. Finally!"

Laurie grinned down at her as he put his arms about her waist. "Yes, and with little pain."

"Little pain!" she said, punching him in the stomach with not inconsiderable effect. Laurie doubled over, the wind knocked out of him. He fell backward, landing upon his bed. Carline came to the edge of the bed and knelt next to him. As he tried to sit up, she pushed him back on the bed with her hand on his chest. "What am I, some dowdy drudge you must endure for the sake of political ambitions?" She playfully pulled at the leather thongs of his tunic. "I should have you thrown in the dungeon. Little pain, you monster."

Gripping a handful of her dress, he yanked her forward, bringing her face close enough to be kissed. With a grin, he said, "Hello, my love." Then they were in each other's arms.

Later, Carline roused from a half-doze to say, "Happy?"

Laurie laughed, causing her head to jiggle on his chest where it lay. "Of course." Stroking her hair, he said, "What was all that about with your brother and Tully?"

She chuckled. "After almost a year of trying to get you to marry me, I wasn't about to let you forget you proposed. For all I knew, you were simply trying to get rid of me so you could sneak away to Sarth."

"Sweet good night!" said Laurie, jumping out of bed. "Arutha!"

Carline turned and settled back into the just-vacated pillow. "So you and my brother are both sneaking off."

"Yes—no, I mean—oh hell." Laurie pulled on his trousers and stood looking about. "Where is my other boot? I'm at least an hour overdue." When he was dressed, he came to sit next to her on the bed. "I must go. Arutha won't let anything stop him. You knew that."

She held tightly to his arm. "I knew you'd both go. How do you plan to get out of the palace?"

"Jimmy."

She nodded. "There's an exit he forgot to mention to the royal architect, I expect."

"Something like that. I must go."

She clung to his arm for a moment. "You didn't take your vows lightly, did you?"

"Never." He bent over to kiss her. "Without you, I am nothing."

Silently she cried, feeling at once filled and empty, knowing for certain she had found her life's mate and fearing to lose him. As if reading her thoughts, he said, "I'll be back, Carline; nothing could keep me from you."

"If you don't, I'll come after you."

With a quick kiss he was gone, the door closing quietly behind him. Carline burrowed deeply into the bed, holding on to the last remaining warmth of him as long as she could.

Laurie slipped through the door into Arutha's suite while the guards in the hall were at the far end of their walking tour. In the dark he heard his name whispered. "Yes," he replied.

Arutha unshuttered a lantern, lighting the room. The single light source made the antechamber of Arutha's suite appear cavernous. Arutha said, "You're late." To Laurie he and Jimmy appeared alien figures as they stood lit from below by the yellow lantern glow. Arutha wore simple mercenary garb: knee-high cavalier boots, heavy woollen trousers, a heavy leather vest over a blue tunic, and his rapier belted at his side. Over all he wore a heavy grey cloak, the deep hood thrown back over his shoulders, but what caused Laurie to stare for a moment was the light that seemed to come from Arutha's eyes. About to embark upon the journey to Sarth at last, he was afire with impatience. "Lead the way."

Jimmy showed them to a low hidden door in the wall, and they entered. Through the ancient tunnels of the palace Jimmy moved quickly, down to a level deeper than even the damp dungeon. Arutha and Laurie kept quiet, though the singer was given to an occasional silent oath when something he stepped on scampered away or squished. He was pleased at the lack of good light.

Suddenly they were moving up rough stone steps. At the top landing, Jimmy pushed upward against a protesting section of seemingly blank stone ceiling. It moved slightly and Jimmy said, "It's a tight squeeze." He wiggled through and took their belongings as they passed them along. The base of an outer stone wall had been cleverly counterweighted to swing from one side, but age and disuse had made it stubborn. Arutha and Laurie managed to wiggle through. Arutha said, "Where are we?"

"Behind a hedge in the royal park. The postern gate to the palace is about a hundred and fifty yards off that way," answered Jimmy. He indicated a direction. "Follow me." He led them through thick shrubbery and into a stand of trees, in which three horses waited.

Arutha said, "I didn't ask you to purchase three mounts."

With an insolent grin, visible in the moonlit night, Jimmy said, "But you also didn't tell me not to, Highness."

Laurie decided it best not to get involved, so he busied himself tying his bundle to the nearest mount. Arutha said, "We move quickly, and I've no patience for this. You may not come, Jimmy."

Jimmy moved toward one of the mounts and nimbly jumped up into the saddle. "I don't take orders from nameless adventurers and unemployed bravos. I'm the Prince of Krondor's Squire." He patted his bundle behind the saddle and removed his rapier—the very one Arutha had given him. "I'm ready. I've stolen enough horses to be a fair rider. Besides, things seem to happen wherever you are. It may get very dull around here without you."

Arutha looked at Laurie, who said, "Better bring him along where we can watch him. He'll only follow behind if we don't."

Arutha seemed about to protest when Laurie said, "We can't call the palace guards to have him arrested."

Arutha mounted, obviously not pleased. Without further conversation, they turned their horses and rode away from the park. Down darkened alleys and narrow streets they moved, riding at a moderate pace so as not to attract undue attention. Jimmy said, "This way lies the eastern gate. I assumed we would leave by the north."

Arutha said, "We'll be heading north soon enough. Should anyone see me leave the city, I'd just as soon have word passed I've gone east."

"Who's going to see us?" said Jimmy lightly, knowing full well that anyone seen riding through the gate at this hour would be noticed.

At the eastern gate two soldiers watched from the gatehouse to see who passed, but as there was neither curfew in effect nor alarm being sounded they barely stirred to watch the three riders pass.

Beyond the walls they were in the outer city, erected when the ancient walls could no longer contain the population. Leaving the main eastern roadway, they moved between darkened buildings toward the north.

Then Arutha pulled up his horse and ordered Jimmy and Laurie to do likewise. Coming around the corner were four riders dressed in heavy black cloaks. Jimmy's sword was out instantly, the chance of two groups of travelers innocently happening across one another on this minor street at this hour being very slight. Laurie began to draw his also, but Arutha simply said, "Put away your weapons."

When the riders closed, Jimmy and Laurie exchanged questioning looks. "Well met," said Gardan as he turned his horse to come alongside Arutha. "All is ready."

"Good," said Arutha. Studying the riders with Gardan, he said, "Three?"

Gardan's good-natured chuckle could be heard in the gloom. "As I hadn't seen him about for some time, I thought Squire Jimmy might have decided to come along, with or without your permission, so I took precautions. Am I incorrect?"

"You are not, Captain," said Arutha, taking no pain to hide his displeasure.

"In any event, David here is your shortest guardsman, and should any attempt pursuit, from a distance he will resemble the boy." He waved the three riders along and they headed back down the street toward the eastern road. Jimmy chuckled as they rode away, for one of the guards had been a slender, dark-haired fellow and the other a blond, bearded man with a lute over his back.

"The guards at the gate seemed to pay scant attention," said Arutha.

"Have no fears on that account, Highness. They're the two biggest gossips in the city watch. Should word of your departure leak from the palace, within hours the entire city will know you were seen riding east. Those three riders will continue on until they reach Darkmoor, if they are not troubled before then. If I may suggest, we'd best be leaving at once."

"We?" said Arutha.

"Orders, Sire. Princess Carline instructed me that should any harm befall either of you"—he indicated Laurie and Arutha—"I needn't return to Krondor."

Sounding a note of mock injury, Jimmy said, "She said nothing about me?"

The others ignored the remark. Arutha looked at Laurie, who sighed deeply. "She had it figured out hours before we left." Gardan indicated that this was so. "Besides, she can be circumspect when the occasion warrants. Sometimes."

Gardan added, "The Princess wouldn't betray her brother or fiancé."

"Fiancé?" said Arutha. "This has been a busy night. Well, you would end up either driven from the palace or married to her. But I'll never understand her taste in men. Very well, it looks as if there's no getting rid of any of you. Let's be off."

The three men and a boy spurred their mounts and resumed their ride and within minutes were through the outer city, heading north toward Sarth.

Near midday, the travelers rounded a bend in the coast road to find a lone traveler sitting by the edge of the King's Highway. He wore a hunter's outfit of green-dyed leather. His dappled horse cropped grass a short way off and he whittled at a piece of wood with his hunting knife. Seeing the band approach, he put away his knife, tossed the wood aside, and gathered up his belongings. He was cloaked and had his longbow over his shoulder when Arutha reined in.

"Martin," said Arutha in greeting.

The Duke of Crydee mounted. "Took you a lot longer to get here than I thought it would."

Jimmy said, "Is there anyone in Krondor who doesn't know the Prince has left?"

"Not so as you would notice," answered Martin with a smile. They commenced riding, and Martin said to Arutha, "Lyam said to tell you he will lay as many false trails as possible."

Laurie said, "The King knows?"

"Of course," said Arutha. He indicated Martin. "The three of us planned this from the start. Gardan had an unusually large number of guards posted near the door to my study when Lyam forbade my going."

Martin added, "Lyam has some of his personal guards impersonating each of us. There's a long-faced fellow and a blond, bearded lout impersonating Arutha and Laurie." With one of his rare grins he said, "There's this handsome brute of a man staying in my suite. Lyam's even managed to borrow that tall, loud-voiced Master of Ceremonies from the Keshian Ambassador. He's to sneak back into the palace after the Keshians leave today. Fitted with a false beard, he's a fair likeness for the captain here. At least he's the right color. He'll be seen popping up here and there in the palace." Gardan laughed.

"Then you've not attempted to leave unnoticed, in truth," said Laurie in admiration.

"No," said Arutha. "I seek to leave under a cloud of confusion. We know whoever is behind this is sending more assassins this way, or so Laughing Jack believed. So if there are spies in Krondor, they'll not know for days what is happening. When we are discovered out of the palace, they'll be unsure of the direction taken. Only those few with us when Pug ensorcelled Anita's suite know we need to travel to Sarth."

Jimmy laughed. "A masterstroke of misdirection. Should someone hear you've gone one way, then another, they'll not know what to believe."

Martin said, "Lyam was thorough. He has another band dressed like you three heading down south toward Stardock with Kulgan and Pug's family today. They'll be just clumsy enough in hiding to be noticed." To Arutha he added, "Pug says he will search for a cure for Anita in Macros's library."

Arutha reined in his horse and the others halted. "We are a half day's ride from the city. If we're not overtaken by sundown, we can count ourselves free of pursuit. We need then only worry about what may lie ahead." He paused, as if what he was about to say was difficult. "Behind all the bantering words, you've chosen danger, all of you." He looked from face to face. "I count myself fortunate for such friendship."

Jimmy seemed the most embarrassed by the Prince's words, but he fought back the urge to quip. "We have—had a vow in the Mockers. It's from an old proverb: 'You can't be sure the cat is dead until the cat is skinned.' When a difficult task lay ahead and a man wished to let others know he was willing to stick it out to the last, he'd say, 'Until the cat is skinned.' " He looked at the others and said, "Until the cat is skinned."

Laurie said, "Until the cat is skinned," and the statement was quickly echoed by Gardan and Martin.

At the last, Arutha said, "Thank you all." He spurred his horse forward and the others followed.

Martin fell in beside Laurie. "What took you so long?"

"I was held up," said Laurie. "It's somewhat complicated. We're going to be married."

"I know that. Gardan and I were waiting for Lyam when he came back from your room. She could, I think, do better." Laurie's face betrayed his discomfort. Then Martin smiled slightly as he added, "But then, maybe she couldn't." Leaning over, he extended his hand. "May you always be happy." After they shook, he said, "That still doesn't account for the delay."

"It's a bit delicate," Laurie said, hoping his future brother-in-law would let the matter drop.

Martin studied Laurie a long moment, then nodded in understanding. "A proper good-bye can take a while."

NINE

FOREST

A band of horsemen appeared on the horizon.

Black figures stood outlined against the reddish sky of late afternoon. Martin sighted them first, and Arutha ordered a halt. Since they had left Krondor, this was the first band of travelers they had encountered obviously not traders. Martin squinted. "I can't see much at this distance, but I think them armed. Mercenaries perhaps?"

"Or outlaws," Gardan said.

"Or something else," Arutha added. "Laurie, you're the most traveled among us. Is there another way?"

Laurie looked about, getting his bearings. Pointing toward the forest on the other side of a narrow stip of farmland, he said, "To the east, about an hour's ride from here, is an old trail that leads up into the Calastius Mountains. It was used by miners once, but it's little traveled now. It will lead us to the inland road."

Jimmy said, "Then we should make for that trial at once. It seems those others have tired of waiting for us to come to them."

Arutha saw the riders on the horizon start in their direction. "Lead the way, Laurie."

They left the road, heading for a series of low stone walls that marked the farms' boundaries. "Look!" shouted Jimmy.

Arutha's companions saw the other band had reacted by spurring their mounts into a gallop. In the orange glow of the late afternoon, they were black figures outlined against a grey-green hillside.

Arutha and the others took the first low stone wall in a smooth jump, but Jimmy was nearly thrown. He managed to right himself without losing too much ground on the others. He said nothing but wished fervently there weren't three more walls between himself and the forest. Somehow he managed to keep seated and still not be too far behind when Arutha's party entered the woods.

The others were waiting for him and he reined in. Laurie pointed. "They can't overtake us, so they parallel us, hoping to intercept us north of here." Then he laughed. "This trail is north-east bound, so our nameless friends will have to travel an additional mile of brush-clogged woodlands to cut our trail. We'll be long past them when they do. If they can find the trail."

Arutha said, "We still must hurry. We've little light, and the woods are not safe at the best of times. How long to this road?"

"We should be there two hours after sunset, maybe a little sooner."

Arutha motioned for him to lead the way. Laurie turned his horse and they all moved deeper into the rapidly darkening forest.

Dark boles bulked on both sides. In the gloom, with scant illumination from middle and large moons filtering down through high branches, the woods seemed a surrounding solid. Throughout the night they had been picking their way along what Laurie insisted was a trail, some ethereal thing that suddenly appeared a few feet before Laurie's horse and just as quickly vanished a few feet behind Jimmy's. To Jimmy one patch of ground looked much like another, except that the meandering way Laurie chose seemed to have slightly less debris cluttering it. The boy constantly looked back over his shoulder, seeking signs of pursuit.

Arutha ordered a halt. "We've seen no signs of being followed. Perhaps we've shaken them."

Martin dismounted. "Not likely. If they have a skilled tracker among them, they've found our spoor. They'll be moving as slowly as we are, but they'll be keeping pace."

Dismounting, Arutha said, "We'll rest here for a while. Jimmy, break out the oats behind Laurie's saddle."

Jimmy grumbled slightly as he began caring for the horses. He had learned after his first night on the road that, as Squire, he was expected to care for his liege's horse—and everyone else's as well.

Martin shouldered his bow and said, "I think I'll backtrack a ways and see if there's anyone close. I'll be back within the hour.

Should anything happen, don't wait for me. I'll find you at the Ishapian abbey tomorrow night." He slipped off into the gloom.

Arutha sat on his saddle, while Jimmy set about caring for the horses, with an assist from Laurie. Gardan kept a vigil, scanning the murk of the forest.

Time passed and Arutha became lost in thought. Jimmy watched him from the corner of his eye. Laurie caught Jimmy studying Arutha in the dim light and moved alongside the boy, helping him brush down Gardan's horse. The singer whispered, "You worry about him."

Jimmy only nodded, a gesture almost lost in the dark. Then he said, "I don't have a family, singer, or a lot of friends. He's . . . important. Yes, I worry."

When he was finished, Jimmy crossed to where Arutha sat staring off into the blackness. "The horses are fed and groomed."

Arutha seemed pulled from his brooding. "Good. Now get some rest. We'll move out at first light." He glanced about. "Where's Martin?"

Jimmy looked back along the trail. "He's still back there somewhere."

Arutha followed his gaze.

Jimmy settled in, his head on his saddle, a blanket pulled about him. He stared off into the darkness for a long time before sleep came.

Something woke Jimmy. Two figures approached and Jimmy made ready to leap to his feet when he saw they were Martin and Gardan. Then Jimmy remembered Gardan had remained on watch. They reached the small campsite, both walking quietly.

Jimmy roused the others. Arutha wasted no time when he saw his brother had returned. "Did you find any sign of pursuit?"

Martin nodded. "A few miles back along the trail. A band of . . . men, moredhel, I don't know which. Their fire was low. One at least is a moredhel. Save that one, to a man they were dressed in black armor, with long black capes. Each wore a strange helm that covered the entire head. I didn't need any more to decide they were not likely to prove friendly. I cut a false trail across ours. It should lead them away for a while, but we should be off at once."

"What of this one moredhel? You say he wasn't attired like the others?"

"No, and he was the biggest damn moredhel I've ever seen, bare-chested except for a leather vest. His head was shaved save for a long scalp lock that was tied so it hung behind like a horse's tail. I could see him clearly in the firelight. I've never seen his like, though I've heard of his sort."

Laurie said, "Yabon mountain clan."

Arutha looked at the singer. Laurie explained, "When I was growing up near Tyr-Sog, we'd hear of raids by the northern mountain clans. They're different from the forest dwellers. The topknot of hair says he's also a chieftain, an important one."

Gardan said, "He's come a long way."

"Yes, and it means some new order has been established since the Riftwar. We knew that many of those driven north by the Tsurani were seeking to join their kin in the Northlands, but now it seems they've brought some of their cousins back with them."

"Or," said Arutha, "it means they're under his command."

Martin said, "For that to have happened . . ."

"Alliance, a moredhel alliance. Something we've always feared," said Arutha. "Come, it's almost light, and we won't puzzle this out any better for standing still."

They readied their horses, and soon they were back on the Forest Road, the major inland road between Krondor and the north. Few caravans used it; while it was a time-saver, most travelers chose to travel through Krondor and up the coast, as that was the safer route. Laurie claimed they were now riding even with the Bay of Ships, about a day's ride from the Ishapian abbey at Sarth. The town of Sarth rested on a peninsula at the north end of the bay. The abbey was in the hills to the northeast of the town, so they'd intercept the road between the abbey and the town. If they pushed, they would reach the abbey just after sundown.

Out in the forest there was no hint of danger, but Martin judged it likely the moredhel-led band was coming. He could hear subtle changes in the early morning sounds of the forest behind that told him something not too distant was disturbing the natural order of things in its passing.

Martin rode beside Arutha, behind Laurie. "I think I might drop back and see if our friends still follow."

Jimmy hazarded a glance over his shoulder, and through the trees behind he could see black-clad figures following. "Too late! They've seen us!" he shouted.

Arutha's party spurred their mounts forward, the thunder of hooves echoing through the trees. All bent low over the necks of their mounts, and Jimmy kept glancing back. They were putting distance between themselves and the black riders, for which Jimmy gave silent thanks.

After a few minutes of hard riding, they came to a deep defile, impossible for horses to jump. Across it stood a sturdy wooden bridge. They sped over it, then Arutha reined it. "Stand here!" They turned their horses, for the sound of pursuit could be heard.

Arutha was about to order them to ready a charge when Jimmy leaped off his horse. He pulled his bundle from in back of his saddle. Running to the end of the bridge, he knelt. Arutha shouted, "What are you doing?"

Jimmy's only answer was "Keep back!"

In the distance the sound of approaching horses grew louder. Martin leaped down from his mount and unshouldered his longbow. He had it strung and an arrow nocked when the first of the black riders hove into view. Without hesitation he loosed the clothyard shaft, and without error it flew, striking the black-armored figure full in the chest with the thundering force only a longbow could deliver at such a distance. The rider was propelled backward out of his saddle. The second horseman avoided the fallen man, but a third was thrown as his mount stumbled over the body.

Arutha moved forward to intercept the second rider, who was about to cross the bridge. "No!" shouted Jimmy. "Keep back!" Suddenly the boy was dashing away from the bridge as the black rider crossed. The horseman was almost upon the spot where Jimmy had knelt when a loud whooshing noise sounded, accompanied by a large cloud of smoke. His horse shied and spun on the narrow bridge, then reared up. The animal stumbled back a step, its rump striking the rails of the bridge. The black-clad warrior was tossed backward over the rail while his horse pawed the air, then he fell, hitting the rocks below the bridge with an audible thud. The horse turned and fled back the way it had come.

Arutha's and the others' horses were far enough away from the explosion of smoke not to panic, though Laurie had to ride forward and quickly grab the reins of Jimmy's mount while Gardan held Martin's. The bowman was busy shooting at the approaching riders, whose animals bucked and shied as their masters fought to bring them back under control.

Jimmy was now racing back toward the bridge, a small flask in his hands. He pulled a stopper from its end and tossed it at the smoke. Suddenly the near end of the bridge erupted in flames. The black riders pulled up, their horses nickering at sight of the fire. The balky animals rode in circles as their riders sought to force them across the bridge.

Jimmy stumbled away from the blaze. Gardan swore. "Look, the fallen ones rise!"

Through the smoke and flame they could see the rider with the arrow in his chest staggering toward the bridge, while another that Martin had felled was slowly rising to his feet.

Jimmy reached his horse and mounted. Arutha said, "What was all that?"

"The smoke bomb I carry out of habit. Many of the Mockers use them to cover escape and create confusion. They make a little fire and a great deal of smoke."

"What was in the flask?" asked Laurie.

"Distillation of naphtha. I know an alchemist in Krondor who sells it to farmers to start fires when they slash and burn."

"That's damned dangerous stuff to be toting around," said Gardan. "Do you always carry it?"

"No," said Jimmy as he mounted. "But then I usually don't travel where I'm likely to run into things you can only stop by roasting. After that business at the whorehouse I thought it might come in handy. I have one more in my bundle."

"Then toss it!" shouted Laurie. "The bridge's not caught yet."

Jimmy pulled out the other flask and nudged his horse forward. With careful aim he tossed the flask into the fire.

Flames rose up, ten, twelve feet in height, as the wooden bridge became engulfed. On both sides of the defile horses whinnied and tried to run as the fire rose higher and higher in the sky.

Arutha looked across the bridge at the enemy horsemen, who now sat patiently waiting for the flames to burn out. From behind them another figure rode into view, the unarmored moredhel with the scalp lock. He sat watching Arutha and the others, no expression evident on his face. Arutha could feel blue eyes boring into his soul. And he felt hate. Here, then, for the first time he saw his enemy, saw one of those who had harmed Anita. Martin began shooting at the black riders, and with a silent signal the unarmored moredhel led his companions back into the trees.

Martin mounted and came to his brother's side. Arutha watched as the moredhel vanished into the trees. Arutha said, "He knows me. We were so clever, and they knew where I was all along."

"But how?" asked Jimmy. "There were so many diversions."

"Some black art," said Martin. "There are powers at play here, Jimmy."

"Come," said Arutha. "They'll be back. This will not stop them. We've gained only a little time."

Laurie led the way toward the northbound road to Sarth. They did not look back as the fire crackled loudly.

They rode nearly continuously for the rest of that day. Of their pursuers they saw nothing, but Arutha knew they were close behind. Near sundown, light fog filled the air as they neared the coast again, where the Bay of Ships turned the road eastward. According to Laurie, they would reach the abbey after sundown.

Martin moved up to ride next to Gardan and Arutha, who stared out into the shadows, absently directing his horse. "Remembering the past?"

Arutha looked at his brother thoughtfully. "Simpler times, Martin. Just remembering simpler times. I rage to be done with this mystery of Silverthorn and have Anita returned to me. I burn for it!" He spoke with sudden passion. With a sigh, his voice softened as he said, "I was wondering what Father would have done in my place."

Martin glanced at Gardan. The captain said, "Exactly what you're doing now, Arutha. Man and boy I knew Lord Borric, and

I'll say there's not another more like him in temper than you. All of you are like him: Martin in the way he watches things closely. Lyam reminds me of him when the lighter moods were upon him, before he lost his lady Catherine."

Arutha asked, "And I?"

It was Martin who answered. "Why, you think like him, little brother, more than Lyam or I do. I'm your eldest brother. I don't take orders from you only because you wear the title Prince to my Duke. I follow your lead because, more than any man I've known since Father, you make the right choices."

Arutha's gaze was distant as he said, "Thank you. That is high praise."

A sound came from the trail behind, just loud enough to be heard without being identified. Laurie tried to lead as quickly as he could, but the dark and fog confounded his sense of direction. The sun was close to setting, so little light penetrated the deep woods. He could see only a small part of the trail in front of him; twice he was forced to slow to separate the true trail from false ones. Arutha rode up beside and said, "Keep it steady. Better to continue at a crawl than halt."

Gardan fell back next to Jimmy. The boy peered into the woods, seeking a glimpse of whatever might be hiding just behind the boles of the trees, but only wisps of grey fog in the last light of the setting sun could be seen.

Then a horse came crashing from out of the brush, one moment not there, the next nearly knocking Jimmy from the saddle. The boy's horse spun in a full circle as the black-armored warrior pushed past. Gardan swung a late blow at the horseman and missed.

Arutha shouted, "This way!" and tried to force his way past another horseman cutting across the trail. He faced the rider, the unarmored moredhel. For the first time Arutha could see the three scars cut into each of the Dark Brother's cheeks. Time froze for an instant as the two confronted one another. There was a strange recognition in Arutha, for here was his enemy made flesh. No longer did he struggle with unseen assassins' hands in the dark or mystic powers without substance; here was someone he could vent his rage upon. Without sound the moredhel swung a vicious blow at Arutha's head, and the Prince avoided being decapitated only by ducking over the neck of his horse. Arutha lashed out with his rapier and felt its point dig in. He came up and saw he had taken the moredhel in the face, cutting deeply across the scarred cheek. But the creature only moaned, a strange tortured sound, half gurgle, half strangled cry. Then Arutha realized the moredhel possessed no tongue. The creature looked at Arutha for a brief moment as his horse turned away.

"Try to break free!" shouted Arutha, spurring his own horse forward. Suddenly Arutha was away, the others behind.

For an instant it seemed the moredhel-led company was too shocked to react to the break, but then the pursuit began. Of all the mad rides in Arutha's life, this one stood out as the maddest. Through the forest, shrouded with fog and night's black cloak, they dashed among trees, following a road little wider than a path. Laurie passed Arutha, taking the lead.

For long minutes they raced through the woods, somehow avoiding the certainly fatal error of leaving the roadway. Then Laurie was shouting, "The road to the abbey!"

Slow to react, Arutha and the others behind Laurie barely made the turn onto a larger road. As they steered their mounts onto the new path, they could see the faint light of the large moon, rising.

Then they were out of the woods, racing down a well-traveled road passing through farmlands. Their horses were lathered and panting, and they spurred them on to more heroic efforts, for while the black riders were not gaining on them, they were not falling behind either.

They sped through the dark, climbing upward, as the road rose out of the gentle hills around a plateau that dominated the valley farmlands near the coast. The road narrowed and they strung out along it in single file, Martin pulling in until the others were past.

The trail became treacherous and they were forced to slow, but so were those behind. Arutha dug his heels into his horse's sides, but the animal had given all it had left to climb this road.

The evening air was heavy with haze and unseasonable cold. The hills were widely spaced, lazy rolling ridges that gently rose and fell. The highest could be climbed in less than an hour. All were covered in wild grasses and brush, but they were free from trees, for this had been farmland.

The abbey at Sarth sat atop a high, craggy place, a small mountain rather than a hill, an upthrust thing of rock and granite facings, flat on top like a table.

Gardan looked downward as they hurried up the side of the mount and said, "I'd not want to attack up this road, Highness. You could hold it with six grandmothers wielding brooms . . . forever."

Jimmy looked back but couldn't see their pursuers in the gloom. "So tell those grannies to get back there and slow down the black riders," he shouted.

Arutha looked behind, expecting to be overtaken by black riders at any second. They rounded a curve and followed the road upward to the summit. Suddenly they stood before the arched entrance to the abbey.

Beyond the wall a tower of some sort could be seen in the moonlight. Arutha pounded on the gates and shouted, "Hello! We seek aid!" Then all heard what they had waited for, the pounding of horses' hooves upon the hard road. Drawing weapons, Arutha's party turned to face those who followed.

The black riders rounded the curve before the abbey gates, and the battle was again joined. Arutha ducked and parried as he tried to protect himself. The attackers seemed possessed of unusual frenzy, as if there was a need to quickly dispatch Arutha and his party. The scar-faced moredhel nearly rode over Jimmy's mount to reach Arutha, his disregard for the boy being the only reason Jimmy survived. The Dark Brother headed straight for Arutha. Gardan, Laurie, and Martin all strove to keep the black riders at bay, but they were on the verge of being overwhelmed at last.

Suddenly it was light on the road. As if full daylight multiplied tenfold had burst forth in the gloom, a dazzling brilliance surrounded the combatants. Arutha and the others were forced to cover their eyes, which teared from the blinding light. They could hear muffled moans from the black-clad figures around them, then the sound of bodies hitting the ground. Arutha peeked through narrowed lids behind his upraised hand and saw enemy horsemen falling stiffly from their saddles. The exceptions were the unarmored moredhel, who shielded his eyes against the sudden light, and three of the armored riders. With a single motion the mute rider waved his three companions away and they turned and fled down the road. As soon as the black riders were out of sight, the brilliant light began to diminish.

Arutha wiped tears from his eyes and began to pursue, but Martin shouted, "Stop! Should you overtake them, it's your death! Here we have allies!" Arutha reined in, loath to lose his opponent. He returned to where the others stood rubbing their eyes. Martin dismounted and knelt over a fallen black rider. He pulled off a helm and quickly stood away. "It's a moredhel, and it smells as if it's been dead for some time." He pointed at its chest. "This is one I killed at the bridge. My broken arrow is still in its chest."

Arutha looked at the building. "That light is gone. Whoever our unseen benefactor is, he must feel we no longer need it." The gates in the wall before them slowly began to open. Martin handed the helm up for Arutha's inspection. It was a strange thing, fashioned with a dragon carved in bas-relief on top, its downswept wings covering the sides. Two narrow slits provided vision for the wearer, and four small holes allowed him to breathe. Arutha tossed the helm back to Martin. "That's an ill-aspected piece of ironmongery. Bring it along. Now let's visit this abbey."

"Abbey!" Gardan observed as they entered. "It looks more like a fortress!" Tall, iron-banded heavy wooden gates straddled the roadway. To the right a stone wall a dozen feet high stretched away, appearing to run to the other edge of the mountaintop. To the left the wall receded, facing upon a vertical drop over a hundred feet to a switchback in the roadway below. Behind the wall they could see a single tower, several floors high. "If that isn't an old-style keep tower, I've never seen one," said the captain. "I'd not want to storm this abbey, Highness. It's the most defensible position I've seen. Look, there's not five feet of clearing between the wall and cliff anywhere." He sat back in the saddle, in obvious appreciation of the military aspects of the abbey's design.

Arutha spurred his horse forward. The gates were now open, and, seeing no reason not to, Arutha led his companions onto the grounds of the Ishapian abbey at Sarth.

TEN

SARTH

The abbey appeared deserted.

The courtyard reflected what they had seen from the road. This had once been as a fortress. Around the ancient tower a larger single-story keep building had been added, as well as two outbuildings that could be seen peeking from behind it. One appeared to be a stable. But before them no sign of movement could be seen.

"Welcome to Ishap's Abbey at Sarth," came a voice from behind one of the gates.

Arutha had his sword halfway from its scabbard before the speaker added, "You have nothing to fear."

The speaker stepped from behind the gate. Arutha put away his weapon. As the others dismounted, the Prince studied the man. He was stocky, of middle years, short, with a youthful smile. His brown hair was cut close and ragged and his face was clean-shaven. He wore a simple brown robe gathered around the waist with a single leather thong. A pouch and some manner of holy symbol hung at his waist. He was unarmed, but Arutha got the impression that the man moved like one who had been trained in arms. Finally Arutha said, "I am Arutha, Prince of Krondor."

The man looked amused, though he didn't smile. "Then welcome to Ishap's Abbey at Sarth, Highness."

"You mock me?"

"No, Highness. We of the Order of Ishap maintain little contact with the outside world, and few visit with us, let alone royalty. Please forgive any insult, if your honor permits, for none was intended."

Arutha dismounted and, fatigue in his voice, said, "It is I who asks forgiveness . . . ?"

"Brother Dominic, but please, no apologies. It is clear from the circumstances of your arrival you were hard-pressed."

Martin said, "Do we have you to thank for that mystic light?"

The monk nodded. Arutha said, "There seems a great deal to speak of, Brother Dominic."

"There are many questions. You'll have to wait upon the Father Abbot's pleasure for most answers, Highness. Come, I'll show you to the stable."

Arutha's impatience wouldn't let him wait a moment longer. "I came on a matter of the utmost urgency. I need to speak with your Abbot. Now."

The monk spread his hands in a gesture indicating it was outside his authority to decide. "The Father Abbot is unavailable for another two hours. He is meditating and praying in the chapel, with the others of our order, which is why I alone am here to greet you. Please, come with me."

Arutha seemed ready to protest, but Martin's hand upon his shoulder settled him. "Again, I am sorry, Brother Dominic. We are, of course, guests."

Dominic's expression indicated that Arutha's temper was a matter of no consequence. He led them to the second of the smaller buildings behind what was once a central keep. It was indeed a stable. The sole occupants at the moment were another horse and a stout little donkey, which cast an indifferent eye upon the newcomers. As they tended their animals, Arutha spoke of their trials over the last few weeks. When he finished, he said, "How did you manage to confound the black riders?"

"My title is Keeper of the Gates, Highness. I may admit any to the abbey, but no one with evil intent can cross the portals without my leave. Once upon the grounds of this abbey, those who sought your life became subject to my power. They took a risk attacking you so close to the abbey. It was a risk that proved deadly to their cause. But further conversation on this and other subjects must wait upon the Father Abbot."

Martin said, "If everyone else is at chapel, you'll need some help disposing of those corpses. They have an irritating habit of coming back to life."

"I thank you for the offer, but I can manage. And they will

remain dead. The magic employed to topple them cleansed them of the controlling evil. Now you must rest."

They left the stable and the monk led them to what appeared to be a barracks. Gardan said, "This place has a martial look to it, brother."

Entering a long room with a single row of cots, the monk said, "In ancient times this fortress was home to a robber baron. The Kingdom and Kesh lay far enough away for him to be a law unto himself, pillaging, raping, and robbing without fear of retribution. After some time he was turned out by the people of the surrounding towns, made bold by his tyranny. The lands below this escarpment were given over to farming, but so deep was their hatred of the baron that this keep stood abandoned. When a mendicant friar of our Order of Wanderers discovered this place, he sent word back to the temple in the city of Kesh. When we sought the use of this place as an abbey, the descendants of those who had turned out the baron had no objection. Today only those of us who serve here remember the history of this place. To those in the towns and villages along the Bay of Ships this has always been the Abbey of Ishap at Sarth."

Arutha said, "I assume this was once a barracks."

Dominic said, "Yes, Highness. We now use it as an infirmary and a place for occasional guests. Make yourselves comfortable, for I must be about my own tasks. The Father Abbot will see you shortly."

Dominic left and Jimmy fell onto one of the cots with an audible sigh. Martin inspected a small stove at one end of the room and found it lit, with the makings for tea next to it. He immediately set a pot to boil. Under a cloth he found bread, cheese, and fruit, which he passed around. Laurie sat examining his lute for possible travel damage and began tuning it. Gardan sat down opposite the Prince.

Arutha sighed long and deeply. "I am on a ragged edge. I fear these monks will have no knowledge of this Silverthorn." For an instant his eyes betrayed his anguish, then he again showed only an impassive expression.

Martin cocked his head to one side as he thought aloud. "Tully seems to think they know a great deal."

Laurie put up his lute. "Whenever I've found myself close to magic, priestly or otherwise, there also I've found trouble."

Jimmy spoke to Laurie. "That Pug seemed a friendly enough fellow for a magician. I wanted to speak to him more, but . . ." He left unsaid the events that had prevented it. "There's little about him that seems remarkable, but the Tsurani seem to fear him, and some of the court whisper about him."

"There is a saga begging to be sung," answered Laurie. He told Jimmy of Pug's captivity and rise among the Tsurani. "Those who practice arcane arts on Kelewan are a law unto themselves, and whatsoever they command is done without hesitation. There is nothing like them on this world. That is why the Tsurani in LaMut hold him in awe. Old habits die hard."

Jimmy said, "He gave up a great deal to return, then."

Laurie laughed. "That wasn't entirely a matter of choice."

Jimmy said, "What's Kelewan like?"

Laurie spun a rich and colorful story of his adventures on that world, with the eye for detail that lay at the heart of his craft, as much as did good voice and playing skills. The others settled in, relaxing and drinking their tea while listening. They all knew the story of Laurie and Pug and their part in the Riftwar, but each time Laurie told the story it was again a riveting adventure, one with the great legends.

When Laurie finished, Jimmy said, "It would be an adventure to go to Kelewan."

"That is not possible," observed Gardan, "I'm glad to say."

Jimmy said, "If it was done once, why not again?"

Martin said, "Arutha, you were with Pug when Kulgan read Macros's letter explaining why he closed the rift."

Arutha said, "Rifts are wild things, spanning some impossible no-place between worlds, possibly across time as well. But something about them makes it impossible to know where they're going to come out. When one is fashioned, then others seem to 'follow' it, coming out in the same general area. But that first one is the one you can't control. That's as much as I understand. You'd have to ask Kulgan or Pug for more details."

Gardan said, "Ask Pug. If you ask Kulgan, you'll get a lecture."

"So Pug and Macros closed down the first one to end the war?" said Jimmy.

"And more," said Arutha.

Jimmy looked around the room, sensing they all knew something he was not privy to. Laurie said, "According to Pug, there was in ancient times a vast evil power known to the Tsurani only as the Enemy. Macros said it would find its way to the two worlds if the rift was left open, drawn to it as steel to a lodestone. It was a being of awesome strength that had destroyed armies and humbled mighty magicians. Or at least that is what Pug explained."

Jimmy cocked his head to one side. "This Pug is that important a magician, then?"

Laurie laughed. "To hear Kulgan tell it, Pug is the most powerful practicer of the magic arts there is since Macros's death. And he's cousin to the Duke and the Prince, and the King."

Jimmy's eyes widened. "It's true," said Martin. "Our father adopted Pug into our family."

Martin said, "Jimmy, you speak of magicians as if you've never had dealings with one."

"I know better. There are a few spellcasters in Krondor, and they tend to be a questionable lot. There was once among the Mockers a thief known as the Grey Cat, for his stealth was unmatched. He was given to bold theft and filched some bauble from a magician who viewed the deed with considerable disfavor."

"What became of him?" asked Laurie.

"He's now the grey cat."

The four listeners sat quietly for a moment, then comprehension dawned and Gardan, Laurie, and Martin burst into laughter. Even Arutha smiled at the joke and shook his head in amusement.

Conversation continued on, easy and relaxed, as the band of travelers felt secure for the first time since leaving Krondor.

The bells sounded from the main building and a monk entered. Silently he motioned for them to come. Arutha said, "We're to follow you?" The monk nodded. "To see the Abbot?" Again the monk nodded.

Arutha was off his cot, all fatigue forgotten. He was the first out the door behind the monk.

The Abbot's chamber befitted one given to a life of spiritual contemplation. It was austere in every aspect. But what was surprising about it was the bookshelves upon the walls, dozens of volumes at every hand. The Abbot, Father John, seemed a kindly man of advancing years, slender and ascetic in appearance. His grey hair and beard showed in stark contrast to dark skin that was lined and wrinkled like carefully carved mahogany. Behind him stood two men, Brother Dominic and one Brother Anthony, a tiny stooped-shouldered fellow of indeterminate age, who constantly squinted at the Prince.

The Abbot smiled, his eyes crinkly at the corners, and Arutha was suddenly put in mind of paintings of Old Father Winter, a mythical figure who gave sweets to children at the Midwinter's Festival. In a deep, youthful voice the Abbot said, "Welcome to Ishap's Abbey, Highness. How may we help you?"

Arutha quickly outlined the history of the last few weeks.

The Abbot's smile vanished as Arutha's story unfolded. When the Prince was finished, the Abbot said, "Highness, we are gravely troubled to hear of this necromancy at the palace. But as to the tragedy that has befallen your Princess, how may we aid you?"

Arutha found himself reluctant to speak, as if at the last his fear of there being no aid overwhelmed him. Sensing his brother's reticence, Martin said, "A conspirator to the assassination attempt claims a moredhel gave him the poison used, one prepared with arcane skills. He called the substance Silverthorn."

The Abbot sat back, sympathy evident in his expression. "Brother Anthony?"

The little man said, "Silverthorn? I'll begin looking in the archives at once, father." With a shuffling step, he quickly departed the Abbot's chambers.

Arutha and the others watched the bent figure leave the room. Arutha asked, "How long will it take?"

The Abbot said, "That depends. Brother Anthony has a remarkable ability to pull facts seemingly from out of the air, remembering things read once in passing a decade before. That is why he has risen to the rank of Head Archivist, our Keeper of Knowledge. But the search could take days."

Arutha clearly didn't understand what the Abbot was speaking about, and the old priest said, "Brother Dominic, why don't you show the Prince and his companions a little of what we do here at Sarth?" The Abbot rose and bowed slightly to the Prince as Dominic moved toward the door. "Then bring him to the base of the tower." He added to Arutha, "I will meet with you shortly, Highness."

They followed the monk out into the main hall of the abbey. Dominic said, "This way." He led them through a door, then down a flight of stairs to a landing from which four passages branched off. He took them past a series of doors. As they walked, he said, "This hill is unlike those around, as you must have noticed when you rode here. It is mostly solid rock. When the first monks came to Sarth, they discovered these tunnels and chambers underneath the keep."

"What are they?" asked Jimmy.

They came to a door and Dominic produced a large ring of keys, which he used to open the heavy lock. The door swung open ponderously, and after they had stepped through, he closed it behind. "The original robber baron used these excavations as storage rooms, against siege, and to hoard booty. He must have grown lax in his defense for the villagers to have laid successful siege. There is enough room here for stores to last years. We have added to them until the entire hill is honeycombed with vaults and passages."

"To what end?" asked Arutha.

Dominic indicated they should follow him through another door, this one unlocked. They entered a large vaulted chamber, with shelving along the walls and free-standing shelves in the center of the room. Each shelf was packed solid with books. Dominic crossed to one and took down a book. He handed it to Arutha.

Arutha studied the old volume. It had faded gilt lettering burned into the binding. There was a faint resistance when Arutha carefully opened it, as if it had not been handled in years. On the first page he saw alien letters of an unknown language, painstakingly written in a stiff script. He lifted the book before his face and sniffed at it. There was a faint, pungent odor on the pages.

As Arutha handed the book back, Dominic said, "Preservative. Every book here has been treated to prevent deterioration." He gave the book to Laurie.

The widely traveled singer said, "I don't speak this tongue, but I think it Keshian, though it is unlike any scribing of the Empire's I know."

Dominic smiled. "The book is from the south part of Great Kesh, near the border of the Keshian Confederacy. It is the diary of a slightly mad but otherwise insignificant noble from a minor dynasty, written in a language called Low Delkian. High Delkian, as best we can ascertain, was a secret language limited to priests of some obscure order."

"What is this place?" asked Jimmy.

"We who serve Ishap at Sarth gather together books, tomes, manuals, scrolls, and parchments, even fragments. In our order there is a saying: 'Those at Sarth serve the god Knowledge,' which is not far from the truth. Wherever one of our order finds a scrap of writing, it or a copy is eventually sent here. In this chamber, and in every other chamber under the abbey, are shelves like these. All are filled, even to the point of being crowded from floor to ceiling, and new vaults are constantly being dug. From the top of the hill to the lowest level there are over a thousand chambers like this one. Each houses several hundred volumes or more. Some of the larger vaults hold several thousand. At last tally we were approaching a half-million works."

Arutha was stunned. His own library, inherited with the throne of Krondor, numbered less than a thousand. "How long have you been gathering these?"

"Over three centuries. There are many of our order who do nothing but travel and buy any scrap they can find, or who pay to have copies made. Some are ancient, others are in languages unknown, and three are from another world, having been obtained from the Tsurani in LaMut. There are arcane works, auguries and manuals of power, hidden from the eyes of all but a few of the most highly placed in our order." He looked about the room. "And with all this, there is still so much we don't understand."

Gardan said, "How do you keep track of it all?"

Dominic said, "We have brothers whose sole task is to catalog these works, all working under Brother Anthony's direction. Guides are prepared and constantly updated. In the building above us and in another room deep below are shelves of nothing but guides. Should you need a work on a subject, you can find it in the guides. It will list the work by vault number—we are standing in vault seventeen—shelf number, and space number upon the shelf. We are attempting to cross-index each work by author, when known, and title as well as subject. The work goes slowly and will take all of another century."

Arutha was again overwhelmed by the sheer size of such an undertaking. "But against what ends do you store all these works?"

Dominic said, "In the first, for the sake of knowledge itself. But there is a second cause, which I will leave for the Abbot to explain. Come, let us join him."

Jimmy was the last through the door, and he cast a rearward glance at the books in the room. He left with the feeling that he was somehow gaining a glimpse of worlds and ideas heretofore unimagined, and he regretted he would never fully understand most of what lay beneath the abbey. He felt somehow lessened for this realization. For the first time, Jimmy felt his world a small one, with a much larger yet to be discovered.

Arutha and his companions waited for the Abbot in a large chamber. Several torches threw flickering illumination upon the walls. Another door opened and the Abbot entered, followed by two men. Brother Dominic was the first through, but the other was unknown to Arutha. He was an old man, large and still erect in his bearing, who despite his robes seemed to resemble a soldier more than a monk, an impression heightened by a war hammer hanging from his belt. His grey-shot black hair had been left to grow to shoulder length but, like his beard, it was neatly trimmed. The Abbot said, "It is time for plain speaking."

Arutha said with a bitter edge, "That would be appreciated."

The unnamed monk broke into a broad grin. "You've your father's gift for blunt speech, Arutha."

Arutha studied the man again, surprised by his tone. Then recognition struck. It had been more than ten years since he had seen this man. "Dulanic!"

"No longer, Arutha. Now I'm simply Brother Micah, Defender of the Faith—which means I crack heads for Ishap now as I used to for your cousin Erland." He patted the hammer at his waist.

"We thought you dead." Duke Dulanic, former Knight-Marshal of Krondor, had vanished when Guy du Bas-Tyra had assumed the viceroyalty over Krondor during the last year of the Riftwar.

The man called Micah seemed surprised. "I thought everyone knew. With Guy on the throne of Krondor and Erland near death from coughing sickness, I feared civil war. I retired from office rather than face your father in the field or betray my King, two unthinkable choices. But I made my retirement no secret."

Arutha said, "With Lord Barry dead, it was assumed you'd both fallen by Guy's hand. No one knew what had become of you."

"Strange. Barry died of a seizure of the heart and I informed du Bas-Tyra of my intention to take holy vows. His man Radburn stood at his side when I gave my resignation."

Martin said, "That would explain it, then. With Jocko Radburn drowned off the Keshian coast and Guy banished from the Kingdom, who would have the truth to tell?"

The Abbot spoke. "Brother Micah came to us a troubled man, called by some agency of Ishap to our service. We tested him and found him worthy, so that now his former life as a noble of the Kingdom is a thing of the past. But I asked him here because he is both a valued adviser and a man of military skills who may help us understand what forces move in the world these days."

"Well enough. Now, what business have we besides finding a cure to Anita's injury?"

"The understanding of that which brought her to injury, that which seeks to end your days, for a start," answered Micah.

Arutha looked slightly abashed. "Of course; forgive my preoccupation. I would welcome anything that made sense out of the madness my life has become over the last month."

The Abbot said, "Brother Dominic has shown you something of our works here. He may have mentioned that we count many auguries and other works by prophets in our collection. Some are as reliable as a child's moods, which is to say not at all. But a few, a very few, are true works of those whom Ishap has given the gift of future seeing. In several of these volumes, among the most reliable we possess, a reference is made to a sign in the sky.

"There is, we fear, a power now loose in the world. What it may be and how it may be combated are yet unknown to us. But this is certain: it is a fell power, and at the end either it shall be destroyed or it shall destroy us. That is inescapable." Pointing upward, the Abbot said, "The tower above us has been converted to study the stars, planets, and moons, using clever devices built for us by some of the more talented artificers in the Kingdom and Kesh. With them we can chart the movements of all the bodies in the sky. We spoke of a sign. You may now see it. Come."

He led them all up a long flight of stairs that took them to the top of the tower. They emerged upon the roof, amid strange devices of confounding configuration. Arutha looked about and said, "It is well you understand this, father, for I do not."

"Like men," said the Abbot, "the stars and planets have both physical and spiritual properties. We know other worlds spin their orbits about other stars. We know this for fact, since"—he pointed to Laurie—"one who has lived for a time on an alien world stands with us at this moment." When Laurie looked astonished, the Abbot said, "We are not so cut off from the rest of the world that something as important as your adventures on Kelewan would not be heard here, Laurie of Tyr-Sog." Returning to his original topic, he said, "But that is the physical side of the stars. They also reveal secrets to those who watch by their arrangement, their pattern, and their movement. Whatever the reason for this phenomenon, this we know: at times a clear message comes to us from the night sky, and we who are bent on gaining knowledge will not refuse to heed such a message; we will remain open to every source of knowledge, including those often held in disrepute.

"The mysteries of these devices, as well as reading the stars, are only a matter of taking the time to master the subject. Any man of sufficient wit can learn. These devices," he said with a sweep of his hand, "are all quite clear in use and purpose once they've been demonstrated. Now, if you'll please look through this device here." Arutha looked through a strange sphere, constructed from a complex latticework of metals. "This is used to chart the relative motion of stars and visible planets."

"You mean there're invisible ones?" asked Jimmy without thinking.

"Correct," said the Abbot, overlooking the interruption. "Or at least there are those we can't see, though if we were close enough they would be visible."

"Part and parcel of the arts of divination is the science of knowing when the auguries are in fruition, at best a chancy business. There is a famous prophecy made by the mad monk Ferdinand de la Rodez. By common account, it has come to pass on three different occasions. Not one can agree which event was the one he predicted."

Arutha studied the sky through the device, only half listening to the Abbot. Through the eyehole he saw a sky ablaze with stars, overlaid with a faint network of lines and notations, which he assumed were somehow inscribed on the inside of the sphere. In the center was a configuration of five stars, reddish in color, one in the center, with lines connecting them in a bright red *X*. "What am I seeing?" he asked. He relinquished his place to Martin, and the former hunter looked through the device.

The Abbot said, "Those five stars are called the Bloodstones."

Martin said, "I know them, but I've never seen that pattern before."

"Nor shall you again for another eleven thousand years—though that is a guess, and we shall have to wait until it occurs again to be sure." He seemed unperturbed by the duration, in fact he seemed quite willing to wait. "What you see is a pattern called the Fiery Cross or Cross of Fire. There is an ancient prophecy concerning it."

"What is this prophecy, and what has it to do with me?" said Arutha.

"The prophecy is ancient, perhaps from the time of the Chaos Wars. It says, 'When the Cross of Fire lights the night and the Lord of the West dead is, shall then return the Power.' It's quite well constructed poetically in the original, though it loses in translation. What we take it to mean is that some agency seeks your death to cause this prophecy's fulfillment, or at least seeks to convince others the prophecy's near fruition. Another germane fact is that the prophecy is one of the few things we have that were created by the Pantathian serpent people. We know little about these creatures. We know that on those rare occasions when they appear they herald troubles, for they are clearly agents of evil working toward ends only they understand. We also know that the prophecy says the Lord of the West is also called Bane of Darkness."

"So someone wants Arutha dead because he is fated to defeat them if he lives?" asked Martin.

"Or so they believe," answered the Abbot.

"But who or what?" said Arutha. "That someone wishes me dead comes as no revelation. What more can you tell me?"

"Little, I'm afraid."

Laurie said, "Still, it gives some small reason behind the Nighthawks' attacks upon you."

"Religious fanatics," said Jimmy, shaking his head, then he looked at the Abbot. "Sorry, father."

The Abbot ignored the remark. "What is important to understand is that they will try again and again and again. You will not be done with them until you root out the ultimate author of the order to kill you."

"Well," said Martin, "we also know that the Brotherhood of the Dark Path is involved."

"North," said Brother Micah. Arutha and the others looked at him questioningly. "Your answers lie northward, Arutha. Look there," he said, his voice still containing a note of command. "To the north lie the High Ranges, all barriers against the denizens of the Northlands. In the west above Elvandar perch the Great Northern Mountains; in the east, the Northern Guardians, the High Fastness, and the Dreaming Mountains. And across the center lies the greatest range of all, the Teeth of the World, thirteen hundred miles of nearly impassable crags. Who knows what lies beyond? What man, save renegade or weapons runner, has ventured there and returned to tell of the Northlands?

"Our ancestors created the Border Baronies ages ago, to bottle up the passes at Highcastle, Northwarden, and Ironpass. The Duke of Yabon's garrisons block the only other major pass to the west of the Thunderhell Steppes. And no goblin or Dark Brother treads upon the Thunderhell and lives, for the nomads do our guarding for us. In short, we know nothing of the Northlands. But that is where the moredhel live and that is where you'll find your answers."

"Or I'll find nothing," said Arutha. "You may be concerned

about prophecy and portents, but I care only for finding the answer to the riddle of Silverthorn. Until Anita is again safe, I shall put my efforts to nothing else." The Abbot appeared disturbed by this. Arutha said, "That there is a prophecy I have no doubt, and that some madman with arcane powers is seeking my death is also not in doubt. But that this spells some great danger to the Kingdom is a long reach. Too long for me. I'll need more proof."

The Abbot was about to answer when Jimmy said, "What is that?"

All eyes turned to look where he pointed. Glowing low on the horizon was a blue light, brightening as if a star were growing before their eyes. Martin said, "It looks like a falling star."

Then they could see it was no star. A faint sound in the distance accompanied the approaching object. Brighter it grew, as the sound grew louder, more angry. Racing across the sky toward them was a blue fire. Suddenly it was speeding directly over the tower with a sizzling sound, like a hot iron passing through water.

Then Brother Dominic shouted, "Off the tower, quickly!"

ELEVEN

CLASH

They hesitated for a moment.

Dominic's warning was followed by a shout from Micah, and the others hurried down the stair. Halfway to the ground floor, Dominic faltered, swaying a little on his feet. "Something approaches."

Reaching the main floor, Arutha and the others hurried to the door and looked out. In the sky above, more of the glowing objects streaked overhead with unbelievable speed. First from one quarter of the sky, then another, they sped, their strange, ominous droning filling the night. Faster and faster they shot through the air, streaks of blue, green, yellow, and red, angry flashes of brilliance ripping through the dark.

"What are they?" shouted Jimmy.

"Magic sentinels of some kind," answered the Abbot. "I can sense they are searching the area they pass over."

Slowly the pattern changed; instead of passing directly overhead, they began to curve and fly off at a tangent to their original course. Those below could see that the objects were slowing in their flight. The curving course tightened, until the glowing objects sped through the night in great arcs overhead. Then they slowed even more, gaining definition. They were large spheres, pulsing with a bright inner light, and inside could be seen strange dark shapes, somehow disturbing in appearance. They continued to slow until they hovered and spiraled, forming a circle above the abbey courtyard. Once the circle was formed, twelve glowing spheres could be seen hanging silently and motionless over the courtyard. Then, with a deep snapping, buzzing sound painful to the ears, lines of energy shot across the gap between each pair and six lines joined the sphere. Then a line formed around the periphery so that now the spheres formed a dodecagon.

"What are these things?" Gardan wondered aloud.

"The Twelve Eyes," the Abbot said in awe, "an ancient and evil spell of legend. No one living is said to have the power to form this thing. It is both a vehicle for seeing and a weapon."

Then the spheres slowly began to move. Gaining speed, they began weaving an intricate pattern, the lines twisting maddeningly, beyond the ability of the eye to follow. Faster they spun, until they became a blurring solid of light. A shaft of energy shot down from the center, striking some invisible barrier above the roofs of the buildings.

Dominic screamed in pain and had to be caught by Martin. The monk's hands pressed hard against his temples and he said, "So powerful. I can scarcely believe . . ." He opened eyes running with tears and said, "The barriers are holding."

Father John said, "Brother Dominic's mind is the keystone to the mystic defenses of the abbey. He is being sorely tested."

Again angry energies shot downward, to be scattered across the invisible barrier, like a multicolored shower above their heads. Shards of mystic rainbow light streaked down the sides of the magic barrier, defining the dome above the abbey for the eye to see.

But again the barrier held. Then another, and another, and soon Arutha and the others could see that the barrier was being pushed lower each time. With each assault, Dominic would cry out in pain. Then, with explosive fury, a single shaft of blinding white light struck the barrier and broke through, searing the ground with an angry hiss and acrid odor.

With the attack, Brother Dominic stiffened in Martin's arms and groaned. "It is entering," he whispered before he passed into unconsciousness.

As Martin lowered the monk to the floor, Father John said, "I must go to my vestry. Brother Micah, you must hold it."

Micah told them, "Whatever is out there has breached a mystic defense second only to that at our father temple. Now I must face it. I am armed and shielded by Ishap," the old monk said in ritual, as he unlimbered the war hammer at his belt.

A roar of impossible volume, like a thousand lions voicing rage at once, shook the abbey. It began as a teeth-jarring shriek and ran down the scale until it seemed to grind at the very stones of the building. Bolts of energy lashed out, seemingly in random directions, and where they struck, destruction ensued. Stones seemed to crumble under the onslaught, whatever was flammable was set afire, and any water touched by the bolts exploded into clouds of steam.

They watched as Micah left the building, striding out to stand below the spinning disk. As if anticipating, he raised his hammer above his head as another bolt of energy lashed downward, blinding those who watched from the door. When the initial blaze of white died down, they could see Micah standing upright, hammer held overhead as the crackling energies cascaded around him, scattering in broken spectrum, so that all the colors of the rainbow danced within the inferno. The very ground at his feet smoked and burned, but he was unharmed. Then the flow of energy halted, and in an instant Micah had pulled back his hammer and made his throw. Almost too quick for the eye to follow, the hammer left his hand and became a blur of blue-white energy as bright and blinding as its target. Higher than was possible for a man to throw, the bolt of flame sped, striking the blazing disk dead center. It seemed to bounce off the disk, and the blue bolt returned to Micah's hand.

The thing lashed out at Micah again, but once more he was protected by the hammer's mystic powers. Again he cast his hammer as soon as the rain of light ceased, striking it at the heart. As the hammer returned, those inside the abbey could see that the thing was beginning to wobble slightly as it spun. A third time he cast his hammer and it struck. Suddenly there was a rending sound, a tearing so loud that Arutha and the others were forced to cover their ears. The circling spheres shattered, and from the center of each plunged small alien shapes. With a wet, plopping noise they struck the ground, wiggled grotesquely, and began to smoke. A high keening shriek filled the night as they erupted into brilliant flame. No one could discern the true forms of the creatures from the spheres, but Arutha was filled with a sense it was something best left undiscovered, for in the instant they ignited, the shapes resembled nothing so much as horribly disfigured babies. Then the night was silent, as a rain of sparkling colors, like fine motes of glass star stuff, began to fall on the abbey. One by one the motes flared and winked out, until the old monk stood silently in the court, his war hammer held before him.

Those who stood in the shelter of the abbey looked at one another, astonishment on their faces. For a long moment they said nothing, then they began to relax. "That was . . . incredible," said Laurie. "I don't know if I could find the words to describe it."

Arutha was about to speak, but something in the way Jimmy and Martin both cocked their heads to one side made him stop. Jimmy said, "I hear something." They all stood silent for a moment, then could hear a distant sound, as if some great bird or bat flapped giant wings in the night.

Jimmy ran from the building before anyone could stop him, nearly spinning as he scanned every quarter of the night sky. Looking back over the roof of the abbey, toward the north, he saw something that made his eyes widen. "Banath!" he exclaimed and dashed to where the old monk still stood, unmoving and silent. Micah seemed in some sort of trance, eyes closed. Jimmy gripped his arm and shook him. "Look!" he shouted as the monk opened his eyes.

Micah looked to where the boy pointed. Blotting out the large moon in the night sky was something that flew toward the abbey, propelled on giant, powerful wings. Instantly the monk shoved the boy away. "Run!"

The push sent Jimmy away from the abbey, so he raced across the courtyard to where a lone wagon sat, filled with fodder for the stables, and dove under it. With a roll and a turn, he lay still, watching.

A thing of despair fashioned in a shape of utter horror descended from the sky. Wings a full fifty feet in width flapped lazily as it dropped down to where the old monk stood. It was a twenty-foot-tall composite of everything loathsome to sane beings. Black talons extended from grotesque parodies of bird claws, atop which rose legs reminiscent of a goat's. But where haunches should have been, only great wattles of fat, huge rings of blubber, shook and quivered, hanging impossibly down from below a manlike chest. Over the body a thick wet-looking substance oozed downward in rivulets. In the center of the thing's chest, a blue-colored but otherwise normal-looking human face stared out in wide-eyed horror, constantly twitching and screaming in gibbering counterpoint to the thing's own loud bellows. Each arm was powerfully fashioned, long and apelike. It shimmered in faint light, rapidly changing, first red, then orange, yellow, and onward through the spectrum until it was again red. And from it emitted a mixture of foul odors, as if the vile smell of every decaying and festering thing in the world had been distilled down and infused into the creature's being.

Most horrid of all was the head, for in supreme cruelty, whatever or whoever had fashioned the misshapen monster had adorned it with a woman's head, large to fit the body, but otherwise normal. And the ultimate jest was in the features of that face, for, in precise imitation, the thing bore the likeness of Princess Anita. Wild tresses seemed to blow in all directions, framing her features in a cloud of red hair. But its expression was one of a street whore, lewd and wanton, as the thing salaciously licked its lips and rolled its eyes toward Arutha. Blood-red lips split into a wide grin, showing long fangs in place of human eyeteeth.

Arutha looked on the thing with a disgust and loathing that rose up to banish any thought save to destroy this obscenity. "No!" he shouted as he began to pull his sword.

Gardan was instantly upon him, driving him to the floor of the building, bringing his strength to bear to hold him down, yelling, "That's what they want!"

Martin lent his strength to stop Arutha, and he and Gardan pulled the Prince away from the door. The creature turned to look at those within the door, absently flexing its claws. Pouting like a little girl, it suddenly leered at Arutha, then stuck out its tongue, wiggling it suggestively. Then with a bellowing laugh, it rose up to its full height and roared at the stars, arms stretched high overhead. With a single step, it moved toward the doorway where the Prince waited. Then suddenly it rocked foreward, shrieked in pain, and turned around.

Arutha and his companions looked past it to see a blue-white bolt of energy returning to Brother Micah's hand. He had struck the first blow while the thing had been distracted. Again he cast his hammer. In a blur it flashed to strike the thing in its huge stomach, bringing another bellow of pain and rage, as a trickle of steaming black blood began to flow.

"My, my!" came a voice from behind Arutha.

Laurie saw that Brother Anthony had come up from some deep vault beneath the abbey and was peering intently at the creature. Laurie said, "What is that thing?"

Showing no emotion except curiosity, the archivist said, "I believe it to be a conjured creature, something fashioned by magic means, brewed up in a vat. I can show you some references in a dozen different works on how to create them. Of course, it could be some rare naturally occurring beast, but that seems highly improbable."

Martin rose, leaving Gardan to restrain Arutha. He unlimbered his ever present bow, quickly strung it, and fitted an arrow to his bowstring. The creature was advancing upon Brother Micah when Martin let fly. The archer's eyes widened as the arrow seemed to pass through the creature's neck without effect.

Brother Anthony nodded. "Yes, it is a conjuration. Notice how it is impervious to mundane weapons."

The creature swung one of its mighty fists down at Brother Micah, but the old fighter simply raised his hammer as if to block. The creature's blow halted a full foot above the monk's upraised hammer, recoiling as if it had hit stone. It bellowed in frustration.

Martin turned to Brother Anthony. "How do you kill it?"

"I don't know. Each of Micah's blows draws energy away from the spell used to create it. But it is a product of tremendous magics, and it might last a day or longer. Should Micah falter . . ."

But the old monk was firm on his feet, answering every blow with a parry and wounding the creature, seemingly at will. While it seemed pained by each wound the hammer made, it gave no sign of being weakened.

"How do you make one?" Martin asked Brother Anthony. Arutha was no longer struggling, but Gardan still knelt with his hand upon his shoulder.

Anthony, caught up for a second in Martin's question, said, "How do you create one? Well, it's rather complex. . . ."

The creature became increasingly enraged by Micah's blows and hammered uselessly at the monk. Tiring of this tactic, it dropped to its knees as it leveled a blow at Micah, overhand as if driving a spike with a hammer, but at the last instant it shifted its aim and slammed its massive fist down on the ground next to the monk.

The jolt caused Micah to stumble slightly, which was the only opening the creature needed. Instantly sweeping its hand sideways, it knocked Micah across the courtyard. The old monk hit the ground heavily, rolled awkwardly, and lay stunned, his hammer bouncing away from him.

Then the thing was again moving toward Arutha. Gardan leaped to his feet, pulling his sword as he dashed forward to protect his Prince. The veteran captain stood before the thing, which grinned hideously down at him, the terrible parody of Anita adding a sickening element to the confrontation. Like a cat playing with a mouse, the creature pawed at Gardan.

From out of an inner door, Father John reappeared, holding a large metal staff topped with an odd-looking seven-sided device. He stepped before Arutha, who was trying to move to aid Gardan, and shouted, "No! You can do nothing."

Something in his voice told Arutha it was futile to attempt to engage the thing, and the Prince retreated a step. The Abbot turned to confront the conjured creature.

Jimmy crawled out from under the wagon and came to his feet. He knew the uselessness of drawing his dirk. Seeing the supine figure of Brother Micah, he ran to see how he fared. The old monk was still senseless, and Jimmy pulled him back toward the relative safety of the wagon. Gardan hacked uselessly at the creature while it played with him.

Jimmy cast about and saw the mystic hammer of Brother Micah lying off to one side. He dove for it and grabbed the haft on the fly, coming to rest on his stomach, eyes upon the monster. The thing had not noticed the boy's recovery of the weapon. Jimmy felt surprise when he lifted it, for it was twice the weight he expected. He rose to his feet and ran to stand behind the monster, confronted by its foul, fur-covered hindquarters, arching above his head as it reached forward to grab Gardan.

The captain was seized in a mammoth hand that lifted him toward the widening mouth. Father John raised up his staff and suddenly waves of green and purple energy flowed from it, washing over the creature. It howled in pain and squeezed Gardan, who cried out in concert.

Martin shouted, "Stop! It's crushing Gardan!"

The Abbot ceased his magic and the thing snorted as it tossed Gardan at the door, seeking to injure its tormentors. The captain slammed into Martin, Brother Anthony, and the Abbot, knocking them to the ground. Arutha and Laurie both sidestepped the flying bodies. The Prince turned to see the leering parody of Anita's face bending toward the door. The creature's wings prevented it from entering the abbey, but long arms came snaking through the door, reaching for Arutha.

Martin rose, helping the shaken Abbot and Brother Anthony to their feet. The archivist said, "Yes! Of course! The face in its chest! Kill it there!"

Martin had an arrow nocked in an instant, but the crouching thing hid the target. It reached through the door for Arutha, then suddenly it was sitting back on its haunches, howling in pain.

For an instant the face in the chest was visible, and Martin pulled back as he said, "Kilian guide my arrow," and let fly. True to the aim, the shaft flew and struck the insane face in the chest square in the forehead. The eyes in that face rolled up and closed as red, human blood billowed from the wound. The creature stopped rock-still.

As all watched in wonder, the creature began to quiver. It grew instantly more brilliant in color as the lights within flashed rapidly. Then all could see it was becoming transparent, insubstantial, a thing of colored glowing smokes and gases, swirling in a mad dance as they slowly dissipated on the night wind. Their lights faded until once again the courtyard was empty and silent.

Arutha and Laurie came up to Gardan, who was still conscious. "What happened?" the Captain asked feebly.

All eyes turned to Martin. He indicated Brother Anthony, who responded, "It was something the Duke asked, how one of those things is made. All the foul arts to make such a being require some animal or human to work upon. That face was all that was left of the poor demented soul who had been used as a focus to create the monster. It was the only mortal part, subject to mundane injury, and when it was killed, the magic . . . unraveled."

Martin said, "I'd not have made that shot had it not reared back like that."

"Most fortunate," said the Abbot.

"Fortune had little to do with it," said a grinning Jimmy. He held Brother Micah's hammer as he approached. "I stuck it up the arse." He indicated the stunned Micah. "He'll do all right," he said as he gave the hammer to the Abbot.

Arutha was still shaken by the sight of Anita's face atop that horror. Laurie, with a weak smile, said, "Father, if it wouldn't be too much trouble, have you some wine we might drink? That was the worst smell I've ever endured."

"Ha!" Jimmy said indignantly. "You should have tried it from my end!"

Arutha watched the dawn break over the Calastius Mountains, the rising sun an angry red orb. In the hours since the attack the abbey had returned to a semblance of order and quiet, but Arutha felt only turmoil within. Whatever lay behind these attempts upon him was powerful beyond anything he had anticipated, despite clear warning from Father Nathan and the High Priestess of Lims-Kragma. He had grown incautious in his haste to discover a cure for Anita, and such was not his nature. He could be bold when needed, and boldness had won him several victories, but of late he had not been bold, only headstrong and impulsive. Arutha felt something alien, something he had not endured since he was a boy. Arutha felt doubt. He had been so confident in his planning, but Murmandamus either had anticipated every move or somehow could react with unbelievable speed each time Arutha made a step.

Arutha came out of his musing to see Jimmy beside him. The boy shook his head. "Just shows you what I've always said."

Despite his concerns, Arutha found himself slightly amused by the boy's tone. "What is that?"

"No matter how canny you think you are, something can come along, bam, and put you on your prat. Then you think, 'That's what I forgot to consider.' Eagle-eye hindsight, old Alvarny the Quick used to call it."

Arutha wondered if the boy had been reading his thoughts. Jimmy continued. "The Ishapians are sitting up here, mumbling prayers to themselves, and convinced they've got a real magic stronghold—'nothing can breach our mystic defenses,' " he mimicked. "Then along come those balls of light and that flying thing and whoops! 'We didn't consider this or that!' They've been jabbering about what they should have done for an hour. Well, I guess they'll have something stronger around here soon." Jimmy leaned back against the stone wall facing the cliff. Beyond the walls of the abbey the valley was emerging from the shadows as the sun reached higher in the sky. "Old Anthony was telling me that the spells necessary for last night's show took some doing, so he doesn't think anything magic will come this way for a while. They'll be strong in their fortress . . . until something comes along that can kick down the gates again, as it were."

"Something of a philosopher, are you?" Arutha smiled slightly as Jimmy shrugged.

"Scared to pissing in my trousers is what I am, and you'd do well to be scared as well. Those undead things in Krondor were bad enough, but last night, well, I don't know how you feel about it, but if I were you, I'd consider moving to Kesh and changing my name."

Arutha smiled ruefully at that, for Jimmy had made him see something he had denied. "To be honest, I am just as scared as you, Jimmy."

Jimmy looked surprised at the admission. "Truth?"

"In truth. Look, only a madman would not be fearful of facing what we have, and what may come, but what matters isn't whether or not you're frightened, but how you behave. My father said once that a hero is someone who simply got too frightened to use his good sense and run away, then somehow lived through it all."

Jimmy laughed, boyish glee making him seem as youthful as his years rather than the man-boy he looked most of the time. "That's a truth, too. Me, I'd rather do what needs be done, quickly, and get on to the fun. This suffering for grand causes is the stuff of sagas and legends."

Arutha said, "See, there's a bit of the philosopher in you, after all." He changed topics. "You acted swiftly last night, and bravely. Had you not distracted the monster so Martin could slay it—"

"We'd be on our way back to Krondor with your bones, assuming it didn't eat them," finished Jimmy with a wry grin.

"Don't look so pleased at the prospect."

Jimmy's grin broadened. "I'd not be, fact is. You're one of the very few I've met worth having around. By most standards this is a merry bunch, though the times are grim. I'm sort of having fun, if the truth be known."

"You have a strange sense of fun."

Jimmy shook his head. "Not really. If you're going to be scared senseless, might as well enjoy it. That's what thieving's about, you know. Breaking into someone's home in the dead of night, not knowing if they're awake and waiting with a sword or club to spread your brains out on the floor when you stick your head in the window. Being chased through the streets by the city watch. It's not fun, but it sort of is, you know? Anyway, it's exciting. And besides, how many can boast they saved the Prince of Krondor by goosing a demon?"

Arutha laughed hard at that. "Hang me, but that's the first thing I've had to laugh aloud at since . . . since the wedding." He placed his hand upon Jimmy's shoulder. "You earned some reward this day, Squire James. What shall it be?"

Jimmy's face screwed up in a display of hard thinking. "Why not name me Duke of Krondor?"

Arutha was thunderstruck. He started to speak, but stopped.

Martin approached from the infirmary and, seeing such a strange expression on Arutha's face, said, "What ails you?"

Arutha pointed at Jimmy. "He wants to be Duke of Krondor."

Martin laughed uproariously. When he quieted, Jimmy said, "Why not? Dulanic's here, so you know his retirement's not bogus. Volney doesn't want the post, so who else are you going to give it to? I've a fair wit, and I've done you a favor or two."

Martin continued laughing while Arutha said, "For which you have been paid." The Prince was caught between outrage and amusement. "Look, you bandit, I might think about having Lyam give you a minor barony—very minor—to take charge of, when you reach your majority, which is at least three years away. For now you'll have to settle for being named Senior Squire of the Court."

Martin shook his head. "He'll organize them into a street gang."

"Well," said Jimmy, "at least I'll have the pleasure of seeing that ass Jerome's face when you give deLacy the order."

Martin stopped his laughing and said, "I just thought you'd like to know Gardan will be fine, as will Brother Micah. Dominic is up and about already."

"The Abbot and Brother Anthony?"

"The Abbot is off somewhere doing whatever abbots do when their abbeys have been desecrated. And Brother Anthony is back looking for Silverthorn. He said to tell you he'll be in chamber sixty-seven if you wish to speak with him."

Arutha said, "I'm going to find him. I want to know what he's discovered." As he walked away, he said, "Jimmy, why don't you explain to my brother why I should elevate you to the second most important dukedom in the Kingdom?"

Arutha walked off in search of the head archivist. Martin turned to look at Jimmy, who grinned back at him.

Arutha entered the vast chamber, musty with age and the faint odor of preservatives. By flickering lantern light Brother Anthony was reading an old volume. Without turning to see who entered, he said, "Just as I thought, I knew it would be here." He sat up. "That creature was similar to one reported killed when the Temple of Tith-Onanka in Elarial was invaded three hundred years ago. It was certain, according to these sources, that Pantathian serpent priests were behind the deed."

Arutha said, "What are these Pantathians, brother? I've only heard the stories told to frighten children."

The old monk shrugged. "We know little, in truth. Most of the intelligent races on Midkemia we can, in some way, understand. Even the moredhel, the Brotherhood of the Dark Path, have some traits in common with humanity. You know, they have a rather rigid code of honor, though it is an odd sort by our standards. But these creatures . . ." He closed the book. "Where Pantathia lies, no one knows. The copies of the maps left by Macros that Kulgan of Stardock sent us show no sign of it. These priests have magics unlike any other. They are the avowed enemies of humanity, though they have dealt with some humans in the past. One thing else is clear, they are beings of undiluted evil. For them to serve this Murmandamus would mark him a foe of all that is good if nothing else did. And that they serve him also marks him a power to fear."

Arutha said, "Then we know little more than what we knew by Laughing Jack's report."

"True," said the monk, "but never discount the worth of knowing he spoke the truth. Knowing what things are not is often as important as knowing what they are."

Arutha said, "In all the confusion, have you discovered anything about Silverthorn?"

"As a matter of fact, I have. I was going to send word as soon as I finished reading this passage. I have little help to offer, I am afraid." Upon hearing this, Arutha's heart sank in his chest, but he indicated the old monk should continue. "The reason I could not quickly bring to mind this Silverthorn is that the name given is a translation of the name with which I am more familiar." He opened another book lying close by. "This is the journal of Geoffrey, son of Caradoc, a monk at the Abbey of Silban west of Yabon—the same one your brother Martin was reared at, though this was several hundred years ago. Geoffrey was a botanist of sorts and spent his idle hours in cataloging what he could of the local flora. Here I've found a clue. I'll read it. 'The plant, which is called Elleberry by the elves, is also known to the people of the hills as Sparkle Thorn. It is supposed to have magic properties when utilized correctly, though the proper means of distillation of the essences of the plant is not commonly known, being required of arcane ritual beyond the abilities of common folk. It is rare in the extreme, having been seen by few living today. I have never beheld the plant, but those with whom I have spoken are most reliable in their knowledge and certain of the plant's existence.' " He closed the book.

"Is that all?" asked Arutha. "I had hoped for a cure, or at least some clue as to how one might be discovered."

"But there is a clue," said the old monk with a wink. "Geoffrey, who was more of gossip than a botanist, attributed the name Elleberry to the plant, as an elven name. This is obviously a corruption of *aelebera,* an elven word that translates to 'silverthorn'! Which means that should any know its magic properties and how to overcome them, it is the Spellweavers of Elvandar."

Arutha was silent for a while, then said, "Thank you, Brother Anthony. I had prayed to end my search here, but at least you've not dashed all hope."

The old monk said, "There is always hope, Arutha conDoin. I suspect that, in all the confusion, the Abbot never got around to telling you the main reason for our gathering all this." His hand waved about him, indicating the masses of books everywhere. "The reason we gather all these works in this mount is hope. Of prophecy and portents there are many, but one speaks of the end of all we know. It states that when all else has succumbed to the forces of darkness, all that will be left will be 'that which was Sarth.' Should that prophecy come true, we hope to save the seeds of knowledge that can again serve man. We work against that day, and pray it will never come."

Arutha said, "You've been kind, Brother Anthony."

"A man helps when he may."

"Thank you." Arutha left the chamber and climbed the stairs, his mind playing over what he knew. He considered his options until he reached the courtyard. Laurie had joined Jimmy and Martin, as had Dominic, who seemed to have recovered from his ordeal, though he was still pale.

Laurie greeted the Prince and said, "Gardan should be well enough tomorrow."

"Good, for we leave Sarth at first light."

"What do you propose?" said Martin.

"I'm going to put Gardan on the first ship bound from Sarth for Krondor, and we'll continue on."

"Continue on where?" asked Laurie.

"Elvandar."

Martin smiled. "It will be good to visit there again."

Jimmy sighed; Arutha said, "What is it?"

"I was just thinking of your palace cooks and bony horsebacks."

Arutha said, "Well, don't think on them too long; you're returning to Krondor with Gardan."

"And miss all the fun?"

Laurie said to Martin, "This lad has a definitely warped sense of fun."

Jimmy started to speak, but Dominic said, "Highness, if I may travel with your captain, I wish to journey to Krondor."

"Of course, but what of your duties?"

"Another will take my office. I will not be fit for that sort of duty for some time, and we cannot wait. There is no shame or dishonor; it is simply necessary."

"Then I am sure Jimmy and Gardan will welcome your company."

"Wait—" began Jimmy.

Ignoring the boy, Arutha asked the monk, "What sends you to Krondor?"

"Simply that it lies on my route to Stardock. Father John thinks it vital we should inform Pug and the other magicians of what we know to be occurring. They practice mighty arts unavailable to us."

"That is well taken. We have need of all the allies we can muster. I should have considered that myself. I will give you some additional intelligence to take to them, if you don't mind. And I'll have Gardan escort you down to Stardock."

"That would be kind."

Jimmy had been trying to be heard as he protested being sent back to Krondor. Ignoring his protests, Arutha said to Laurie, "Take our aspiring young duke here and go down to town and find a ship. We'll follow tomorrow. Also see about some fresher mounts, and don't get into trouble."

Arutha walked away toward the barracks with Dominic and

Martin, leaving Laurie and Jimmy in the courtyard. Jimmy was still trying to make himself heard, and was saying, ". . . but . . ."

Laurie clapped Jimmy on the shoulder and said, "Come along, 'Your Grace.' Let's get down the road. If we can finish our business early, we'll see if we can find a game at the inn."

An evil light seemed to come into Jimmy's eyes at that. "Game?" he said.

"You know, something like pashawa, or over-under-man-in-between. Knucklebones or stones. Gambling."

"Oh," said the boy. "You'll have to show me how."

As he turned for the stable, Laurie fetched him a kick in the rump, propelling him along. "Show you how, indeed. I'm not some rube in from the farmlands here. I heard that the first time I lost my poke."

Running forward, Jimmy laughed. "It was worth a try!"

Arutha entered the darkened room. Looking down at the figure on the cot, he said, "You sent for me?"

Micah raised himself up and leaned back against the wall. "Yes. I hear you're leaving this hour. Thank you for coming." He indicated Arutha should sit upon the bed. "I need a little sleep, but I'll be fit enough in a week or so.

"Arutha, your father and I were friends as youngsters. Caldric was just establishing the practice of bringing squires to court that's now taken for granted. We were quite a bunch. Brucal of Yabon was our Senior Squire, and he ran us ragged. In those days we were a fiery crew, your father, myself, and Guy du Bas-Tyra." At mention of Guy's name, Arutha stiffened but said nothing. "I like to think we were the backbone of the Kingdom in our day. Now you are. Borric did well with you and Lyam, and Martin brings no shame. I am now serving Ishap, but I still love this Kingdom, son. I just wanted you to know my prayers are with you."

Arutha said, "Thank you, my lord Dulanic."

He eased himself on his pillows. "No longer. I'm just a simple monk now. By the way, who rules in your place?"

"Lyam is in Krondor and will remain until I return. Volney acts as Chancellor."

At this Micah laughed, which brought a wince of pain. "Volney! Ishap's teeth! He must hate it."

"He does," said Arutha with a smile.

"You going to have Lyam name him Duke?"

"I don't know. As much as he protests, he's the most able administrator available. We lost some good young men during the Riftwar." Arutha smiled his crooked smile. "Jimmy suggests I name *him* Duke of Krondor."

"Don't sell that one short, Arutha. Train him while you have him. Pile the responsibility on him until he yells, and give him more. Educate him well, then take stock. He's a rare one."

Arutha said, "Why is this, Micah? Why this concern for matters you've put behind?"

"Because I'm a vain old man and a sinner, despite my repentance. I still admit to pride in how my city fares. And because you're your father's son."

Arutha was silent for a long time, then he said, "You and Father were close once, weren't you?"

"Very. Only Guy was closer to Borric."

"Guy!" Arutha couldn't believe his father's most hated enemy could have ever once been his friend. "How is that possible?"

Micah studied Arutha. "I thought your father would have told you before he died." He was silent for a long moment. "Then again, Borric wouldn't." He sighed. "We who were friends to both your father and Guy, we all took a vow. We vowed never to speak of the shame which caused them to end the closest of friendships, and which caused Guy to wear black every day for the rest of his life, earning him the name Black Guy."

Arutha said, "Father once mentioned that strange act of personal courage, though he had no other good to speak of Guy."

"He wouldn't. And I will not either, for Guy would have to release me from the vow, or be proved dead, before I would speak. But I can say that before that schism they were as brothers. Whether wenching, brawling, or in war, neither was more than a voice's call from the other's aid.

"But look you, Arutha. You have to rise early, and you must get rested. You've no more time to idle away over matters long buried. You must be off to find a cure for Anita. . . ." The old man's eyes misted over, and Arutha realized that in his own dark concern for her he had ignored the fact that Micah had long been a member of Erland's household. He had known Anita since birth. She would be like a granddaughter to him.

Micah swallowed hard. "These damn ribs! Breathe deeply and your eyes tear like you're eating raw onion." He let out a long sigh. "I held her in my arms when the priests of Sung the White blessed her, less than an hour after her birth." His eyes took on a far-off look; he turned his face away and said, "Save her, Arutha."

"I will find a cure."

Whispering to control his emotions, Micah said, "Then go, Arutha. Ishap protect you."

Arutha squeezed the old monk's hand for a moment, rose, and left his quarters. Walking across the main hall of the abbey building, he was intercepted by a silent monk who indicated he should follow. He was led to the Abbot's quarters and found the Abbot and Brother Anthony waiting for him.

"It is good you took time to visit with Micah, Highness," said the Abbot.

Suddenly Arutha became alarmed. "Micah will recover, won't he?"

"If Ishap wills it. He is an old man to be withstanding such an ordeal."

Brother Anthony seemed incensed by the notion and almost snorted. The Abbot ignored the sound and said, "We have given some thought to a problem that needs be dealt with." He pushed a small case toward Arutha, who reached over and lifted it from the table.

The case was clearly ancient, of delicately carved wood, and time had worn it almost smooth. When it was opened it revealed a velvet cushion upon which rested a small talisman. It was a bronze hammer, a miniature of that which Micah had carried, a thong passing through a tiny hole in the haft. "What is it?"

Anthony said, "You must have considered how your foe was able to locate you seemingly at will. It is likely that some agency, perhaps the serpent priest, had located you with a scrying spell of one sort or another. That talisman is a legacy from our ancient past. It was fashioned at the oldest known enclave of our faith, the Ishapian abbey at Leng. It is the most powerful artifact we possess. It will mask your movements from all scrying magic. To any who have been following you by arcane means, you will simply vanish from sight. We have no protection from mundane eyes, but if you are cautious and mask your identity, you should be able to reach Elvandar without being intercepted. But never remove it, or you will again be subject to location by sorcery. It will also render you impervious to the sort of attack we endured last night. Such a creature would be unable to harm you—though your enemy may still strike through those about you, for they will not be so protected."

Arutha placed the talisman around his neck and said, "Thank you."

The Abbot rose. "Ishap protect you, Highness, and know you may always find haven here at Sarth."

Arutha said thank you again and left the Abbot. As he returned to his quarters and finished rolling his travel bundle, he considered what he had learned. Pushing doubt aside, he determined once again to save Anita.

TWELVE

NORTHWARD

A lone rider raced up the road.

Arutha looked back as Martin warned of the approaching horseman. Laurie turned his horse, drawing his sword, as Martin began to laugh. Arutha said, "If that's who I think, I'll have his ears."

Martin said, "Then sharpen your knife, brother, for look at the way those elbows flap as he rides."

Within moments Martin's prediction proved correct, for a grinning Jimmy reined in. Arutha took no pains to hide his displeasure. He said to Laurie, "I thought you told me he was safely upon the ship for Krondor with Gardan and Dominic."

Laurie looked on with an expression of helplessness. "He was, I swear."

Jimmy looked at the three. "Isn't anyone going to say hello?"

Martin tried to look serious, but even his elven-learned composure was being tested. Jimmy had all the ingenuousness of an eager puppy, as false a pose as most others he assumed, and Arutha was trying hard to keep a stern demeanor. Laurie hid his laughter behind a quickly raised hand and a cough.

Arutha shook his head, looking down at the ground. Finally he said, "All right, what is the tale?"

Jimmy said, "First of all, I swore an oath; it might not mean much to you, but it is still an oath, and it binds us 'until the cat is skinned.' And there was one other little thing."

Arutha said, "What was it?"

"You were being watched while you left Sarth."

Arutha sat back in the saddle, as startled by the boy's offhanded tone as much as by the revelation. "How can you be certain?"

"In the first, the man was known to me. He's a certain merchant from Questor's View, by name Havram, who is in fact a smuggler employed by the Mockers. He's been absent since the Nighthawks' infiltration was made known to the Upright Man, and he was in the inn where Gardan, Dominic, and I waited for the ship. I went aboard ship with the good captain and the monk and slipped over the side just before they weighed anchor. Then, in the second, the man was without the normal retinue he employed when working at his normal trade. He is usually a vocal, affable man, given to public display when acting the merchant, but in Sarth he lurked under a heavy cowl and hugged dark corners. He would not be in such a place, ignoring his usual role, unless forced to by unusual circumstances. And he followed you from the inn, until he was clear as to which way you had ridden. But most important of all, he was an ofttime companion of both Laughing Jack and Golden Dase."

Martin said, "Havram! That was the man Laughing Jack said recruited Golden and him into the Nighthawks."

"They'll be relying on spies and agents now that they can't use magic to find you," added Laurie. "It makes sense they had someone in Sarth waiting for you to come down from the Abbey."

"Did he see you leave?" asked the Prince.

Jimmy laughed. "No, but I saw him leave." They all looked at him with questions on their faces, and the boy said, "I took care of him."

"You did what?"

Jimmy looked pleased with himself. "Even a town as small as Sarth has its underside if you know where to look. Using my reputation as a Mocker of Krondor, I made myself known and established my bona fides. Certain people who wish to remain anonymous were made to understand I knew who they were—and would be willing to neglect mentioning it to the local garrison in exchange for a service. As they thought I still enjoyed a favored position in the Mockers, they chose not to deposit me in the bay, especially when I sweetened the deal with a small pouch of gold I carried. I then mentioned there was not a single person in the Western Realm who would miss a certain merchant taking his ease at the inn. They took my meaning. The false merchant is most likely on his way to Kesh via the Durbin slave route even as we speak, learning the finer points of menial labor."

Laurie slowly shook his head. "The boy has a definite hard edge to him."

Arutha heaved a resigned sigh. "It seems I am again in your debt, Jimmy."

Jimmy said, "There's a small caravan coming up the coast about an hour behind. If we ride slowly they may overtake us by nightfall. We could most likely hire on as additional guards and ride in with wagons and a few other mercenaries when Murmandamus is out looking for the three riders who left Sarth."

Arutha laughed. "What am I to do with you?" Before Jimmy could answer, he said, "And don't say anything about being Duke of Krondor." As he turned his mount, he said, "And don't tell me where you got that horse."

Fate, or the efficacy of the Ishapian talisman, served Arutha and his three companions, for they encountered no trouble along the road to Ylith. Jimmy's prediction of a caravan's overtaking them proved accurate. It was a poor thing, consisting of five wagons served by only two bravos hired as guards. Once the merchant in charge was satisfied they were not brigands, he welcomed them as traveling companions—for he gained four additional bodyguards for the price of a few meals.

For two weeks they traveled with little to disrupt the monotony of the journey. Peddlers, traders, and caravans of all sizes, with up to a score of mercenary guards, passed both ways along the coast between Questor's View and Sarth. Arutha was satisfied that should some spy or agent discover him among the throng of bravos riding along the road, it would be by pure chance.

Finally, near sundown, they could see the lights of Ylith in the distance. Arutha rode point with Yanov the merchant's two guards. He held back until the lead wagon was even with him and said, "Ylith ahead, Yanov."

The lead wagon passed, and the stout merchant, a silk and finecloth peddler from Krondor, waved happily. Arutha had been relieved to discover Yanov an ebullient man, for he paid little attention to what others had to say and Arutha's quickly contrived history had stood up to scrutiny. As far as the Prince could tell, Yanov had never seen him before.

Martin was the first to overtake Arutha, as the last wagon in the train moved past him. "Ylith," said Arutha, kicking his mount into motion.

Jimmy and Laurie crossed the road from where they had ridden flank as Martin said, "Soon we'll be shed of this train and can see to new mounts. These need a rest."

Laurie said, "I'll be pleased to be rid of Yanov. He cackles like a fishwife, without a halt."

Jimmy shook his head in mock sympathy. "And he hardly ever lets anyone else tell a story around the campfire."

Laurie glared. Arutha said, "Enough. We'll be another band of travelers. If Baron Talanque discovers I'm here, it's a state affair. We'll have feasting, tourneys, hunting, receptions, and everyone between the Great Northern Mountains and Kesh will know I'm in Ylith. Talanque's a fine fellow, but he does enjoy his revels."

Jimmy laughed. "He's not the only one." With a whoop and a shout, he spurred his horse forward. Arutha, Laurie, and Martin sat amazed for a moment, then the relief of reaching Ylith struck and they were off after the boy.

As Arutha raced past the lead wagon, he shouted, "Good trading, Master Yanov!" The merchant looked after them as if they'd become bereft of reason. Etiquette required he pay them a token for their stint at guard.

Reaching the gates of the city, they slowed, as a caravan of some size had just finished passing into Ylith and several other travelers were waiting for it to clear the portals before they could enter. Jimmy reined in behind a farmer's hay cart and spun his horse to face his companions as they rode up, laughing at the momentary frolic. Without words they fell into line, watching as soldiers passed the cart through. In these peaceful days, the soldiers seemed to be giving only the most cursory inspection to those passing into the city.

Jimmy looked about, for Ylith was the first large city encountered since they'd left Krondor, and the busy metropolitan rhythm was already making him feel at home. Then near the gates he noticed a lone figure hunkered down, watching those who passed through. From his tartan plaid and leather breeches, it was clear he was a Hadati hillman. His hair fell past his shoulders, but a warrior's topknot was bound high, and he wore a rolled scarf tied above his eyes. Across his knees rested a pair of wooden sheaths, protecting the sharp edges of the long, slender sword and a shorter half-sword common to his people. Most striking about the man was his face, for around the eyes, from forehead down to cheekbones, his face was painted bone-white, as was his chin directly below his mouth. He clearly studied the Prince as he passed, then slowly rose as Jimmy and Martin followed Arutha and Laurie into the city.

Jimmy suddenly laughed aloud, as if Martin had joked, and stretched, affording himself a quick glance behind. The hillman was slowly walking through the gates behind them, putting his sword and half-sword in his belt-sash.

Martin said, "The Hadati?" When Jimmy nodded, the Duke said, "You've a quick eye. Is he following?"

"He is. Shall we lose him?"

Martin shook his head. "We'll deal with him once we settle somewhere. If we need to."

As they rode up the narrow streets of the city, they were greeted by signs of prosperity on all sides, for shops burned brightly with lantern light as merchants showed their wares to those out shopping in the cool of the evening.

Even at this early hour of the evening, celebrants were about in numbers, as guards from caravans and sailors in from months at sea were out in force, seeking whatever pleasures gold could buy. A band of rowdy fighting men, mercenaries by their look, pushed across the street, obviously working on a heroic drunk, yelling and laughing. One bumped against Laurie's horse and, in a display of mock anger, shouted, "Here now! Watch where you're pointing that beastie. Shall I teach you manners?" He feigned pulling his sword, to the delight of those with him. Laurie laughed along with the man as Martin, Arutha, and Jimmy kept an eye on potential trouble.

"Sorry, friend," said the singer. The man made a half-grimace, half-laugh as he again motioned as if to draw his sword.

Another from the mercenary band pushed him roughly aside and said, "Go have a drink," to his companion. Smiling up at Laurie, he said, "Still can't ride any better than you can sing, Laurie?"

Laurie was off his mount instantly and embraced the man in a bear hug. "Roald, you son of a whoremonger!"

They exchanged backslaps and hugs, then Laurie presented the man to the others. "This black heart is Roald, a friend since boyhood and more than once a companion on the road. His father owned the farm next to my father's."

The man laughed. "And our fathers threw the both of us out of home on almost the same day."

Laurie introduced Martin and Jimmy, but when he reached Arutha used the agreed-upon name of Arthur. "Pleased to know your friends, Laurie," said the mercenary.

Arutha cast a quick glance about. "We're blocking the thoroughfare. Let's find lodgings."

Roald waved a hand for them to follow. "I'm staying at a place the next street over. It's almost civilized."

Jimmy spurred his horse forward and kept an eye on this boyhood friend of the singer, studying the man with a practiced eye. He had all the earmarks of a seasoned mercenary, one who had been earning a living with his sword long enough to be considered an expert by dint of his still being alive. Jimmy glimpsed Martin looking rearward and wondered if the Hadati still stalked them.

The inn was called the Northerner, respectable enough for a place so near the docks. A stableboy roused himself from a sorry-looking meal to take their horses. Roald said, "Keep them well, lad." The boy obviously knew him. Martin tossed the boy a silver coin.

Jimmy watched the boy catch the coin in midair, and as he gave over his horse's reins, he placed the thumb of his right hand between fore- and middle fingers, so the boy could see. A flash of recognition passed between them and the boy gave Jimmy a curt nod.

When they were inside, Roald signaled for the serving girl to bring ale as he pointed to a table in the corner, near the door to the stable yard and away from the normal flow of customers. Pulling out a chair for himself, Roald discarded his heavy leather gauntlets as he sat. He spoke just loud enough for those at the table to hear. "Laurie, last time I saw you was what? Six years ago? You went riding off with a LaMutian patrol to look for Tsurani to write songs about. Now here you are with"—he indicated Jimmy—"this short thief here."

Jimmy grimaced. "Highsign?"

"Highsign," agreed Roald. When the others looked confused, Roald said, "This lad Jimmy gave the stableboy a sign so the local thieves will keep hands off his kick. Tells them a thief from another city is in town and respecting the conventions and should have the courtesy returned. Right?"

Jimmy nodded appreciatively. "Right. It tells them I won't . . . work without their leave. Keeps things civilized. The boy will pass the word."

Quietly Arutha said, "How did you know?"

"I'm no outlaw, but I'm no saint either. Over the years I've kept all manner of company. Mostly I'm a simple fighting man. Up to a year ago I was a mercenary in the Yabonese Free Levies. Fought for King and country for a silver piece a day and found." His eyes got a distant look. "We'd been on and off the line for seven years. Of the lads who signed aboard with our captain that first year, one in five was left. Each winter we'd stay in LaMut and our captain would go out recruiting. Each spring we'd return to the front with fewer men." His eyes lowered to the ale before him. "I've fought against bandits and outlaws, renegades of all stripe. I served marine duty on a warship hunting pirates. I stood at Cutter's Gap when fewer than thirty of us held back two hundred goblins for three days until Brian, Lord Highcastle, could come fetch us out. But I never thought I'd live to see the day the bloody Tsurani would quit. No," he said, "it's glad I am to be standing guard on piddly little caravans the hungriest outlaw in the land wouldn't bother with. My biggest problem these days is keeping awake." The mercenary smiled. "Of all my old friends, you were the best, Laurie. I'd trust you with my life, if not my women and money. Let's hoist a round for old times' sake, then we can start telling lies."

Arutha liked the openness of the fighter. The serving woman brought another round, and Roald paid, over Laurie's protest. "I'm in this very day with a great creaking caravan from the Free Cities. My mouth is caked with a month's worth of road dust, and I'll only waste my gold sooner or later. It might as well be now."

Martin laughed and said, "Only the first, friend Roald. The rest are our pleasure."

Jimmy said, "Have you seen a Hadati hillman around?"

Roald waved his hand. "They're around. Anyone in particular?"

Martin said, "Green and black tartan on his plaid, white paint on his face."

Roald said, "Green and black's a far northwest clan, couldn't say which. But the white paint . . ." He and Laurie exchanged glances.

Martin said, "What?"

Laurie said, "He's on a Bloodquest."

Roald said, "A personal mission. Some matter of clan honor or another. And let me tell you, honor's no joke to a Hadati. They're as intractable about it as those damn Tsurani up in LaMut. Maybe he has to avenge a wrongdoing, or pay back a debt for his tribe, but whatever it is, only a fool would get in the way of a Hadati on Bloodquest. They tend to be a forward lot with a sword."

Roald finished his drink and Arutha said, "If you will join us, let's share a meal."

The fighter smiled at that. "In truth, I am hungry."

The call was given and soon the food was served, and conversation turned to an exchange of histories between Laurie and Roald. Roald had listened raptly while Laurie recounted his adventures during the Riftwar, though he left out his involvement with the royal family and the news he was to wed the King's sister. The mercenary's mouth hung open. "I've never known a singer not given to overboasting, and you're the worst I've known, Laurie, but that tale is so outlandish I believe what you've said. It's incredible."

Laurie looked stung. "Overboast? Me?"

While they ate, the innkeeper came over and said to Laurie, "I see you to be a singer." Laurie had brought along his lute, a nearly instinctive habit. "Will you honor this house with your songs?"

Arutha looked ready to object, but Laurie said, "Of course." To Arutha he said, "We can leave later, Arthur. In Yabon, even when a singer pays for his meals, it is expected he will sing when asked. I build accounts. If I pass this way, I can sing and eat even if I have no money." He crossed to a dais in the corner near the front door to the inn and sat upon a stool. He tuned his lute until the pitch of each string was correct, then began his song. It was a common tune, sung in all parts of the Kingdom and known by all who sang in alehouses and inns. It was a favorite of those who listened. The melody was pleasant, but the words were mawkish.

Arutha shook his head. "That's awful."

The others laughed. "True," said Roald, "but they like it," indicating the crowd.

Jimmy said, "Laurie plays what is popular, not always what is good. That way he eats."

Laurie finished to a loud round of applause and began another song. It was a bright, ribald chanty, sung by sailors throughout the Bitter Sea, telling of a drunken seaman's encounter with a mermaid. A group of sailors fresh off a ship set up a clapping accompaniment to the song, and one took out a simple wooden pipe and played a clever countermelody. As the rowdy mood of the room increased, Laurie slipped into another bawdy chanty regarding what occupies the captain's wife while her husband is out to sea. The sailors cheered at this, and the one with the pipe danced before the bar while he played.

As the festive feeling in the room increased, the front door opened and three men entered. Jimmy watched them as they slowly made their way through the room and said, "Uh oh, trouble."

Martin looked to where Jimmy was watching. "You know them?"

"No, but I recognize the type. It's the big one in front who'll start it."

The man in question was the obvious leader of the three. He was a tall, red-bearded fighter, a barrel-chested mercenary who had let most of his powerful frame run to fat. He wore two dirks but was otherwise unarmed. His leather vest barely closed over his gut. The two behind him looked like fighting men. One was armed with a variety of knives, varying from a tiny stiletto to a long dagger. The other wore a long hunting knife at his belt.

The red-bearded man led his companions toward Arutha's table, speaking rudely as he pushed all aside who blocked his way. His manner wasn't entirely unfriendly, for he exchanged loud, coarse jokes with several men in the inn who obviously knew him. Soon all three stood before Arutha's table. Looking at the four seated there, the red-bearded man let a grin spread slowly across his face. "You sit at my table." His accent betrayed him as being from one of the southern Free Cities.

He leaned forward, fists on the table between the plates of food, and said, "You are strangers. I forgive you." Jimmy's mouth dropped open and he instinctively pulled away, for the man's breath betrayed a day already spent drinking and teeth long gone to rot. "If you were Ylithmen, you'd know when Longly is in town, every night he sits this table in the Northerner. Leave now, and I won't kill you dead." With that he threw back his head and laughed.

Jimmy was the first on his feet, saying, "We didn't know, sir." He smiled weakly as the others exchanged glances. Arutha indicated he wished to quit the table and avoid trouble. Jimmy made a show of being scared to death of the fat fighter. "We'll find another table."

The man called Longly grabbed Jimmy's left arm above the elbow. "This is pretty boy, no?" He laughed and looked at his companions. "Or maybe it's girl, dressed like boy, he's so pretty." He laughed again, then looked at Roald. "This boy your friend? Or is he pet?"

Jimmy's eyes rolled heavenward as he said, "I wish you hadn't said that."

Arutha reached across the table and put his hand upon the man's arm. "Let the boy go."

Longly swung a backhanded blow at Arutha with his free hand, knocking the Prince backward.

Roald and Martin exchanged resigned looks as Jimmy quickly raised his right leg so he could reach the dirk in his right boot top. Before anyone could move, Jimmy had the point of the dirk placed firmly in Longly's ribs. "I think you'd better find another table, friend."

The huge man looked down at the thief, who barely reached his chin, then at the dagger. With a roaring laugh, he said, "Little fellow, you are very funny." His free hand shot out and gripped Jimmy's wrist with unexpected speed. With slight effort, he forced the dirk away.

Jimmy's face became beaded with sweat as he struggled to escape the viselike grip of the red-bearded man. In the corner Laurie sang on, ignorant of what was occurring at his friends' table. Others nearby, used to the activities of a seaport inn, were making room for impending trouble. Arutha sat on the floor, still groggy from the blow, then reached down and loosened his rapier in its scabbard.

Roald nodded to Martin and both slowly stood, making a show of not pulling weapons. Roald said, "Look, friend, we mean no harm. Had we known this to be your usual table, we'd have stayed clear. We'll find another. Let the boy go."

The man threw back his head and laughed. "Ha! I think I keep him. I know fat Quegan trader give me a hundred gold for a boy so pretty." With a sudden scowl he looked about the table, then his gaze locked on Roald. "You go. The boy will say he's sorry for poking Longly in ribs, then maybe I let him go. Or maybe to fat Quegan he goes."

Arutha slowly rose. It was difficult to know if Longly was seriously intending trouble, but after being struck, Arutha was not about to give the man the benefit of the doubt. The locals obviously knew Longly, and if he was only intending some simple brawling and Arutha was first to pull steel, he could bring down their wrath. The fat man's two companions looked on cautiously.

Roald exchanged another glance with Martin and raised his flagon as if to finish his ale. With a sudden jerk he tossed the contents of the mug into Longly's face, then backhanded the knife bearer in the side of the head with the pewter ale jack. The slender man's eyes rolled upward as he slumped to the floor. The third man was distracted by Roald's sudden move and didn't see Martin's fist as the Duke unloaded a thundering blow, knocking Longly's companion backward over another table. With the sudden action, more prudent customers began a quick exit from the inn. Laurie stopped playing and stood up on the dais to see what the problem was.

One of the barmen, not interested in who was responsible for trouble, sprang over the bar and landed atop the nearest combatant, who happened to be Martin. Longly held fast to Jimmy's wrist, wiping ale from his own face. Laurie carefully put down his lute and with a running jump leaped from the dais to a tabletop and vaulted onto Longly's back. Wrapping his arms around the large man's throat, he began choking him.

Longly rocked forward under the impact, then regained his balance while Laurie clung to him. Ignoring the singer, he looked at Roald, who was ready to fight. "You should not have thrown ale on Longly. Now I'm mad."

Jimmy's face was turning white from the pain of the large man's grip. Laurie said, "Somebody help me! This giant's got a tree trunk for a neck!"

Arutha sprang to his right just as Roald struck Longly in the face. The large man blinked, then, with an insolent toss, threw Jimmy into Roald, knocking the mercenary into Arutha. All three went down in a heap. With his other hand he reached back over his shoulder and grabbed Laurie by the tunic. He flipped the singer overhead, tumbling him over the table. The table leg nearest Jimmy collapsed and Laurie rolled off into Roald and Arutha as they struggled to rise.

Martin had been grappling with the barman and finished off the encounter by tossing him back over the bar. He then reached out and seized Longly by the shoulder, turning him. The red-bearded man's eyes seemed to light at finding an opponent worthy of his mettle. At four inches over six feet, Martin was taller, though giving up pounds to Longly in bulk. Longly's voice sounded in a gleeful shout as he reached out and grabbed at Martin. Instantly they were in a wrestlers' hold, each with his hand around the back of the other's neck, opposite hand holding the other's wrist. For a long moment they swayed, then moved slightly as each sought a better advantage for a throw.

Laurie sat up, shaking his head. "It's not human." Suddenly he realized he was sitting on Roald and Arutha and began disentangling himself.

Jimmy got to his feet, wobbling as he stood. Laurie looked up at the boy as Arutha stood up. "What were you trying to accomplish by pulling that dirk?" Laurie asked the thief. "Get us killed?"

Jimmy looked angrily to where the two big men struggled for advantage. "Nobody talks about me that way. I'm no fop's delight."

Laurie said, "Don't take things so personally." He started to rise. "He just wants to play." Laurie's knees buckled and he had to grab Jimmy to keep his feet. "I think."

Longly was giving out with a strange assortment of grunts as he strove against Martin, while the Duke remained silent. Martin leaned forward, countering Longly's larger bulk with greater height. What had started as a possible bloodletting had settled into a passably friendly wrestling contest, albeit a rough one. Longly suddenly pulled back, but Martin simply followed the move, releasing his hold on Longly's neck but holding on to his wrist. In a single move he was behind the heavy man, holding Longly's arm in a painful position behind his head. The fat man grimaced as Martin put pressure on the hold, slowly forcing him to his knees.

Laurie helped Roald to his feet as the mercenary shook his head, trying to gather his wits. When his vision had cleared, he studied the contest. He said to Laurie, "That can't be very comfortable."

Jimmy said, "I expect that's why his face is turning purple."

Roald started to speak to Jimmy, but something caused his head to turn suddenly toward Arutha. Jimmy and Laurie followed his gaze and their eyes widened.

Arutha, seeing all three staring at him, spun. A black-cloaked figure had managed to approach the table silently while the brawl was in progress. He stood stiffly behind Arutha, a dagger in his right hand poised to strike. The man's eyes stared forward and his mouth moved silently.

Arutha's hand shot out, knocking aside the dagger, but his eyes studied the figure behind the black-clad man. The Hadati warrior Jimmy and Martin had seen at the gate was poised, sword ready for another blow. He had struck silently at the assassin from behind, preventing a successful attack on the Prince. As the dying man collapsed, the Hadati quickly put up his slender sword and said, "Come, there are others."

Jimmy quickly examined the dead man and held up an ebon hawk on a chain. Arutha turned to Martin and said, "Martin! Nighthawks! Finish it!"

Martin nodded to his brother, then, with a wrenching movement that almost dislocated Longly's shoulder, drove him to his knees. Longly looked upward at Martin, then closed his eyes in resignation as the Duke raised his right hand. Halting his strike, Martin said, "What use?" and shoved Longly forward.

The large man fell face downward on the floor and then sat up, rubbing at his painful shoulder. "Ha!" He laughed loudly. "You come back sometime, big hunter. You give Longly good thrashing, by gods!"

They raced out of the inn to the stables. The stableboy nearly fainted at the sight of all these armed men running toward him. Arutha said, "Where are our horses?" The boy pointed toward the rear of the stable.

Martin said, "They'll not stand up to a long run tonight."

Seeing other mounts, fresh and fed, Arutha said, "Who owns these?"

The boy said, "My master, sir. But they are to be sold at auction next week."

Arutha signaled for the others to saddle the fresh mounts. The boy's eyes teared as he said, "Please, sir, don't kill me."

Arutha said, "We'll not kill you, boy."

The boy cowered away while the animals were saddled. The Hadati took a saddle from what was obviously the inn's supply of tack and made a sixth horse ready. Arutha mounted and tossed a pouch at the boy. "Here, tell your master to sell our mounts and make up the difference from what's in the bag. Keep something for yourself."

When all were ready, they rode from the stable, through the gates of the inn courtyard, and down a narrow street. If an alarm was going out, the city gates would soon be closed. A death in a bar brawl was a chancy thing. They could be pursued or not, depending upon which officer of the city watch was on duty that night, as much as for any other cause. Arutha decided to take no chances and they raced for the city's western gate.

The city guards barely took notice when the six horsemen galloped past and disappeared down the highway toward the Free Cities. No alarm had been sounded.

Down the road they flew, until the lights of Ylith were a distant glow in the night behind them. Then Arutha gave the signal to rein in.

He turned to the Hadati. "We must speak."

They dismounted and Martin led them to a small glade some distance from the road. As Jimmy tethered the horses, Arutha said, "Who are you?"

"I am Baru, called the Serpentslayer," answered the Hadati.

Laurie said, "That is a name of power." He explained to Arutha, "To earn his name, Baru killed a wyvern."

Arutha looked at Martin, who inclined his head in respect. "To hunt dragonkind takes courage, strength of arm, and luck." Wyverns were first cousins to dragons. The difference was mainly of size. To face one was to face rage and talons, speed and fangs, twelve feet high at the shoulder.

The Hadati smiled for the first time. "You are a hunter, as your bow proclaims, Duke Martin." At this Roald's eyes widened. "Mostly, it takes luck."

Roald stared at Martin. "Duke Martin . . ." He then looked at Arutha. "Then you'd be . . ."

The Hadati said, "He is Prince Arutha, son of Lord Borric and brother to our King. Did you not know?"

Roald sat back silently shaking his head in an emphatic no. He looked at Laurie. "This is the first time you've *ever* told only part of a story."

Laurie said, "It's a long one and even stranger than the other."

He said to Baru, "I see you are a northerner, but I do not know your clan."

The Hadati fingered his plaid. "This signifies I am of Ordwinson's family of the Iron Hills Clan. My people live near the place you city men call Lake of the Sky."

"You Bloodquest?"

He indicated the rolled scarf about his forehead. "I quest. I am Wayfinder."

Roald said, "He's a sort of holy man . . . ah, Highness."

Laurie said, "A consecrated warrior. The scarf contains the names of all his ancestors. They can have no rest until he finishes his mission. He's taken a vow to complete the Bloodquest or die."

"How do you know me?" asked Arutha.

"I saw you on your way to the peace conference with the Tsurani at the end of the war. There is little about those days any of my clan will forget." He looked off into the night. "When our King called to us, we came to fight the Tsurani, and for nine years and more we did so. They were strong foemen, willing to die for honor, men who understood their place on the Wheel. It was a worthy struggle.

"Then, in the spring of the last year of the war, the Tsurani came in great number. For three days and nights we fought, surrendering ground at great cost to the Tsurani. On the third day we who came from the Iron Hills were surrounded. Every fighting man of the Iron Hills Clan was numbered among those who stood at bay. To a man we should have died, save that Lord Borric saw us imperiled. Had not your father sortied to save us, our names would be but whispers upon yesterday's wind."

Arutha recalled that Lyam's letter about his father's death had mentioned Hadati. "What has my father's death to do with me?"

Baru shrugged. "I don't know. I was seeking knowledge at the gate. Many pass there, and I was asking questions to aid my quest. Then I saw you pass. I thought it would be interesting to discover why the Prince of Krondor would enter one of his own cities as a common fighter. It would help pass the time while I sought information. Then the assassin came, and I couldn't stand idly by and watch him slaughter you. Your father saved the manhood of my people. I saved your life. Perhaps that pays a debt in part. Who can know how the Wheel turns?"

Arutha said, "At the inn you said there were others?"

"The man who tried to kill you followed you into the inn, watched you for a moment, then returned outside. There he spoke to a street boy, giving him money, and the boy ran off. He saw the three who fought with you and stopped them before they could pass. I heard nothing that was said, but he pointed to the inn and the three entered."

Arutha said, "Then the fight was staged."

Jimmy, who had finished with the horses, said, "More likely he knew Longly's temper and made sure he knew some strangers were at his usual table, in case they were heading somewhere else and might miss us."

Laurie said, "He might have wanted to keep us busy until others arrived, then saw what he thought was too good a chance to miss."

Arutha said, "Had you not been there, Baru, it would have been too good a chance to miss."

The Hadati took this as thanks and said, "There is no debt. As I said, it may be I who am paying off a debt."

Roald said, "Well then, I guess you've sorted everything out. I'll be off for Ylith."

Arutha exchanged glances with Laurie. The minstrel said, "Roald, old friend, I think you should change your plans."

"What?"

"Well, should you have been noticed with the Prince, which seems likely, as there were thirty or forty people in the inn when the brawl broke out, those who are looking for him may decide to ask you where we're bound."

With false bravado Roald said, "Just let them try."

Martin said, "We'd rather not. They can be determined. I've had dealings with moredhel before, and they lack tenderness."

Roald's eyes widened. "The Brotherhood of the Dark Path?"

Martin nodded and Laurie said, "Besides, you're presently at liberty."

"Which is how I plan to stay."

Arutha tried a sterner stand. "You'd say no to your Prince?"

"No disrespect intended, Highness, but I'm a free man not in your service and I've broken no laws. You have no authority over me."

"Look," said Laurie, "there's a likelihood these assassins are going to look hard for anyone seen with us. And even though you're as tough a boot as I've known, I've seen what they can do and I'd not risk being taken alone by them." Roald's resolve seemed unshaken.

Martin said, "We could certainly find some reward for service."

Roald, visibly brightening, said, "How much?"

Arutha replied, "Stay until we complete our quest and I'll pay you . . . a hundred golden sovereigns."

Without hesitation Roald said, "Done!" It was easily four months' wages for even a seasoned caravan guard.

Arutha then looked at Baru. "You spoke of needing information. Can we aid your Bloodquest?"

"Perhaps. I seek to find one of those you know as the Brotherhood of the Dark Path."

Martin raised an eyebrow at Arutha. "What have you to do with the moredhel?"

"I seek a large moredhel of the Yabon hills, who wears a topknot, so"—he pantomimed a horsetail of hair—"and three scars upon each cheek. I have been told he has come to the south on some black mission. I had hoped to hear of him from travelers, for one like that will stand out among the moredhel of the south."

Arutha said, "If he has no tongue, then he attacked us on our way to Sarth."

"That is him," said Baru. "The tongueless one is called Murad. He is a chieftain of the Clan Raven moredhel, blood enemies of my people since the dawn of time. Even his own people fear him. The scars upon his face speak of pacts with dark powers, though little beyond that is known. He has not been seen in years, since before the Riftwar when moredhel moss-troopers raided across the hill borders of Yabon.

"He is the cause of the Bloodquest. He was seen again two months ago when he led a band of black-armored warriors past one of our villages. For no good reason he paused long enough to destroy the village, burning every building and killing everyone there except the herdsboy who described him to me. It was my village."

With an almost resigned sigh he said, "If he was near Sarth, then there I must go next. This moredhel has lived too long."

Arutha nodded to Laurie, who said, "Actually, Baru, if you stay with us, he'll most likely come looking for you." Baru looked quizzically at the Prince, and Arutha told him of Murmandamus and his servants and the quest for Anita's cure.

When he had finished, the Hadati grinned and there was no humor in it. "Then I shall take service with you, Highness, if you will accept me, for fate has thrown us together. You are hunted by my enemy and I will have his head before he can have yours."

"Good," said Arutha. "You will be welcome, for we follow a dangerous road."

Martin stiffened, and in almost the same instant Baru was coming to his feet, moving toward the trees behind the Duke. Martin signaled for silence, and before the others could move, he vanished into the trees, a step behind the hillman. The others began to move until Arutha motioned for them to hold. As they stood motionless in the dark, they heard what had alerted Martin and the Hadati. Echoing through the night was the sound of riders coming down the road from Ylith.

Long minutes passed, then the sound of hoofbeats passed, heading southwest. A few more minutes after, Martin and Baru reappeared. Martin whispered, "Riders, a dozen or more, moving down the road as if there were demons coming behind."

"Black armor?" asked Arutha.

Martin said, "No, these were human, and hard to see in the dark, but I judge them a rough crew."

"The Nighthawks could have hired extra bashers if they needed. Ylith's that sort of town," Laurie said.

Jimmy agreed. "Maybe only one or two were Nighthawks, but hired knives kill as quickly as any others."

Baru said, "They head toward the Free Cities."

"They'll be back," said Roald. Arutha turned to look at the mercenary in the gloom, barely seeing his face in the faint moonlight. "Your Baron Talanque has a new customs shed down the road five miles. My caravan passed it this afternoon. Seems there's been some new smuggling from Natal of late. They'll find out from the guards no one passed this night, and they'll be back."

"Then," said Arutha, "we must be away. The question is how we reach Elvandar. I planned on traveling the road north to Yabon, then going west."

Roald said, "From Ylith north you'll meet some who know you from the war, Highness. Especially around LaMut. Had I any wits about me, I'd have figured it out after a while."

"Then which way?" asked the Prince.

Martin said, "We could head straight west from here, take the South Pass, and run the Grey Towers along the western face through the Green Heart. It's dangerous, but . . ."

Arutha said, "But goblins and trolls are known enemies. That is how we shall travel. Now let's be off."

They mounted and moved out, Martin in the lead. Slowly they wended their way through the dark and silent forests, heading west. Arutha hid his anger, forcing it down within. The uneventful trip from Sarth to Ylith had lulled him, making him forget for a while what dangers existed. But the ambush at the inn and the pursuing riders had turned his awareness back to the dangers. Murmandamus and his agents might have been denied their magic means of finding him, but they still had a net out, one that had nearly caught him.

Jimmy rode last in line, and he watched behind for a while, hoping not to see signs of followers. Soon sight of the road was lost in the darkness, and the boy returned his attention to Roald's and Laurie's backs, the only things he could see before him.

THIRTEEN

STARDOCK

The wind whipped the water to white foam.

Gardan looked at the distant shore of Stardock, wishing he could ride to the academy instead of trusting fate to keep a barge right side up. Still, it was on an island. He had endured sea voyages before, but despite a lifetime living in a seaport he hated traveling over water, though he would never openly admit as much.

They had left Krondor by ship, traveling down the coast until they entered the narrows between the Bitter Sea and the Sea of Dreams, which was more of a giant saltwater lake than a true sea. At Shamata they had commandeered horses and followed the river Dawlin to its source, the Great Star Lake. Now they stood waiting for the barge to put in. It was poled by two men in simple tunics and trousers, local peasants by the look of them. In a moment Gardan, Brother Dominic, Kasumi, and six Tsurani guards would step aboard and be poled to Stardock Island, almost a mile away.

Gardan shivered in the unseasonably cool air. It was spring, but the late afternoon air had none of the warmth expected at this time of year. "I'm the fugitive from a hot land, Captain," said Kasumi with a chuckle.

Gardan's voice had little humor in it as he replied, "No, it is cold here, but there's something else. I've felt nothing but dark foreboding since leaving the Prince." Brother Dominic said nothing, but his expression showed he shared the feeling.

Kasumi nodded. He had stayed in Krondor to guard the King, and when Arutha's messages arrived he had accepted Lyam's charge to accompany Gardan and the Ishapian monk to Stardock. Besides his desire to visit Pug again, there had been something in Lyam's orders that made him believe the King counted the monk's safe arrival at Stardock vital.

The barge put in to shore and one of the two bargemen stepped ashore. "We'll have to make two trips to carry the horses, sir," he said.

Kasumi, who was senior, said, "That will be fine." He indicated five of his men and said, "These will go first; we will follow."

Gardan said nothing about going second; he had no desire to rush the coming ordeal. The five Tsurani led their animals aboard and took up position silently. Whatever they might think about journeying on the wallowing barge, they maintained their stoic demeanor.

The barge put out, and Gardan watched quietly. Save for faint signs of activity on the far island, the southern shore of the Great Star Lake was deserted. Why, wondered Gardan, would anyone choose to live in such isolation? Legend had it a star fell from the sky, creating the lake. But whatever the lake's origins, no community had ever arisen upon its shores.

The lone remaining Tsurani guard said something in his own language to Kasumi, pointing to the northeast. Kasumi looked where the man pointed.

Gardan and Dominic looked as well. In the distance, close to the horizon and coming before the approaching night, several winged figures could be seen gliding swiftly toward them. "What are they?" asked Kasumi. "Those are the biggest birds I've seen on your world so far. They appear to be nearly man-sized."

Gardan squinted. Suddenly Dominic shouted, "Ishap's grace! Everyone back to shore."

The bargemen looked back from where they were making slow, steady progress. Seeing Gardan and the others draw weapons, they quickly pushed back for land. The approaching figures could now be seen as they raced toward the party on shore. One of the boatmen cried out in fear and prayed to Dala for protection.

The nude creatures were grotesquely human-shaped, male, with blue skins and powerfully muscled torsos. Shoulder and chest muscles flexed as giant batlike wings beat the air. Their heads resembled those of hairless monkeys, and each waved a long, prehensile tail. Gardan counted: there were an even dozen of them. With impossibly high shrieks, they dove straight at the party on shore.

As his horse bolted, Gardan lunged to one side, barely avoiding the outstretched claws of one of the creatures. A scream sounded behind, and Gardan glimpsed one of the bargemen being carried aloft by a creature. It hovered for an instant with a powerful beat of its wings, holding the man by the neck. With a contemptuous cry it ripped out the bargeman's throat and dropped him. In a spray of blood, the man fell to the water.

Gardan struck out at one of the creatures, which sought to grab him in the same manner. The blade struck it squarely in the face, but the creature only withdrew with a back beat of its wings. There was no apparent mark upon it where the sword had struck. It grimaced, shook its head, then launched another attack. Gardan fell back, focusing his entire concentration on the creature's outstretched hands. Very humanlike fingers ending in long talons raked across the steel of his blade as he parried. The captain wished his horse had stood long enough for him to retrieve his shield.

"What manner of beings are these?" Kasumi shouted as the barge got close enough for the five Tsurani to leap for the shore.

Dominic's voice could be heard somewhere behind. "They are elemental creatures, fashioned by black arts. Our weapons have no effect."

The Tsurani seemed unperturbed despite that fact, attacking the creatures as they would any enemy, with no hesitation. While the blows received did no damage to the creatures, they obviously inflicted pain, for the Tsurani's onslaught caused the creatures to withdraw and hover for a moment.

Gardan looked and found Kasumi and Dominic close by. They both had shields and stood at the ready. Then the creatures were on them again. A soldier screamed, and Gardan caught a glimpse of a Tsurani falling nearby.

Gardan saw Kasumi avoid the rush of two of the creatures, using sword, shield, and agility to good advantage. But the captain knew there was no hope of survival, for it would be only a matter of time before they tired and slowed. The creatures showed no sign of fatigue and were attacking with as much fury as when they arrived.

Dominic lashed out with his mace, and a creature warbled a high-pitched note of pain. If weapons could not cut the magically constructed hide, then at least they could break bones. The creature fluttered in a circle, trying desperately to stay aloft, but slowly it approached the ground. From the way one wing lamely flapped, it was obvious Dominic had broken its shoulder.

Gardan dodged another attack and danced to one side. Behind the two creatures attacking him he saw the wounded one touch the ground. As soon as its feet made contact with the earth, the creature emitted an ear-splitting howl of pain and burst into a shower of sparkling energies. With a flash, near-blinding in the evening gloom, it vanished, leaving only a smoking patch on the ground. Dominic shouted, "They are elementals of the air! They cannot abide the touch of earth!"

Gardan swung a mighty overhand blow at the creature on his right. The force of the blow drove the creature downward. It made the briefest contact with the earth, but that was enough. Like the other, it exploded into sparks. In panic, it had reached out a hand and gripped the trailing tail of the creature beside it, as if trying to pull itself away from the destruction below. The sparking energy traveled up the tail of the second creature and it, too, was consumed.

Kasumi whirled about and saw that three of his six men lay dead. The creatures now numbered nine, and they swarmed the remaining fighters, though there was now an element of caution in their approach. One swooped down toward Dominic, who braced for the attack. Instead of reaching out for the monk, the elemental beat backward against the air, buffeting the cleric, seeking to knock him down. Gardan raced up behind the creature, ducking to avoid claws reaching for him. He lunged forward, barely keeping sword in hand, and threw his arms about the dangling legs of the creature facing Dominic. He hugged them close, his face buried against the naked thigh of the thing. His stomach churned at the stench from the elemental's body, the odor of things long dead and best buried. His unexpected weight pulled the thing downward. It shrieked and beat its wings furiously, but it was off balance and Gardan pulled it to the ground. Like the others, it burst into sparks.

Gardan rolled away, feeling pain erupt along his arms and chest, where he had gripped the creature when it exploded: he had been burned in the process of destroying it. He ignored the pain and felt a growing hope. Those on the shore numbered seven—Gardan, Kasumi, Dominic, three soldiers, and a boatman wielding a pole—and the creatures were now only eight.

For a moment the attacking elementals chose to circle overhead, out of reach of the surviving soldiers' weapons. As they began to peel off for a swooping attack, a shimmering began a short distance down the beach from the defenders. Gardan prayed to Tith, god of soldiers, that it wasn't the arrival of another attacker. One more foe would surely tip the balance and overwhelm them.

With a flickering of light a man appeared upon the beach, dressed in simple black tunic and trousers. Gardan and Kasumi at once recognized Pug and shouted a warning to him. The magician calmly surveyed the situation. One creature, seeing an unarmed opponent, howled with maniacal glee and dove for him.

Pug stood his ground, showing no defense. The diving creature reached a point less than ten feet from him, then crashed into an invisible barrier. As if it had struck a stone wall, the creature crumpled to the ground. It vanished in another blinding flash.

Shrieks of panic sounded overhead, as the remaining creatures now understood that here was a foe beyond their powers to harm. As one, the seven remaining creatures turned and began a headlong flight northward.

Pug waved his hands and suddenly a blue fire danced upon his upraised palms. He cast it after the fleeing creatures. The sphere of blue fire sped after the elementals and caught up with them as they winged furiously over the water. Like a cloud of pulsating light, it enveloped them. Strangled cries of pain could be heard as the elementals contorted in midair and fell twitching into the lake. As each touched the surface of the water, it erupted into green flame, consumed as it vanished under the rippling surface of the lake.

Gardan watched Pug as he approached the nearly exhausted soldiers. There was something unusually somber in Pug's expression and his gaze held a hint of power Gardan had never seen before. Abruptly, Pug's expression changed as he relaxed. His face now looked young, boyish in spite of his nearly twenty-six years of age. With a sudden smile he said, "Welcome to Stardock, gentlemen."

A warm fire filled the room with a cozy glow. Gardan and Dominic rested in large chairs set before the fireplace, while Kasumi sat on cushions, Tsurani fashion.

Kulgan dressed the captain's burns, fussing like a mother over her idiot child. The two had known each other for years at Crydee, well enough for Kulgan to take a rough tone with the captain. "How you could be foolish enough to grab on to one of those things—anyone knows that contact with an elementally dependent creature when it returns to a primal state involves the release of energies, mostly heat and light."

Gardan, tired of being scolded, said, "Well, I didn't know. Kasumi, did you know? Dominic?"

Kasumi sat laughing as Dominic said, "As a matter of fact, I did know."

"You are no help at all, priest," muttered the captain. "Kulgan, if you are done, can we eat? I've been smelling that hot food for nearly an hour and it's close to making me go mad."

Pug laughed, leaning against the wall next to the hearth. "Captain, it's more like ten minutes."

They were sitting in a room in the first floor of a large building under construction. Kasumi said, "I am glad the King permitted me to visit your academy, Pug."

"And I as well," said Brother Dominic. "While we at Sarth appreciate those copies of works you've forwarded to us so far, we are still vague about what your plans are. We seek to know more."

Pug said, "I am pleased to host any who come with the love of learning, Brother Dominic. Perhaps someday we may claim repayment of our slight hospitality and visit your fabled library."

Kulgan's head came around at that. "I would be pleased to claim that right, friend Dominic."

"Anytime you call, you'll be welcome," answered the monk.

"Watch this one," said Gardan with a tilt of his head toward Kulgan. "Lose him in those underground vaults and you'll never find him. He's as passionate for books as a bear for honey."

A striking woman with dark hair and large, dark eyes entered the room, followed by two servants. All carried platters with food, and as she placed hers upon the long table at the other end of the room from where the men were gathered, she said, "Please, it is time for supper."

Pug said, "Brother Dominic, this is my wife, Katala."

The monk nodded deferentially and said, "My lady."

She smiled at him. "Please, Katala. We tend to the informal here."

The monk again inclined his head as he came to the indicated chair. He turned at the sound of a door opening, and for the first time since the captain had met him, the monk's composure cracked. William came hurrying into the room, the green-scaled form of Fantus behind.

"Ishap's mercy! Is that a firedrake?"

William ran to where his father stood and hugged him, eyeing the newcomers cautiously. Kulgan said, "This is Fantus, lord of this estate. The rest of us live here by his sufferance, though he suffers William's company best." The drake's gaze shifted to Kulgan for a moment as if he agreed totally. Then his large red eyes returned to contemplating the table and what lay upon it.

Pug said, "William, say hello to Kasumi."

William bowed his head slightly, smiling. He spoke in the Tsurani tongue, and Kasumi answered, laughing.

Dominic looked interested. Pug said, "My son is fluent in both the King's Tongue and the Tsurani language. My wife and I keep him practicing both, for many of my works are in the Tsurani language. That is one of the problems I have in bringing the art of the Greater Path to Midkemia. Much of what I do is the result of how I think, and I think magic in the Tsurani language. William's going to be a great help someday, aiding me in discovering ways to do magic in the King's Tongue so I can teach those who live here."

Katala said, "Gentlemen, the food grows cold."

"And my wife does not permit talking of magic at this table," said Pug.

Kulgan snorted at this, and Katala said, "If I did, these two would hardly get a mouthful."

Gardan moved with alacrity, despite his discomfort, saying, "I don't have to be warned more than once." He sat down and immediately one of the servants began filling his platter.

Dinner proceeded pleasantly, with talk of small things. As if the terrors of the day had vanished with the night, all mention of the grim events that had brought Gardan, Dominic, and Kasumi to Stardock were ignored. Nothing about Arutha's quest, the threat of Murmandamus, or the portent of the abbey was said. For a short time no discord existed. For a brief hour, the world was a pleasant place with old friends, and new guests, enjoying one another's company.

Then William was making his good-nights. Dominic was struck by the resemblance between boy and mother, though his manner of moving and speaking was in open imitation of his father. Fantus had been fed from William's plate and padded out of the room behind him.

"I still can hardly credit my senses where that drake is concerned," said Dominic after they had left.

"He's been Kulgan's pet as long as I can remember," said Gardan.

Kulgan, who was lighting a pipe, said, "Ha! No longer. That boy and Fantus have been inseparable since the day they met."

Katala said, "There is something beyond the ordinary with those two. At times I think they understand each other."

Dominic said, "Lady Katala, there is little about this place which is not beyond the ordinary. This gathering together of magicians, this construction, that is all extraordinary."

Pug rose and led the others to the chairs near the fire. "But understand that upon Kelewan, when I studied at the Assembly, what you see aborning here was ancient and established. The brotherhood of magicians was an accepted fact, as was the common sharing of knowledge."

Kulgan puffed contentedly upon his pipe. "Which is as it should be."

Pug said, "We can discuss the rise of the academy at Stardock tomorrow, when I can show you our community. I'll read the messages from Arutha and the Abbot tonight. I know all that led up to Arutha's leaving Krondor, Gardan. What occurred between there and Sarth?"

The captain, who had been feeling drowsy, forced himself alert and quickly told of the events from Krondor to Sarth. Brother Dominic remained silent, since the captain forgot nothing of significance. Then it was the monk's turn, as he explained what he knew of the attack upon the abbey. When he had finished, Pug and Kulgan asked several questions but withheld comment.

Pug said, "The news you carry is cause for the deepest concern. Still, the hour is late, and I think there are others upon this island who should be consulted. I suggest we show these tired and sore gentlemen to their rooms and begin discussions in earnest tomorrow."

Gardan, who could feel a yawn beginning, stifled it and nodded. Kasumi, Brother Dominic, and the captain were escorted from the room by Kulgan, who bade the others good night.

Pug left the fireside and crossed to a window, where he stood watching the little moon's light reflecting off the water as it peeked through the cloud cover. Katala came up behind her husband and her arms went around his waist.

"You are troubled by this news, husband." It was a statement, not a question.

"As always, you know my mind." He turned within the circle of her arms and drew her closer, smelling the sweetness of her hair as he kissed her cheek. "I had hoped we would live out our lives with the building of this academy and the raising of children our only concerns."

She smiled up at him, dark eyes mirroring the unending love she felt for her man. "Among the Thuril we have a saying: 'Life is problems. Living is solving problems.' " He smiled at this. She said, "Still, it is true. What do you think of the news Kasumi and the others brought?"

"I do not know." He stroked her brown hair. "Lately I have felt a growing gnawing feeling inside. I have thought it simply worry over the progress we make here in building the academy, but it is more than that. My nights have been filled with dreams."

"I know, Pug. I have seen you struggle in your sleep. You have yet to speak to me of them."

He looked at her. "I had no wish to trouble you, love. I thought them mere ghosts of memories from the times of trouble. But now I . . . I am not sure. One returns with frequency, coming more often lately. A voice in a dark place cries out to me. It seeks my aid, begs for help."

She said nothing, for she knew her husband and would wait until he was ready to share his feelings. Finally he said, "I know the voice, Katala. I have heard it before, when the time of troubles was full upon us at its most dreadful moment, when the outcome of the Riftwar hung in the balance, when the fate of two worlds rested upon my shoulders. It's Macros. It's his voice I hear."

Katala shivered and hugged her husband close. The name of Macros the Black, whose library served as the seed for this growing academy of magic, was one she knew well. Macros was the mysterious sorcerer, neither of the Greater Path like Pug, nor of the Lesser Path like Kulgan, but something else. He had lived long enough to seem eternal and he could read the future. He had always had a hand in the conduct of the Riftwar, playing some cosmic game with human lives for stakes only he understood. He had rid Midkemia of the rift, the magic bridge between her own homeworld and her new one. She nestled closer to Pug, her head on his chest. Most of all, she knew why Pug was troubled. Macros was dead.

Gardan, Kasumi, and Dominic stood at ground level admiring the work proceeding above. Workers contracted in Shamata were laying course after course of stone, building up the high walls of the academy. Pug and Kulgan stood nearby, inspecting the newest plans submitted by the Masterbuilder in charge of construction. Kulgan motioned for the newcomers to join them. "This is all vital to us, so you will please indulge us a bit, I trust," said the stout mage. "We have been at work for only a few months and we are anxious to see the work uninterrupted."

Gardan said, "This building will be immense."

"Twenty-five stories tall, with several higher towers for observing the heavens."

Dominic said, "That is incredible. Such a building could house thousands."

Kulgan's blue eyes sparkled merrily. "From what Pug has told me, it is but a part of what he knew in the City of Magicians on the other world. There an entire city has grown together into a single gigantic edifice. When we have completed our work, years from now, we shall have only one-twentieth part of that, or less. Still, there is room to grow, if needs be. Someday, perhaps, the academy may cover this entire island of Stardock."

The Masterbuilder left, and Pug said, "I am sorry for the interruption, but some decisions needed to be made. Come, let's continue the inspection."

Following the wall, they rounded a corner to come upon a group of buildings looking like nothing so much as a small village. Here they could see men and women in various manner of dress, Kingdom and Keshian, moving among the buildings. Several children played in a square at the center of the village. One of them was William. Dominic looked about and saw Fantus lying near a doorway in the sunlight, a short distance away. The children were frantically trying to kick a ball fashioned of rags bound in leather into a barrel. The game seemed devoid of rules of conduct or play.

Dominic laughed at the sight. "I used to play the same game on Sixthdays when I was a boy."

Pug smiled. "As did I. Much of what we plan has yet to be implemented, so for the present the children's duties are occasional things. They don't seem to mind."

"What is this place?" asked Dominic.

"For the time being, it is the home of our young community. The wing where Kulgan and my family have our rooms, as well as some instruction rooms, is the only part of the academy ready for use. It was the first section completed, though construction still continues above on the upper floors. Those who travel to Stardock to learn and serve at the academy live here, until more quarters can be made ready in the main building." He motioned for them to follow him into a large building that dominated the village. William left the game and tagged along beside his father. Pug placed his hand upon the boy's shoulder. "How are your studies today?"

The boy made a face. "Not so good. I gave up today. Nothing works as it should."

Pug's expression turned serious, but Kulgan gave William a playful push back toward the game. "Run along, boy. Worry not, your father was equally hardheaded when he was my student. It will come in time."

Pug half smiled. "Hardheaded?"

Kulgan said, "Perhaps 'slow-witted' would be a better way to put it."

Entering the door, Pug said, "Until the day I die, Kulgan will make sport of me."

The building turned out to be a hollow shell. Its only purpose seemed to be to house a large table running the length of it. The only other feature of the room was a hearth. The high ceiling was supported by rafter beams, from which hung lanterns that gave off a cheery light.

Pug pulled out a chair at the end of the table, signaling for the others to sit as well.

Dominic was pleased with the fire. Even if it was late spring, this day was chilly. He said, "What of the women and children about?"

Kulgan withdrew his pipe from his belt and began to stuff the bowl with tabac. "The children are the sons and daughters of those who have come here. We have plans to organize a school for them. Pug has some strange notions about educating everyone in the

Kingdom someday, though I don't see universal education becoming the vogue. The women are either the wives of magicians or magicians themselves, women commonly regarded as witches."

Dominic appeared troubled. "Witches?"

Kulgan lit his pipe with a flame on the end of his finger and exhaled a cloud of smoke. "What is in a name? They practice magic. For reasons I do not understand, men have at least been somewhat tolerated for practicing magic in many places, while women have been driven from nearly every community where they are discovered to have power."

Dominic said, "But it is held that witches gain their powers by serving dark forces."

Kulgan waved the notion aside. "Nonsense. That is superstition, if you'll forgive my being blunt. The source of their power is no more dark than your own, and their behavior is usually a great deal kinder than that of some of the more enthusiastic, if misguided, servants of some temples."

Dominic said, "True, but you are speaking of a recognized member of a legitimate temple."

Kulgan looked directly at Dominic. "Forgive the observation, but in spite of the Ishapian reputation for a more worldly view than that of other orders, your remarks are profoundly provincial. So what if these poor wretches do not toil within a temple?

"If a woman serves in a temple she is holy, and if she comes to her power in a hut in the woods she is a witch? Even my old friend Father Tully wouldn't swallow that piece of dogmatic tripe. You are not speaking of any inherent question of good or evil; you're talking about who's got a better guild."

Dominic smiled. "You, then, seek to build a better guild?"

Kulgan blew out a cloud of smoke. "In a sense, yes, though that is less the reason for what we do than is trying to codify as much magic lore as possible."

Dominic said, "Forgive my harsh questions, but one of my charges was to determine the source of your motivation. The King is your powerful ally, and our temple was concerned that there might be some hidden purpose behind your activities. It was thought, as long as I was coming here . . ."

Pug finished, "You might as well challenge what we do and see what we say?"

Kasumi said, "As long as I have known Pug, he has acted with honor."

Dominic went on, "Had I a single doubt, I would have said nothing now. That your purposes are only the highest is not in doubt. Just . . ."

Pug and Kulgan both said, "What?"

"It is clear you seek to establish a community of scholars, more than anything else. That, in and of itself, is laudable. But you will not always be here. Someday this academy could be a powerful tool in the wrong hands."

Pug said, "We are taking every precaution to avoid that pitfall, believe me."

Dominic said, "I do."

Pug's expression changed, as if he had heard something. "They are coming," he said.

Kulgan watched with rapt attention. "Gamina?" he asked in a whisper.

Pug nodded, and Kulgan made a satisfied "Ah" sound. "The contact was better than ever. She grows in power each week."

Pug explained to the others, "I read the reports you brought last night and have summoned here one who I think may help. With him comes another."

Kulgan said, "The other is . . . one able to send thoughts and receive them with remarkable clarity. At present she is the only one we have found able to do so. Pug has told of a similar ability on Kelewan, used during his training, but it required preparation of the subject."

Pug said, "It is like the mind touch used by some priests, but there is no need for physical contact, or even proximity, it seems. Nor is there the attendant danger of being caught up in the mind of the one touched. Gamina is a rare talent." Dominic was impressed. Pug continued, "She touches the mind and it is as if she speaks. We have hopes of someday understanding this wild talent and learning a way to train others to it."

Kulgan said, "I hear them approaching." He rose. "Please, gentlemen, Gamina is something of a timid soul, one who has undergone difficult times. Remember that and be gentle with her."

Kulgan opened the door and two people entered. The man was ancient, with a few stray wisps of hair, like white smoke, falling to his shoulders. His hand was on the other's shoulder and he walked stooped over, showing some slight deformity under his red robe. From the milky orbs that stared blankly ahead it was obvious the old man was blind.

But it was the girl who commanded their attention. She wore homespun and appeared about seven years old, a tiny thing who clutched at the hand upon her shoulder. Her blue eyes were enormous, illuminating a pale face of delicate features. Her hair was almost as white as the old man's, holding only a hint of gold. What struck Dominic, Gardan, and Kasumi was an overwhelming feeling that this child was perhaps the most beautiful they had ever seen. Already they could see in those childish features the promise of a woman of unsurpassed beauty.

Kulgan guided the old man to a chair next to his own. The girl did not sit, but chose to stand beside the man, both hands on his shoulder, fingers flexing nervously, as if she feared to lose contact with him. She looked at the three strangers with the expression of a cornered wild thing. She took no pains to disguise her distrust.

Pug said, "This is Rogen."

The blind man leaned forward. "Whom do I meet?" His face, despite the age it showed, was alive and smiling, uptilted as if to hear better. It was evident that he, unlike the girl, enjoyed the prospect of meeting newcomers.

Pug introduced the three men, who sat opposite Kulgan and Rogen. The blind man's smile broadened. "I am pleased to meet you, worthy gentlemen."

Then Pug said, "This is Gamina."

Dominic and the others were startled when the girl's voice sounded in their heads. *Hello.*

The girl's mouth had not moved. She was motionless, her enormous blue eyes fixed upon them.

Gardan said, "Did she speak?"

Kulgan answered, "With her mind. She has no other power of speech."

Rogen reached up to pat the girl's hands. "Gamina was born with this gift, though she nearly drove her mother crazy with her silent crying." The old man's face became solemn. "Gamina's mother and father were stoned to death by the people of her village, for having birthed a demon. Poor, superstitious people they were. They feared to kill the baby, thinking she would revert to her 'natural' form and slay them all, so they left her in the forest to die of exposure. She was not yet three years old."

Gamina looked at the old man with penetrating eyes. He turned to face her, as if he could see her, and said, "Yes, that is when I found you."

To the others he said, "I was living in the forest, in an abandoned hunter's lodge I had discovered. I also was driven from my home village, but that was years earlier. I foretold the death of the town miller and was blamed for it. I was branded a warlock."

Pug said, "Rogen has the power of second sight, perhaps to compensate for his blindness. He has been without sight since birth."

Rogen smiled broadly and patted the girl's hands. "We are alike, we two, in many ways. I had grown to fear what would become of the girl when I die." He interrupted himself to speak to the girl, who had become agitated at his words. She stood shaking, her eyes welling up with tears. "Hush," he scolded gently. "I will, too—everyone does. I hope not too soon, though," he added with a chuckle. He returned to his narrative. "We came from a village near Salador. When word reached us of this wondrous place, we started our journey. It took six months to walk here, mostly because I am so old. Now we have found people like ourselves, who view us as a source of knowledge, not a source of fear. We are home."

Dominic shook his head, amazed that a man his age and a child had walked hundreds of miles. He was obviously moved. "I am beginning to understand another part of what it is you do here. Are there many more like these two?"

Pug said, "Not as many as I would like. Some of the more established magicians refuse to join us. Others fear us. They will not reveal their abilities. Others simply do not yet know we exist. But some, like Rogen, seek us out. We have nearly fifty practitioners of magic here."

"That is a great many," said Gardan.

Kasumi said, "In the Assembly there were two thousand Great Ones."

Pug nodded. "We also had nearly that number who followed the Lesser Path. And of those who rose to the black robe, the sign of the Greater Magician, each was but one in five who began training, under conditions more rigorous than we are capable of here or would desire."

Dominic looked at Pug. "What of the others, those who failed their training?"

"They were killed," Pug answered flatly.

Dominic judged it a topic Pug did not wish to pursue. A flicker of fear crossed the girl's face and Rogen said, "Hush, hush. No one will hurt you here. He was speaking of a faraway place. Someday you will be a great teacher."

The girl relaxed, and a faint flicker of pride in her expression could be seen. It was obvious she doted upon the old man.

Pug said, "Rogen, there is something taking place that your powers may aid us in understanding. Will you help?"

"Is it that important?"

"I would not ask if it were not vital. Princess Anita lies in peril and Prince Arutha is at constant risk from some unknown enemy."

The girl became worried, or at least that was how Gardan and Dominic read her expression. Rogen cocked his head, as if listening, then said, "I know it is dangerous, but we owe Pug a great deal. He and Kulgan are the only hope for people like ourselves." Both men appeared embarrassed by this but said nothing. "Besides, Arutha is the King's brother, and it was their father who gave us all this wonderful island to live on. How would people feel if they knew we could have helped but didn't?"

Pug spoke softly to Dominic. "Rogen's second sight . . . is different from any I've heard of. Your order is reputed to have some knowledge of prophecy." Dominic nodded. "He sees . . . probabilities is the best way I can describe it. What *may* happen. It seems to require a great deal of his energies, and though he is tougher than he looks, he is still quite old. It is easier if only one person speaks to him, and as you have the best understanding of the nature of the magic that has occurred, I think it would be better for you to tell him all you know." Dominic agreed. Pug said, "If everyone else will please remain silent."

Rogen reached across the table and took the cleric's hands. Dominic was surprised at the strength remaining in those withered old fingers. While not able to foretell himself, Dominic was familiar with the process as performed by those of his order. He cleared his mind, then began to tell his story from when Jimmy first ran afoul of the Nighthawk upon the rooftop to when Arutha left Sarth. Rogen remained silent. Gamina did not move. When Dominic spoke of the prophecy naming Arutha "Bane of Darkness," the old man shuddered and his lips moved silently.

The mood in the room became ominous as the monk spoke. Even the fire seemed to dim. Gardan found he was hugging himself as he sat.

When the monk halted, Rogen continued to clutch his hand, not allowing the other to pull away. His head was raised, neck arched slightly backward, as if he were listening to something distant. His lips worked without sound for a while, then slowly words were forming, though so quietly they were not distinguishable. All at once he spoke clearly, his voice firm. "There is a . . . presence . . . a being. I see a city, a mighty bastion of towers and walls. Upon its walls stand proud men willing to defend it to the end. Now . . . it's a city under siege. I see it overwhelmed, with its towers ablaze. . . . It's a city being murdered. A great savage host runs in its streets as it falls. Those who fight are sorely pressed and withdraw to a keep. Those who rape and loot . . . all are not human. I see those of the Dark Path and their goblin servants. They roam the streets, their weapons dripping blood. I see strange ladders being raised to storm the keep, and strange bridges of blackness. Now it burns, all burns; all is in flames . . . it is over."

There was a moment of silence, then Rogen continued. "I see a host, gathered on a plain, with strange banners flying. Black-armored figures sit silently on horseback, showing twisted shapes on shields and tabards. Above them stand a moredhel. . . ." The old man's eyes teared. "He is . . . beautiful. . . . He . . . is evil. He wears the mark of the dragon. He stands upon a hill while below him armies march past singing battle songs. Great machines of war are pulled by miserable human slaves."

Again there was silence. Then: "I see another city. The image shifts and wavers, for its future is less certain. Its walls lie breached, and its streets are stained red. The sun hides its face behind grey clouds . . . and the city cries out in anguish. Men and women are chained in lines without end. They are . . . whipped by creatures who taunt and torment them. They are being herded to a great square, where they face their conqueror. A throne is erected atop a mound . . . a mound of bodies. Upon it sits . . . the beautiful one, the evil one. At his side stands another, a black robe hides his features. Behind them both is another something. . . . I cannot see it, but it is real, it exists, it is . . . dark. . . . It is insubstantial, without being, not truly there, but . . . it is also there. It touches the one on the throne." Rogen tightly clutched Dominic's hands. "Wait . . ." he said, then hesitated. His hands began to tremble, then in piteous tones, nearly a sob, he cried, "Oh gods of mercy! It can see me! *It can see me!*" The old man's lips trembled, while Gamina clutched at his shoulder, eyes wide, holding him closely, terror written upon her little face. Suddenly Rogen's lips parted to emit a terrible groan, a sound of the purest agony and despair, and his body went rigid.

Without warning a lance of fire, a stab of pure pain, erupted in the minds of all who sat in the room. Gamina screamed in silence.

Gardan clutched at his head, nearly fainting from the white-hot flash of searing agony. Dominic's face went ashen and he reeled back in his chair under the onslaught of the cry as if struck a physical blow. Kasumi's eyes screwed closed as he fought to rise. Kulgan's pipe fell from slack lips as he clutched his temples. Pug staggered to his feet, using every shred of his magic power to erect some sort of mental barrier against the tearing in his mind. He pushed back the blackness that sought to overwhelm him, reaching out to touch the girl. "Gamina," he croaked.

The girl's mental screaming continued unabated and she tore frantically at the old man's tunic, a mindless act, as if she sought somehow to snatch him back from whatever horror he faced. Her large eyes were wide and her voiceless hysterics nearly drove those around her to madness. Pug lunged forward and grabbed her shoulder. Gamina ignored the touch, continuing to scream for Rogen.

Mustering his powers, Pug forced aside the terror and pain in the girl's projected thoughts for a brief moment.

Gardan's head fell forward onto the table, as did Kasumi's. Kulgan lurched upright, then fell back into his chair, stunned. Besides Pug and Gamina, only Dominic had managed to retain consciousness. Something inside him had struggled to reach out to the girl, no matter how much he wished to retreat from the pain being visited upon him by her.

The girl's primitive terror nearly brought Pug to his knees, but he forced himself on. He cast a spell, and the girl fell forward. At once the pain ceased. Pug caught her, but the effort drove him back and he staggered into his chair. He sat cradling the unconscious girl, stupefied by the onslaught.

Dominic felt as if his head would burst but hung on to consciousness. The old man's body was still rigid, nearly bowed back with pain, his lips working feebly. Dominic incanted a spell of healing, one used to cease pain. Finally Rogen went limp, seeming to collapse into his chair. But his face was still a mask of terror and pain, and he cried out in a hoarse whisper words the monk could not understand, before he lapsed into unconsciousness.

Pug and the monk exchanged confused looks. Dominic felt blackness overtake him and, before he passed out, wondered why the magician suddenly looked so frightened.

Gardan paced the room where they had dined the night before. Next to the fire, Kulgan said, "You'll wear a furrow in the stones of the floor if you don't sit down."

Kasumi rested quietly on a cushion beside the magician. Gardan lowered himself next to the Tsurani and said, "It's this infernal waiting." Dominic and Pug, with the aid of some healers in the community, were tending to Rogen. The old man had lain near death since he had been carried from the meeting house. Gamina's mental scream had touched all within a mile of her, though striking those at a distance with less force. Still, several people near the building had been rendered senseless for a time. When the cries had stopped, those with their wits about them had rushed to see what had occurred. They had found all in the meeting house unconscious.

Katala was soon on the scene and ordered them all carried to the quarters where she could oversee their care. The others had recovered in a few hours, but Rogen had not. The vision had begun in midmorning, and now it was after supper.

Gardan struck hand with fist and said, "Damn! I was never meant for this sort of business. I am a soldier. These monsters of magic, these nameless powers . . . Oh for an enemy of flesh and blood!"

"Too well do I know what you can do to a flesh-and-blood enemy," Kasumi said. Kulgan looked interested, and Kasumi said, "In the early years of the war, the captain and I faced one another at the siege of Crydee. It wasn't until we were exchanging histories that I discovered he was second to Prince Arutha during the siege, or he that I led the assault."

The door opened and a large man entered, removing a great cloak. He was bearded and weather-beaten in appearance, looking like a hunter or woodcutter. He smiled slightly and said, "I go away for a few days and look who wanders in."

Gardan's dark face broke into a broad smile and he rose, extending his hand. "Meecham!"

They shook and the man called Meecham said, "Well met, Captain." Kasumi followed suit, for Meecham was an old acquaintance. He was a franklin, a free man with his own land in service to Kulgan, though he was more a friend to the magician than any sort of servant.

Kulgan said, "Any luck?"

The forester absently stroked the scar on his left cheek as he said, "No. All fakes."

Kulgan said to the others, "We heard of a traveling caravan of fortunetellers and gypsies, camped a few days this side of Landreth. I sent Meecham to discover if any of them were true talents."

"There was one," said Meecham. "Might have been what he seemed, but he quieted down when I told him where I was from. Maybe he'll show up on his own hook." He looked around the room. "All right, isn't anyone going to tell me what's going on here?"

As Kulgan finished recounting everything to Meecham, the door opened and further conversation was interrupted. William entered leading Gamina by the hand. The old man's ward looked even more pale than when Gardan had seen her the day before. She looked at Kulgan, Kasumi, and Gardan and her voice entered their minds. *I am sorry I caused so much pain. I was frightened.*

Kulgan slowly extended his arms, and the girl gingerly allowed him to gather her up onto his ample lap. With a gentle hug, he said, "It is all right, lass. We understand."

The others smiled at the girl reassuringly and she seemed to relax. Fantus came padding into the room. William threw him a quick look and said, "Fantus is hungry."

Meecham said, "That beast was born hungry."

No, came the thought. *He said he was hungry. No one remembered to feed him today. I heard.*

Kulgan gently held the little girl away from him so he could look at her. "What do you mean?"

He told William he was hungry. Just now. I heard him.

Kulgan looked at William. "William, can you hear Fantus?"

William looked at Kulgan with a curious expression. "Of course. Can't you?"

They talk to each other all the time.

Kulgan's face became animated. "This is wonderful! I had no idea. No wonder you two have been so close. William, how long have you been able to speak to Fantus this way?"

The boy shrugged. "Ever since I can remember. Fantus has always talked to me."

"And you could hear them speak to each other?" Gamina nodded. "Can you speak to Fantus?"

No. But I can hear him when he talks to William. He thinks funny. It is hard.

Gardan was astonished by the conversation. He could hear Gamina's answers in his head, as if he were listening. From observing the girl's private remarks to Rogen the day before, he realized that she obviously was able to speak with whomever she chose in a selective way.

William turned toward the drake. "All *right!*" he said in aggravated tones. He said to Kulgan, "I'd better go to the kitchen and get him something. Can Gamina stay here?"

Kulgan gave the girl a gentle hug and she nestled deeply into his lap. "Of course."

William dashed from the room, and Fantus hurried after, the prospect of a meal motivating him to an atypical display of speed. When they were gone, Kulgan said, "Gamina, can William speak to other creatures besides Fantus?"

I don't know. I'll ask him.

They watched in fascination as the girl's head cocked to one side, as if she were listening to something. After a moment she nodded. *He said only sometimes. Most animals aren't very interesting. They think a lot about food and other animals, is all.*

Kulgan looked as though he had been given a present. "This is wonderful! Such a talent. We have never heard of a case of a human communicating directly with animals. Certain magicians have hinted at such an ability in the past, but never like this. We shall have to investigate this fully."

Gamina's eyes widened as her face took on an expectant look. She sat up and her head came around to face the door, and an instant later Pug and Dominic entered. Both looked weary, but there was no sign of the sorrow Kulgan and the others had feared.

Before the question could be asked, Pug said, "He still lives, though he was deeply afflicted." He noticed Gamina in Kulgan's lap, looking as if that physical contact were somehow vital to her. "Are you better?" Pug asked. She ventured a slight smile and a nod.

Some communication passed between them and Pug said, "I think he will recover. Katala will stay at his side. Brother Dominic has proved a great help, for he is versed in healing arts. But Rogen is very old, Gamina, and if he doesn't recover, you must understand and be strong."

Gamina's eyes rimmed with moisture, but she nodded slightly. Pug came over and drew up a chair, as did the monk. Pug seemed to notice the addition of Meecham for the first time and they greeted each other. A quick introduction to Dominic was made, and then Pug said, "Gamina, you could be a big help to us. Are you willing?"

How?

"There has never been an occurrence like today's to my knowledge. I must know what made you so afraid for Rogen." There was something in Pug's manner that revealed deep concern. He masked it well, so as not to distress the child, but it still wasn't completely hidden.

Gamina looked frightened. She shook her head and something passed between the little girl and Pug. Pug said, "Whatever it was, it could make the difference in Rogen's living. Something we do not understand is involved in this; we should know about it."

Gamina bit her lower lip slightly. Gardan was struck by the fact the girl was showing considerable bravery. From what little he had heard of the girl's lot, it had been a terrible one. To grow up in a world where people were always suspicious and hostile, and those thoughts were always heard, must have kept the child on the edge of madness. For her to trust these men at all bordered on the heroic. Rogen's kindness and love must have been endless to counterbalance the pain this child had known. Gardan thought that if any man deserved the occasionally bestowed title of "saint" the temples used for their heroes and martyrs, then it was Rogen.

More conversation passed between Pug and Gamina, all silent. Finally Pug said, "Speak so we might all hear. All these men are your friends, child, and they will need to hear your story to stop Rogen and others from being hurt again."

Gamina nodded. *I was with Rogen.*

"What do you mean?" asked Pug.

When he used his second sight, I went with him.

"How were you able?" said Kulgan.

Sometimes when someone thinks things, or sees things, I can see or hear what they do. It's hard when they aren't thinking at me. I can do it best with Rogen. I could see what he saw, in my mind.

Kulgan pushed the child slightly away so he might better look at her. "Do you mean to say you can see Rogen's visions?" The girl nodded. "What about dreams?"

Sometimes.

Kulgan hugged her tightly. "Oh, what a fine child you are! Two miracles in one day! Thank you, wonderful child!"

Gamina smiled, the first happy expression any of them had seen. Pug threw him a questioning look, and Kulgan said, "Your son can speak to animals." Pug's jaw dropped, and the stout magician continued, "But that is not important for the moment. Gamina, what did Rogen see that hurt him so badly?"

Gamina began to tremble and Kulgan held her closely. *It was bad. He saw a city burning and people being hurt by bad creatures.*

Pug said, "Do you know the city? Is it some place you and Rogen have seen?"

Gamina shook her head, her big eyes seemingly as round as saucers. *No. It was just a city.*

"What else?" asked Pug gently.

The girl shivered. *He saw something . . . a man?* There was a strong feeling of confusion, as if she was dealing with concepts she could not fully comprehend. *The man? saw Rogen.*

Dominic said softly, "How could something in a seeing sense the seer? A vision is a prophetic look at what might happen. What sort of thing could sense a magic witness across the barriers of time and probability?"

Pug nodded. "Gamina, what did this 'man' do to Rogen?"

It? He? reached out and hurt him. He? said some words.

Katala entered the room, and the child looked up at her expectantly. Katala said, "He's fallen into a deep, normal sleep. I think he will recover now." She came up behind the chair Kulgan sat in and leaned on the back; she reached down and cupped Gamina's chin. "You should be getting to bed, child."

Pug said, "A little longer." Katala sensed her husband was concerned with something vital and nodded agreement. He said, "Just before he fainted, Rogen used a word. It is important for me to know where he heard that word. I think he heard the thing, the bad man, in the vision use the word. I need to know what Rogen heard the bad man say. Can you remember the words, Gamina?"

She laid her head down on Kulgan's chest and nodded only slightly, obviously afraid to remember them. Pug spoke in reassuring tones. "Would you tell them to us?"

No. But I can show you.

"How?" asked Pug.

I can show you what Rogen saw, she answered. *I just can.*

"All of us?" asked Kulgan. She nodded. The tiny girl sat up in Kulgan's lap and took a deep breath, as if steeling herself. Then she closed her eyes and took them all into a dark place.

Black clouds raced overhead, angry on the bitter wind. Storms threatened the city. Massive gates lay shattered, for engines of war had worked their destruction on wood and iron. Everywhere fires burned out of control as a city died. Creatures and men savaged those found hiding in cellars and attics, and blood pooled in the gutters of the streets. In the central market a mound of bodies had been piled nearly twenty feet high. Atop the corpses rested a platform of dark wood, upon which a throne had been placed. A moredhel of striking appearance sat on the throne, surveying the chaos his servants had visited upon the city. At his side stood a figure draped all in black robes, deep hood and large sleeves hiding every physical clue as to what manner of creature it was.

But the attention of Pug and the others was drawn to something beyond the pair, a presence of darkness, some strange unseen thing that could be felt. Lurking in the background, it was the true source of power behind the two upon the platform. The black-robed creature pointed at something, and a green-scaled hand could be seen. Somehow, the presence behind the two made contact, made itself known to the onlookers. It knew it was being observed, and its response was one of anger and disdain. It reached out with alien powers and spoke, carrying to those in the room a message of grey despair.

All in the room shook themselves from the girl's vision. Dominic, Kulgan, Gardan, and Meecham appeared disturbed, chilled by the menace in what the girl had showed them, though it could only be a shadow of the firsthand experience.

But Kasumi, Katala, and Pug were rocked. When the child had finished, tears streaked down Katala's face and Kasumi had lost his usual Tsurani mask, his face ashen and drawn. Pug appeared hardest hit of all as he sat back heavily on the floor. He lowered his head, withdrawing inside himself for a moment.

Kulgan looked about in alarm. Gamina seemed more distressed by the reaction than by recalling the image. Katala sensed the child's distress and picked her up from Kulgan's lap, hugging her closely. Dominic said, "What is it?"

Pug looked up and, more than anything, appeared suddenly fatigued, as if the weight of two worlds once again was his to bear. Finally he spoke, slowly. "When Rogen was at last freed of the pain, the last words he spoke were 'the Darkness, the Darkness.' That is what he saw behind those two figures. The Darkness Rogen saw spoke these words: 'Intruder, whoever you are, wherever you are, know my power is coming. My servant prepares the way. Tremble, for I come. As was in the past, so shall be in the future, now and forever. Taste my power.' He, it, must have somehow reached out and touched Rogen then, causing the terror, the pain."

Kulgan said, "How can this be?"

Softly, hoarsely, Pug spoke. "I do not know, old friend. But now a new dimension is added to the mystery of who seeks Arutha's death and what lies behind all the black arts being thrown at him and his allies."

Pug buried his face in his hands a moment, then looked around the room. Gamina clung to Katala, and all eyes were upon Pug.

Dominic said, "But there is something else." He looked at Kasumi and Katala. "What is that tongue? I heard it as well as you, as I heard Rogen's foreign words, but know it not at all."

It was Kasumi who said, "The words were . . . ancient, a language used in the temples. I could only understand a little. But the words were Tsurani."

FOURTEEN

ELVANDAR

The forest was silent.

Large branches, ancient beyond memory, arched high overhead, blocking out most of the day's sunlight; the surrounding environment revealed a soft green glow, devoid of direct shadows and full of deep recesses of dimly perceived paths, winding away.

They had been in the elven forests for over two hours, since midmorning, and as yet had seen no sign of an elf. Martin had thought they would be intercepted shortly after crossing the river Crydee.

Baru spurred his horse forward and pulled even with Martin and Arutha. "I think we are being watched," said the Hadati.

Martin said, "For some minutes now. I only caught a glimpse a while ago."

"If the elves are watching, why don't they come forward?" asked Jimmy.

Martin said, "It may not be elves who watch us. We will not be completely free from care until we are within the bounds of Elvandar. Keep alert."

For several minutes they rode, then even the chirping birds ceased their noise. The forest seemed to be holding its breath. Martin and Arutha pushed their mounts through narrow paths, barely wide enough for a man afoot. Suddenly the silence was broken by a raucous hooting, punctuated by shrieks. A stone came hurling past Baru's head and a storm of rocks, twigs, and sticks followed. Dozens of small hairy figures jumped from behind trees and brush, howling furiously while pelting the riders with missiles.

Arutha charged forward, fighting to keep his mount under control, as did the others. He steered through the trees while ducking under branches. As he moved toward four or five child-sized creatures, they shrieked in terror and leaped away in different directions. Arutha singled out one and rode up behind it. The creature found itself blocked by a deadfall, a jumbled mass of fallen trees, heavy brush, and a large rock. It turned to face the Prince.

Arutha had his sword drawn and reined in, ready to strike. Then all anger flowed out of him at the sight before him. The creature made no effort to attack, but instead backed as far as possible into the tangle, an expression of pure terror on its face.

It was a very manlike face, with large, soft brown eyes. A short but human nose was set above a wide mouth. The creature's lips were drawn back in a mock snarl, showing an impressive arrangement of teeth, but the eyes were wide with fear and large tears flowed down its hairy cheeks. Otherwise it looked like a small ape or large monkey.

A loud racket erupted around Arutha and the creature as more of the small man-things surrounded them. They howled fiercely, pounding on the ground with savage fury, but Arutha saw it was all show; there was no real threat in their actions. Several feigned attacks, but ran shrieking in terror if Arutha turned to face them.

The others came riding up behind, and the little creature Arutha had trapped cried piteously. Baru pulled up alongside the Prince and said, "As soon as you charged, these others fled after you."

The riders could see that the gathered creatures were abandoning their mock fury and their expressions were now concerned. They chattered to one another in what sounded like words.

Arutha put away his sword. "We will not hurt you."

As if they understood, the creatures quieted. The one who was trapped watched guardedly.

Jimmy said, "What are they?"

Martin said, "I don't know. Man and boy I've hunted these woods and I've never seen their like."

"They are gwali, Martin Longbow."

The riders turned in their saddles and were greeted by the sight of a company of five elves. One of the creatures raced to stand before the elves. He pointed an indicting finger toward the riders. In a singsong voice he said, "Calin, mans come. Hurt Ralala. Make stop hurt her."

Martin left his horse. "Well met, Calin!" He and the elf embraced, and the other elves greeted him in turn. Then Martin led them to where his companions waited and said, "Calin, you remember my brother."

"Greetings, Prince of Krondor."

"Greetings, Elf Prince." He cast a sidelong glance at the surrounding gwali. "You save us from being overwhelmed."

Calin smiled. "I doubt it. You look a capable company." He came up to Arutha. "It has been a while since we last spoke. What brings you to our forests, Arutha, and with so strange an entourage? Where are your guardsmen and banners?"

"That is a long tale, Calin, and one I wish to share with your mother and Tomas."

Calin agreed. To an elf patience was a way of life.

With the tension broken, the gwali cornered by Arutha broke and ran to join the others of her kind, who stood around watching. Several examined her, grooming her hairy hide, patting her reassuringly after her ordeal. Satisfied she was unharmed, they quieted down and watched the elves and humans. Martin said, "Calin, what are these creatures?"

Calin laughed, his pale blue eyes crinkling at the corners. He stood as tall as Arutha but was even more slender than the rangy Prince. "As I have said, they are called gwali. This rascal is named Apalla." He patted the head of the one who had spoken to him. "He is something of a leader among them, though I doubt they really entertain the concept. It may be he is simply more talkative than the others." Looking at the rest of Arutha's company, he said, "Who are these with you?"

Arutha made introductions and Calin said, "You are welcome to Elvandar."

"What is a gwali?" asked Roald.

Calin said, "These are, and that is the best answer I can give. They have lived with us before, though this is their first visit in a generation. They are simple folk, without guile. They are shy and tend to avoid strangers. When afraid, they will run unless they are cornered, then they will feign attack. But don't be misled by those ample teeth; they're for tough nuts and insect carapaces." He turned his attention to Apalla. "Why did you try to scare these men?"

The gwali jumped up and down excitedly. "Powula make little gwali." He grinned. "She don't move. We afraid mans hurt Powula and little gwali."

"They are protective of their young," said Calin in understanding. "Had you actually tried to hurt Powula and the baby, they would have risked attacking you. Had there been no birthing, you never would have seen them." He said to Apalla, "It is all right. These men are friends. They will not hurt Powula or her baby."

Hearing this, the other gwali came pouring out from the protecting trees and began examining the strangers with open curiosity. They tugged at the riders' clothing, which was quite different from the green tunics and brown trousers the elves wore. Arutha suffered the examination for only a minute, then said, "We should get to your mother's court soon, Calin. If your friends are finished?"

"Please," said Jimmy, his nose wrinkling as he pushed away a gwali who hung from a branch next to him. "Don't they ever bathe?"

"Unfortunately, no," answered Calin. He said to the gwali, "That's enough, we must go." The gwali accepted the instruction with good grace and quickly vanished among the trees, except Apalla, who seemed more assertive than the rest. "They will continue that sort of thing all day if you allow them to, but they don't mind when you shoo them off. Come." He told Apalla, "We go to Elvandar. Tend to Powula. Come when you will."

The gwali grinned and nodded vigorously, then scampered off after his brethren. In a moment there was no hint that a gwali existed within miles.

Calin waited until Martin and Arutha had remounted. "We are only a half day's travel to Elvandar." He and the other elves began their run through the forest. Except for Martin, the riders were surprised at the pace the elves set. It was not taxing for the mounts, but for a human runner to keep it up for a half day would be close to impossible.

After a short while Arutha drew even with Calin, who loped along at an easy pace. "Where did those creatures come from?"

Calin shouted, "No one knows, Arutha. They're a comic lot. They come from some place to the north, perhaps beyond the great mountains. They will show up, stay a season or two, then vanish. We sometimes call them the little wood ghosts. Even our trackers can't follow them after they depart. It's been nearly fifty years since their last visit, and two hundred since the one before that." Calin breathed easily as he ran in long, fluid strides.

"How fares Tomas?" asked Martin.

"The Prince Consort fares well."

"What of the child?"

"He is well. He is a fit, handsome child, though he may prove somewhat different. His heritage is . . . unique."

"And the Queen?"

"Motherhood agrees with her," answered her elder son with a smile.

They fell into silence, for Arutha found it difficult to continue the conversation while negotiating the trees, even if Calin did not. Swiftly through the forest they traveled, each passing minute bringing them closer to Elvandar and hopes fulfilled . . . or hopes dashed.

The journey was soon completed. One moment they were traveling through heavy forest, then they entered a large clearing. This was the first glimpse any of them, save Martin, had had of Elvandar.

Giant trees of many colors rose high above the surrounding forest. In the afternoon light the topmost leaves seemed ablaze with color where golden sunlight struck them. Even from this distance, figures could be seen along the high paths spanning the gaps between boles. Several of the giant trees were unique to this place, their leaves a dazzling silver, gold, or even white. As the day's shadows deepened, they could be seen to have a faint glow of their own. It was never truly dark in Elvandar.

As they crossed the clearing, Arutha could hear the astonished comments of his companions.

Roald said, "Had I known . . . you'd have had to tie me up to keep me from coming along."

Laurie agreed. "It makes the weeks in the forest worth it."

Baru said, "The tales of our singers do not do justice to it."

Arutha awaited a comment from Jimmy, but when the voluble lad said nothing, Arutha looked behind. Jimmy rode in silence, his eyes drinking in the splendor of this place, so alien from anything seen in his life. The usually jaded boy had finally encountered something so outside his experience, he was truly awestruck.

They reached the outer boundary of the tree-city and on all sides could hear the soft sounds of a busy community. A hunting party approached from another quarter, bearing a large stag, which they carried off to be butchered. An open area outside the trees was set aside for the dressing of carcasses.

They reached the trees and reined in. Calin instructed his companions to care for the horses and led Arutha's party up a circular stairway carved into the trunk of the biggest oak the Prince and the others had ever seen. Reaching a platform at the top, they passed a group of elven fletchers practicing their craft. One saluted Martin, who returned the greeting and briefly inquired if he might impose upon their generosity. With a smile, the fletcher handed Martin a bundle of finely crafted bowshafts, which the Duke placed in his nearly empty quiver. He spoke quick thanks in the elven tongue and he and his companions continued onward.

Calin led them up another steep stairway to a platform. He said, "From here it may prove difficult for some of you. Keep to the center of the paths and platforms and do not look down if you feel discomforted. Some humans find the heights distressing." He said the last as if it was almost incomprehensible.

They crossed the platform and mounted more steps, passing other elves hurrying about their business. Many were dressed like Calin, in simple woods garb, but others wore long colorful robes, fashioned of rich fabrics, or bright tunics and trousers, equally colorful. The women were all beautiful, though it was a strange, inhuman loveliness. Most of the men looked young, about Calin's age. Martin knew better. Some elves hurrying past were young, twenty, thirty years of age, while others, equally young in appearance, were several hundred years old. Though he looked younger than Martin, Calin was past a hundred and had taught Martin hunting skills when the Duke had been a boy.

They continued along a walkway, nearly twenty feet wide, stretching along enormous branches, until they came to a ring of trunks. In the midst of the trees a large platform had been constructed, almost sixty feet across. Laurie wondered if even a single drop of rain could worm its way through the thick canopy of branches overhead to fall on a royal brow. They had reached the Queen's court.

Across this platform they walked, to a dais upon which two thrones were erected. In the slightly higher of the two sat an elven woman, serenity enhancing her already near-flawless beauty. Her face with its arched brows and finely chiseled nose was dominated by her pale blue eyes. Her hair was light red-brown, with streaks of gold—like Calin's—giving it the appearance of being struck by sunlight. Upon her head rested no crown, only a simple circlet of gold that pulled back her hair, but there was no mistaking Aglaranna, the Elf Queen.

Upon the throne to her left sat a man. He was an imposing figure, taller than Martin by two inches. His hair was sandy-blond and his face looked young, while still holding some elusive ageless quality. He smiled at the sight of the approaching party, giving him an even younger look. His face was similar to the elves', yet with a difference. His eyes lacked color to the point of being grey, and his eyebrows were less arched. His face was less angular, possessing a strong, square jaw. His ears, revealed by the golden circlet that held back his hair, were slightly pointed, less upswept than those of the elves. And he was much more massive in the chest and shoulders than any elf.

Calin bowed before them. "Mother and Queen, Prince and Warleader, we are graced by guests."

Both rulers of Elvandar rose and walked forward to greet their guests. Martin was greeted with affection by the Queen and Tomas, and the others were shown courtesy and warmth. Tomas said to Arutha, "Highness, you are welcome."

Arutha replied, "I thank Her Majesty and His Highness."

Seated around the court were other elves. Arutha recognized the old counselor Tathar, from his visit to Crydee years before. Quick introductions were made. The Queen bade them rise and led everyone to a reception area adjoining the court, where they were all informally seated. Refreshments were brought, food and wine, and Aglaranna said, "We are pleased to see old friends"—she nodded at Martin and Arutha—"and to welcome new"—she indicated the others. "Still, men rarely visit us without cause. What is yours, Prince of Krondor?"

Arutha told them his tale while they dined. From first to last the elves sat silently listening. When Arutha was finished, the Queen said, "Tathar?"

The old counselor nodded. "The Hopeless Quest."

Arutha asked, "Are you saying you know nothing of Silverthorn?"

"No," replied the Queen. "The Hopeless Quest is a legend among our people. We know the aelebera plant. We know of its properties. That is what the legend of the Hopeless Quest tells us. Tathar, please explain."

The old elf, the first Jimmy and the others had seen who showed some signs of age—faint lines around the eyes and hair so pale it bordered on white—said, "In the lore of our people, there was a Prince of Elvandar who was betrothed. His beloved had been courted by a moredhel warrior, whom she spurned. In his wrath the moredhel poisoned her with a draught brewed from the aelebera and she fell into a sleep unto death. Thus the Prince of Elvandar began the Hopeless Quest, in search of that which could cure her, the aelebera, the Silverthorn. Its power is such that it can cure as well as kill. But the aelebera grows only in one place, Moraelin, in your language the Black Lake. It is a place of power, sacred to the moredhel, a place where no elf may go. The legend says the Prince of Elvandar walked the edge of Moraelin until he had worn a canyon around it. For he may not enter Moraelin, nor will he leave until he has found that which will save his beloved. It is said he walks there still."

Arutha said, "But I am not an elf. I will go to Moraelin, if you'll but show me the way."

Tomas looked around the assembly. "We shall place your feet upon the path to Moraelin, Arutha," he said, "but not until you've rested and taken counsel. Now we shall show you places where you may refresh yourselves and sleep until the nighttime meal."

The meeting broke up as the elves moved away, leaving Calin, Tomas, and the Queen with Arutha's group. Martin said, "What of your son?"

With a broad smile, Tomas motioned for them to follow. He led them through a bough-covered passage to a room, its vault formed by a giant elm, where a baby lay sleeping in a cradle. He was less than six months old from the look of him. He slept deeply, dreaming, little fingers flexing slightly. Martin studied the child and could see what Calin meant by saying his heritage was unique. The child looked more human than elven, his ears being only slightly pointed and possessing lobes, a human trait unknown among elves. His round face looked more like that of any chubby infant, but there was an edge to it, something which said to Martin that this was a child who was more his father's than his mother's. Aglaranna reached down and gently touched him while he slept.

Martin said, "What have you named him?"

Softly the Queen said, "Calis." Martin nodded. In the elven tongue it meant "child of the green," referring to life and growth. It was an auspicious name.

Leaving the baby, Martin and the others were taken to rooms within the tree-city of Elvandar, where they found tubs for bathing and sleeping mats. All were quickly clean and asleep, save Arutha, whose mind wandered from an image of Anita asleep to a silver plant growing on the shore of a black lake.

Martin sat alone, enjoying the first evening of his first visit to Elvandar in a year. As much as any place, even Castle Crydee, this was his home, for as a boy he had played and been one with the elven children.

Soft elven footsteps caused him to turn. "Galain," he said, happy to see the young elf, cousin to Calin. He was Martin's oldest friend. They embraced and Martin said, "I expected to see you sooner."

"I've just returned from patrolling along the northern edge of the forests. Some strange things are going on up there. I hear you may have some light to shed on what they may be."

"A small candle flicker, perhaps," said Martin. "Some evil is at play up there, have no doubt."

He filled Galain in, and the young elf said, "Terrible deeds, Martin." He sounded genuinely sorry to hear about Anita. "Your brother?" The question, in elvish fashion, carried a variety of nuances in the intonation, each concerning itself with a different aspect of Arutha's trials.

"He perseveres, somehow. He puts it all out of his mind sometimes; other times he is nearly overwhelmed by it. I don't know how he keeps from going mad. He loves her so very deeply." Martin shook his head.

"You've never wed, Martin. Why?"

Martin shrugged. "I've never met her."

"You are sad."

"Arutha's a difficult man at times, but he is my brother. I remember him as a child. Even then it was hard to get close to him. Perhaps it was his mother's death, when he was still so young. He kept things distant. For all the toughness, for all the hard edges, he's easily hurt."

"You two are much alike."

"There is that," Martin agreed.

Galain stood quietly next to Martin awhile. "We shall help, as much as we can."

"We must go to Moraelin."

The young elf shivered, an unusual display even in one so inexperienced. "That is a bad place, Martin. It is called Black Lake for a reason that has nothing to do with the color of the water. It is a well of madness. The moredhel go there to dream dreams of power. It lies on the Dark Path."

"It was a Valheru place?"

Galain nodded yes.

"Tomas?" Again the question carried a variety of meanings. Galain was especially close to Tomas, having followed him during the Riftwar.

"He will not go with you. He has a new son. Calis will be tiny for so short a time, only a few years. A father should spend that time with his baby. Also, there is the risk." Nothing more needed to be said, for Martin understood. He had watched the night Tomas had almost succumbed to the mad spirit of the Valheru within him. It had nearly cost Martin his life. It would be some time before Tomas felt secure enough to challenge his own heritage, to again awaken that dread being contained within. And he would venture into a Valheru place of power only when he felt circumstances were grave enough to justify the risk.

Martin smiled his crooked smile. "Then we shall go alone, we humans of meager talents."

Galain returned the smile. "You are many things, so I doubt your talents meager." Then he lost the smile. "Still, you would do well to take counsel with the Spellweavers before you go. There is dark power at Moraelin, and magic overcomes much in the way of strength and courage."

Martin said, "We will. We speak soon." He looked to where an elf approached, Arutha and the others behind. "I think now. Will you come?"

"I've no place in the circle of elders. Besides, I have not eaten for a day. I will rest. Come talk if you need."

"I will."

Martin hurried to join Arutha. They followed the elf, who led the humans back to the council. When all were seated before Aglaranna and Tomas, the Queen said, "Tathar, speak for the Spellweavers: say what counsel you have for Prince Arutha."

Tathar stepped into the center of the court circle and said,

"Strange things have been occurring for some turns of the middle moon. We expected southward movement of the moredhel and goblins back to the homes they were driven from during the Riftwar, but this has not come to be. Our scouts in the north have tracked many bands of goblins heading across the Great Northern Mountains into the Northlands. Moredhel scouts have come unusually close to our borders.

"The gwali come to us again because they say they don't like the place they lived in anymore. It is hard to make sense of them at times, but we know they came from the north.

"What you have told us, Prince Arutha, causes us deep concern. First, because we share your sorrow. Second, because the manifestations you tell of bespeak a power of great evil with a long reach and far-flung minions. But most of all, because of our own ancient history.

"Long before we drove the moredhel from our forests, for taking to the Dark Path of Power, the elven people were one. Those of us who lived in the forests were farther from our masters, the Valheru, and because of this were less attracted to the intoxication of power dreams. Those of us who lived close to our masters were seduced by those dreams and became the moredhel." He looked to the Queen and Tomas, and both nodded. "What is little spoken of is the cause of our divorcement from the moredhel, who once were our blood. Never before has any human been told all.

"In the dark era of the Chaos Wars, many changes in the lands occurred. From the people of the elves, four groups rose." Martin leaned forward, for as much as he knew of elvenkind, more than almost any man alive, this was all new to him. Until this moment he had always believed only the moredhel and elves were the sum total of elvenkind. "The most wise and powerful, numbering the greatest Spellweavers and scholars, were the eldar. They were the caretakers for all that their masters had plundered from across the cosmos, arcane works, mystical knowledge, artifacts, and riches. It was they who first began fashioning what is now Elvandar, lending it magic aspect. They vanished during the Chaos Wars, for they were among our masters' first servants, and it is supposed that, being very close to them, they perished with them. Of the elves and Brotherhood of the Dark Path, the eledhel and moredhel in our tongue, you know something. But there were yet other kin of ours, the glamredhel, which name means 'the chaotic ones' or 'the mad ones.' They were changed by the Chaos Wars, becoming a nation of insane, savage warriors. For a time elves and moredhel were one, and both were warred upon by the mad ones. Even after the moredhel were driven from Elvandar, they remained the sworn enemy of the glamredhel. We speak little of these days, for you must remember that while we speak of eledhel, moredhel, and glamredhel, all elvenkind is one race, even to this day. It is simply that some of our people have chosen a dark way of life."

Martin was astonished. For all he knew of elven culture, he had, like other humans, always supposed the moredhel a race apart, related to the elves but somehow different. Now he realized why the elves had always been reticent in discussing their relationship to the moredhel. They saw them as being one with themselves. In an instant Martin understood. The elves mourned the loss of their brothers to the lure of the Dark Path.

Tathar continued. "Our lore tells of the time when the last great battle in the north was fought, when the armies of the moredhel and their goblin servants at last crushed the glamredhel. The moredhel rampaged, obliterating our mad cousins in a terrible war of genocide. Even to the smallest infant, the glamredhel were supposedly slaughtered, lest they again rise and challenge the supremacy of the moredhel. It is the single blackest shame in the memory of our race that one segment of our people utterly destroyed another.

"But what concerns you is this: at the heart of the moredhel host stood a company called the Black Slayers, moredhel warriors who had renounced their mortality to become monsters with but one purpose: to kill for their master. Once dead, the Black Slayers rise again to do their master's bidding. Once risen from the dead, they may be halted only by magic means, by utterly destroying the body, or by cutting the hearts from out of their bodies. Those who rode against you on the road to Sarth were Black Slayers, Prince Arutha.

"Before the battle of obliteration, the moredhel had already gone far down the Dark Path, but something caused them to descend to these new depths of horror, the Black Slayers and the genocide.

They had become a tool of an insane monster, a leader who sought to emulate the vanished Valheru and bring all the world under his dominion. It was he who had gathered the moredhel under his banner and who had given rise to the abomination that was the Black Slayers. But in that last battle he was wounded unto death, and with his passing the moredhel ceased to be a nation. His captains gathered and sought to determine a successor. They quickly fell out with one another and became much like the goblins—tribes, clans, families, never able to combine under one leader for long. The siege of Carse Keep, fifty years past, was but a skirmish compared to the might the moredhel mustered under this leader. But with his passing, an era of moredhel might came to an end. For he was unique, a charismatic, hypnotic being of strange abilities, able to weld the moredhel into a nation.

"The leader's name was Murmandamus."

Arutha said, "Is it possible he's somehow returned?"

"Anything may be possible, Prince Arutha, or so it seems to one who has lived as long as I," answered Tathar. "It may be that one seeks to unite the moredhel by invoking that ancient name, gathering them together under one banner.

"Then there is this business of the serpent priest. So despised are the Pantathians that even the moredhel slaughter them when they find them. But that one of them is a servant of this Murmandamus hints at dark alliances. It warns us we may be facing forces beyond our expectations. If the nations of the north are rising, we all must again face a testing, one which will rival that of the outworlders in peril for our peoples."

Baru stood, in Hadati fashion, indicating he wished to speak. Tathar inclined his head in Baru's direction, and he said, "Of moredhel lore my people know little, save that the Dark Brothers are enemies of our blood. This much I may add: Murad is counted a great chieftain, perhaps the greatest living today, one who might command many hundreds of warriors. That he serves with the Black Slayers speaks of Murmandamus's power. Murad would serve only one whom he feared. And one who could visit fear upon Murad is one to be feared indeed."

Arutha said, "As I told the Ishapians, much of this is speculation. I must be concerned with finding Silverthorn." But even as he uttered those words, Arutha knew he was speaking falsely. Too much indicated that the threat from the north was real. This was no rash of goblin raids on northern farmers. This was a potential for invasion surpassing that of the Tsurani. In the face of this, his refusal to set aside all considerations except finding a cure for Anita was shown for what it was: an obsession.

"They may be one and the same, Highness," said Aglaranna. "What seems to be unfolding here is a madman's desire to gather the moredhel and their servants and allies under his dominion. To do so he must bring a prophecy to fruition. He must destroy the Bane of Darkness. And what has he accomplished? He has forced you to come to the one place he is certain to find you."

Jimmy sat upright, his eyes wide. "He's waiting for you!" he blurted, ignoring protocol. "He's at this Black Lake!"

Laurie and Roald put their hands upon his shoulders, in reassurance. Jimmy sat back, looking embarrassed.

Tathar said, "From the lips of youth . . . I and the others have considered, and in our judgment, that is what must be occurring, Prince Arutha. Since the gift of the Ishapian talisman, Murmandamus must devise another way to find you, or he risks his alliances dissolving. The moredhel are much as others—they need to raise crops and tend herds. Should Murmandamus tarry overlong in bringing the prophecy to fruition, they may desert him, save for those who have taken dark vows, such as the Black Slayers. His agents will have passed word that you have quit Sarth, and by now intelligence from Krondor will tell him you are upon a quest for that which will save your Princess. Yes, he will know you seek Silverthorn, and he, or one of his captains, such as Murad, will be waiting for you at Moraelin."

Arutha and Martin looked at each other. Martin shrugged. "We never thought it would be easy."

Arutha regarded the Queen, Tomas, and Tathar. "My thanks for your wisdom. But we will go to Moraelin."

Arutha looked up as Martin came to stand nearby. "Brooding?" asked the elder brother.

"Just . . . considering things, Martin."

Martin sat next to Arutha, at the edge of a platform near the rooms they had been given. In the night, Elvandar glowed with a faint light, a phosphorescence that kept the elven city cloaked in a soft magic. "What things are you considering?"

"That I may have let my preoccupation with Anita get in the way of my duty."

Martin said, "Doubt? Well then, you reveal yourself at last. Listen, Arutha, I've had doubts about this journey from the start, but if you let doubt block you, nothing gets done. You must simply make your best judgment and act."

"And if I'm wrong?"

"Then you're wrong."

Arutha lowered his head until it rested against a wooden rail. "The problem is one of stakes. When I was a child, if I was wrong I lost a game. Now I could lose a nation."

"Perhaps, but it still doesn't change the need to make your best judgment and act."

"Things are getting out of hand. I wonder if it might not be best to return to Yabon and order Vandros's army into the mountains."

"That might do it. But then there are places six may go an army may not."

Arutha smiled a wry smile. "Not very many."

Martin returned the smile, almost a mirror image. "True, but still there are one or two. From what Galain said about Moraelin, stealth and cunning will be more important than strength. What if you marched Vandros's army up there and found Moraelin lay just the other side of a lovely road like the one up to the abbey at Sarth? Remember the one Gardan avowed could be held by a half-dozen grannies with brooms? I'll warrant Murmandamus has more than a half-dozen grandmothers up there. Even if you could battle Murmandamus's hordes and win, could you order one soldier to give his life so Anita should live? No; you and this Murmandamus play a game, for high stakes, but still a game. As long as Murmandamus thinks he can lure you up to Moraelin, we have a chance of stealing in and getting Silverthorn."

Arutha looked at his brother. "We do?" he asked, already knowing the answer.

"Of course. As long as we don't spring the trap, it remains open. That is the nature of traps. If they don't know we're already inside, we might even get out." He spent a quiet moment looking northward, then said, "It's so close. It's just up in those mountains, a week from here, no more. It's so close." He laughed at Arutha. "It would be a shame to come so close and quit."

Arutha said, "You're mad."

"Perhaps," said Martin. "But just think, it's so close."

Arutha had to laugh. "All right. We leave tomorrow."

The six riders set out the next morning, with the blessings of the Elf Queen and Tomas. Calin, Galain, and two other elves ran alongside the horsemen. As they lost sight of the Queen's court, a gwali swung along through the trees, crying, "Calin!"

The Elf Prince signaled a halt and the gwali dropped from the branches and grinned at them. "Where mans going with Calin?"

"Apalla, we take them to the northern road. Then they travel to Moraelin."

The gwali became agitated and shook his furry head. "No go, mans. Bad place. Little Olnoli eaten there by bad thing."

"What bad thing?" said Calin, but the gwali ran off shrieking in fright before an answer was forthcoming.

Jimmy said, "Nothing like a happy send-off."

Calin said, "Galain, return and find Apalla and see if you can glean any sense from what he says."

Galain said, "I'll find out what he means and follow after." He waved to the travelers and headed back after the gwali. Arutha motioned for the party to continue.

For three days the elves guided them to the edge of their forests, up into the foothills of the Great Northern Mountains. Then, at midday on the fourth day, they came to a small stream, and on the other side they could see the trail leading through the woodlands, toward a canyon. Calin said, "Here is the limit of our holdings."

Martin said, "What of Galain, do you think?"

"It may be he discovered nothing of worth, or it may have taken him a day or two to find Apalla. The gwali can be difficult to locate if they decide to be. If Galain meets us, we'll direct him after you. He will overtake you as long as you haven't crossed over into the heart of Moraelin."

"Where would that be?" said Arutha.

"Follow that trail for two days until you come to a small valley. Cross it, and on the north face you'll see a waterfall. A trail leads up from there, and atop the plateau you'll be near the top of the falls. Follow the river upward, until you reach its source. From that lake you'll find a trail again moving upward, again to the north. That is the only way to Moraelin. You'll find a canyon, which winds around the lake in a complete circle. Legend says it is the tracks made by the mourning Elf Prince, wearing the ground down around the lake. It is called the Tracks of the Hopeless. There is only one way into Moraelin, across a bridge made by the moredhel. When you cross the bridge over the Tracks of the Hopeless, you will be in Moraelin. There you will find the Silverthorn. It is a plant with a light silver-green leaf of three lobes, with fruit like red holly berries. You will recognize it at once, for its name describes it: the thorns are silver. If nothing else, get a handful of the berries. It will lie close to the edge of the lake. Now go, and may the gods protect you."

With brief farewells the six riders moved off, Martin and Baru in the lead, Arutha and Laurie following, Jimmy and Roald bringing up the rear. As they followed a turn, Jimmy glanced back, until he could no longer see the elves. He turned eyes forward, knowing they were now on their own, without allies or haven. He said a silent prayer to Banath and took a deep breath.

FIFTEEN

RETURN

Pug stared into the fire.

The small brazier in his study threw a dancing pattern of lights on the walls and ceiling. He ran his hand over his face, feeling fatigue in the very fabric of his being. He had labored since Rogen's vision, sleeping and eating only when Katala pushed him from his studies. Now he carefully closed one of Macros's many books; he had been reading them exhaustively for a week. Since confronted with the impossibilities of Rogen's vision, he had sought every shred of information available to him. Only one other magic user upon this world had known anything pertaining to the world of Kelewan, and that had been Macros the Black. Whatever that dark presence in the vision, it had spoken a language that fewer than five thousand on Midkemia might even recognize—Pug, Katala, Laurie, Kasumi and his Tsurani garrison at LaMut, and a few hundred ex-prisoners scattered around the Far Coast. And of them all, only Pug could fully understand the words spoken in Gamina's vision, for that language was a distant, dead ancestor of the present-day Tsurani tongue. Now Pug searched in vain through Macros's library for some hint of what this dark power might be.

Of the hundreds of volumes Macros had bequeathed to Pug and Kulgan, only a third had been cataloged. Macros, through his strange goblin-like agent, Gathis, had provided a listing of each title. In some cases that had proved helpful, for the work was well known by title alone. In other cases it was useless until the book was read. There were seventy-two works alone called *Magic,* and a dozen other instances of several books with like nomenclature. Looking for possible clues to the nature of what they faced, Pug had closeted himself with the remaining works and begun skimming them for any hint of useful information. Now he sat, the work upon his knee, with a growing certainty about what he must do.

Pug placed the book carefully upon his writing table and left his study. He walked down the stairs to the hall that connected all the rooms in use in the academy building. Work upon the upper level next to the tower that housed his workrooms had been halted by the rain that now beat down upon Stardock. A cold gust blew through a crack in the wall, and Pug gathered his black robe about himself as he entered the dining hall, which was used as a common room these days.

Katala looked up from where she sat embroidering, near the fireplace, in one of the comfortable chairs that occupied the half of the room used as common quarters. Brother Dominic and Kulgan had been talking, the heavyset magician puffing on his ever present pipe. Kasumi watched as William and Gamina played chess in the corner, their two little faces masks of concentration as they pitted their newly emerging skills against each other. William had been an indifferent student of the game until the girl had shown an interest. Being beaten by her seemed to bring out his sense of competition, heretofore limited to the ball yard. Pug thought to himself that, when time permitted, he would have to explore their gifts more closely. If time permitted . . .

Meecham entered, carrying a decanter of wine, and offered a wine cup to Pug. Pug thanked him and sat down next to his wife. Katala said, "Supper is not for another hour. I had expected I would have to come fetch you."

"I've finished what work I had and decided to relax a little before dining."

Katala said, "Good. You drive yourself too hard, Pug. With teaching others, supervising the construction of this monstrous building, and now locking yourself away in your study, you have had little time to spend with us."

Pug smiled at her. "Nagging?"

"A wifely prerogative," she said, returning his smile. Katala was not a nag. Whatever displeasure she felt was openly voiced, and quickly resolved, by either compromise or one partner's acceptance of the other's intractability.

Pug looked about. "Where is Gardan?"

Kulgan said, "Bah! You see. If you hadn't been locked up in your tower, you'd have remembered he left today for Shamata, so he can send Lyam messages by military pouch. He'll be back in a week."

"He went alone?"

Kulgan settled back in his chair. "I cast a foretelling. The rain will last three days. Many of the workers returned home for a short visit rather than sit in their barracks for three days. Gardan went with them. What have you been delving into in your tower these last few days? You've barely said a civil word for a week."

Pug surveyed those in the room with him. Katala seemed absorbed by her needlework, but he knew she was listening closely for his answer. The children were intent upon their game. Kulgan and Dominic watched him with open interest. "Reading Macros's works, seeking to discover something that might give a clue to what can be done. You?"

"Dominic and I have counseled with others in the village. We've managed to come to some conclusions."

"Such as?"

"Now that Rogen is healing, and has been able to tell us in detail what he saw in his vision, some of our more talented youngsters have thrown themselves upon the problem." Pug detected a mixture of amusement and pride in the older magician's words. "Whatever it is out there that seeks to bring harm to the Kingdom, or Midkemia, is limited in power. Assume for a moment that it is, as you fear, some dark agency slipped through the rift from Kelewan, somehow, during the Riftwar. It has weaknesses, and fears to reveal itself fully."

"Explain, please," said Pug, his interest driving aside all fatigue.

"We will assume this thing is from Kasumi's homeworld and not seek some other more exotic explanation for its use of an ancient Tsurani dialect. But unlike Kasumi's former allies, it comes not in open conquest, but rather seeks to use others as tools. Assume it came by the rift somehow. The rift is a year closed, which means it has been here for at least that long, and perhaps as long as eleven years, gathering servants like the Pantathian priests. Then it seeks to establish itself, by using a moredhel, the 'beautiful one,' as Rogen described him, as an agent. What we need truly fear is the dark presence behind that beautiful moredhel and the others. That is the ultimate author of this bloody business.

"Now, if all this is true, it seeks to manipulate and employ guile rather than direct force. Why? Either it is too weak to act, and must employ others, or it is biding its time until it is able to reveal its true nature and come to the fore."

"Which all means we still must discover the identity and nature of this thing, this power."

"True. Now, we also have done some speculation predicated upon the assumption that what we face is not of Kelewan."

Pug interrupted. "Do not waste time with that, Kulgan. We must proceed on the assumption that what we face *is* from Kelewan, for that, at least, provides us with a possible avenue of approach. If Murmandamus is simply some moredhel witch-king come into his own, one who just happens to speak a long-dead Tsurani tongue, we can counter that. But an invasion by some dark power from Kelewan . . . that is the assumption we must make."

Kulgan sighed loudly and relit his cold pipe. "I wish we had more time, and more idea of how to proceed. I wish we could examine some aspect of this phenomenon without risk. I wish a hundred things, but most of all I wish for one work by one reliable witness to this thing."

"There is a place where such a work may exist."

Dominic said, "Where? I would gladly accompany you or anyone else to such a place, no matter what the risk."

Kulgan barked a bitter laugh. "Not likely, good brother. My former student speaks of a place upon another world." Kulgan looked hard at Pug. "The library of the Assembly."

Kasumi said, "The Assembly?"

Pug saw Katala stiffen. "In that place there may be answers that would aid our coming battle," he said.

Katala never took her eyes from her work. In controlled tones she said, "It is good the rift is closed and cannot be reopened save by chance. Your life may already be ordered forfeit. Remember that your status as a Great One was called into question before the attack on the Emperor. Who can doubt you are now named outlaw? No, it is good there is no way you might return."

Pug said, "There is a way."

Instantly Katala's eyes were ablaze as she looked hard at him. "No! You cannot return!"

Kulgan said, "How can there be a way back?"

"When I studied for the black robe, I was given a final task," Pug explained. "Standing upon the Tower of Testing, I saw a vision of the time of the Stranger, a wandering star that imperiled Kelewan. It was Macros who intervened at the last to save Kelewan. Macros was again on Kelewan on the day I nearly destroyed the Imperial Arena. It was obvious all the time and only this week did I understand."

"Macros could travel between the worlds at will!" said Kulgan, comprehension dawning in his eyes. "Macros had the means to fashion controllable rifts!"

"And I have found it. Clear instructions are in one of his books."

Katala whispered, "You cannot go."

He reached over and took her white-knuckled hands in his own. "I must." He faced Kulgan and Dominic. "I have the means of returning to the Assembly, and I must use it. Otherwise, should Murmandamus be a servant of some dark Kelewanese power, or simply a diversion while such a power comes into its own, we will be lost without hope. If we are to find a way of dealing with such a one, we must first identify it, discover its true nature, and to do that I must go to Kelewan." He looked at his wife, then at Kulgan. "I will return to Tsuranuanni."

It was Meecham who spoke first. "Well then. When do we leave?"

Pug said, "We? I must go alone."

The tall franklin said, "You can't go alone," as if that thought was the sheerest absurdity. "When shall we leave?"

Pug looked up at Meecham. "You don't speak the language. You're too tall to be a Tsurani."

"I'll be your slave. There are Midkemian slaves there, you've said often enough." His tone indicated the argument was over. He looked from Katala to Kulgan and said, "There wouldn't be a moment's peace around here should anything happen to you."

William came over, Gamina behind him. "Papa, please take Meecham with you."

Please.

Pug put his hands in the air. "Very well. We'll establish some charade."

Kulgan said, "I feel a little better, which is a relative statement not to be taken as approval."

"Your objection is duly noted."

Dominic said, "Now the issue has been broached, I, too, wish to again offer to accompany you."

"You offered before you knew where I was going. One Midkemian I can look after, two would prove too burdensome."

"I have my uses," replied Dominic. "I know the healer's arts and can perform my own brands of magic. And I have a good arm and can wield a mace."

Pug studied the monk. "You are taller than I by only a little. You might pass as a Tsurani, but there's the problem of language."

"In Ishap's order we have magic means to learn languages. While you prepare your rift spells, I can learn the Tsurani tongue and aid Meecham in learning it as well, if the Lady Katala or Earl Kasumi will help."

William said, "I can help. I speak Tsurani."

Katala didn't look pleased, but agreed. Kasumi said, "I also." He looked troubled.

Kulgan said, "Of all here, Kasumi, I expected you would be the most likely to wish a return, yet you've said nothing."

"When the last rift closed, my life on Kelewan ended. I am now Earl of LaMut. My tenure within the Empire of Tsuranuanni is but a memory. Even if it is possible to return, I would not, for I have taken oath to the King. But," he said to Pug, "will you carry messages for me to my father and brother? They have no way to know I live, let alone prosper."

"Of course. It is only right." He said to Katala, "Beloved, can you fashion two robes of the Order of Hantukama?" She nodded. He explained to the others, "It is a missionary order; its members are commonly seen traveling about. Disguised as such, we shall attract little attention as we wander. Meecham can be our begging slave."

Kulgan said, "I still don't like this idea. I am not happy."

Meecham looked at Kulgan. "When you worry, you're happy."

Pug laughed at this. Katala put her arms around her husband and held him closely. She also was not happy.

Katala held up the robe and said, "Try this."

Pug found it a perfect fit. She had carefully chosen fabrics that would most closely resemble those used upon Kelewan.

Pug had been meeting daily with others in the community, delegating authority for his absence—and, as was understood but not spoken, against the probability that he would not return. Dominic had been learning Tsurani from Kasumi and William and aiding in Meecham's mastery of that language. Kulgan had been given Macros's work on rifts to study so he could aid Pug in the formation of one.

Kulgan entered Pug's private quarters as Katala was inspecting her handiwork. "You'll freeze in that."

Katala said, "My homeworld is a hot place, Kulgan. These light robes are what is commonly worn."

"By women as well?" When she said yes, he said, "Positively indecent," as he pulled out a chair.

William and Gamina ran into the room. The little girl was a changed child now that Rogen's recovery was assured. She was William's constant companion, playing, competing, and arguing as if she were a sister. Katala had kept her in the family's quarters while the old man healed, in a room next to William's.

The boy shouted, "Meecham's coming!" and broke out in gleeful laughter as he spun in a circle of delight. Gamina laughed aloud as well, imitating William's spin, and Kulgan and Pug exchanged glances, for it was the first audible sound the child had ever made. Meecham entered the room, and the adults' laughter joined with the children's. The burly forester's hairy legs and arms stuck out from the short robe, and he stood awkwardly in the imitation Tsurani sandals.

He looked around the room. "So what's funny?"

Kulgan said, "I've grown so used to seeing you in hunter's togs, I couldn't imagine what you'd look like."

Pug said, "You just look a little different than I had expected," and tried to stifle a laugh.

The franklin shook his head in disgust. "If you're done? When do we leave?"

Pug said, "Tomorrow morning, just after dawn." Instantly all laughter in the room died.

They waited quietly around the hill with the large tree, on the north side of Stardock Island. The rain had stopped, but a damp, cold wind blew, promising more rain shortly. Most of the community had come to see Pug, Dominic, and Meecham on their way. Katala stood next to Kulgan with her hands upon William's shoulders. Gamina clutched tightly to Katala's skirt, looking nervous and a little frightened.

Pug stood alone, consulting the scroll he had fashioned. A short way off, Meecham and Dominic waited, shivering against the cold, while they listened to Kasumi. He was intensively speaking of every detail of Tsurani custom and life he could recall that might prove important. He was constantly remembering details he had almost forgotten. The franklin held the travel bag Pug had prepared, containing the usual items a priest would carry. Also inside, under those items, were a few things uncommon to a priest on Kelewan, weapons and coins of metal, a fortune by Kelewanese standards.

Kulgan came to where Pug indicated, holding a staff fashioned by a woodcarver in the village. He planted it firmly in the soil, then took another handed to him and placed it four feet away. He stepped back as Pug began to read aloud from the scroll.

Between the staves a field of light grew, rainbow colors dancing up and down. A crackling noise could be heard, and the air began to smell as it did after a lightning strike, acrid and pungent.

The light began to expand and change in color, moving faster through the spectrum until it gleamed whitely. It grew in intensity until it was too bright to look upon. Still Pug's voice droned on. Then came a loud explosion of noise, as if a thunderclap had pealed between the staves, and a short gust of wind toward the gap between them, as if a sudden drawing in of air had occurred.

Pug put away his scroll and all looked at what he had fashioned. A shimmering square of grey "nothingness" stood between the upright staves. Pug motioned to Dominic and said, "I'll go through first. The rift is targeted to a glade behind my old estate, but it might have appeared elsewhere."

If the environment proved hostile, he would have to step around the pole, entering it from the same side again, appearing back on Midkemia as if he had passed through a hoop. If he was able.

He turned and smiled at Katala and William. His son jiggled around nervously, but Katala's reassuring pressure on the boy's shoulders quieted him. She only nodded, her face composed.

Pug stepped into the rift and vanished. There was an audible intaking of breath at the sight, for only a few there knew what to expect. The following moments dragged on, and many unconsciously held their breath.

Suddenly Pug appeared from the other side of the rift and an audible sigh of relief came from those who waited. He came back to the others and said, "It opens exactly where I had hoped it would. Macros's spellcraft was flawless." He took Katala's hands. "It is next to the reflecting pool in the meditation glade."

Katala fought back the tears. She had tended flowers around that pool, where a solitary bench looked over calm waters, when she had been mistress of that great estate. She nodded understanding, and Pug embraced her, then William. As Pug knelt before William, Gamina suddenly threw her arms around his neck. *Be careful.*

He hugged her in return. "I will, little one."

Pug motioned Dominic and Meecham to follow and walked through the rift. They hesitated the barest instant and followed him into the greyness.

The others stood watching for long minutes after the three had vanished, and the rain began again. No one wished to leave. Finally, as the rain took on a more insistent quality, Kulgan said, "Those set to watch, remain. The rest, back to work." Everyone slowly moved off, no one resenting Kulgan's sharp tone. They all shared his concern.

Yagu, chief gardener on the estate of Netoha, near the city of Ontoset, turned to find three strangers walking the path from the meditation glade to the great house. Two were priests of Hantukama, the Bringer of Blessed Health, though both were unusually tall for priests. Behind walked their begging slave, a captive barbarian giant from the late war. Yagu shuddered, for he was an ugly sort, with a horrible scar down his left cheek. In a culture of warriors, Yagu was a gentle man, preferring the company of his flowers and plants to that of men who spoke only of warfare and honor. Still, he had a duty to his master's house and approached the three strangers.

When they saw him coming, they halted, and Yagu bowed first, as he was initiating the conversation—common courtesy until rank was established. "Greetings, honored priests. It is Yagu the gardener who presumes to interrupt your journey."

Pug and Dominic bowed. Meecham waited to the rear, ignored, as was the custom. Pug said, "Greetings, Yagu. For two humble priests of Hantukama your presence is no interruption. Are you well?"

Yagu said, "Yes, I am well," finishing off the formal greeting of strangers. Then he took on a lofty stance, crossing his arms and sticking his chest out. "What brings the priests of Hantukama to the house of my master?"

Pug said, "We travel from Seran to the City of the Plains. As we passed by, we saw this estate and hoped to beg a meal for poor missionaries. Is this possible?" Pug knew it was not Yagu's prerogative to say, but he let the scrawny gardener play out the role of deciding.

The gardener stroked his chin for a moment. "It is permitted for you to beg, though I cannot say if you will be turned away or fed. Come, I will show you the kitchen."

As they walked toward the house, Pug said, "May I inquire who lives in this wondrous abode?"

Showing pride in the reflected glory of his master, Yagu said, "This is the house of Netoha, called 'He Who Rises Quickly.' "

Pug feigned ignorance, though he was pleased to know his former servant was still in possession of the estate. "Perhaps," said Pug, "it would not be too offensive for humble priests to pay respects to so august a personage."

Yagu frowned. His master was a busy man, but he also made time for such as these. He would not be pleased to find the gardener had presumed to fend them off, though they were little more than beggars, not being from a powerful sect, such as the servants of Chochocan or Juran. "I will ask. It may be my master will have a moment for you. If not, then perhaps a meal may be had."

The gardener led them to a door Pug knew led into the kitchen area. The afternoon sun beat down upon them as the gardener disappeared inside. The house was a strange design of interconnecting buildings Pug had built nearly two years before. It had started something of a revolution in Tsurani architecture, but Pug doubted the trend had continued, given the Tsurani sensitivity to political fortune.

The door slid open and a woman stepped out, followed by Yagu. Pug bowed before she could get a look at his face. It was Almorella, a former slave Pug had freed, now wed to Netoha. She had been Katala's closest friend.

Yagu said, "My mistress graciously agrees to speak with the priests of Hantukama."

From his bowing position Pug said, "Are you well, mistress?"

Hearing his voice, Almorella gripped the doorframe as she fought for breath. When Pug straightened, she forced herself to breathe and said, "I . . . am well." Her eyes widened and she began to speak his Tsurani name.

Pug shook his head. "I have met your honored husband. I hoped he might spare a moment for an old acquaintance."

Almost inaudibly Almorella said, "My husband always has time for . . . old friends."

She bade them enter and closed the door behind. Yagu stood outside a moment, perplexed at his mistress's behavior. But as the door slid shut, he shrugged and returned to his beloved plants. Who could understand the rich?

Almorella led them quickly and silently through the kitchen. She struggled to maintain her composure, barely concealing her shaking hands as she brushed past three startled slaves. They never noticed their mistress's agitated state, for their eyes were riveted on Meecham, the biggest barbarian slave they had ever seen, truly a giant among giants.

Reaching Pug's former workroom, she slid aside the door and whispered, "I will get my husband."

They entered and sat, Meecham awkwardly, upon plump cushions on the floor. Pug looked about the room and saw that little had changed. He felt a strange sense of being in two places at the same time, for he could almost imagine opening the door to find Katala and William outside in the garden. But he wore the saffron-colored robe of a priest of Hantukama, not the black of a Great One, and a terrible peril was possibly about to descend upon the two worlds with which his fate seemed forever intertwined. Since beginning the search for a return to Kelewan, a faint nagging had started at the back of Pug's mind. He sensed that his unconscious mind was operating as it often did, working on a problem while his attention was elsewhere. Something about all that had occurred on Midkemia had a faintly familiar quality to it, and he knew the time was soon coming when he would intuit what that quality was.

The door slid open and a man entered, Almorella behind. She closed the door, while the man bowed low. "You honor my home, Great One."

"Honors to your house, Netoha. Are you well?"

"I am well, Great One. How may I serve?"

"Sit, and tell me of the Empire." Without hesitation, Netoha sat. "Does Ichindar still rule the Holy City?"

"The Light of Heaven still rules the Empire."

"What of the Warlord?"

"Almecho, he you knew as Warlord, acted with honor and took his own life after you shamed him at the Imperial Games. His nephew, Axantucar, wears the white and gold. He is of the Oaxatucan Family, one who gained by the death of others when . . . the peace was betrayed. All with stronger claims were killed, and many with claims as valid as his to the office of Warlord were . . . dealt with. The War Party is still firmly in control of the High Council."

Pug considered. With the War Party still in control of the nations, there would be scant chance of finding sympathetic ears in the High Council, though the Game of the Council would continue. That terrible, seemingly never-ending struggle for power might provide the opportunity for discovering alliance.

"What of the Assembly?"

"I sent those things which you instructed, Great One. The others were burned as you commanded. I received only a note of thanks from the Great One Hochopepa, nothing more."

"What is the talk in the market?"

"I have not heard your name mentioned in many months. But just after you departed, it was said you attempted to lure the Light of Heaven into a trap, bringing dishonor on yourself. You have been named outlaw and outcast by the Assembly, the first to have the black robe stripped away. Your words are no longer as law. Any who aid you do so at peril of their lives, and the lives of their families, and the lives of their clan."

Pug rose, "We shall not tarry here, old friend. I would not risk your lives, nor the lives of your clan."

Netoha spoke as he moved to open the door. "I know you better than most. You would not do what they accused you of, Great One."

"Great One no longer, by edict of the Assembly."

"Then I honor the man, Milamber," he said, using Pug's Tsurani name. "You have given us much. The name Netoha of the

Chichimecha is upon the rolls of the Hunzan Clan. My sons will grow in greatness because of your generosity."

"Sons?"

Almorella patted her stomach. "Next planting season. The healer priests think twins."

"Katala will be doubly pleased. First, to know the sister of her heart is well, and second, that you will be a mother."

Almorella's eyes brimmed with moisture. "Katala is well? And the boy?"

"My wife and son are well and send you their love."

"Return with our greetings and affection, Milamber. I have prayed that someday we may again meet."

"Perhaps we shall. Not soon, but someday. . . . Netoha, is the pattern intact?"

"It is, Milamber. Little has changed. This is still your home."

Pug rose and motioned for the others to follow him. "I may have need of it for a quick return to my own lands. If I sound the arrival gong twice, have everyone quit the house at once, for there may be others behind me who will harm you. I hope it will not be so."

"Your will, Milamber."

They walked out of the room and made for the pattern room. Pug said, "In the glade by the pool is the means for my return home. I would it remained undisturbed until I close it."

"It is done. I will instruct the grounds keepers to allow no one in the glade."

At the door Almorella said, "Where are you bound, Milamber?"

"That I will not tell you, for what you do not know cannot be forced from you. You are already in jeopardy for simply having me under your roof. I will add no more."

Without further word he led Dominic and Meecham into the pattern room and closed the door behind. Removing a scroll from his belt pouch, Pug placed it on the center of a large tile pattern, a depiction of three dolphins. It was sealed with black wax, embossed with a large chop, from the ring of the Great One. "I send a message to a friend. With this symbol upon it, no one will dare touch it but him to whom it is addressed." He closed his eyes for a moment, then suddenly the scroll wasn't there.

Pug motioned Dominic and Meecham to stand next to him on

the pattern. "Every Great One in the Empire has a pattern in his home. Each is unique, and when it is remembered exactly, a magician can transport himself or send an object to it. In a few cases, a location that is very familiar, such as the kitchen at Crydee where I worked as a boy, might serve as well as a pattern. It is usual to will a gong to sound, announcing our arrival, though I shall avoid that this time, I think. Come." He reached out and gripped each of them, closed his eyes, and incanted. There seemed to be a sudden blur and the room appeared to change about them.

Dominic said, "What . . . ?" then realized they had transported to another place. He looked down at a different pattern, resembling an ornamental flower of red and yellow.

Pug said, "The one who lives here is brother to one of my old teachers, for whom the pattern was emplaced. That Great One called here often. I hope we may still find friends here."

Pug went to the door and slid it slightly ajar. He peered up and down the corridor. Dominic stepped up behind him. "How far did we travel?"

"Eight hundred miles and more."

"Amazing," Dominic said softly.

Pug led them swiftly to another room, where the afternoon sunlight could be seen coming through a window, casting the shadow of the room's lone occupant upon the door. Without announcing himself, Pug slid it open.

Before a writing desk sat an old man, his once powerful body shrunken by age. He squinted at the parchment before him, and his lips moved silently as he read. His robe was a deep blue, simple, but finely made. Pug was shocked, for he remembered this man as a tower despite his advancing years. The last year had taken a toll.

The man looked up at the intruders. His eyes grew large as he said, "Milamber!"

Pug motioned his companions through the door and slid it behind. "Honors to your house, Lord of the Shinzawai."

Kamatsu, Lord of the Shinzawai, did not rise in greeting. He stared at the former slave who had risen to the rank of Great One and said, "You are under edict, branded traitor, and without honor. Your life is forfeit should you be found." His tone was cold, his expression hostile.

Pug was taken aback. Of all his allies in the plot to end the Riftwar, Kamatsu had been among the staunchest. Kasumi, his son, had carried the Emperor's message of peace to King Rodric.

"Have I caused you offense, Kamatsu?" Pug asked.

"I had a son among those lost when you attempted to entrap the Light of Heaven with your deceit."

"Your son still lives, Kamatsu. He honors his father and sends affection." Pug handed Kamatsu the message from Kasumi. The old man peered at it for a long time, reading every character slowly. When he had finished, tears ran unashamedly down his leathery cheeks. "Can all this be true?" he said.

"It is true. My King had nothing to do with the deception at the truce table. Nor had I a hand in it. That mystery is long in explaining, but first hear of your son. He not only is alive, but is now counted highly in my nation. Our King sought no vengeance upon our former enemies. He granted freedom to all who would serve him. Kasumi and the others are freemen in his army."

"All?" said Kamatsu incredulously.

"Four thousand men of Kelewan are now soldiers of my King's army. They are counted among the most loyal of his subjects. They bring honor to their families. When King Lyam's life was in danger, the task of guaranteeing his safety was given to your son and his men." Pride shone in Kamatsu's eyes. "The Tsurani live in a city called LaMut, and fight well against the enemies of our nation. Your son is named Earl of that city, as important a rank as Lord of a family, closer to clan Warchief. He is married to Megan, the daughter of a powerful merchant of Rillanon, and someday you will be a grandfather."

The old man seemed to gain in strength; he said, "Tell me of his life." Pug and Kamatsu began to speak of Kasumi, his life for the last year, and his rise, his meeting Megan just before Lyam's coronation, and their rapid courtship and marriage. For nearly a half hour they spoke, the urgency of Pug's mission forgotten for the moment.

When they were done, Pug said, "And Hokanu? Kasumi asked after his brother."

"My younger son is well. He patrols the northern frontier against the Thūn raiders."

"Then the Shinzawai rise to greatness on two worlds," said Pug. "Alone among Tsurani families can the Shinzawai make that claim."

Kamatsu said, "That is a strange thing to contemplate." His voice turned serious. "What has caused your return, Milamber? It is not only to ease an old man's loss, I am certain."

Pug introduced his companions and then said, "A dark power rises up against my nation, Kamatsu. We have faced only a part of its might and we seek to understand its nature."

Kamatsu said, "What has this to do with your return here? What cause have you to return?"

"In a vision, one of our seers confronted this dark agency and was addressed in the ancient temple language." He spoke of Murmandamus and the dark power behind the moredhel.

"How can this be?"

"That is what has caused me to risk a return. I hope to find an answer in the library of the Assembly."

Kamatsu shook his head. "You risk much. There is a certain tension within the High Council, beyond what is usual for the Great Game. I suspect we are on the verge of some major upheaval, as this new Warlord seems even more obsessed with controlling the nations than was his uncle."

Understanding at once the Tsurani subtlety, Pug asked, "Do you speak of a final schism between Warlord and Emperor?"

With a heavy sigh, the old man nodded. "I fear civil war. Should Ichindar press forward with the certainty he showed to end the Riftwar, Axantucar would be blown away as chaff upon the wind, for the majority of the clans and families still hold the Emperor as supreme, and few trust this new Warlord. But the Emperor has lost much face. For him to have forced the five great clans to the peace table only to be betrayed has robbed him of his moral authority. Axantucar is free to act without opposition. I think this Warlord seeks to unite the two offices. The gold trim on white is not enough for this one. I think he seeks to wear the gold of the Light of Heaven."

" 'In the Game of the Council, anything is possible,' " quoted Pug. "But look you, all were betrayed at the peace talks." He spoke of the last message of Macros the Black, reminding Kamatsu of the ancient teachings of the Enemy's attacks upon the nation, and speaking of Macros's fear that the rift would draw that terrible power.

"Such duplicity shows that the Emperor was no more a fool than the rest, but it still does not forgive him the mistake. Yet such a tale may win him a little more support in the High Council—if support has any meaning."

"You think the Warlord ready to act?"

"Anytime now. He has neutralized the Assembly by having his own pet magicians call its own autonomy into question. Great Ones sit in debate over their own fate. Hochopepa and my brother, Fumita, dare not take a hand in the Great Game at this time. Politically, the Assembly might as well not exist."

"Then seek allies in the High Council. Tell them this: somehow our two worlds stand linked again by some dark power of Tsurani origin. It moves against the Kingdom. It is power beyond human understanding, perhaps power to challenge the gods themselves. I cannot tell you how I know, but I feel certain that, should the Kingdom fall, then will Midkemia fall; should Midkemia fall, then surely will Kelewan fall after."

Kamatsu, Lord of the Shinzawai, former Warchief of the Kanazawai Clan, showed an expression of concern. Softly he said, "Can it be?"

Pug's expression showed he believed it true. "It may be I will be captured or killed. If so, I must have allies on the High Council who will speak this cause to the Light of Heaven. It is not my life I fear for, Kamatsu, but the lives of two worlds. If I fail, the Great Ones Hochopepa or Shimone must return to my world with whatever can be learned of this dark power. Will you help?"

Kamatsu rose. "Of course. Even had you not brought word of Kasumi, even had our doubts about you been true, only a madman would be unwilling to put aside former grievances in light of such warning. I will leave at once by fast boat downriver to the Holy City. Where will you be?"

"Seeking help from another. If I am successful, I shall plead my case before the Assembly. No one gains the black robe without having learned to listen before acting. No, my true risk is falling into the Warlord's hands. If you do not hear of me in three days, assume that has come to pass. I will be either dead or captive. Then you must take action. Only silence will aid this Murmandamus. In this you must not fail."

"I will not fail, Milamber."

Pug, once known as Milamber, greatest of the Great Ones of Tsuranuanni, rose and bowed. "We must leave. Honors to your house, Lord of the Shinzawai."

Kamatsu bowed lower than was required of his station and said, "Honors to your house, Great One."

Hawkers shouted to passing buyers as the sun beat down. The market square at Ontoset was athrong with business. Pug and his companions had taken a place in the section of the plaza set aside for licensed beggars and priests. For three mornings they rose from under the protective wall of the square and spent the day preaching to those willing to stop and listen. Meecham would pass among the small crowds, holding out the beggar's bowl. There was only one temple of Hantukama east of the Holy City of Kentosani—in the city of Yankora, far from Ontoset—so there was little risk of them being discovered by another wandering priest in the short time they would be staying in the city. The order was widely and thinly spread, and many who served had not seen another priest of the order for years.

Pug finished his sermon for the morning and returned to Dominic's side as the monk instructed an injured girl's mother in proper care for the child. Her broken leg would be fully mended within days. The woman's grateful thanks were all she could give, but Dominic's smile indicated that was sufficient. Meecham joined them, showing several of the tiny gemstones and slivers of metal that served as currency in the Empire. "A man could make a decent living this way."

Pug said, "You scared them into giving."

A commotion in the crowd made them all look as a company of horsemen rode past. They wore the green armor of a house known to Pug by reputation, the Hoxaka. They were members of the War Party. Meecham said, "They've taken to riding, for certain."

"Like the Tsurani in LaMut," Pug whispered back. "It seems once a Tsurani gets over being terrified of horses, he becomes mad for them. I know Kasumi did. Once upon a horse, it was near-impossible to get him off." It appeared the horse had become accepted in the Empire and cavalry firmly established in the arsenal of Tsurani weapons.

When the horses had passed, another noise made them turn; standing before them was a heavyset man in black robes, his bald head gleaming in the noonday sun. On every side citizens were bowing and moving away, not wishing to crowd the august presence of a Great One of the Empire. Pug and his companions bowed.

The magician said, "You three will come with me."

Pug made a show of stammering, "Your will, Great One." They hurried to follow after.

The black-robed magician walked directly to the nearest building, a leatherworkers' establishment. The magician entered and said to the proprietor, "I have need of this building. You may return in an hour."

Without hesitation the owner said, "Your will, Great One," and called for his apprentices to join him outside. In a minute the building was empty except for Pug and his friends.

Pug and Hochopepa embraced, then the stout magician said, "Milamber, you are mad to return. When I received your message, I could scarcely believe my senses. Why did you risk sending it through the pattern, and why this meeting in the heart of the city?"

Pug said, "Meecham, watch the window." To Hochopepa he said, "What better place to hide than in plain sight? You receive messages by the pattern often, and who would think of questioning you about speaking to common priests?" He turned and said, "These are my companions," and made the introductions.

Hochopepa swept clear a bench and sat. "I have a thousand questions. How did you manage to return? The magicians who serve the Warlord have been trying to relocate your homeworld, for the Light of Heaven, may the gods protect him, is determined to avenge the betrayal of the peace conference. And how did you manage to destroy the first rift? And live?" He saw Pug's amusement at his flood of questions and ended, "But most important, why have you returned?"

Pug said, "There is loose upon my homeworld some dark power of Tsurani origin, an evil thing of dark magic. I seek knowledge, for it is of Kelewan." Hochopepa looked questioningly at him. "Many strange things occur on my world, and it is the most elegant answer, Hocho. I hope to discover some clue to the nature of this dark power. And it is a fearful agency." He went into detail about what had occurred since the first, from explaining the reason for the betrayal, to the attempts on Prince Arutha, to his own interpretation of Rogen's seeing.

Hochopepa said, "This is strange, for we know of no such power upon Kelewan—at least, none I have heard about. One advantage to our organization is that two thousand years of cooperative effort by the Black Robes has rid this world of a great many such menaces. In our lore we know of demon lords and witch-kings, spirits of dark powers and things of evil, all of whom fell before the combined might of the assembly."

From the window Meecham said, "Seems you might have missed one."

Hochopepa appeared taken aback at being addressed by a commoner, then he chuckled. "Perhaps, or perhaps there is another explanation. I do not know. But," he said to Pug, "you have always been a force for social good within the Empire, and I have no doubt that all you have said is truth. I will act as your agent, seeking safe passage to the library, and I will aid in your research. But understand, the Assembly is hamstrung by internal politics. The vote to let you live is by no means a certainty. I shall have to return and lobby. It may take days before I can openly voice the question.

"But I think I can succeed at this. You raise too many questions to ignore. I will convene a meeting as soon as possible and return for you once I have pleaded your case. Only a madman would fail to heed your warning, even should it prove to be something not of this world that plagues your land. At worst you gain a parole to use the library and depart; at best, perhaps a reinstatement. You will have to justify your past actions."

"I can and will, Hocho."

Hochopepa left the bench and stood before his old friend. "It may be we can yet have peace between our nations, Milamber. Should the old wound somehow be healed, we could benefit both worlds. I, for one, would love to visit this academy you build and meet this seer who predicts the future and this child who speaks with the mind."

"I have many things I would share, Hocho. The making of controllable rifts is but a tenth part of it. But all that later. Go now."

Pug began to guide Hochopepa to the door, but something in Meecham's pose caught his eye. It was too stiff and awkward. Dominic had been closely following the magicians' conversation and had not seemed to notice any change in the franklin. Pug studied Meecham a second, then shouted, "A spell!"

Pug moved toward the window and touched Meecham. The tall man was unable to move. Past him Pug could see men running toward the building. Before Pug could react and incant a spell of protection, the door exploded inward with a thunderous sound, knocking everyone inside to the floor and stunning them momentarily.

Senses reeling, Pug tried to regain his feet, but his ears rang from the sound and his vision blurred. As he staggered upright, an object was hurled in through the door. It was a ball-like object the size of a man's fist. Pug again tried to establish a spell of protection around the room, but the sphere emitted a blinding orange light. Pug's eyes felt seared and he closed them, breaking the pattern of his spell. He began again, but the object made a high-pitched whine, which seemed to somehow drain away his strength. He heard someone hit the floor and couldn't tell if Hochopepa or Dominic had tried to rise and failed or if Meecham had toppled. Pug fought against the magic of the sphere with all his considerable might, but he was off balance and confused. He staggered to the door, trying to get away from the object, for once free of its debilitating effects he could easily save his friends. But its own spell was too quick and strong. At the threshold of the shop he collapsed. He fell to his knees, blinking against the double vision the sphere or explosion had inflicted upon him. He could make out men approaching the building from across the plaza. They wore the armor of the Warlord's Imperial Whites, his personal honor guard. Sinking downward into darkness, Pug could see that the one who led them wore a black robe. Pug could hear the magician's voice, as if coming from a vast distance through the ringing in his ears, saying, "Bind them."

SIXTEEN

MORAELIN

Mist blew through the canyon.

Arutha signaled a halt; Jimmy peered downward through the blowing moisture. A waterfall thundered beside the trail that was their route toward Moraelin. Now they were properly in the Great Northern Mountains, in that area between the elven forests and the Northlands. Moraelin lay higher in the mountains, in a rocky, barren place just below the crest. They waited while Martin scouted the pass ahead. Since leaving their elven guides they had become a military mission in enemy-held lands. They could trust Arutha's talisman to hide them from Murmandamus's scrying magic, but that he knew they would soon come to Moraelin was beyond question. It was never to be a question of if they would encounter his minions, but simply when.

Martin returned, signaling that the way ahead was clear, then he put up his hand for a halt again. He dashed past the others, heading back down the trail. As he passed Baru and Roald, he motioned for them to follow. They jumped down from their mounts, and Laurie and Jimmy took the reins. Arutha looked back, wondering what Martin had seen, while Jimmy kept eyes ahead.

Martin and the others returned, another figure walking easily with them. Arutha relaxed when he saw it was the elf Galain.

The oppressive nature of their journey was such that when they spoke, it was in hushed tones, lest echoes in the hills betray them. Arutha greeted the elf. "We thought you not coming."

Galain replied, "The Warleader sent me after you with this intelligence but a few hours after you departed. After he was found, the gwali Apalla said two things of importance. First, a beast of some ferocious nature unclear from the gwali's description inhabits the area near the lake. Tomas pleads caution. Second, there is another entrance to Moraelin. He felt it of sufficient import to dispatch me after." Galain smiled. "Besides, I thought it might also prove useful to see if you were being followed."

"Were we?"

Galain nodded. "Two moredhel scouts cut your trail less than a mile north of our forests. They were marking your way, and one surely would have run ahead to warn when you got close to Moraelin. I would have joined you earlier, but I needed to be certain neither could escape to give warning. Now there is no such risk." Martin nodded, knowing the elf would have killed them both suddenly and without chance for alarm. "There are no signs of others."

Martin asked, "Do you return?"

"Tomas gave me discretion. It is not of much use to go back at this point. I may as well travel with you. I may not pass over the Tracks of the Hopeless, but until that portal is reached, another bow may prove useful."

"Welcome," said Arutha.

Martin mounted and, without words, Galain ran on ahead to scout the way. They moved swiftly upward, the falls chilling them despite the early summer warmth. At these heights hail and occasionally snow were not uncommon except in the hottest months of summer, still weeks away. The nights had been damp, though not as bitter as had been feared, for they made cold camp. The elves had given them trail rations, dried meat and hard cakes of nut flour and dried fruit—nourishing but cheerless fare.

The trail led along the face of the cliffs, until it came out in a high meadow, overlooking the valley. A silver, sparkling lake lapped its shores gently in the late afternoon light, the only sound being the singing of birds and the rustling of the wind in the trees. Jimmy looked about. "How can . . . how can the day be so nice when we move toward nothing but trouble?"

Roald said, "One thing about soldiering: if you're going to risk dying, there's no sense doing it wet, cold, and hungry unless absolutely necessary. Enjoy the sunshine, lad. It's a gift."

They watered their horses. After a welcome rest, they continued onward. The path Calin had spoken about, north of the lake, was easily found but steep and difficult to negotiate.

As sunset approached, Galain returned with news of a promising cave in which they might safely build a small fire. "It is curved, twice, and the air moves upward through fissures that will carry smoke away. Martin, if we leave now, we might have time to hunt game near the lake's edge."

Arutha said, "Don't be overly long in the hunt. Signal your approach with that raven's honk you do so well, or you'll be greeted by some sword points."

Martin nodded once, giving the reins of his horse to Jimmy. He said, "Two hours after sunset at the latest," and he and Galain were heading back down the trail toward the lake.

Roald and Baru took point, and after a five-minute ride found the cave Galain had mentioned. It was flat, wide, and free of other occupants. Jimmy explored back and found it narrow after a hundred feet, so that unexpected visitors would have to come through the mouth. Laurie and Baru gathered wood and the first fire in days was built, though it was a small one. Jimmy and Arutha settled in with the others, waiting for Martin and Galain.

Martin and Galain lay in wait. They had constructed a natural-looking blind, using brush gathered from other parts of the woods. They were certain they could observe any animal coming down to the lake's edge without being seen. They had lain downwind from the lake, neither speaking, for half an hour when the sound of hooves upon the rocks sounded from below the cliff.

Both nocked arrows, but otherwise remained silent. Into the meadow from the trail below rode a dozen horsemen, dressed in black. Each wore the strange dragon helm seen at Sarth, and their heads moved constantly, as if they looked for something—or someone. Then behind them came Murad, his cheek still showing the additional cut Arutha had given him on the road to Sarth.

The Black Slayers reined in and watered their mounts, staying in the saddle. Murad seemed relaxed but alert. For a silent ten minutes they let the horses drink.

When they were finished watering the horses, they moved out, turning up the trail after Arutha's band. When they were out of sight, Martin said, "They must have come in between Yabon and Stone Mountain to have avoided your forests. Tathar is correct in his assumption that they will move to Moraelin to wait for us."

Galain said, "Few things in life disturb me, Martin, but those Black Slayers are one."

"You're just now coming to that conclusion?"

"You humans are given to overreaction upon occasion." Galain looked to where the riders had gone.

Martin said, "They will overtake Arutha and the others shortly. If this Murad can track, then they will find the cave."

Galain stood. "Let us hope the Hadati knows his trail craft. If not, at least we will be attacking from the rear."

Martin smiled a grim smile. "That will certainly be of comfort to those in the cave. Thirteen against five, and only one way in or out."

Without further comment, they shouldered their bows and began to lope up the trail behind the moredhel.

"Riders come," said Baru. Jimmy was instantly covering the fire with dirt, carried in against the need. That way the fire would die quickly without smoke. Then Laurie touched Jimmy on the arm and motioned that he should come to the rear of the cave to help quiet the horses. Roald, Baru, and Arutha moved forward to where they could, they hoped, see out of the cave mouth without being seen.

The evening looked murky dark after the bright fire, but soon their eyes adjusted and they could see the riders passing by the cave. The rearmost pulled up a moment before the others answered some silent command and halted. He looked about, as if sensing something nearby. Arutha fingered his talisman, hoping the moredhel was simply cautious and not feeling his presence.

A cloud passed from before the little moon, the only one up this early, and the vista before the cave became slightly more illuminated. Baru stiffened at sight of Murad, for the hillman could now clearly see the moredhel. He had begun to draw his sword when Arutha's hand gripped his wrist. The Prince hissed in the hillman's ear, "Not yet!"

Baru's body trembled as he struggled against his desire to avenge his family's death and complete his Bloodquest. He burned to attack the moredhel without regard for his own safety, but there were his companions to consider.

Then Roald gripped the back of the Hadati's neck and put his cheek against Baru's, so he could speak into his ear almost without sound. "If the twelve in black cut you down before you reach Murad, what honor do you to your village's memory?"

Baru's sword slipped noiselessly back into its sheath.

Silently they watched as Murad surveyed the surroundings. His eyes fell on the mouth of the cave. He peered at the entrance, and for a moment Arutha could feel the scar-faced moredhel's eyes upon him. Then they were moving again . . . then they were gone.

Arutha crept forward until he hung out of the cave, watching for signs the riders were returning. Suddenly a voice behind said, "I thought a cave bear might have run you all out of there."

Arutha spun, his heart racing and his sword coming out of its scabbard, to find Martin and Galain standing behind. He put up his weapon and said, "I could have run you through."

The others appeared and Galain said, "They should have investigated, but they seemed determined to be somewhere in a hurry. So we might do well to follow. I'll keep them under watch and mark the trail."

Arutha said, "What if another band of Dark Brothers comes along? Won't they find your trail markings?"

"Only Martin will recognize my trail markings. No mountain moredhel can track like an elf." He shouldered his bow and began to run after the riders.

As he vanished into the night's gloom, Laurie said, "What if the Dark Brothers are forest dwellers?"

Galain's voice came back out of the dark: "I'll have almost as much to worry about as you will."

After Galain was out of earshot, Martin said, "I wish he were only joking."

Galain ran back down the trail, motioning toward a stand of trees off to the left of the road. They hurried to the trees and dismounted. They led the mounts down into a draw, as deep into the woods as possible. Galain whispered, "A patrol comes." He, Martin, and Arutha hurried back to the edge of the trees where they could spy anyone on the trail.

A few minutes passed with agonizing slowness; then a dozen riders came down the mountain road, a mixed band of moredhel and men. The moredhel were wearing cloaks and were clearly forest dwellers from the south. They rode past without pause, and when they were out of sight, Martin said, "Renegades now flock to Murmandamus's banner." He almost spit as he said, "There are few I'd gladly kill, but humans who would serve the moredhel for gold are among them."

As they returned to the others, Galain said to Arutha, "There is a camp athwart the road a mile above here. They are clever, for it is a difficult passage around the camp, and we would need to leave your horses here. It is that or ride through the camp."

"How far to the lake is it?" asked the Prince.

"Only a few miles. But once past the camp we rise above the tree line and there is little cover, save down among the rocks. It will be a slow passage, and better done at night. There are bound to be scouts around and many guards on the road to the bridge."

"What about the second entrance the gwali told of?"

"If we understood rightly, by descending down into the Tracks of the Hopeless, you'll find a cave or fissure that will lead through the rock up to the surface of the plateau near the lake."

Arutha considered. "Let us leave our mounts here. . . ."

Laurie said, with a faint smile, "Might as well tether the horses to the trees. If we die, we won't need them."

Roald said, "My old captain used to get downright short with soldiers who harped on death before a battle."

"Enough!" said Arutha. He took a step away, then turned. "I've been worrying this over and over. I've come this far and I'll continue, but . . . you may leave now if you wish, and I'll not object." He looked at Laurie and Jimmy, then Baru and Roald. He was answered by silence.

Arutha looked from face to face, then nodded brusquely. "Very well. Tie up the horses and lighten your packs. We walk."

The moredhel watched the trail below, well lit by large and middle moons, as little moon rose. He perched atop an outcropping of rock, nestled behind a boulder. He was positioned so he would be unobserved by any coming up the trail.

Martin and Galain took aim at the moredhel's back as Jimmy slipped behind the rocks. They would try to win past without being seen, but if the moredhel twitched in the wrong direction, Martin and Galain meant to see him dead before he could speak. Jimmy had gone first, as he was judged the least likely to make noise. Next came Baru, and the hillman moved through the rocks with the practiced ease of one mountain-born. Laurie and Roald moved very slowly, and Martin wondered if he could hold his target for the week it was taking them to pass. Then at last Arutha slipped past, the light breeze making enough noise to disguise the faint scuff of boot upon rock as he stepped down into a shallow depression. He scampered along until he joined with the others, out of sight of the sentry. Within seconds Martin, then Galain, followed, and the elf went past to again take point.

Baru signaled he would go after, and Arutha motioned agreement. In a moment Laurie and Roald followed. Just before he turned to follow, Jimmy put his face before Martin and Arutha's and whispered, "When we get back, the first thing I'm going to do is scream my bloody head off."

With a playful swat, Martin sent him along. Arutha looked at Martin and silently mouthed the words, "Me too." Then the Prince was going down the wash. Martin took a last backwards glance, then followed.

Silently they lay in a depression near the road, a small ridge of rock hiding them from the passing moredhel horsemen. Reluctant even to breathe, they remained motionless as the riders seemed to pause in their slow passage. For a long, torturous moment, Arutha and his companions feared discovery. Just as every nerve seemed to scream for action, as every muscle demanded motion, the riders continued along their patrol. With a sigh of relief close to a sob, Arutha rolled over and discovered the trail empty. With a nod to Galain, Arutha ordered a resumption of the trek. The elf was off along the defile, and the others slowly rose and followed.

The night wind blew bitter along the face of the mountains. Arutha sat back against the rocks, looking where Martin pointed. Galain hugged the opposite wall of the crevice they crouched in.

They had taken a rise over a crest to the east of the trail, seeming to take them away from their destination, but a necessary detour to avoid increasing moredhel activity. Now they looked down upon a broad canyon, in the middle of which a high plateau rose upward. In the center of the plateau a small lake could be seen. To their left they could see the trail returning as it ran past the edge of the canyon, then disappeared over the crest of the mountains farther up, clearly shown in the light of all three moons.

Where the trail came closest to the edge of the canyon, twin towers of stone had been erected. Another pair stood opposite on the plateau. Between them a narrow suspension bridge swayed in the wind. On top of all four towers torches burned, their flames dancing madly in the wind. Movement along the bridge and atop the towers told them the entire area around the plateau was heavily guarded. Arutha leaned back against the rocks. "Moraelin."

Galain said, "Indeed. It appears they feared you might bring an army with you."

Martin said, "It was a thought."

Arutha said, "You were right about its comparing to the road to Sarth. This would have been almost as bad. We'd have lost a thousand men reaching this point alone—if we could have gotten this far. Across the bridge, single file . . . ? It would have been mass slaughter."

Martin asked, "Can you see that black shape across the lake?"

"A building of some sort," said Galain. He looked perplexed. "It is unusual to see a building, that building, any building, though the Valheru were capable of anything. This is a place of power. That must be a Valheru building, though I've never heard of its like before."

"Where shall I find Silverthorn?" asked Arutha.

Galain said, "Most of the stories say it needs water, so it grows on the edge of the lake. Nothing more specific."

Martin said, "Now, as to gaining entrance."

Galain signaled them away from the front end of the crevice, and they returned to where the others waited. The elf knelt and drew in the ground. "We are here, with the bridge here. Somewhere down at the base is a small cave or large fissure, large enough for a gwali to run through, so I'd guess it would be big enough for you to crawl through. It might be a chimney in the rock you can climb up, or it might be connecting caves. But Apalla was emphatic that he and his people had spent some time on that plateau. They didn't stay long because of the 'bad thing,' but he remembered enough to convince Tomas and Calin he wasn't confused about being here.

"I've spotted a broken facing on the other side of the canyon, so we'll work along past the bridge entrance until we have that black building between myself and the bridge guards. You'll find what appears to be the start of a way down there. Even if you can only get a short way down, you can lower yourself with ropes. Then I'll pull them up and hide them."

Jimmy said, "That'll be real handy when we want to climb back up."

Galain said, "At sundown tomorrow I'll lower the ropes again. I'll leave them down until just before sunrise. Then I'll pull them up again. I'll lower them again the next night. I think I can stay hidden in the crack in the broken facing. I may have to scamper into the brush, but I'll stay free of any moredhel who are looking about." He didn't sound too convinced. "If you need the ropes sooner than that," he added with a smile, "simply shout."

Martin looked at Arutha. "As long as they don't know we're here, we have a chance. They still look to the south, thinking us somewhere between Elvandar and here. As long as we don't give ourselves away . . ."

Arutha said, "It's as good a plan as I can come up with. Let's go."

Quickly, for they needed to be down in the canyon before sunrise, they moved among the rocks, seeking to reach the far side of the canyon rim.

Jimmy hugged the face of the plateau, hiding in the shadow below the bridge. The rim of the canyon was some hundred fifty feet above them, but there was still a chance of being seen. A narrow black crack in the face of the plateau presented itself. Jimmy turned his head to Laurie and whispered, "Of course. It has to be right under the bridge."

"Let's just hope they don't bother to look down."

Word was passed back, and Jimmy entered the fissure. It was a tight squeeze for only ten feet, then opened into a cave. Turning back toward the others, he said, "Pass a torch and flint through."

As he took them, he heard a movement behind him. He hissed a warning and spun, his dirk almost flying into his hand. The faint light coming from behind was more a hindrance than a help, for it caused most of the cave to be inky black to his eyes. Jimmy closed his eyes, relying on his other senses. He backed up and toward the crack, saying a silent prayer to the god of thieves.

From ahead he heard a scrabbling sound, like claws on rock, and heard a slow, heavy breathing. Then he remembered the gwali talking of a "bad thing" that ate one of his tribe.

Again came the noise, this time much closer, and Jimmy wished fervently for a light. He moved to the right as he heard Laurie speak his name in a questioning tone. The boy hissed, "There's some kind of animal in here."

Jimmy could hear Laurie say something to the others and the scramble as the singer moved back, away from the cave entrance. Faintly he could hear someone, perhaps Roald, saying, "Martin's coming."

Holding on to the knife with fierce intensity, Jimmy thought to himself, yes, if it comes to fighting animals, I'd send in Martin, too. He expected the large Duke of Crydee to leap in beside him at any moment and wondered what was taking so long.

Then there was sudden movement toward the boy and he leaped back and up, instinctively, almost climbing a rock face. Something struck his lower leg, and he could hear the snapping of jaws. Jimmy turned in midair and, using his native abilities, tucked and rolled with the fall, coming down on something that wasn't rock. Without hesitation, Jimmy lashed out with his dirk, feeling the point dig into something. He continued to roll off the back of the creature while a reptilian hiss and snarl filled the cave. The boy twisted as he came to his feet, pulling the dirk free. The creature spun, moving quickly, almost as quickly as Jimmy, who leaped away from the creature, blindly, and struck his head against a low-hanging outcropping of rock.

Stunned, Jimmy fell hard aginst the wall as the creature launched itself again, again missing by only a little. Jimmy, half stunned, reached out with his left hand and found his arm wrapping around the thing's neck. Like the legendary man riding the tiger, Jimmy couldn't release his hold, for the creature could not reach him as long as he held fast. Jimmy sat, letting the animal drag him around the cave, while he stabbed repeatedly at the leathery hide. With little leverage, his blows were mostly ineffective. The creature thrashed about, and Jimmy was battered against the rock walls and scraped as he was dragged about the cave. Jimmy felt panic rising up inside, for the animal seemed to be gaining in fury, and his arm felt as if it would be torn from his shoulder. Tears of fear ran down the boy's cheeks, and he hammered at the creature in terror. "Martin," he half shouted, half gulped. Where was he? Jimmy felt with sudden certainty that he was at last at the end of his vaunted luck. For the first time he could remember, he felt helpless, for there was nothing he could do to extricate himself from this situation. He felt himself go sick to his stomach and numb all over and, with dread certainty, felt fear for his life: not the exhilarating thrill of danger during a chase across the Thieves' Highway, but a horrible numbing sleepiness as if he wished to curl up in a ball and end it all.

The creature leaped about, banging Jimmy against the wall repeatedly, and suddenly was still. Jimmy continued to stab at it for a moment, then a voice said, "It's dead."

The still-woozy thief opened his eyes and saw Martin standing over him. Baru and Roald stood behind, the mercenary with a lit torch. Next to the boy lay a lizardlike creature, seven feet in length, looking like nothing as much as an iguana with a crocodile's jaws, Martin's hunting knife through the back of its skull. Martin knelt before Jimmy. "You all right?"

Jimmy scuttled away from the thing, still showing signs of panic. When it penetrated his fear-clouded senses that he was unhurt, the boy shook his head vigorously. "No, I'm not all right." He wiped away the tearstains on his face and said, "No, damn it all, I'm not." Then, with tears again coming, he said, "Damn it. I thought I . . ."

Arutha came through the fissure last and took stock of the boy's condition. He moved next to the boy, who leaned tearfully against the rock wall. Gently placing his hand upon Jimmy's arm, he said, "It's over. You're all right."

His voice betraying a mixture of anger and fear, Jimmy said, "I thought it had me. Damn, I've never been so scared in my life."

Martin said, "If you're going to be scared of something at long last, Jimmy, this beastie is a good choice. Look at the jaws on it."

Jimmy shivered. Arutha said, "We all get scared, Jimmy. You've just finally found something to be truly fearful of."

Jimmy nodded. "I hope it doesn't have a big brother about."

Arutha said, "Did you sustain any wounds?"

Jimmy took quick inventory. "Just bruises." Then he winced. "A lot of bruises."

Baru said, "A rock serpent. Good-sized one. You did well killing it with that knife, Lord Martin."

In the light the creature looked respectable, but nothing near the horror Jimmy had imagined in the dark. "That's the 'bad thing'?"

Martin said, "Most likely. As bad as it looked to you, imagine what it looks like to a three-foot-tall gwali." He held up his torch as Laurie and Arutha entered. "Let's see what this place is like."

They were in a narrow but high-ceilinged chamber, mostly limestone, from its look. The floor climbed slightly as it moved away from the fissure that led outside.

Jimmy appeared ragged, but went to the fore, taking Martin's torch and saying, "I'm still the expert at climbing into places I'm not welcome."

They moved quickly through a series of chambers, each slightly larger and located higher up than the others. The connecting chambers had an odd appearance and strange feel to them, somehow disquieting. The plateau was large enough that they moved for some time without much sense of moving upward, until Jimmy said, "We move in a spiral. I'll swear we're now above the place where Martin killed that rock serpent."

They continued their progress until they came to an apparent dead end. Looking about, Jimmy pointed upward. Above their heads by three feet was an opening in the roof. "A chimney," said Jimmy. "You climb up by putting your back to one side and feet to the other."

"What if it widens too much?" asked Laurie.

"Then it's usual to come back down. The rate of descent is up to you. I suggest you do it slowly."

Martin said, "If the gwali can get up there, we should be able."

Roald said, "Beggin' Your Grace's pardon, but do you think you could swing through the trees like them, too?"

Ignoring the remark, Martin said, "Jimmy?"

"Yes, I'll go first. I'll not end my days because one of you lost his grip and fell on me. Keep clear of the opening until I call down."

With assistance from Martin, Jimmy easily made it into the chimney. It was a good fit, with just enough room to negotiate easily. The others, especially Martin and Baru, would find it a tight fit, but they would squeeze through. Jimmy quickly made it to the top, about thirty feet from the chamber below, and found another cave. Without light he couldn't tell its size, but faint echoes of his breathing told him it was a good size. He lowered himself down just far enough to call the come ahead, then scrambled up to the lip.

By the time the first head, Roald's, popped into view, Jimmy had a torch lit. Quickly they all climbed up the chimney. The cave was large, easily two hundred feet across. The roof averaged a full twenty-five feet high. Stalagmites rose from the floor, some joining together with the stalactites above to form limestone pillars. The cave was a forest of stone. In the distance several other caves and passages could be seen.

Martin looked about. "How high do you judge we've climbed, Jimmy?"

"No more than seventy feet. Not yet halfway."

"Now which way?" asked Arutha.

Jimmy said, "Nothing for it except to try them one at a time." Picking one of the many exits, he marched toward it.

After hours of searching, Jimmy turned to Laurie and said, "The surface."

Word was passed and Arutha squeezed up past the singer to look. Above the boy's head was a narrow passage, little more than a crack. Arutha could see light above, almost blinding after the faintly lit passages. With a nod, Jimmy climbed up until he blocked out the brilliance above.

When he returned, he said, "It comes out in an outcropping of rocks. We're about a hundred yards from the bridge side of the black building. It's a big thing, two stories tall."

"Any guards?"

"None I could see."

Arutha considered, then said, "We'll wait until dark. Jimmy, can you hang close to the surface and listen?"

"There's a ledge," said the boy and scrambled back upward.

Arutha sat and the others did likewise, waiting for darkness to come.

Jimmy tensed and relaxed muscles to avoid cramping. The top of the plateau was deathly silent, except for an occasional sound carried by the wind. Mostly he heard a stray word or the sounds of boots coming from the direction of the bridge. Once he thought he heard a strange, low sound coming from the black building, but he couldn't be certain. The sun had dipped beneath the horizon, although the sky still glowed. It was certainly two hours after normal suppertime, but this high on the face of the mountains, this close to Midsummer, and this far north, the sun set long after it did in Krondor. Jimmy reminded himself that he had worked jobs before where he'd had to skip meals, but somehow that didn't stop his stomach from demanding attention.

At last it was dark enough. Jimmy, for one, was glad, and it seemed the others shared his feelings. Something about this place brought them to the edge of outright agitation. Even Martin had several times been heard muttering curses at the need to wait. No, there was something alien about this place, and it was a subtle sort of effect they were feeling. Jimmy knew he wouldn't feel secure again until this place was miles behind him and a dim memory.

Jimmy climbed out and kept watch while Martin came next, followed by the others. By agreement they split up into three groups: Baru with Laurie, Roald with Martin, and Jimmy with the Prince. They would scout the lakeshore for the plant, and as soon as one found it he would return to the crack in the rocks, waiting down below for his companions.

Arutha and Jimmy were slated to move toward the big black building, and by agreement had decided to begin their search behind the building. It seemed wise to check for guards before searching near the ancient Valheru edifice. It was impossible to know the moredhel attitude toward the place. They might hold it in similar awe to the elves' and refuse to enter, give it wide berth until some ceremony, as if it were a shrine, or they might be inside the building in numbers.

Slipping through the dark, Jimmy reached the edge of the building and hugged it. The stones felt unusually smooth. Jimmy ran his hand over them and discovered they were textured like marble. Arutha waited, weapons ready, while Jimmy did a quick circumnavigation of the building. "No one in sight," he whispered, "except at the bridge towers."

"Inside?" Arutha hissed.

Jimmy said, "Don't know. It's a big place, but only one door. Want to look?" He hoped the Prince would say no.

"Yes."

Jimmy led Arutha down along the wall and around the corner, until he came to the solitary door to the large building. Above it was a half-circle window, with a faint light showing. Jimmy signaled for Arutha to give him a boost, and the young thief scampered up to the cornice above the door. He gripped it and pulled himself up to peek through the window.

Jimmy peered about. Below him, behind the door, was an anteroom of some sort, with a stone slab floor. Beyond, double doors opened into darkness. Jimmy noticed something strange about the wall below the window. The exterior stone was only facing.

Jimmy jumped back down. "There's nothing I can see from the window."

"Nothing?"

"There's a passage into the darkness, that's all; no sign of any guards."

"Let's start looking around the lake's edge, but keep an eye on this building."

Jimmy agreed and they headed down toward the lake. The building was beginning to make his "something's odd" bump itch, but he shoved aside any distraction and concentrated on the search.

Hours were spent stalking the shore. Few water plants lined the lake's edge; the plateau was almost devoid of flora. In the distance there would be an occasional faint rustling sound, which Arutha supposed came from one of the other pairs who searched.

When the sky became grey, Jimmy alerted Arutha to the coming dawn. Giving up in disgust, the Prince accompanied the boy thief back to the crevice. Laurie and Baru were already there and Martin and Roald joined them a few minutes later. All reported no sight of Silverthorn.

Arutha remained silent, turning slowly until his back was to the others. Then he clenched his fist, looking as if he had been struck a terrible blow. All eyes were on him as he stared away into the darkness of the cave, his profile etched in relief by the faint light from above, and all saw tears upon his cheeks. Suddenly he spun to confront his companions. Hoarsely he whispered, "It must be here." He looked at each of them in turn, and they glimpsed something in his eyes: a depth of feeling, a sense of overwhelming loss that caused them to share his dread. All of them saw suffering and something dying. If there was no Silverthorn, Anita was lost.

Martin shared his brother's pain, and more, for in this instant he saw his father, in those quiet moments before Arutha had been old enough to know the depths of Borric's loss of his Lady Catherine. The elven-taught hunter felt his own chest constrict at the thought of his brother reliving those lonely nights before the hearth, beside an empty chair, with only a portrait over the fire to gaze upon. Of the three brothers, only Martin had glimpsed the profound bitterness that had haunted their father's every waking moment. If Anita died, Arutha's heart and joy might well die with her. Unwilling to surrender hope, Martin whispered, "It will be here somewhere."

Jimmy added, "There is one place we haven't looked."

Arutha said, "Inside that building."

Martin said, "Then there's only one thing to do."

Jimmy hated to hear himself say, "One of us must get inside and take a look."

SEVENTEEN

WARLORD

The cell stank of damp straw.

Pug stirred and found his hands tethered to the wall with needra-hide chains. The skin of the stolid, six-legged Tsurani beast of burden had been treated to almost the hardness of steel and was anchored firmly to the wall. Pug's head ached from the encounter with the strange magic-disrupting device. But there was another irritation. He fought off his mental sluggishness and looked at the manacles. As he began to incant a spell that would cause the chains to change to insubstantial gases, a sudden wrongness occurred. He could put no other name to it but a *wrongness.* His spell would not work. Pug sat back against the wall, knowing the cell had been blanketed by some ensorcellment neutralizing any other magic. Of course, he thought: how else does one keep a magician in jail?

Pug looked about the room. It was a dark pit of a cell with only a little light coming through a small barred opening high in the door. Something small and busy bustled through the straw near Pug's foot. He kicked and it scurried off. The walls were damp, so he judged that he and his companions were belowground. He had no way of telling how long they had been here, nor had he any idea where they were: they could be anywhere upon the world of Kelewan.

Meecham and Dominic were chained to the wall opposite Pug, while to his right Hochopepa was likewise bound. Pug knew at once that the Empire rested upon a fine balancing point for the Warlord to risk bringing harm to Hochopepa. To capture a denounced renegade was one thing, but to incarcerate a Great One of the Empire was another. By rights, a Great One should be immune to the dictates of the Warlord. Besides the Emperor, a Great One was the only possible challenge to the Warlord's rule. Kamatsu had been correct. The Warlord was nearing some major ploy or offensive in the Game of the Council, for the imprisonment of Hochopepa showed contempt for any possible opposition.

Meecham groaned and slowly looked up. "My head," he mumbled. Finding himself chained, he tugged experimentally at his bonds. "Well," he said, looking at Pug, "what now?"

Pug looked back and shook his head. "We wait."

It was a long wait, perhaps three or four hours. When someone appeared, it was suddenly. Abruptly the door had swung open and a black-robed magician entered, followed by a soldier of the Imperial Whites. Hochopepa nearly spat as he said, "Ergoran! Are you mad? Release me at once!"

The magician motioned for the soldier to release Pug. He said to Hochopepa, "I do what I do for the Empire. You consort with our enemies, fat one. I will bring word to the Assembly of your duplicity when we have finished with our punishment of this false magician."

Pug was quickly herded outside and the magician named Ergoran said, "Milamber, your display at the Imperial Games a year ago has earned you some respect—enough to ensure you do not wreak any more havoc upon those around you." Two soldiers fastened rare and costly metal bracelets upon his wrists. "The wards placed in this dungeon prevent any spell from operating within. Once you are outside the dungeon, these bracelets will cancel your powers." He motioned for the guards to bring Pug and one pushed him from behind.

Pug knew better than to waste time on Ergoran. Of all those magicians called the Warlord's pets, he had been among the most rabid. He was one of the few magicians who believed that the Assembly should be an arm of the ruling body of the Empire, the High Council. It was supposed by some who knew him that Ergoran's ultimate goal was to see the Assembly become the High Council. It had been rumored that while the hot-tempered Almecho had publicly ruled, as often as not Ergoran had been the one behind him deciding the policy of the War Party.

A long flight of stairs brought Pug into sunlight. After the darkness of the cell he was blinded for a moment. As he was pushed along through the courtyard of some immense building, his eyes quickly adjusted. He was taken up a broad flight of stairs, and as he climbed, Pug looked over his shoulder. He could see enough landmarks to know where he was. He saw the river Gagajin, which ran from the mountains called the High Wall down to the city of Jamar. It was the major north–south thoroughfare for the Empire's central provinces. Pug was in the Holy City itself, Kentosani, the capital of the Empire of Tsuranuanni. And from the dozens of white-armored guards, he knew he was in the Warlord's palace.

Pug was pushed along through a long hall until he reached a central chamber. The stone walls ended, and a rigid, painted wood-and-hide door was slid aside. A personal council chamber was where the Warlord of the Empire chose to interrogate his prisoner.

Another magician stood near the center of the room, waiting upon the pleasure of a man who sat reading a scroll. The second magician was one Pug knew only slightly, Elgahar. Pug realized he could expect no aid here, even for Hochopepa, for Elgahar was Ergoran's brother; magic talent had run deep in their family. Elgahar had always seemed to take his lead from his brother.

The man sitting upon a pile of cushions was of middle years, wearing a white robe with a single golden band trimming the neck and sleeves. Remembering Almecho, the last Warlord, Pug couldn't think of a more striking contast. This man, Axantucar, was the antithesis of his uncle in appearance. While Almecho had been a bullnecked, stocky man, a warrior in his manner, this man looked more like a scholar or teacher. His wire-thin body made him appear the ascetic. His features were almost delicate. Then he lifted his gaze up from the parchment he had been reading and Pug could see the resemblance: this man, like his uncle, had the same mad hunger for power in his eyes.

Slowly putting away his scroll, the Warlord said, "Milamber, you show courage, if not prudence, in returning. You will of course be executed, but before we have you hung, we would like to know one thing: why have you returned?"

"Upon my homeworld a power grows, a dark and evil presence that seeks to advance its cause, and that cause is the destruction of my homeland."

The Warlord seemed interested and motioned for Pug to continue. Pug told all he knew, completely and without embellishment or exaggeration. "Through magic means I have determined that this thing is of Kelewan; somehow the fate of both worlds are again intertwined."

When he was finished, the Warlord said, "You spin an interesting tale." Ergoran appeared to brush aside Pug's story, but Elgahar looked genuinely troubled. The Warlord went on, "Milamber, it is truly a shame you were taken from us during the betrayal. Had you remained, we might have found employment for you as a storyteller. A great power of darkness, aborning from some forgotten recess within our Empire. What a wonderful tale." The man's smile vanished and he leaned forward, elbow upon knee, as he looked at Pug. "Now, to the truth. This shabby nightmare you spin is but a weak attempt to frighten me into ignoring your true reasons for returning. The Blue Wheel Party and its allies are on the verge of collapse in the High Council. That is why you return, for those who counted you as ally before are desperate, knowing the utter domination of the War Party to be all but a fact. You and the fat one are again in league with those who betrayed the Alliance for War during the invasion of your homeworld. You fear the new order of things we represent. Within days I shall announce the end of the High Council, and you have come to thwart that event, true? I don't know what you have in mind, but we shall have the truth from you, if not now, then soon. And you shall name those who stand arrayed against us.

"And we will have the means of your return. Once the Empire is secure under my rule, then shall we return to your world and quickly do what should have been done under my uncle."

Pug looked from face to face and knew the truth. Pug had met and spoken with Rodric, the mad King. The Warlord was not as mad as the King had been, but there was no doubt that he was not entirely sane. And behind him stood one who betrayed little, but just enough, for Pug to understand. Ergoran was the power to be feared here, for he was the true genius behind the dominance of the War Party. It would be he who would rule in Tsuranuanni, perhaps, someday, even openly.

A messenger arrived and bowed before the Warlord, handing him a parchment. The Warlord read quickly, then said, "I must go to the council. Inform the Inquisitor I require his services the fourth hour of the night. Guards, return this one to his cell." As the guards pulled Pug about by his chain, the Warlord said, "Think on this, Milamber. You may die slowly or quickly, but you will die. The choice is yours. Either way, we shall have the truth from you eventually."

Pug watched as Dominic entered his trance. Pug had told his companions of the Warlord's reaction, and after Hochopepa had raged on for a time, the fat magician had lapsed into silence. Like others of the black robe, Hochopepa found the notion of any whim of his being ignored almost unfathomable. This imprisonment was nearly impossible to contemplate. Meecham had shown his usual taciturnity, while the monk had also seemed unperturbed. The discussion had been short and resigned.

Dominic had soon after begun his exercises, fascinating to Pug. He had sat and begun meditating until he was now entering some sort of trance. In the silence, Pug considered the monk's lesson. Even in this cell, apparently without hope, there was no need for them to surrender to fear and become mindless wretches. Pug turned his mind back, remembering his boyhood at Crydee: the frustrating lessons with Kulgan and Tully, as he sought to master a magic that he would discover, years later, he was unsuited to practice. A shame, he thought to himself. There were many things he had observed during his time at Stardock that had convinced him the Lesser Magic of Midkemia was significantly further advanced than on Kelewan. Most likely, it was a result of there being only one magic on Midkemia.

For variety, Pug tried one of the cantrips taught him by Kulgan as a boy, one he had never mastered anyway. Hmmm, he mused, the Lesser Path spell isn't affected. He began to encounter the strange blocking from within himself and almost felt amusement at it. As a boy he had feared that experience, for it signaled failure. Now he knew it was simply his mind, attuned to the Greater Path, rejecting Lesser Path discipline. Still, somehow the effects of the anti-magic wards caused him to attack the problem more obliquely. He closed his eyes, imagining the one thing he had tried on innumerable occasions, failing each time. The pattern of his mind balked at the requirements of that magic, but as it shifted to take on its normal orientation, it somehow rebounded against the wards, recoiled, and . . . Pug sat up, eyes wide. He had almost found it! For the briefest instant he had almost understood. Fighting down excitement, he closed his eyes, head down, and concentrated. If he could only find that one instant, that one crystalline instant when he had understood . . . an instant that had fled as soon as it had come . . . In this dank, squalid cell he had stood upon the brink of perhaps one of the most important discoveries in the history of Tsurani magic. If only he could recapture that instant . . .

Then the doors to the cell opened. Pug looked up, as did Hochopepa and Meecham. Dominic remained in his trance. Elgahar entered, motioning for a guard to close the door behind him. Pug stood, uncramping legs that had succumbed to the cold stones beneath the straw while he had meditated upon his boyhood.

"What you say is disturbing," said the black-robed magician.

"As it should be, for it is true."

"Perhaps, but it may not be, even if you believe it to be true. I would hear everything."

Pug motioned for the magician to sit, but he shook his head in negation. Shrugging, Pug returned to his place on the floor and began his narrative. When he reached the portion relating Rogen's vision, Elgahar became observably agitated, halting Pug to ask a series of questions. Pug continued, and when he was through, Elgahar shook his head. "Tell me, Milamber, on your homeworld, are there many who could have understood what was said to this seer in the vision?"

"No. Only myself and one or two others could have understood it; only the Tsurani in LaMut would have recognized it as ancient High Temple Tsurani."

"There is a frightening possibility. I must know if you've considered it."

"What?"

Elgahar leaned close to Pug and whispered a single word in his ear. Color drained from Pug's face and he closed his eyes. Back on Midkemia, his mind had begun the process of intuiting what it could from the information at hand. He had subconsciously known all along what the answer would be. With a single, long sigh, he said, "I have. At every turn I have shied from admitting that possibility, but it is always there."

Hochopepa said, "What is this you speak of?"

Pug shook his head. "No, old friend. Not yet. I want Elgahar to consider what he has deduced without hearing your opinion or mine. This is something that must make him reevaluate his loyalties."

"Perhaps. But even if I do, it will not necessarily alter our present circumstance."

Hochopepa exploded in rage. "How can you say such a thing! What circumstance can matter in the face of the Warlord's crimes? Have you come to the point where all your free will has been surrendered to your brother?"

Elgahar said, "Hochopepa, you of all who wear the black robe should understand, for it was you and Fumita who played in the Great Game for years with the Blue Wheel Party." He spoke of those two magicians' part in helping the Emperor end the Riftwar. "For the first time in the history of the Empire, the Emperor is in a unique position. With the betrayal at the peace conference, he has come to the position of having ultimate authority while having lost face. He may not use his influence, and he will not again utilize his authority. Five clan Warchiefs died in that betrayal, the five most likely to achieve the office of Warlord. Many families lost position in the High Council because of their deaths. Should he again attempt to order the clans, he may be refused."

"You speak of regicide," said Pug.

"It has happened before, Milamber. But that would mean civil war, for there is no heir. The Light of Heaven is young and has yet to father sons. Of his issue there are only three girls as yet. The Warlord desires only the stabilization of the Empire, not the overthrow of a dynasty more than two thousand years old. I have neither affection nor disaffection for this Warlord. But the Emperor must be made to understand that his position in the order of things is spiritual only, surrendering all final authority to the Warlord. Then shall Tsuranuanni enter an era of endless prosperity."

Hochopepa barked a bitter laugh. "That you can believe such drivel shows only that our screening at the Assembly is not rigorous enough."

Ignoring the insult, Elgahar said, "Once the internal order of the Empire has been made stable, then we can counter any possible threat you may herald. Even should what you say be true and my speculation prove accurate, there may be years before we need deal with the issue upon Kelewan—ample time to prepare. You must remember, we of the Assembly have reached new pinnacles of power never dreamed of by our ancestors. What may have been a terror to them may prove only a nuisance to ourselves."

"You fail in your arrogance, Elgahar. All of you. Hocho and I have discussed this before. Your assumption of supremacy is in error. You have not surpassed your ancestors' might; you have yet to equal it. Among the works of Macros the Black I have found tomes that reveal powers undreamed of in the millennia the Assembly's existed."

Elgahar seemed intrigued by the notion and was silent for a long time. "Perhaps," he said in a thoughtful tone at last. He moved toward the door. "You have accomplished one thing, Milamber. You convince me it is vital to keep you alive longer than the Warlord's pleasure dictates. You have knowledge we must extract. As to the rest, I must . . . think upon it."

Pug said, "Yes, Elgahar, think upon it. Think upon one word: that which you whispered in my ear."

Elgahar seemed on the verge of saying something, then spoke to the guard outside, ordering the door opened. He left, and Hochopepa said, "He's mad."

"No," said Pug. "Not mad; he simply believes what his brother tells him. Anyone who can look into Axantucar's and Ergoran's eyes and think they are the ones to bring prosperity to the Empire is a fool, a believing idealist, but not mad. Ergoran is the one we must truly fear."

They settled back to silence, and Pug returned to brooding on what Elgahar had whispered to him. The chilling possibility that represented was too dreadful to dwell upon, so he turned his mind to consider again the strange moment where for the first time in his life he glimpsed the true mastery of the Lesser Path.

Time had passed. Pug didn't know how long, but he assumed it was four hours past sunset, the time the Warlord had set for interrogation. Guards entered the cell, unshackling Meecham, Dominic, and Pug. Hochopepa was left behind.

They were marched to a room equipped with devices of torture. The Warlord stood resplendent in green and golden robes, speaking to the magician Ergoran. A man in a red hood waited silently while the three prisoners were shackled to pillars in the room, situated so they could see one another.

"Against my better judgment, Ergoran and Elgahar have convinced me it would be beneficial to keep you alive, though each has different reasons. Elgahar seemed inclined to believe your story somewhat, at least enough to think it prudent to learn all we may. Ergoran and I are not so disposed, but there are other things we wish to know. Therefore we shall begin to ensure we have only the truth from you." He signaled to the Inquisitor, who tore Dominic's robes from him, leaving him wearing only a loincloth. The Inquisitor opened a sealed pot and took out a stick heavy with some whitish substance. He daubed some on Dominic's chest and the monk stiffened. Without metals, the Tsurani had developed methods of torture different from those used on Midkemia, but equally as effective. The substance was a sticky caustic that began to blister the skin as soon as administered. Dominic screwed his eyes shut and bit back a cry.

"For reasons of economy, we thought you'd be more likely to tell us the truth if your companions were given attention first. From what your former compatriots tell us, and from that unforgivable outburst at the Imperial Games, you seem to have a compassionate nature, Milamber. Will you tell us the truth?"

"Everything I have said is true, Warlord! Torturing my friends will not change that!"

"Master!" came a cry.

The Warlord looked at his Inquisitor. "What?"

"This man . . . look." Dominic had lost his pained expression. He hung from the pillar, beatific peace upon his face.

Ergoran stepped up before the monk and examined him. "He's in some manner of trance?"

Both Warlord and magician looked at Pug, and the magician said, "What tricks does this false priest practice, Milamber?"

"He is no priest of Hantukama, true, but he is a cleric of my world. He can place his mind at rest regardless of what occurs with his body."

The Warlord nodded toward the Inquisitor, who removed a sharp knife from the table. He stepped before the monk and, with a sudden cut, sliced open his shoulder. Dominic did not move, not even an involuntary twitch, in reaction. Using pincers, the Inquisitor took a hot coal and applied it to the cut. Again the monk did not react.

The Inquisitor put away his pincers and said, "It is useless, master. His mind is blocked away. We've had this problem with priests before."

Pug's brow furrowed. While not free of politics, the temples tended to be circumspect in their relationships with the High Council. If the Warlord had been interrogating priests, that indicated movement on the part of the temples toward those allied against the War Party. From Hochopepa's ignorance of this fact, it also meant the Warlord was moving covertly and had stolen the march on his opposition. As much as anything, this told Pug that the Empire was in serious straits, even now poised on the brink of civil war. The assault upon those who stood with the Emperor would come soon.

"This one's no priest," said Ergoran, coming up to Meecham. He looked up at the tall franklin. "He's a simple slave, so he should prove more manageable." Meecham spit full in the magician's face. Ergoran, used to the unhesitating fear and respect due a Great One, was as stunned as if he had been clubbed. He staggered back, wiping spittle from his face. Enraged, he said coldly, "You've earned a slow, lingering death, slave."

Meecham smiled, for the first time Pug could remember, a broad grin, almost leering. His face was rendered impossibly demonic by the scar on his cheek. "It was worth it, you genderless mule."

In his anger, Meecham had spoken in the King's Tongue, but the tone of the insult was not lost on the magician. He reached over, pulled the sharp blade from the Inquisitor's table, and slashed a long furrow on Meecham's chest. The franklin stiffened, his face draining of color as the wound began to bleed. Ergoran stood before him in triumph. Then the Midkemian spit again.

The Inquisitor turned to the Warlord. "Master, the Great One is interfering with delicate work."

The magician stepped back, letting the knife drop. He again wiped the spittle from his face as he returned to the Warlord's side. With hatred in his voice, he said, "Don't be too hasty in speaking what you know, Milamber. I wish this carrion a long session."

Pug struggled to battle the magic neutralizing properties of the bracelets upon his wrists, but to no avail. The Inquisitor began to work upon Meecham, but the stoic franklin refused to cry out. For half an hour the Inquisitor practiced his bloody trade, until at last Meecham sounded a strangled groan and passed into semiconsciousness. The Warlord said, "Why have you returned, Milamber?"

Pug, feeling Meecham's pain as if it were his own, said, "I've told you the truth." He looked at Ergoran. "You know it's the truth." He knew his plea fell on deaf ears, for the enraged magician wished Meecham to suffer for spite, not caring that Pug had told all.

The Warlord indicated to the Inquisitor that he was to begin upon Pug. The red-hooded man tore Pug's robes open. The pot of caustic was opened and a small daub was applied to Pug's chest. Years of hard work as a slave in the swamp had left Pug a lean, muscled man, and his body tensed as the pain began. At first daub there had been no sensation, then an instant later pain seared his flesh as the chemicals in the paste reacted. Pug could almost hear the skin blister. The Warlord's voice cut through the pain. "Why have you returned? Whom have you contacted?"

Pug closed his eyes against the fire on his chest. He sought refuge in the calming exercises Kulgan had taught him as an apprentice. Another daub of paste and another fire erupted, this time on the sensitive flesh inside his thigh. Pug's mind rebelled and sought to find refuge in magic. Again and again he battled to break through the barrier imposed by the magic limiting bracelets. In his youth he had been able to find his path to magic only under great stress. When his life had been threatened by trolls, he had found his first spell. When battling Squire Roland, he had lashed out magically, and when he had destroyed the Imperial Games, it had been from a deeply held well of anger and outrage. Now his mind was an enraged animal, bouncing off the bars of a magically imposed cage, and like an animal, he reacted blindly, striking against the barrier again and again, determined either to be free or to die.

Hot coals were placed against his flesh and he screamed. It was an animal cry, mixed pain and rage, and his mind lashed out. His thoughts became blurred, as if he existed in a landscape of reflecting surfaces, a mad spinning room of mirrors, each casting back an image. He saw the kitchen boy of Crydee looking back at him in one surface, then Kulgan's student in another. In a third was the young squire, and the fourth, a slave in the Shinzawai swamp camp. But in the reflections behind the reflections, the mirrors seen within the mirrors, in each he saw a new thing. Behind the boy in the kitchen he saw a man, a servant, but there was no doubt who that man was. Pug, without magic, without training, grown to manhood as a simple member of the castle's serving staff, labored in the kitchen. Behind the image of the young squire he saw a Kingdom noble, with Princess Carline upon his arm, his wife. His mind whirled. He frantically sought something. He studied the image of Kulgan's student. Behind him he saw the reflected image of an adult practitioner of the Lesser Art. In his mind Pug spun, seeking the origin of that reflected image within an image, of the Pug grown to be a master of the Lesser Magic. Then he saw the source of that image, a possible future never realized, a chance of fate having diverted his life from that outcome. But in the alternate probabilities of his life he found what he sought. He found an escape. Suddenly he understood. A way was opened to him and his mind fled down that path.

Pug's eyes snapped open and he looked past the red-hooded figure of the Inquisitor. Meecham hung groaning, again conscious, while Dominic was still lost in a trance.

Pug used a mental ability to turn off his awareness of the injury done his body. In an instant he stood without feeling pain. Then his mind reached toward the black-robed figure of Ergoran. The Great One of the Empire almost staggered as Pug's gaze locked upon his own. For the first time in memory, a magician of the Greater Path employed a talent of the Lesser Path, and Pug engaged Ergoran in a contest of wills.

With mind-shattering force, Pug overwhelmed the magician, stunning him instantly. The black-robed figure sagged for a moment until Pug took control of his body. Closing his own eyes, Pug now saw through Ergoran's. He adjusted his senses, then had complete command over the Tsurani Great One. Ergoran's hand shot forward and a cascade of energies sprang from his fingers, striking the Inquisitor from behind. Red and purple lines of force danced along the man's body as he arched and shrieked. Then the Inquisitor danced across the room like a mad puppet, his movements jerky and spastic as he cried out in agony.

The Warlord stood briefly stunned, then screamed, "Ergoran! What insanity is this?" He grabbed at the magician's robe as the Inquisitor slammed against the far wall and fell to the stone floor. The instant the Warlord came into contact with the magician, the painful energies ceased to strike the Inquisitor and engulfed the Warlord. Axantucar writhed as he fell back from the onslaught.

The Inquisitor rose from the floor, shaking his head to clear it, and staggered back toward the captives. The red-hooded torturer pulled a slender knife from the table, sensing Pug to be the author of his pain. He stepped toward Pug, but Meecham gripped his chains and hoisted himself up. With a heave, Meecham reached out and encircled the Inquisitor's neck with his legs. In a scissors grip he held the struggling Inquisitor, squeezing with tremendous power. The Inquisitor struck at Meecham's leg with the knife, slashing it across the flesh over and over, but Meecham kept pressure on. Again and again the knife cut, until Meecham's legs were covered in his own blood, but the Inquisitor couldn't cut deeply with the blood-slick little knife. Meecham only gave a joyous cry of victory. Then, with a grunt and a jerk, he crushed the man's windpipe. As the Inquisitor collapsed, strength flowed out of the franklin. Meecham dropped, held up only by his chains. With a weak smile he nodded toward Pug.

Pug broke off the pain spell and the Warlord fell back from Ergoran. Pug commanded the magician to approach. The Great One's mind felt like a soft, malleable thing under Pug's magic control, and somehow Pug knew how to command the magician to act, while keeping aware of what he himself was doing.

The magician began freeing Pug from his chains, while the Warlord struggled to his feet. One hand was free. Axantucar staggered to the outer door. Pug made a decision. If he could be free of the bonds, he could handle any number of guards called in by the Warlord, but he couldn't control two men and he didn't think he could keep control of the magician long enough to destroy the Warlord and free himself. Or could he? Then Pug recognized the danger. This new magic was proving difficult and his judgment was slipping. Why was he allowing the Warlord to gain his freedom? The pain of torture and the exertion were taking a terrible toll, and Pug felt himself weakening by the moment. The Warlord pulled open the door, screaming for guards, and when it opened, Axantucar grabbed at a spear. With a heave, he struck Ergoran full in the back. The blow knocked the magician to his knees before he could loosen Pug's other hand. It also had the effect of sending a psychic shock back to strike Pug. Pug screamed in concert with Ergoran's dying pain.

Fog shrouded Pug's mind. Then something within cracked, and his thoughts became a sea of glittering shards as the mirrors of memory shattered; scraps of past lessons, images of his family, smells, tastes, and sounds rang through his consciousness.

Lights danced through his mind, first scattering motes of starlight, reflections of new vistas within. They weaved and danced, forming a pattern, a circle, a tunnel, then a way. He plunged through the way and found himself upon a new plane of consciousness. New paths were walked, new understandings achieved. That path opened to him before, through pain and terror, was now his to walk at will. At last he stood in command of those powers which were his legacy.

His vision cleared and he saw soldiers struggling on the stairs. Pug turned his attention to the remaining shackle upon his wrist. Suddenly he remembered an old lesson of Kulgan's. With a caress of his mind, the hardened leather shackle was made soft and supple again and he pulled his hand free.

Pug concentrated and the magic-inhibiting bracelets fell away, broken in half. He looked up at the stairs, and for the first time the full impact of what he saw registered. The Warlord and his soldiers had fled the room as some sort of struggle took place above. A soldier in the blue armor of the Kanazawai clan lay dead next to an Imperial White. Pug quickly released Meecham, easing him to the ground. He was bleeding heavily from the leg wounds and cuts to his body. Pug sent Dominic a questing mental message: *Return.* Dominic's eyes opened at once as his shackles fell off and Pug said, "Tend to Meecham." Without asking for explanation, the monk turned to treat the wounded franklin.

Pug dashed up the stairs and ran to where Hochopepa lay imprisoned. He entered the cell and the startled magician said, "What is it? I heard some noise outside."

Pug bent over and changed the manacles to soft leather. "I don't know. Allies, I think. I suspect the Blue Wheel Party is attempting to free us." He pulled Hochopepa's hands free of the now soft restraints.

Hochopepa stood on wobbly legs. "We must help them help us," he said with resolution. Then he considered his freedom and the softened restraints. "Milamber, how did you do that?"

Passing though the door, Pug answered, "I don't know, Hocho. It will be something to discuss."

Pug raced up the stairs toward the upper level of the palace. In the central gallery of the Warlord's palace, armed men struggled in hand-to-hand combat. Men in armor of various colors battled the Warlord's Imperial Whites. Looking about the bloody combat, Pug saw Axantucar fighting past a struggling pair of soldiers. Two white-armored soldiers covered his retreat. Pug closed his eyes and reached out. His eyes opened and he could see the invisible hand of energy he had created. He could feel it as he could his own. As if picking up a kitten by the neck, he reached out and gripped the Warlord. Raising him up, he drew the struggling, kicking man toward him. The soldiers halted their struggle at the sight of the Warlord above them. Axantucar, supreme warrior of the Empire, shrieked in unashamed terror at the invisible force that had grabbed him.

Pug pulled him back toward where he and Hocho stood. Some of the Imperial Whites recovered from their shock and deduced that the renegade magician must be the cause of their master's dilemma. Several broke off from their struggles with the soldiers in colored armor and ran to aid the Warlord.

Then a loud voice cried out, "Ichindar! Ninety-one times Emperor!"

Instantly every soldier in the room, regardless of which side he struggled for, dropped to the floor, putting forehead against the stone. The officers stood with heads bowed. Only Hochopepa and Pug watched as a cortege of Warchiefs, all in the armor of those who constituted the Blue Wheel Party, entered the room. In the forefront, wearing armor not seen in years, came Kamatsu, again for a time Warchief of the Kanazawai Clan. Forming up, they parted to allow the Emperor to enter. Ichindar, supreme authority of the Empire, walked into the hall, resplendent in his ceremonial golden armor. He stalked to where Pug waited, the Warlord still hanging in midair above him, and surveyed the scene. At last he said, "Great One, you do seem to cause difficulty whenever you appear." He looked up at the Warlord. "If you'll put him down, we can get to the bottom of this mess."

Pug allowed the Warlord to fall, striking the ground heavily.

"That is an amazing tale, Milamber," said Ichindar to Pug. He sat on the pillows occupied earlier that day by the Warlord, sipping a cup of the Warlord's chocha. "It would be simple to say I believe you and that all is forgiven, but the dishonor visited upon me by those you call elves and dwarves is an impossible thing to forget." Around him stood the Warchiefs of the clans of the Blue Wheel, and the magician Elgahar.

Hochopepa said, "If the Light of Heaven will permit me? Remember they were but tools, soldiers, if you will, in a game of shāh. That this Macros was attempting to prevent the arrival of the Enemy is but another concern. That he is responsible for the betrayal rids you of the responsibility of avenging yourself upon anyone but Macros. And as he is presumed dead, it is a moot issue."

The Emperor said, "Hochopepa, your tongue is as facile as a relli's." He referred to the water-snake-like creature known for its supple movement. "I will not be punitive without good cause, but I also am reluctant to take my former stance of conciliation toward the Kingdom."

Pug said, "Majesty, that would not be wise at this time, in any event." When Ichindar looked interested in the comment, Pug continued. "While I hope that someday our two nations may meet again as friends, at this time there are more pressing matters that demand attention. For the short term, it must be as if the two worlds were never rejoined."

The Emperor sat up. "From what little I understand of such matters, I suspect you are correct. Larger issues need to be resolved. I must make a decision shortly that may forever change the course of Tsurani history." He lapsed into silence. For a long time he held his own council, then said, "When Kamatsu and the others came to me, telling me of your return and your suspicion of some black terror of Tsurani origin upon your world, I wished to ignore it all. I cared nothing for your problems or those of your world. I was even indifferent to the possibility of once more invading your land. I was fearful of acting again, for I had lost much face before the High Council after the attack on your world." He seemed lost in thought a brief moment. "Your world was lovely, what little I saw before the battle." He sighed, his green eyes fastening on Pug. "Milamber, had Elgahar not come to the palace, confirming what your allies in the Blue Wheel Party reported, you most likely would be dead, and I would soon follow after, and Axantucar on his way to bloody civil war. He gained the white and gold only because of the outrage against the betrayal. You prevented my death, if not some greater calamity for the Empire. I think that warrants some consideration, though you know the turmoil in the Empire is just beginning."

Pug said, "I am enough a product of the Empire to understand that the Game of the Council will become even more vicious."

Ichindar looked outside the window, where the body of Axantucar hung twisting in the wind. "I will have to consult the historians, but that is the first Warlord hung by an Emperor, I believe." Hanging was the ultimate shame and punishment for a warrior. "Still, as he no doubt planned the same fate for myself, I don't think I'm likely to have a rebellion, at least not this week."

The Warchiefs of the High Council who were in attendance looked at one another. Finally Kamatsu said, "Light of Heaven, if I may? The War Party retires in confusion. The betrayal by the Warlord has robbed them of any base for negotiation within the High Council. Even as we speak, the War Party is no more, and its clans and families will be meeting to discuss which parties to join to regain some shred of their influence. For now the moderates rule."

The Emperor shook his head and in surprisingly strong tones said, "No, honored lord, you are wrong. In Tsuranuanni I rule." He stood, surveying those around him. "Until these matters Milamber brought to our attention are resolved and the Empire is truly safe, or the threat has been shown to be false, the High Council is recessed. There will be no new Warlord until I have commanded an election within the council. Until I decree otherwise, I am the law."

Hochopepa said, "Majesty, the Assembly?"

"As before, but be warned, Great One, see to your brothers. If another Black Robe is ever discovered involved in a plot against my house, the status of Great Ones outside the law will end. Even should I be forced to pit all the armies of the Empire against your magic might, even to the utter ruination of the Empire, I will not allow any to challenge the supremacy of the Emperor again. Is that understood?"

Hochopepa said, "It will be done, Imperial Majesty. Elgahar's renunciation and his brother's and the Warlord's acts will give others in the Assembly pause to think. I shall bring the matter before the membership."

The Emperor said to Pug, "Great One, I cannot instruct the Assembly to reinstate you, nor am I entirely comfortable having you around. But until this matter is resolved, you are free to come and go as long as you need. When you again depart for your homeworld, inform us of your findings. We shall be willing to accommodate you somewhat in preventing the destruction of your world, if we may. Now"—he started for the door—"I must return to my palace. I have an Empire to rebuild."

Pug watched as the others left. Kamatsu came up to him and said, "Great One, it seems to have ended well for a time."

"For a time, old friend. Seek to aid the Light of Heaven, for his life may be a short one when tonight's decrees are made public tomorrow."

The Lord of the Shinzawai bowed before Pug. "Your will, Great One."

To Hochopepa, Pug said, "Let's fetch Dominic and Meecham from where they rest and go to the Assembly, Hocho. We have work to do."

"In a moment, for I have a question of Elgahar." The stout magician faced the former Warlord's pet. "Why the sudden reversal of position? I had always counted you your brother's tool."

The slender magician replied, "What Milamber carried warning of, upon his homeworld, gave me pause to think. I spent time weighing all possibilities, and when I suggested the obvious answer to Milamber, he concurred. It was a risk too grave to ignore. Compared to this, all other matters are inconsequential."

Hochopepa turned to face Pug. "I do not understand. What does he speak of?"

Pug sagged in fatigue and something more, a deep-hidden terror coming to the fore. "I hesitate even to speak of it." He looked at those about him. "Elgahar concluded something I suspected but was afraid to admit, even to myself."

For a moment he was silent, and those in the room seemed to hold their breath, then he said, "The Enemy has returned."

Pug pushed back the leather-covered volume before him and said, "Another dead end." He passed a hand over his face, closing tired eyes. He had so much to deal with and a sense of fleeing time. The discovery of his ability as a Lesser Path magician he kept to himself. There was a side to his nature he had never suspected, and he wished more private conditions under which to explore these revelations.

Hochopepa and Elgahar looked up from where they sat reading. Elgahar had worked as hard as any, demonstrating some wish to make amends. "These records are in a shambles, Milamber," he commented.

Pug agreed. "I told Hocho two years ago that the Assembly had become lax in its arrogance. This confusion is but one example." Pug adjusted his black robe. When his reasons for returning were made known, he had, on a motion by his old friends, seconded by Elgahar, been reinstated to full membership without hesitation. Of the members in attendance, only a few abstained and none voted in opposition. Each had stood upon the Tower of Testing and had seen the rage and might of the Enemy.

Shimone, one of Pug's oldest friends in the Assembly and his former instructor, entered with Dominic. Since the encounter with the Warlord's Inquisitor the night before, the priest had shown remarkable recuperative powers. He had used his magic healing arts on Meecham and Pug, but something in the way they worked prevented him from using them upon himself. However, he had also possessed the knowledge to instruct the magicians at the Assembly in concocting a poultice that prevented festering in the cuts and burns he had endured.

"Milamber, this priest friend of yours is a wonder. He has some marvelous means of cataloging our works here."

Dominic said, "I have only shared what we have learned at Sarth. There is a great deal of confusion here, but it is not as bad as it appears on casual inspection."

Hochopepa stretched. "What has me concerned is that there is little here we don't already know. It is as if the vision we shared upon the tower is the earliest recollection of the Enemy, and no other has been recorded."

"That may be true," said Pug. "Remember that most of the truly great magicians perished at the golden bridge, leaving only apprentices and Lesser Magicians behind. It may have been years before any attempt to keep records commenced."

Meecham entered carrying a huge bundle of ancient tomes heavily bound in treated skins. Pug indicated a spot on the floor nearby and Meecham put them down. Pug opened the bundle and handed copies of the works around. Elgahar carefully opened one, the book's binding creaking as he did. "Gods of Tsuranuanni, these works are old."

"Among the oldest in the Assembly," Dominic said. "It took Meecham and myself an hour just to locate them and another to dig them out."

Shimone said, "This is almost another dialect, it's so ancient. There are verb usages here, inflections I've never heard of."

Hocho said, "Milamber, listen to this: 'And when the bridge vanished, still did Avarie insist on council.' "

Elgahar said, "The golden bridge?"

Pug and the others stopped what they were doing and listened as Hochopepa continued reading. " 'Of the Alstwanabi, those remaining were but thirteen, numbering Avarie, Marlee, Caron'—the list goes on—'and little comfort among them, but Marlee spoke her words of power and calmed their fears. We are upon this world made for us by Chakakan'—could that be an ancient form of 'Chochocan'?—'and we shall endure. *Those who watched say we are safe from the Darkness.'* The Darkness? Can it be?"

Pug reread the passage. "This is the same name used by Rogen after his vision. It is too far a stretch to be called coincidence. There is our proof: the Enemy is somehow involved in the attempts upon Prince Arutha."

Dominic said, "There is something else there as well."

Elgahar agreed. "Yes, who are *'those who watched'?"*

Pug pushed away the book, the toll of the last day bringing on sleep unbidden. Of all those who had searched through the day with him, only Dominic remained. The Ishapian monk seemed able to disregard fatigue at will.

Pug closed his eyes, intent on resting them for a short while only. His mind had been occupied with many things, and many things he had put aside. Now images flickered past, but none seemed to abide.

Soon Pug was asleep, and while he slept, he dreamed.

He stood upon the roof of the Assembly again. He wore the grey of a trainee, as he was shown the tower steps by Shimone. He knew he must mount, again to face the storm, again to pass that test which would gain him the rank of Great One.

He mounted and climbed in his dream, seeing something at each step, a string of flashing images. A stover bird struck the water for a fish, its scarlet wings flashing against the blue of sky and water. Then other images came flooding in, hot jungles where slaves toiled, a clash of warriors, a dying soldier, Thūn running over the tundra of the north, a young wife seducing a guard of her husband's household, a spice merchant at his stall. Then his vision traveled to the north, and he saw . . .

Ice fields, bitter-cold and swept by a steel-edged wind. He could smell the bitterness of age here. From within a tower of snow and ice, figures emerged bundled against the wind. Human-shaped, they walked with a smooth tread that marked them other than human. They were beings old and wise in ways unknown to men, and they sought a sign in the sky. They looked up and they watched. They watch. Watchers.

Pug sat up, eyes open. "What is it, Pug?" asked Dominic.

"Get the others," he said. "I know."

Pug stood before the others, his black robes blowing in the morning breeze. "You'll have no one with you?" Hochopepa asked again.

"No, Hocho. You can help by getting Dominic and Meecham back to my estate so they may return to Midkemia. I've passed along all I've learned here for Kulgan and the others, with messages for all who need know what we've discovered so far. I may be seeking a legend, trying to find these Watchers in the north. You can help more by getting my friends back."

Elgahar stepped forward. "If it is permitted, I would accompany your friends to your world."

Pug said, "Why?"

"The Assembly has little need for one caught up in the affairs of the Warlord, and from what you have said, there are Great Ones in training at your academy who need instruction. Count it an act of appeasement. I will remain there, at least for a while, continuing the education of these trainees."

Pug considered. "Very well. Kulgan will instruct you in what needs be done. Always remember that the rank of Great One means nothing on Midkemia. You will be simply one among a community. It will prove difficult."

Elgahar said, "I shall endeavor."

Hochopepa said, "That's a capital idea. I've long wondered about this barbaric land you hail from, and I could use a vacation from my wife. I'll go, too."

"Hocho," said Pug, laughing, "the academy is a rough place, devoid of your usual comforts."

He stepped forward. "Never mind that. Milamber, you'll require allies on your world. I may speak lightly, but your friends will need help and soon. The Enemy is something beyond the experience of any of us. We'll start now to combat it. As for the discomfort, I'll manage."

"Besides," said Pug, "you've been licking your lips over Macros's library ever since I've spoken of it."

Meecham shook his head. "Him and Kulgan. Two peas in a pod."

Hochopepa said, "What's a pea?"

"You'll discover soon, old friend." Pug embraced Hocho and Shimone, shook hands with Meecham and Dominic, and bowed to the other members of the Assembly. "Follow the instructions on activating the rift as I've written them. And be certain to close it, once through; the Enemy may still seek a rift to enter our worlds.

"I go to the Shinzawai estate, the northernmost destination where I can use a pattern. From there I'll take horse and cross the Thūn tundra. If the Watchers still exist, I shall find them and return to Midkemia with what they know of the Enemy. Then shall we meet again. Until then, my friends, care for one another."

Pug incanted the required spell, and with a shimmer he was gone.

The others stood about awhile. Finally Hochopepa said, "Come, we must make ready." He looked at Dominic, Meecham, and Elgahar. "Come, my friends."

EIGHTEEN

VENGEANCE

Jimmy woke with a start.

Someone had walked by on the surface. Jimmy had slept through the day with the others, awaiting the fall of night for the investigation of the black building. He had taken the position closest to the surface.

Jimmy shivered. Throughout the day his dreams had been alien, haunted by troubling images—not true nightmares, but rather dreams filled with odd longings and dim recognitions. It was almost as if he had inherited another's dreams, and that other hadn't been human. Somehow he felt lingering memories of rage and hatred. It left him feeling dirty.

Shaking off the odd, fuzzy feeling, he looked down. The others were dozing, except for Baru, who seemed to be meditating. At least, he sat upright with legs crossed and his hands before him, eyes closed and breath even.

Jimmy cautiously pulled himself upward, until he was just below the surface. Two voices sounded some distance away. ". . . here somewhere."

"If he was stupid enough to go inside, then the fault is his," came another voice with a strange accent. A Dark Brother, Jimmy thought.

"Well, I'm not going in after him—not after being warned to keep clear," said a second human voice.

"Reitz said to find Jaccon, and you know how he is about desertion. If we don't find Jaccon, he'll likely have our ears just for spite," complained the first human.

"Reitz is nothing," came the voice of the moredhel. "Murad has ordered that none should enter the black building. Would you invoke his wrath and face his Black Slayers?"

"No," said the first human voice, "but you better think of something to tell Reitz. I'm fresh out . . ."

The voices trailed off. Jimmy waited until the voices couldn't be heard, then chanced another brief look. Two humans and a moredhel were walking toward the bridge, one of the humans gesturing. They halted at the end of the bridge, pointing toward the house and explaining something. It was Murad they were speaking to. At the far end of the bridge, Jimmy could see an entire company of human horsemen waiting as the four crossed over.

Jimmy dropped down and woke Arutha. "We've got company upstairs," the boy whispered. Lowering his voice so Baru would not hear, he said, "And your old scar-faced friend is back with them."

"How close is it to sundown?"

"Less than an hour, perhaps two to full darkness."

Arutha nodded and settled in to wait. Jimmy dropped past him to the floor of the upper cavern and foraged through his pack for some jerked beef. His stomach had been reminding him he had not eaten for the last day, and he decided that if he was going to die tonight, he might as well eat first.

Time passed slowly, and Jimmy noticed that something beyond

the normal tension expected in this situation had infected the mood of each of Arutha's company. Martin and Laurie had both fallen into deep, brooding silences, and Arutha seemed introverted almost to the point of being catatonic. Baru silently mouthed chants and appeared in a trance, while Roald sat facing a wall, staring at some unseen image. Jimmy shook off distant images of strange people, oddly dressed and engaged in alien undertakings, and forced himself alert. "Hey," he said with just enough authority to jar everyone and turn their attention to him. "You all look . . . lost."

Martin's eyes seemed to focus. "I . . . I was thinking of Father."

Arutha spoke softly. "It's this place. I was . . . nearly without hope, ready to give up."

Roald said, "I was at Cutter's Gap again, only Highcastle's army wasn't going to arrive in time."

Baru said, "I was singing . . . my death chant."

Laurie crossed to stand next to Jimmy. "It's this place. I was thinking Carline had found another while I was gone." He looked at Jimmy. "You?"

Jimmy shrugged. "It hit me funny, too, but maybe it's my age or something. It only made me think of strange people dressed in weird clothing. I don't know. It sort of makes me angry."

Martin said, "The elves said the moredhel come here to dream dreams of power."

Jimmy said, "Well, all I know is you looked like those walking dead." He moved toward the crevice. "It's dark. Why don't I go look about, and if things are quiet, then we can all go."

Arutha said, "I think perhaps you and I should go together."

"No," said the boy thief. "I hate to show a lack of deference, but if I'm to risk my life doing something I'm expert in, let me do it. You need to have someone crawl about inside that place, and I'll not have you tagging after."

"It's too dangerous," said Arutha.

"I'll not deny that," answered Jimmy. "I'll guarantee that Dragon Lord shrine will need some skill cracking, and if you've any sense you'll let me go alone. Otherwise you'll be dead before I can say, 'Don't step there, Highness,' and we might as well not have bothered in the first place. We could have just let the Nighthawks skewer you, and I'd have spent many more comfortable nights in Krondor."

Martin said, "He's right."

Arutha said, "I don't like this, but you are right." As the boy turned to go, he added, "Have I told you that you put me in mind of that pirate Amos Trask sometimes?"

In the darkness they could sense the boy's grin.

Jimmy scampered up through the crevice and peered out. Seeing no one, he made a quick run for the building. Coming up against the wall, he edged around until he was before the door. He stood quietly for a moment, judging the best way to approach the problem. He studied the door once again, then quickly clambered up the wall, finding finger- and toeholds in the molding next to the door. Again he studied the anteroom through the window. Double doors opened up into darkness beyond. Otherwise the room was empty. Jimmy glanced upward and was confronted by a blank ceiling. What was waiting inside to kill him? As sure as dogs had fleas, there was a trap inside. And if so, what sort and how to get around it? Again Jimmy was visited by the nagging itch of something odd about this place.

Jimmy dropped back to the ground and took a deep breath. He reached out and lifted the latch of the door. With a shove, he leaped aside, to the left, so the swinging door, hinged on the right, would shield him from anything behind it for an instant. Nothing happened.

Jimmy peered cautiously inside, letting his senses seek out inconsistencies, flaws in the design of the place, any clue to reveal a trap. He saw none. Jimmy leaned against the door. What if the trap were magic? He had no defenses against some enchantment meant to kill humans, non-moredhel, anyone wearing green, or whatever it might be. Jimmy stuck his hand across the portal, ready to snatch it back. Nothing happened.

Jimmy sat. Then he lay down. From the low angle everything looked different and he hoped he might see something. As he rose, something did register. The floor was made of marble slabs of equal size and texture, with slight cracks between them. He lightly placed his foot on the slab before the door, slowly permitting his weight to fall upon it, feeling for any movement. There was none.

Jimmy entered and moved around toward the far doors. He inspected every stone slab before he stepped upon it, and decided none were trapped. He inspected the walls and ceiling, gauging everything about the room that might provide him with some intelligence. Nothing. The old, familiar feeling plagued Jimmy: something was wrong here.

With a sigh, Jimmy faced the open doors into the heart of the building and entered.

Jimmy had seen many unsavory characters in his former occupation, and this Jaccon would have fitted in perfectly. Jimmy lay flat and rolled the corpse over. As the dead man's weight landed upon the other stone before the door, there was a faint snapping sound and something sped overhead. Jimmy examined Jaccon and found a small dart stuck in the man's chest near the collarbone. Jimmy didn't touch it; he didn't have to: he knew it contained a quick-acting poison. Another item of interest on the fellow was a beautifully carved dagger with a jeweled hilt. Jimmy plucked it from the man's belt and stuck it inside his tunic.

Jimmy sat back upon his heels. He had walked through a long, blank hall, with no doors, down into a subterranean level of the building. He judged he stood less than a hundred yards from the caverns where Arutha and the others waited. He had stumbled upon the corpse at the only door leaving the hall. The stone slab directly beyond the door was ever so slightly depressed.

He rose and stepped through the door, diagonally to the stone next to the one before the door. The trap was so obvious it shouted for caution, but this fool, in his rush toward fabled wealth, had walked into it. And paid the price.

Something bothered Jimmy. The trap was *too* obvious. It was as if someone wanted him to feel confident in defeating it. He shook his head. Whatever tendency toward incaution he'd had was gone. Now he was fully professional, a thief who understood that any misstep would likely be his last.

Jimmy wished for more light than was provided by the single torch he had brought along. He inspected the floor below Jaccon and saw another displaced stone. He ran his hand along the doorjamb and found no trip wire or other triggering device. Stepping across the threshold, avoiding the stones before the door, Jimmy passed the corpse and continued on toward the heart of the building.

It was a circular room. In the center of it a slender pedestal rose. Upon the pedestal sat a crystal sphere, lit from above by some unseen light source. And within the sphere rested a single branch with silver-green leaves, red berries, and silver thorns. Jimmy walked cautiously. He looked everywhere but where the pedestal rested. He explored every inch of the room he could reach without entering the pool of light about the sphere, and found nothing resembling a trap-springing device. But the nagging at the back of Jimmy's mind, which had been with him all along, kept shouting that something was wrong about this place. Since discovering Jaccon, he had avoided three different traps, all easy enough for any competent thief to spot. Now here, where he expected the last trap to be, he found none.

Jimmy sat down on the floor and began to think.

Arutha and the others came alert. Jimmy came scrambling back down into the crevice, to land with a thud on the floor of the cave. "What did you find?" asked Arutha.

"It's a big place. It's got lots of empty rooms, all cleverly fashioned so that you can only move one way from the door to the center of the building and out. There's nothing in there but some sort of little shrine in the center. There're a few traps, simple enough ones to get around.

"But the whole thing's too off-center. Something's not right. The building's a fake."

"What?" said Arutha.

"Just suppose you wanted to catch you, and you were worried about you being very clever. Don't you think you might just add one last catchall in case all the bright lads you hired to catch you were a mite slow?"

"You think the building's a trap?" said Martin.

"Yes, a big elaborate, clever trap. Look, suppose you got this mystic lake and all your tribe comes here to make magic or get power from the dead or whatever it is the Dark Brothers do up here? You want to add this one last catchall, so you think like a human. Maybe Dragon Lords don't build buildings, but humans do, so you build this building, this big building with nothing in it. Then you put a sprig of Silverthorn in some place, like in a shrine inside, and you rig a trap. Someone finds the little hellos you put along the way, gets around them, thinking they're being very, very clever, wanders about, finds the Silverthorn, pulls it, and . . ."

"And the trap springs," said Laurie, his tone appreciative of the boy's logic.

"And the trap springs," said Jimmy. "I don't know how they did it, but I'll bet the last trap is magic of some sort. The rest were too easy to find, then, at the end, nothing. I bet you touch the sphere with the Silverthorn in it and a dozen doors between you and the outside slam shut, a hundred of those dead warriors come out of the walls, or the whole building simply falls on you."

Arutha said, "I'm not convinced."

"Look, you've got a greedy pack of bandits up there. Most of them aren't very smart or they wouldn't be outlaws living in the mountains. They'd be self-respecting thieves in a city. Besides being stupid, they're greedy. So they come up here to earn some gold looking for the Prince and they're told, 'Don't go in the building.' Now, each one of these clever lads thinks the moredhel are lying, because he knows everyone else is as stupid and greedy as he is. One of these clever lads goes up there looking around, and gets a dart in the gullet for his efforts.

"After I found the sphere on the pedestal, I doubled back and really looked around. That place was built by the moredhel, recently. It's about as ancient as I am. It's mostly a wood building, with stone facing. I've been in old buildings. This isn't one. I don't know how they did it. Maybe with magic, or just a whole lot of slave labor, but it's no more than a few months old."

"But Galain said this was a Valheru place," said Arutha.

Martin said, "I think him right, but I think Jimmy right as well. Remember what you told me of Tomas's rescue from the Valheru underground hall by Dolgan, just before the war?" Arutha said he did. "That place sounds much like this."

"Light a torch," said Arutha. Roald did so, and they moved away from the crevice.

Laurie said, "Has anyone noticed that for a cave the ground is fairly flat?"

"And the walls're pretty regular," added Roald.

Baru looked about. "In our haste we never examined this place closely. It is not natural. The boy is right. The building is a trap."

Martin said, "This cave system has had two thousand years or more to wear away. With that fissure above us, rain comes through here every winter, as well as seepage from the lake above. It has worn away most of what was carved upon the walls." He ran his hand over what seemed at first glance to be swirls in the stone. "But not all." He indicated some design on the walls, rendered abstract by years of erosion.

Baru said, "And so we dream ancient dreams of hopelessness."

Jimmy said, "There are some tunnels we haven't explored yet. Let's have a look."

Arutha looked at his companions. "Very well. You take the lead, Jimmy. Let's backtrack to that cave with all the tunnels, then you pick a likely one and we'll see where it leads."

In the third tunnel they found the stairway leading down. Following it, they came to a large hallway, ancient from the look of the sediment upon the floor. Regarding it, Baru said, "No foot has trod this hall in ages."

Tapping the surface of the floor with his boot, Martin agreed. "This is years of buildup."

Jimmy led them along, under giant vaulted arches from which hung dust-laden torch holders, long rusted to near-uselessness. At the far end of the hall they discovered a chamber. Roald inspected the giant iron hinges, now grotesquely twisted lumps of rust, barely recognizable, where once huge doors had hung. "Whatever wanted through the door that was here didn't seem willing to wait."

Passing through the portal, Jimmy halted. "Look at this."

They faced what seemed a large hall, with faint echoes of ancient grandeur. Tapestries, now little more than shredded rags with no hint of color, hung along the walls. Their torches cast flickering shadows upon the walls, giving the impression that ancient memories were awakening after eons of sleep. What might have once been any number of recognizable things were now scattered piles of debris tossed about the hall. Splinters of wood, a twisted piece of iron, a single gold shard, all hinted at what might have once been, without revealing lost truths. The only intact object in the room was a stone throne atop a raised dais halfway along the right-hand wall. Martin approached and gently touched the centuries-old stone. "Once a Valheru sat here. This was his seat of power." As if remembering a dream, all in the hall were visited with a sense of how alien this place was. Millennia gone, the power of the Dragon Lord was still a faint presence. There was no mistaking it now: here they stood in the heart of an ancient race's legacy. This was a source of the moredhel dreams, one of the places of power along the Dark Path.

Roald said, "There's not much left. What caused this? Looters? The Dark Brotherhood?"

Martin looked about, as if seeing ages of history in the dust upon the walls. "I don't think so. From what I know of ancient lore, this may have endured from the time of the Chaos Wars." He indicated the utter destruction. "They fought on the backs of dragons. They challenged the gods, or so legends say. Little that witnessed that struggle survived. We will probably never know the truth."

Jimmy had been scampering about the chamber, poking here and there. At last he returned and said, "Nothing growing here."

"Then where is the Silverthorn?" Arutha asked bitterly. "We have looked everywhere."

Everyone was silent for a long minute. Finally Jimmy said, "Not everywhere. We've looked around the lake, and"—he waved his hand around the hall—"under the lake. But we haven't looked *in* the lake."

"In the lake?" said Martin.

Jimmy said, "Calin and Galain said it grew very close to the edge of the water. So, had anyone thought to ask the elves if there have been heavy rains this year?"

Martin's eyes widened. "The water level's risen!"

"Anyone want to go swimming?" asked Jimmy.

Jimmy pulled his foot back. "It's cold," he whispered.

Martin said to Baru. "City boy. He's seven thousand feet up in the mountains and he's surprised the lake's cold."

Martin waded into the water, slowly, so as not to splash. Baru followed. Jimmy took a deep breath and followed, wincing every step as the water reached higher. When he stepped off a ledge, he plunged in up to his waist and opened his mouth in a silent gasp of pain. Upon the shore, Laurie winced in sympathy. Arutha and Roald kept watch for any sign of alarm on the bridge. All three crouched low, behind the gentle slope down to the water. The night was quiet, and most of the moredhel and human renegades slept on the far side of the bridge. They had decided to wait until the hours just before dawn. It was likely the guards would be half-asleep if they were humans, and even moredhel were likely to make the assumption that nothing would occur just before sunrise.

Faint sounds of movement in the water were followed by a gasp as Jimmy ducked his head underwater for the first time and came right up again. Gulping air, he ducked back under. Like the others, he worked blind, feeling along. Suddenly his hand smarted as he stuck himself on something sharp among the moss-covered rocks. He came up with what seemed a noisy gasp, but nothing at the bridge indicated he was heard. Ducking under, he felt the slimy rocks. He located the thorny plant by sticking himself again, but he didn't jump up. He took two more punctures getting a grip on the plant and pulling, but suddenly it came up. Breaking the surface, he whispered, "I've got something."

Grinning, he held up a plant that gleamed almost white in the light of the little moon. It looked like red berries stuck onto the branches of a rose branch with silver thorns. Jimmy turned it in appreciation. With a tiny "Ah" of triumph, he said, "I've got it."

Martin and Baru waded over and inspected the plant. "Is this enough?" asked the Hadati.

Arutha said, "The elves never told us. Get some more if you can, but we wait only a few more minutes." Gingerly he wrapped the plant in a cloth and stowed it in his pack.

In ten minutes they had found three more plants. Arutha was convinced this was enough and signaled it was time to return to the cave. Jimmy, Martin, and Baru, dripping and chilled, hurried to the crevice and entered, with the others keeping watch.

Inside the cave, Arutha looked a man reborn as he inspected the plants under the faint light of a small brand Roald held aloft.

Jimmy couldn't keep his teeth from chattering as he grinned at Martin. Arutha could not take his eyes from the plant. He marveled at the odd sensations that coursed through his body as he regarded the branches with their silver thorns, red berries, and green leaves. For beyond the branches, in a place only he could see, he knew a soft laugh might be heard again, a soft hand might touch his face, and the embodiment of every happiness he had known might somehow be his again.

Jimmy looked at Laurie. "Damn me if I don't think we're going to do it."

Laurie threw Jimmy his tunic. "Now all we have to do is get back down."

Arutha's head came up. "Dress quickly. We leave at once."

As Arutha breasted the rim of the canyon, Galain said, "I was about to pull the ropes up again. You cut it fine, Prince Arutha."

"I thought it best to be down the mountain as soon as possible, rather than wait another day."

"That I cannot argue," agreed the elf. "Last night there was some argument between the chief of the renegades and the moredhel leaders. I couldn't get close enough to hear, but as the dark ones and humans don't get along very well, I judge this arrangement soon to end. If that happens, this Murad may decide to cease waiting and begin looking once more."

"Then we had best get as far from here as we can before light."

Already the sky was turning grey as false dawn visited the mountains. Fortune was with them in part, for on this side of the mountains they would have shadows to hide within awhile longer than had they faced the sunrise. It would be only a little help, but any was welcome.

Martin, Baru, and Roald were quickly up the ropes. Laurie struggled a little, not having the knack of climbing, a fact he had failed to mention to the others. With silent urging from his companions, he finally cleared the rim.

Jimmy scampered quickly upward. The morning light was growing. Jimmy feared being seen against the rock face of the canyon should anyone move from the bridge. In his haste, he became incautious and slipped on an outcropping, the toe of his boot skidding off the rock. He gripped the rope as he fell a few feet and grunted as he slammed into the face of the canyon. Then pain exploded along his side and he bit back a shout. Gasping silently for breath, he turned his back to the wall of the canyon. With a spasm of movement he wrapped the rope under his left arm and gripped it tightly. Gingerly he reached inside his tunic and felt the knife he had pilfered from the dead man. When dressing, he had hastily returned it to his tunic rather than place it in his pack as he should have done. Now at least two inches of steel stuck in his side. Keeping his voice in control, he whispered, "Pull me up."

Jimmy nearly lost his grip with the first wave of pain that struck as they hauled the rope upward. He slipped and gritted his teeth. Then he was over the rim.

"What happened?" asked the Prince.

"I got careless," answered the boy. "Lift my tunic."

Laurie did so and swore. Martin nodded at the boy, who returned the gesture. Then he pulled the knife and Jimmy almost fainted. Martin cut a section of a cloak and bound the boy's side. He motioned to Laurie and Roald, who supported the boy between them as they moved away from the canyon. As they hurried through the quickly brightening morning, Laurie said, "You just couldn't do it the easy way, could you?"

They had managed to avoid detection while carrying Jimmy, for the first half of the day. The moredhel still did not know Moraelin had been invaded, and looked outward, awaiting the approach of those who now sought to escape.

But now they watched a moredhel lookout. He sat perched upon the outcropping that had caused so much trouble getting past before, and under which they must again pass. It was near noon, and they huddled down inside a depression, barely out of sight. Martin signaled to Galain, asking if the elf wanted to move first or second. The elf moved out, letting Martin follow. The afternoon was still, the day lacking even the slight breeze that had covered small movements when they had passed three nights earlier. Now it took all the skill the elf and Martin possessed to move a scant twenty feet without alerting the sentry.

Martin nocked an arrow and took aim over Galain's shoulder.

Galain pulled his hunting knife and rose up beside the moredhel. Galain tapped him on the shoulder. The dark elf spun at the unexpected contact, and Galain slashed his knife across his throat. The moredhel reared up and Martin's arrow took him in the chest. Galain grabbed him about the knees, lowering him back to his sitting position. He twisted Martin's arrow, breaking it off rather than trying to pull out the barb. In only moments the moredhel had been killed and still seemed at his post.

Martin and Galain ducked back down and faced the others. "He'll be discovered in a few hours. They may think us on our way in and search above us first, but then they'll be down the mountain. Now we must fly. We're two days to the outer reaches of the elven forests if we don't stop. Come."

They scrambled down the trail, Jimmy wincing as he was half carried by Laurie. "If the horses are still there," muttered Roald.

"If they're not," said Jimmy weakly, "at least it's all downhill."

They stopped only to let the horses get the minimal rest they required to survive a cross-country run. It would be likely the animals would not be usable after the dash, but that could not be helped. Arutha would let nothing prevent his return now that he possessed the means for Anita's cure. Before, he had been a man on the edge of despair; now a flame burned within, and he would let nothing extinguish it. Through the night they rode.

Lathered, panting horses were led by exhausted riders down the woodland trail. They had entered deep forest, still in the foothills of the mountains, but close to the boundary of the elven forests. Jimmy was half-conscious from loss of blood, fatigue, and pain. The wound had opened again sometime during the night and he had been unable to do more than clutch his side. Then the boy's eyes rolled up and he fell face down onto the trail.

When he regained consciousness, he sat up, held by Laurie and Baru while Martin and Roald wrapped him in fresh bandages cut from Martin's cloak. "This'll have to do until we reach Elvandar," said Martin.

Arutha said, "If it opens again, say something. Galain, ride double with him, and don't let him fall off."

Once again they were in the saddle, and once again they endured the nightmare ride.

Near sundown of the second day, the first horse faltered. Martin put it down quickly and said, "I'll run for a while."

For nearly three miles the Duke ran; though the fatigued horses' pace was slower than normal, this was still an impressive feat. Baru took to the trail for a while, then Galain, but still they were reaching their limit. The horses were reduced to a loping canter and trotting. Then they could only walk.

In silence they moved through the night, simply counting the passing yards as each minute took them closer to safety, knowing that, somewhere behind, the mute moredhel captain and his Black Slayers followed. Near morning they crossed a small trail and Martin said, "Here they must split forces, for they can't know we haven't turned east for Stone Mountain."

Arutha said, "Everyone dismount."

They did and the Prince said, "Martin, lead the horses toward Stone Mountain for a while, then turn them loose. We'll continue on foot."

Martin did as he was bidden while Baru masked the tracks of those on foot. Martin caught up with them an hour later. As he ran down a woodland trail toward them, he said, "I think I heard something behind. I can't be sure. The wind is picking up and the noise was faint."

Arutha said, "We continue toward Elvandar, but keep alert for a defensible position." He started a stagger-legged run, and the others took off after him, Jimmy supported in part by Martin.

For nearly an hour they half ran, half stumbled along, until the sounds of pursuit could be heard echoing through the woods. They felt a surge of energy as fear drove them onward. Then Arutha pointed toward an outcropping of rock, in a semicircle that formed an almost perfect natural breastwork. He asked Galain, "How far until help?"

The elf studied the woods in the early morning light and said, "We are near the edge of our forests. My people will be an hour away, perhaps two."

Arutha quickly gave the elf the pack containing the Silverthorn and said, "Take Jimmy. We'll hold them here until you return." They all knew the pack was against the possibility the elf didn't return in time. At least Anita could still be cured.

Jimmy sat down on the rock. "Don't be ridiculous. I would double the time he'll take to find help. I can fight standing still better than I can run." With that he crawled over the stone breastwork and pulled out his dirk.

Arutha looked at the boy: tired, bleeding again, almost collapsing from fatigue and blood loss, but grinning at him while holding his dirk. Arutha gave a curt nod and the elf was off. Quickly they got behind the rocks, drew weapons, and waited.

For long minutes they huddled down behind the rocks, knowing that as each minute passed, their chances of rescue increased. Almost with each breath they could feel rescue and obliteration racing toward them. Chance as much as anything would determine their survival. If Calin and his warriors were waiting close to the edge of the forest, and Galain could quickly locate them, there was hope; if not, no hope. In the distance the sound of riders grew louder. Each moment passed slowly, each instant of possible discovery dragging by, and the agony of waiting increased. Then, in almost welcome relief, a shout was sounded and the moredhel were upon them.

Martin rose up, his bow already drawn by the time he had a target. The first moredhel to see them was propelled backward out of his saddle by the force of the arrow taking him in the chest. Arutha and the others made ready. A dozen moredhel riders milled about, startled at the sudden bow fire. Before they could react, Martin had another down. Three turned and rode away, but the others charged.

The outcropping reared up and spread out, making it impossible for the moredhel to overrun them, but they came at full gallop anyway, their horses' hooves making dull thunder upon the still-damp ground. Though they rode close to the necks of their horses, two more were taken by Martin's bow before they reached the stone redoubt. Then the moredhel were upon them. Baru leaped atop the rocks, his long sword a blur as he sliced through the air. A moredhel fell, his arm severed from his body.

Arutha ran up and jumped from the rocks, dragging a Dark

Brother from the saddle. The moredhel died under his knife. He spun in place, his rapier coming from its sheath as another rider charged. The Prince stood his ground until the last, then with a sideways leap and a slash unseated the rider. A quick thrust, and the moredhel died.

Roald pulled one from his saddle and they both slid down into the protection of the rocks. Jimmy waited as they rolled about, then, when he saw an opening, another Dark Brother died as the boy used his dirk.

The two remaining saw Laurie and Martin ready, and chose to retreat. Both died as Martin's bow sang in the morning light. As soon as they were out of the saddle, Martin was over the rocks. He quickly scavenged the bodies and returned with a short bow and two quivers of arrows. "I'm almost out," he said, indicating his depleted quiver. "These are no cloth-yard shafts, but I can use this little horse bow if I need."

Arutha looked about. "There'll be more along soon."

"Do we run?" asked Jimmy.

"No. We would only gain a little, and we might not find a place nearly as defensible. We wait."

Minutes passed and all waited with eyes turned toward the trail they knew the moredhel would use to attack them. Laurie whispered, "Run, Galain, run."

For what seemed an eternity the woods were silent. Then in clouds of dust, with hooves pounding the ground, horsemen came into view.

The giant mute, Murad, rode in the van, a dozen Black Slayers behind him. Other moredhel and human renegades followed. Murad reined in, signaling for the others to halt.

Jimmy groaned. "There's a hundred of them."

Roald said, "Not a hundred, more like thirty."

Laurie said, "That's enough."

Arutha looked over the rock, saying, "We may be able to hold for a few minutes." They all knew it was hopeless.

Then Baru stood. And before anyone could prevent him, he started shouting at the moredhel, in a language unknown to Jimmy, the Prince, and Martin. Laurie and Roald shook their heads.

Arutha began to reach for the hillman, but Laurie said, "Don't. He's challenging Murad to personal combat. A matter of honor."

"Will he accept?"

Roald shrugged. "They're a funny lot. I've fought the Dark Brothers before. Some of them are cutthroat renegades. But most are caught up in honor and ritual and the like. Depends on where you find them. If that lot's a gang of moss-troopers from north Yabon, they'll simply attack. But if Murad's got a band of old-fashioned deep-forest Dark Brothers under his command, they may not take kindly to him saying no. If he's trying to show some magic powers are backing him, he can't rightly refuse and keep their loyalty. But mostly it depends on what Murad thinks about matters of honor."

"Whatever's the outcome, Baru's thrown them into confusion," observed Martin.

Arutha could see the moredhel standing about while the mute stared impassively at Baru. Then Murad waved his hand toward Baru and the others. A moredhel in a cloak rode forward, turning his horse to face Murad, and said something in a questioning tone.

The mute motioned again, and the moredhel who confronted him waved the other away. The moredhel riders, except for those wearing black armor, retreated their mounts several yards. One of the humans rode up and turned his horse to face Murad. He shouted something at the moredhel leader, several other humans behind echoing the tones.

"Martin," said Arutha, "can you make out what's being said?"

"No. But whatever it is, it isn't flattering, that's for certain."

Suddenly Murad drew his own sword and struck the offending human. Another human shouted something and seemed ready to ride forward, but two moredhel rode to intercept him. With a sullen expression the first brigand turned his horse and rode back to join the other humans.

Murad again gestured toward the humans, and charged his horse.

Baru leaped from the rocks and ran a short way forward to take up position. He stood his ground, his sword drawn back to strike. As the horse was almost upon him, Baru lashed out with a circling step that took him from harm's way, and the horse nickered in pain as it stumbled.

The wounded animal went down. Murad, despite his bulk, rolled from the falling animal and came up, sword still in hand. He was quick and turned in time to meet Baru's attack. The two combatants clashed, steel ringing on steel.

Arutha looked about. The dozen Black Slayers waited quietly, though for how long Arutha did not know. With Murad involved in a matter of honor, they might wait until the issue was decided. The Prince fervently hoped so.

All eyes watched; Martin said, "Don't let down your guard. As soon as this is over, either way, they'll hit us again."

"At least I can catch my breath," said Jimmy.

Arutha surveyed the area. Twenty more moredhel were approaching the area. All Baru did was buy them time.

Murad struck out and was struck in return. Within minutes both combatants were a mass of bleeding wounds, testimony to how each was able to almost deliver a death blow, but not quite. Cut and parry, lunge and riposte, slash and dodge, the struggle went on. The Hadati was equal in height to the moredhel, but the dark elf bulked larger. With a series of overhead, clubbing blows, Murad began to drive Baru back.

Martin brought his bow to the ready. "Baru's tiring. It'll be over soon."

But like a dancer timing his moves to the music, Baru let Murad fall into a pattern. Up and down the sword rose and fell, then, when it was rising, Baru ceased his retreat, instead stepping forward and to the side. With a sweeping cut, he sliced Murad's ribs. It was a deep cut that bled fiercely.

"That's a surprise," Martin said calmly.

"Damn fine move," said Roald in professional appreciation.

But Murad didn't let the surprising blow finish him. He turned in place and grabbed the Hadati's sword arm. Murad was off balance, but he pulled Baru down with him. They grappled and rolled down the hill toward the rocks where Arutha stood. Weapons slipped from blood-wet fingers and the two combatants struck at each other with fists.

Then they were up again, but Murad had his arms about Baru's waist. Hoisting the Hadati into the air, the moredhel placed interlocked hands in the small of Baru's back, squeezing to break his spine. Baru's head went back as he cried out in pain. Then he brought his hands together in a thunderous slap over the moredhel's ears, rupturing his eardrums.

Murad gave a warbling, gurgling cry of pain as he dropped Baru. The creature covered his ears with his hands, blinded by pain for a moment. Baru reared back and struck the moredhel in the face with his fist, a staggering blow that pulped Murad's nose, broke some teeth, and split his lip.

Again Baru struck him in the face, jerking his head back, and again. The Hadati seemed on the verge of clubbing the moredhel to death. But Murad gripped Baru's wrist and pulled him down, and again they rolled upon the ground.

Then Murad was atop Baru, and each had his hands around the other's neck. With grunts of pain and exertion, the two began choking each other.

Jimmy reached down and took a dagger from the body of the dead moredhel at his feet, to supplement his dirk. Martin said, "Soon. Soon."

Murad bore down with all his weight, his face turning red, as did Baru's. Neither could breathe, and it was only a question of who succumbed first. Baru bore the bulk of the moredhel atop him, but Murad had a deep wound in his side, which still bled, weakening him as every second passed.

Then, with a grunt and sigh, Murad fell forward onto Baru. There was silence in the woods for a long moment before Murad moved. With a roll he fell over, off Baru. The Hadati slowly rose. Taking a knife from the moredhel's own belt, he slowly cut Murad's throat. Sitting back upon his heels, Baru breathed deeply. Then, with deliberate contempt for his own danger, he plunged his knife deep into Murad's chest.

"What's he doing?" asked Roald.

Martin said, "Remember what Tathar said about the Black Slayers. He's cutting Murad's heart out, just in case he might try to rise again."

More moredhel and renagades had joined the company overlooking the combat, and now more than fifty riders watched the Hadati butcher the moredhel chieftain. The Hadati cut down into the chest, then his hand plunged deep within the wound and with a single jerk he pulled Murad's heart free. Holding his hand up, so that all might see, he showed the assembled moredhel and humans that Murad's heart beat no longer. Then he tossed it aside and rose drunkenly to his feet.

With a staggering, wobbling run, he tried for the rocks, only ten yards away. A moredhel rider moved to strike him from the side, and Jimmy threw his dagger. The point took the creature in the eye, causing him to scream as he fell back out of the saddle. But another came at Baru and cut at him. The sword took him in the side, and the Hadati fell forward.

"Damn you!" shouted Jimmy, near tears. "He won. You could have let him come back!" He threw his dirk, but the other rider dodged. The moredhel who had struck Baru stiffened and turned, and Arutha and his companions saw an arrow in his back. Another moredhel shouted something as he put away his bow. This brought an angry shout from a third and one of the humans.

"What is all this?" asked Arutha.

Roald said, "The one who killed Baru is a renegade: no honor. That fellow on the horse seems to have had the same opinion as Jimmy. The Hadati won, he should have been allowed to return to die with his companions. Now the slayer, another renegade, and the human bandits are all shouting at one another. We might gain a little time, or at least have some of them quit, now that their big chieftain is dead."

Then the Black Slayers charged.

Martin reared up and began firing. The archer's speed was phenomenal, and three riders were unhorsed before they reached the rock abutment.

Steel clashed upon steel and the battle was joined. Roald leaped atop the rock, as had Baru before, and his sword also struck out at all who came within his reach. No moredhel could ride in close enough to strike him with their short swords, while his broadsword delivered death to whoever rode within reach.

Arutha parried a blow aimed at Laurie, then struck upward from a crouch to take a rider. Roald leaped and dragged one from saddle and clubbed him with the hilt of his sword. Seven moredhel died before the others withdrew.

Arutha said, "They didn't all charge."

The others could see that some of the moredhel had held back, and others were still arguing, along with two human renegades. A few of the Black Slayers were still mounted, and they were ignoring what transpired with their companions, forming for another charge.

Jimmy liberated another dagger from a moredhel just at the edge of the rocks, then noticed something. He tugged at Martin's sleeve. "See that ugly-looking fellow with the fancy red breastplate and all those gold rings and things?"

Martin saw such a one sitting at the head of the human riders. "Yes."

"Can you kill him now?"

"It's a difficult shot. Why?"

"Because as sure as there's elves in the woods, that's Reitz. He's captain of that band of outlaws. You knock him off and the others will most likely run away, or at least keep holding back until a new captain's elected."

Martin rose up, took aim, and let fly. The shaft sped between the boles of the trees and took the indicated rider in the throat. With a snap his head came up and he somersaulted backward out of his saddle.

"Amazing," said Jimmy.

Martin said, "I had to clear the top of that breastplate."

Laurie said dryly, "Not very sporting, shooting without warning."

"You may convey my apologies," said Martin. "I forgot you singers always have the heroes acting that way in your sagas."

"If we're the heroes," said Jimmy, "the outlaws should run away."

True to Jimmy's prediction, the human renegades began muttering among themselves, and were suddenly riding away. One moredhel shouted after them angrily, then waved another attack upon the Prince's party. Another moredhel spit on the ground before the first and turned his horse, motioning some companions away as well. Twenty or so rode after the humans.

Arutha counted. "Fewer than twenty this time, and the Slayers."

The riders dismounted, including those who had held back during the previous attack. They had discovered they couldn't close in to the rocks while on horseback. They ran close, using the trees as cover and fanned out, to surround Arutha's position.

Roald said, "This is what they should have done the first time."

"They're a little slow, but not entirely stupid," commented Laurie.

Jimmy clutched his dagger as the Dark Brothers charged. "I'd have preferred stupidity."

The moredhel came in a wave, and suddenly there was fighting on all sides. Jimmy leaped away as a sword came crashing down from above. He thrust upward with his dagger and took the moredhel in the stomach.

Roald and Laurie battled, back to back, surrounded by Dark Brothers. Martin shot until he was out of arrows, when he grabbed up the moredhel bow and arrows. His firing was rapid and accurate and a dozen more Dark Brothers were struck before he dropped the bow and pulled his sword.

Arutha fought like a man possessed, his rapier delivering injury at every quarter. No moredhel could get close and remain free of wounds. But the Prince knew time would eventually win. The defenders would fatigue and slow and then they would die.

Arutha could feel the strength drain from his arms as the certainty of death came to him. There was little point in hoping. There were more than twenty moredhel still standing, and they were but five.

Martin hewed with his sword, cutting all who came before him. Roald and Laurie lunged and parried, giving up only inches, but slowly being worn down by the attackers.

A moredhel leaped over the stone breastwork and spun to face Jimmy. Jimmy acted without hesitation, his stiff side slowing him only slightly. He lashed out and sliced the moredhel's hand, causing it to drop its sword. The Dark Brother yanked its belt knife loose as Jimmy slashed again. But the moredhel leaped back, avoiding the boy's cut. Then it closed and was upon Jimmy. The boy slashed widly, losing his balance and his knife, and the moredhel was atop him. A knife blade came rushing toward the boy's face, but he dodged and it struck rock. Jimmy gripped at the creature's wrist, holding the blade away. The blade came toward his face, for the weakened boy could not hold back the moredhel's superior strength.

Then the moredhel's head snapped backward and Jimmy could see a knife drawn across the dark elf's throat, leaving a bloody track. The moredhel was pulled off by the hand gripping his hair, then the hand was extended to Jimmy.

Galain stood over the boy and helped him to his feet. Stunned, Jimmy looked about. Hunting horns sounded in the forests and the air was filled with arrows. The moredhel retreated before the attacking elves.

Martin and Arutha dropped their weapons, slumping in exhaustion. Roald and Laurie collapsed where they stood. Calin ran toward them, directing his elven warriors in pursuit.

Arutha looked up, relief bringing tears unbidden to his eyes. In a hoarse voice he said, "Is it over?"

Calin said, "It is, Arutha. For a while. They'll be back, but by then we will all be safely within the boundary of our forests. Unless they plan invasion, the moredhel will not cross that border. Our magic is still too strong there."

An elf leaned over the body of Baru. "Calin! This one still lives!"

Martin lay back on the rocks, panting. "That Hadati is tough."

Arutha waved away Galain's hand as he stood, his legs feeling like water. "How far?"

"Less than a mile. We need only to cross a small stream, and we are in our forests."

Slowly the survivors of the attack felt a lifting of their hopelessness, for they knew their chances now were excellent. With the elven escort, it would be unlikely the moredhel would muster enough strength to overwhelm them, even should they mount another attack. And with Murad dead, it was likely their leadership would crumble. From the behavior of many of the Dark Brothers it was clear he had been of major importance to them. His death would surely weaken Murmandamus's plans for some time.

Jimmy hugged himself, wondering at the chill he felt, for suddenly he was returned to the moment he stood in the cave at Moraelin. He felt the strange dislocation in time, and knew where he had experienced that chill before—twice before, in the palace and in the cellar of the House of Willows. He felt the hair on the back of his neck stand on end and knew with dread certainty that some magic was being visited upon them. He leaped away from the rock and looked about the glade. Pointing, he shouted, "Then we'd better start now! Look!"

The body of a Black Slayer began to move.

Martin said, "Can we cut their hearts out?"

"Too late," cried Laurie. "They're armored, and we should have acted at once."

A dozen Black Slayers were slowly rising and turning to face Arutha's party, weapons in hand. With tentative steps they began to advance upon the Prince. Calin shouted orders and elves grabbed up the near-exhausted and wounded men. Two carried Baru between them, and they started to run.

The dead warriors staggered after, their wounds still bleeding, and as they moved, their movements smoothed out, as if some agency was perfecting its control over them.

With increasing speed the undead followed. Elven bowmen ran, halted, turned, and fired, to no effect. The shafts struck the dead moredhel and would rock them, knocking a few to the ground, but they would only rise again.

Jimmy looked back, and somehow the view of these creatures running through the bright morning light in the lovely forests was far more horrible than anything he had seen at the palace or in the sewers of Krondor. Their movements were surprisingly smooth as they ran after, weapons at the ready.

Those elves carrying the injured and fatigued humans kept running while Calin ordered others to slow the moredhel. Elven warriors drew swords and engaged the undead creatures; after a few parries, they would retreat. The rear guard slowed the Black Slayers, but they could not be halted.

The elves worked themselves into a pattern. They would turn, fight, retreat a little, fight again, then flee. But the inability to visit harm on their foes served only to delay these, not to end their threat. Panting, fatigued elves labored to halt an inexorable flood. After several minutes the humans were being half carried, half dragged across a small stream.

Calin said, "We enter our forests. Here we will stand."

The elves drew swords and waited. Arutha, Martin, Laurie, and Roald readied weapons and waited. The first moredhel entered the water, sword in hand, splashing toward them. He reached the shore as an elf made ready to strike, but the moment the undead creature placed his foot upon the shore, it seemed to sense something behind the elves. The elf struck it to no effect, but the dead Black Slayer staggered back, raising its hands, as if seeking protection.

Suddenly a rider sped past the defenders, a figure resplendent in white and gold. Upon the back of a white elf steed, a legendary mystic horse of Elvandar, Tomas charged the moredhel. The elf steed reared, and Tomas leaped down from its back and, with a golden arc of his sword, nearly split the Black Slayer in twain.

Like a raging flame incarnate, Tomas sped along the shore, visiting destruction upon each Black Slayer as they set foot across the stream. Despite their arcane origin, each was helpless before the combined might of his arm and Valheru magic. Several managed single blows, which he easily turned aside, answering with terrible swiftness. His golden sword lashed out and black armor was cracked as if little more than brittle hide. But none of the undead sought to flee; each came on, and each was quickly dispatched. Of those with Arutha, only Martin alone had seen Tomas in battle before, and even he had never seen such a display. Soon it was over, and only Tomas stood upon the edge of the stream. Then came the sound of more horses. Arutha looked behind and saw more elf steeds approaching, ridden by Tathar and the other Spellweavers.

Tathar said, "Greetings, Prince of Krondor."

Arutha looked up and smiled weakly. "Thanks to you all."

Tomas resheathed his sword and said, "I could not travel with you, but once these dared cross the boundaries of our forest, I could act. Elvandar is mine to preserve. Any who dares invade will be treated as these." To Calin he said, "Build a funeral pyre. Those black demons shall never rise again." And he said to the others, "When it is done, we shall return to Elvandar."

Jimmy fell back upon the grass of the stream bank, his body too sore and tired to move. Within moments he was asleep.

They feasted the next night. Queen Aglaranna and Prince Tomas hosted Arutha and his companions. Galain approached where Martin and Arutha sat and said, "Baru will live. Our healer says he's the toughest human he's seen."

"How long before he's up again?" asked Arutha.

"A long time," said Galain. "You'll have to leave him with us. By rights he should have died an hour before we got here. He's lost a lot of blood, and some of those cuts are severe. Murad almost crushed his spine and his windpipe."

"But other than that, he'll be as good as new," said Roald across the table.

Laurie said, "When I get home to Carline, I promise never to leave again."

Jimmy came to sit next to the Prince. "You look thoughtful for one who's pulled off the impossible. I'd thought you'd be happy."

Arutha ventured a smile. "I won't be until Anita is cured."

"When do we ride home?"

"We go to Crydee in the morning; the elves will escort us there. Then we take ship to Krondor. We should be back in time for the Festival of Banapis. If Murmandamus can't find me with his magic, a ship should be safe enough. Unless you'd prefer riding back the way we came?"

Jimmy said, "Not likely. There might still be more of those Black Slayers about. I'll take drowning over another run-in with them, anytime."

Martin said, "It will be good to see Crydee again. I'll have much to see to, getting my house in order. Old Samuel will be at wits' end with the estate management, though I'm sure the Baron Bellamy has done well enough running things in my absence. But there will be much to do before we leave."

"Leave for where?" said Arutha.

In an innocent tone Martin said, "Why, for Krondor, of course." But his gaze traveled northward, and silently he echoed his brother's thoughts. Up there was Murmandamus, and a battle yet unjoined. The issue was not decided, only the first skirmish. With the death of Murad the forces of the Darkness had lost a captain, had been pushed back, retiring in disorder, but they were not vanquished, and they would return, if not tomorrow, then some other day.

Arutha said, "Jimmy, you have acted with wit and bravery beyond what is required of a squire. What reward shall you have?"

Biting a large rib of elk, the boy replied, "Well, you still need a Duke of Krondor."

NINETEEN

CONTINUATION

The riders reined in.

Staring upward, they studied the mountaintops that marked the boundary of their lands, the great peaks of the High Wall. For two weeks twelve riders had picked their way through the mountains, until they had journeyed beyond the normal limits of Tsurani patrols, above the timberline. They moved slowly through a pass it had taken days to locate. They were seeking something no Tsurani had searched for in ages, a way through the High Wall into the northern tundra.

It was cold in the mountains, an alien experience for most of the riders, except those who had served on Midkemia during the years of the Riftwar. To the younger soldiers of the Shinzawai Household Guard, this cold was a strange and almost frightening thing. But they showed no sign of their discomfort, except to absently draw their cloaks more tightly about their shoulders as they studied the odd whiteness on the peaks, hundreds of feet yet above their heads. They were Tsurani.

Pug, still in the black robes of a Great One, turned to his companion. "A short way from here, I think, Hokanu."

The young officer nodded and signaled his patrol forward. For weeks the younger son of the Lord of the Shinzawai had led this escort beyond the limits of the Empire's northern borders. Following the river Gagajin to its highest source, a nameless lake in the mountains, the hand-picked warriors had passed the trails followed by patrols of the Empire of Tsuranuanni. Here were the wild, rock-strewn, seemingly desolate lands between the Empire and the tundra of the north, home of the Thūn nomads. Even with a Great One in attendance, Hokanu felt vulnerable. Should a Thūn tribe be migrating nearby when they came out of the mountains, there would be a score or more of their young warriors running as flankers, seeking any excuse to take a Tsurani head as a trophy.

They rounded a bend in the trail and a narrow gap in the mountains provided a glimpse of the lands beyond. For the first time they could see the vast expanse of the tundra. Vaguely perceived in the distance, a long, low white barrier could be made out. "What is that?" said Pug.

Hokanu shrugged, his face an implacable Tsurani mask. "I do not know, Great One. I suspect it is another range of mountains, across the tundra. Or perhaps it is that thing you described, the wall of ice."

"A glacier."

Hokanu said, "Whatever; it lies to the north, where you said the Watchers may be."

Pug looked behind him at the ten silent riders. Then he asked, "How far?"

Hokanu laughed. "Farther than we can ride in another month without starving. We shall have to stop to hunt."

"I doubt there is a great deal of game about."

"More than one would think, Great One. The Thūn struggle to reach their traditional southern ranges every winter, the lands we have held for over a thousand years, but they still somehow survive the winters here. Those of us who have wintered on your world know how to forage in snow country. There will be creatures like your rabbits and deer once we drop back down below the timberline. We shall survive."

Pug weighed his choices. After a moment of silent consideration he said, "I don't think so, Hokanu. You may be right, but if what I hope to find is only a legend, then we shall have all come for no good reason. I may return to your father's home by my arts, and I could manage to take a few of you with me, three or even four, but the rest? No, I think it is time for a parting."

Hokanu began to object, for his father had ordered him to protect Pug, but Pug wore the black robe. "Your will, Great One." He signaled to his men. "Pass up half your food." He said to Pug, "There will be enough here to keep you fed for a few more days if you eat sparingly, Great One." When the food had been gathered in two large travel bags and hung behind Pug's saddle, Hokanu motioned his men to wait.

The magician and the officer rode forward a short way, and the son of the Shinzawai said, "Great One, I have given thought to the warning you bring and your quest." He seemed to find it difficult to speak his mind. "You have brought much into my family's life, not all of it good, but like my father, I've always believed you to be a man of honor, one without guile. If you believe this legendary Enemy to be the cause behind all the troubles on your homeworld you have spoken of, and if you think it about to find your world and ours, I must also believe. I admit to fear, Great One. I am ashamed."

Pug shook his head. "There is no shame, Hokanu. The Enemy is something beyond any of our understanding. I know you think it a thing of legend, something spoken of when you were a small boy and your teachers began to instruct you in the history of the Empire. Even I, who have seen it in mystic vision, even I do not fathom it, save to count it the greatest threat to our worlds imaginable. No, Hokanu, there is no shame. I fear its coming. I fear its power, and its madness, for it is a thing mindless in rage and hate. I doubt the sanity of any who did not fear it."

Hokanu lowered his head in agreement, then looked the magician in the eyes. "Milamber . . . Pug. I thank you for the ease you brought to my father." He spoke of the message Pug had carried from Kasumi. "May the gods of both worlds watch over you, Great One." He bowed his head as a sign of respect and then silently turned his mount around.

In a short while Pug sat alone atop the pass through which no Tsurani had ridden in ages. Below him lay the forests of the north slope of the High Wall, and beyond them the ranges of the Thūn. And beyond the tundra? A dream or legend perhaps. The alien creatures seen briefly in a vision each magician endured as he passed his final testing for the black robe. Those creatures known only as the Watchers. It was Pug's hope they possessed some knowledge of the Enemy, some knowledge that might prove the difference in the coming battle. For as Pug sat atop his tired mount, on the wind-swept heights of the greatest mountains on Kelewan's largest continent, he was certain some great struggle had begun, a struggle that could mean the destruction of two worlds.

Pug urged his horse forward, and the animal began moving downward, toward the tundra and the unknown.

Pug pulled back on the reins. Since leaving Hokanu's patrol he had seen nothing in the hills as he rode down toward the tundra. Now, a day out of the foothills, a band of Thūn were speeding to meet him. The centaur-like creatures hooted their battle songs as they ran, their powerful hooves beating the tundra in rhythmic concussion. But unlike the legendary centaur, the upper portion of this creature looked as if some form of lizard had grown to man shape above the torso of a heavy horse or mule. Like all other native life forms on Kelewan, they were hexapedal, and as with the other intelligent native race, the insectoid cho-ja, the upper limbs had developed into arms. Unlike humans, they had six fingers.

Pug waited quietly until the Thūn were almost upon him, then he erected a mystic barrier and watched as they crashed into it. The Thūn were all large, warrior males, though Pug couldn't really imagine what a female of the species must look like. Still, these creatures, for all their alien appearance, acted as Pug would have expected young human warriors to act under the same circumstance, confused and angry. Several beat ineffectively against the barrier while the others retreated a short way off to observe. Then Pug removed the cape the Shinzawai lord had given him for the journey. Through the haze of the mystic barrier, one of the young Thūn saw him wearing the black robe and shouted to his companions. They turned and fled.

For three days they followed him at a respectful distance. Some ran off, and for a time those remaining were joined by other Thūn. This leaving and returning, with some Thūn always behind him, continued unabated. At night, Pug erected a circle of protection about himself and his mount, and when he awoke the next morning, the Thūn still watched. Then, on the fourth day, the Thūn finally made peaceful contact.

A single Thūn trotted toward him, awkwardly holding his hands above his head, palms together in the Tsurani parley sign. Pug could see as he came up to him that they had sent an elder.

"Honors to your tribe," said Pug, hoping the creature could speak Tsurani.

An almost human chuckle answered. "A first that is, black one. Never honor have man given to me." The speech was heavily accented, but understandable, and the strange, saurian features were surprisingly expressive. The Thūn was unarmed, but old scars showed it had once been a powerful warrior. Now age had robbed it of much of its vigor.

Pug expressed a suspicion. "You are the sacrifice?"

"My life is yours to take. Bring down your sky fire, if that your wish. But not, I think, your wish." Again the chuckle. "Black ones the Thūn have faced. And why a one near the age of leaving should you take, when sky fire can a whole band burn? No, you move for purposes your own, do you not? Troubling those soon left to face the ice hunters, the pack killers, a purpose of yours is not." Pug studied the Thūn. He was almost at the day when he would be too old to keep pace with the moving band, when the tribe would abandon him to the predators of the tundra.

"Your age brings wisdom. I have no contention with the Thūn. I simply seek to pass to the north."

"Thūn a Tsurani word. We are Lasura, the people. Black ones have I seen. You a troublesome lot. Fight almost won, then black ones sky fire bring. Tsurani fight bravely, and Tsurani head a great trophy is, but black ones? Leaving Lasura in peace, your business usually is not. Why our ranges seek you to cross?"

"There is a grave danger, from ages long gone. It is a danger to all on Kelewan, to Thūn as well as Tsurani. I think there are those who may know how that danger may be met, those who live high in the ice." He pointed to the north.

The old warrior reared up, like a startled horse, and Pug's own mount shied away. "Then, mad black one, northward go. Death waits there. Find that out you shall. Those who in the ice live none welcome, and the Lasura no contest with madmen seek. Those who do a mad one harm are by the gods harm done. Touched by the gods you are." He dashed off.

Pug felt both relief and fear. For the Thūn to know "those who live in the ice" showed there was a chance the Watchers were neither fiction nor long vanished into the past. But the Thūn's warning caused him to fear for his mission. What waited for him high in the ice of the north?

Pug moved away as the Thūn band vanished over the horizon. Winds blew down off the ice, and he pulled his cloak about him. Never had he felt this alone.

More weeks had passed, and the horse had died. It was not the first time Pug had subsisted on horsemeat. Pug used his arts to transport himself short distances, but mostly he walked. Vagueness about time disturbed him more than any danger. He had no sense of the Enemy's imminent attack. For all he knew, the Enemy might need years to actually enter Midkemia. Whatever else, he knew it couldn't still possess the power it displayed in the vision of the time of the golden bridge, otherwise it would have swept into Midkemia and no power on the planet could have stopped it.

Pug's routine became dully monotonous as he continued northward. He would walk until he topped some slight rise and would fix his vision on a distant point. With concentration, he could transport himself there, but it was tiring and a little dangerous. Fatigue dulled the mind, and any mistake in the spell used to gather the energy needed to move him could cause him harm, or even kill him. So he would walk, until he felt sufficiently alert and at a place conducive to such spell casting.

Then one day he had seen something strange in the distance. An odd feature seemed to rear up above the icy cliff. It appeared vague, too far away to be seen clearly. He sat down. There was a spell of far seeing, one used by magicians of the Lesser Path. He remembered it as if he had read it a moment before, a faculty of his mind that had somehow been enhanced by his torture by the Warlord and the odd spell fashioned to keep him from his magic. But he lacked the strenuous stimulation, the fear of death, that had allowed him to use a Lesser Magic, and he could not cause the spell to work for him. Sighing, he stood and began again to trudge northward.

For three days he had seen the ice spire, rising high into the sky above the leading edge of a great glacier. Now he trudged up to a high rise and gauged his distance. Transporting himself without a known location, a pattern to focus his mind upon, was dangerous unless he could see his destination. He picked a small outcropping of rock before what seemed to be an entrance and incanted a spell.

Suddenly he stood before what was clearly a door into an ice tower, fashioned by some arcane art. At the door appeared a robed figure. It moved silently and with grace, and was tall, but nothing of its features could be seen in the deep dark of its hood.

Pug waited and said nothing. The Thūn were obviously frightened of these creatures, and while Pug had little fear for himself, a blunder could cost him the only source of aid he could think of to help stem the Enemy. Still, he was ready to instantly defend himself if necessary.

As winds whipped snowflakes in swirls about him, the robed figure motioned for Pug to follow and turned back in to the door. Pug hesitated a moment, then followed the robed figure into the spire.

Inside the spire were stairs, carved into its walls. The spire itself seemed to be fashioned from ice, but somehow there was no cold here; in fact, the spire seemed almost warm after the bitter wind of the tundra. The stairs led up, toward the pinnacle of the spire, and down, into the ice. The figure was vanishing down the stairs, almost out of sight when Pug entered. Pug followed. They descended what seemed an impossible distance, as if their destination lay far below the glacier. When they halted, Pug was certain they were many hundreds of feet below the surface.

At the bottom of the stairs they came to a large door, fashioned from the same warm ice as the walls. The figure moved through the door, and again Pug followed. What he saw on the other side caused him to halt, dumbfounded.

Below the mighty edifice of ice, in the frozen wastes of the Arctic of Kelewan, was a forest. Moreover, it was a forest like none upon Kelewan, and Pug's heart raced as he beheld mighty oaks and elms, ash and pine. Dirt, not ice, lay under his boots, and all around a soft, gentle light was diffused by the green branches and bowers. Pug's guide pointed toward a path and again took the lead. Deep in the forest they came to a large clearing. Pug had never seen the like of the sight before him, but he knew there was another place, a far distant place, that looked much as this did. In the center of the clearing, gigantic trees rose, with mighty platforms erected amid them, connected by roads upon the backs of branches. Silver, white, gold, and green leaves all seemed to glow with mystic light.

Pug's guide raised his hands to his hood and slowly lowered it. Pug's eyes widened in wonder, for before him stood a creature unmistakable to one reared upon Midkemia. Pug's expression was one of open disbelief and he was nearly speechless. Before him stood an old elf, who with a slight smile said, "Welcome to Elvardein, Milamber of the Assembly. Or would you prefer to be called Pug of Crydee? We have been expecting you."

"I prefer Pug," he half whispered. He was able to muster up only a shred of his composure, so shocked was he to find Midkemia's second most ancient race living among this impossible forest, deep in the ice of an alien planet. "What is this place? Who are you, and how did you know I was coming here?"

"We know many things, son of Crydee. You are here because it is time for you to face that greatest of terrors, what you call the Enemy. You are here to learn. We are here to teach."

"Who are you?"

The elf motioned Pug toward a gigantic platform. "There is much you must learn. A year shall you abide with us, and when you leave, you will come to power and understanding you only glimpse now. Without that teaching, you will not be able to survive the coming battle. With it, you may save two worlds." Nodding as Pug moved forward, the elf fell in beside him. "We are a race of elvenkind long vanished from Midkemia. We are the eldest race of that world, servants to the Valheru, those whom men called the Dragon Lords. Long ago did we come to this world, and for reasons you shall learn we chose to abide here. We watch for the return of that which has brought you to us. We prepare against the day we see the return of the Enemy. We are the eldar."

Stunned by this, Pug could only wonder. Silently he entered the twin of the city of elves, Elvandar, the place deep in the ice that the eldar had called Elvardein.

Arutha strode down the hall. Lyam walked at his side. Behind them hurried Volney, Father Nathan, and Father Tully. Fannon, Gardan and Kasumi, Jimmy and Martin, Roald and Dominic, Laurie and Carline all followed in a pack. The Prince still had on the stained and tattered travel clothing he had worn on the ship from Crydee. They had had a fast, and blessedly uneventful, journey.

Two guards still waited without the room Pug had ensorcelled. Arutha motioned for them to open the door. When it was open, he waved them aside, and with the hilt of his sword, he smashed the seal as Pug had instructed.

The Prince and the two priests hurried to the Princess's bedside. Lyam and Volney kept the rest outside. Nathan opened the vial containing the curative fashioned by the elven Spellweavers. As instructed, he poured a drop upon Anita's lips. For a moment nothing happened, then the Princess's lips flickered. Her mouth moved, and she licked the drop from her lips. Tully and Arutha held her up; Nathan raised the vial to her mouth and poured. She drank it all.

Before their eyes color returned to Anita's cheeks. As Arutha knelt at her side, her eyes fluttered and opened. She turned her head slightly, and said, "Arutha," in almost a silent whisper. Her hand gently came and touched his cheek as tears of thanks ran unashamedly down his face. He took her hand and kissed it.

Then Lyam and the others were in the room. Father Nathan rose and Tully barked, "Only a minute, now! She has to rest."

Lyam laughed, his loud happy laugh. "Listen to him. Tully, I'm still the King."

Tully said, "They may make you Emperor of Kesh, King of Queg, and Grand Master of the Brothers of the Shield of Dala as well, for all I care. To me you'll always be one of my less-gifted students. A moment, then out you go." He turned away, but as with the others, his face was wet.

The Princess Anita looked around at all the smiling faces and said, "What happened?" She sat up and with a wince said, "Oh, I hurt," then smiled an embarrassed smile. "Arutha, what did happen? All I remember was turning to you at the wedding . . ."

"I'll explain later. You rest, and I'll see you again soon."

She smiled and yawned, covering her mouth. "Excuse me. But I am sleepy." She snuggled down and was soon asleep.

Tully began shooing them from the room. Outside, Lyam said, "Father, how soon before we can finish this wedding?"

"In a few days," said Tully. "The restorative powers of that mixture are phenomenal."

"Two weddings," said Carline.

Lyam said, "I was going to wait until we returned to Rillanon."

"Not on your best horse's rump," snapped Carline. "I'm taking no chances."

"Well, Your Grace," said the King to Laurie, "I guess it's been decided."

Laurie said, " 'Your Grace'?"

With a laugh and a wave, as he walked away, Lyam said, "Of course, didn't she tell you? I can't have my sister married to a commoner. I'm naming you Duke of Salador."

Laurie looked more shaken than before. "Come along, love," said Carline, taking him by the hand. "You'll survive."

Arutha and Martin laughed, and Martin said, "Have you noticed the peerage has been going to hell lately?"

Arutha turned to Roald. "You were in this for gold, but my thanks go beyond mere gold. A bonus you shall have. Volney, this man is to have a bag of a hundred gold sovereigns, our agreed-upon price. Then he is to have ten times that as bonus. And then another thousand for thanks."

Roald grinned. "You are generous, Highness."

"And if you'll accept, you're welcome to be my guest here as long as you wish. You might even find it in your heart to consider joining my guard. I've a captaincy about to open."

Roald saluted. "Thanks, but no, Your Highness. I've thought of late it was time to settle down, especially after this last business, but I have no ambitions to enlist."

"Then feel free to guest with us as long as you desire. I'll instruct the Royal Steward to prepare a suite for your use."

With a grin, Roald said, "My thanks, Highness."

Gardan said, "Does that remark about a new captaincy mean I'm finally done with this duty and can return to Crydee with His Grace?"

Arutha shook his head. "Sorry, Gardan. Sergeant Valdis will become captain of my guard, but no retirement for you yet. From those reports of Pug's you brought from Stardock, I'm going to need you around. Lyam is about to name you Knight-Marshal of Krondor."

Kasumi clapped Gardan upon the back. "Congratulations, Marshal."

Gardan said, "But . . ."

Jimmy cleared his throat in expectation. Arutha turned and said, "Yes, Squire?"

"Well, I thought . . ."

"You had something to ask?"

Jimmy looked from Arutha's face to Martin's. "Well, I just thought as long as you were passing out rewards . . ."

"Oh yes, of course." Turning, Arutha spotted one of the squires and shouted, "Locklear!"

The young squire came running to bow before his Prince. "Highness?"

"Escort Squire Jimmy back to Master deLacy and inform the Master of Ceremonies that Jimmy is now Senior Squire."

Jimmy grinned as he and Locklear walked away. He seemed about to say something, then thought better of it and followed Locklear.

Martin put his hand on Arutha's shoulder. "Keep an eye on that boy. He seriously means to be Duke of Krondor someday."

Arutha said, "Damn me if he just might not do it."

EPILOGUE

RETREAT

The moredhel silently raged.

To the three chieftains before him he betrayed no hint of his anger. They were leaders of the most important lowland confederations. As they approached, he knew what they would say before it was spoken. He listened patiently, the light from the large bonfire before his throne casting a flicker across his chest, giving the illusion of movement to the birthmark dragon there.

"Master," said the centermost chieftain, "my warriors grow restless. They chafe and they complain. When shall we invade the southlands?"

The Pantathian hissed, but a restraining gesture from the leader quieted him. Murmandamus sat back in his throne and silently brooded on his setback. His finest general lay dead, irretrievable even to those powers at his command. The balky clans of the north were demanding action, while the mountain clans were drifting away by the day, confounded by Murad's death. Those who had come from the southern forests whispered among themselves of traveling the lesser passes back into the lands of men and dwarves, seeking to return to their homelands in the foothills near the Green Heart and among the highland meadows of the Grey Towers. Only the hill clans and the Black Slayers remained steadfast, and they were too small a force, despite their ferocity. No, the first battle had been lost. The chieftains before him demanded some promise, some sign or portent, to reassure their nervous alliances, before old feuds erupted. Murmandamus knew he could hold the armies here for only a few more weeks without marching. This far north, there were only two short months of warm weather left before the fall, then quickly the harsh northern winter would strike. If war was not forthcoming, to bring booty and plunder, the warriors would soon need to return to their homes. Finally Murmandamus spoke.

"O my children, the auguries are not in fruition." Pointing above, to stars seen faintly against the glare of the camp's fires, he continued. "The Cross of Fire heralds only the beginning. But we have not reached the time. Cathos says the fourth Bloodstone is not yet properly aligned. The lowest star will be in proper position at the summer solstice, *next year.* We cannot hurry the stars." Inwardly he raged at the dead Murad for having failed him in so critical a mission. "We trusted our fate to one who acted too swiftly, who may have been uncertain in his resolve." The chieftains exchanged glances. All knew Murad as one above reproach in visiting destruction on the hated humans. As if reading their minds, Murmandamus said, "For all his might, Murad underestimated the Lord of the West. That is why this human is to be feared, why he must be destroyed. With his death, the way south becomes open, for then shall we visit destruction upon all who oppose our will."

Standing, he said, "But the time is not yet. We shall wait. Send home your warriors. Let them prepare against winter. But carry forth the word: let all the tribes and clans gather here next summer, let the confederations march with the sun when it again begins its journey south. For before next Midsummer's Day, the Lord of the West shall die." His voice rose in volume. "We were tested against the powers of our forefathers and found wanting. We were judged guilty of failing in our resolve. We shall not again so fail." He struck fist to palm, his voice rising to a near-shriek. "In a year's time we shall bring forth the news that the hated Lord of the West is destroyed. Then shall we march. And we shall not march alone. We shall call our servants, the goblins, the mountain trolls, the land-striding giants. All shall come to serve us. We shall march into human lands and burn their cities. I shall erect my throne upon a mountain of their bodies. Then, O my children, shall we spill blood."

Murmandamus gave permission for the chieftains to withdraw. This year's campaign was at an end. Murmandamus signaled to his guards to attend him as he swept past the crooked form of the serpent priest. Silently he brooded upon Murad's death and the loss that death had caused. The Cross of Fire would look much as it did now for the next year and a bit more, so the lie about the configuration would hold. But time was now an enemy. A winter would be spent in preparation, and remembrance. No, this defeat would rankle as the freezing nights of winter slowly passed, but those nights would see the birth of another plan, which would bring the death of the Lord of the West, he who was the Bane of Darkness. And with that death, the onslaught against the nations of men would begin, and the killing would not halt until all lay prostrate at the feet of the moredhel, as was proper. And the moredhel would serve one master, Murmandamus. He turned and faced those most loyal to him. In the flickering light of their torches, madness danced in his eyes. His voice was the only sound in the ancient halls, a harsh whisper that grated upon the ear. "How many human slaves have our raiders captured to pull our siege engines?"

One of the captains said, "Several hundred, Master."

"Kill them all. At once."

The captain ran to carry out the order, and Murmandamus felt a lessening of the rage within as the prisoners' deaths atoned for Murad's failure. In near-hissing tones, Murmandamus said, "We have erred, O my children. Too soon did we gather to regain that which is rightfully our heritage. In a year, when the snows again have melted from the peaks, we again will gather, and then shall all who oppose us know terror." He paced about the hall, a figure of stunning power, a fey brilliance surrounding him in an almost perceptible halo. His magnetism was nearly palpable. After a silent time, he spun toward the Pantathian. "We leave. Prepare the gate."

The serpent nodded, while the Black Slayers took their positions along the wall. When each was situated in a niche, a field of green energy surrounded them. Each became rigid, a statue in his private nook, awaiting the summons that would come next summer.

The Pantathian finished a long incantation and a shimmering silver field appeared in the air. Without another word, Murmandamus and the Pantathian stepped through the gate, leaving Sar-Sargoth for some place known only to himself and Cathos. The gate winked out of existence.

Silence dominated the hall. Then, outside, the screams of the dying prisoners began to fill the night.

The final confrontation between Arutha and Murmandamus, as well as Pug and Tomas's search for Macros the Black, will be chronicled in *A Darkness at Sethanon,* to be published by Doubleday & Company, Inc.